GERMS OF TRUTH

ALSO BY HEATHER TOSTESON

Visible Signs

Hearts as Big as Fists & Other Stories

God Speaks My Language, Can You?

The Sanctity of the Moment: Poems from Four Decades

Wising Up Press
P.O. Box 2122
Decatur, GA 30031-2122
www.universaltable.org

Copyright © 2013 by Heather Tosteson

All rights reserved. No part of this book may be used or reproduced in any manner whatsoever without written permission, except in the case of brief quotations embodied in critical articles or reviews.

This is a work of fiction. Names, characters, places and incidents either are the product of the author's imagination or are used fictitiously. Any resemblance to actual persons, living or dead, events, or locales is entirely coincidental.

Catalogue-in-Publication data is on file with the Library of Congress.
LCCN: 2013936996

Wising Up ISBN: 978-0-9827262-8-0

GERMS OF TRUTH

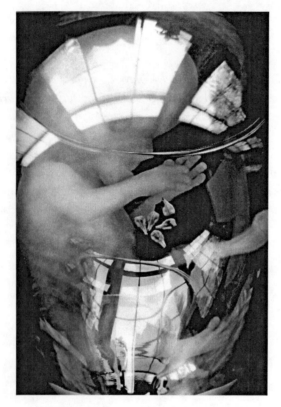

Heather Tosteson

Wising Up Press Collective
Wising Up Press
Decatur, Georgia

DEDICATION

For each of the beloved members of my several far from blended families for all the generous rapprochements and equally fertile schisms that have taught me, and keep teaching me, what it means to love and be loved.

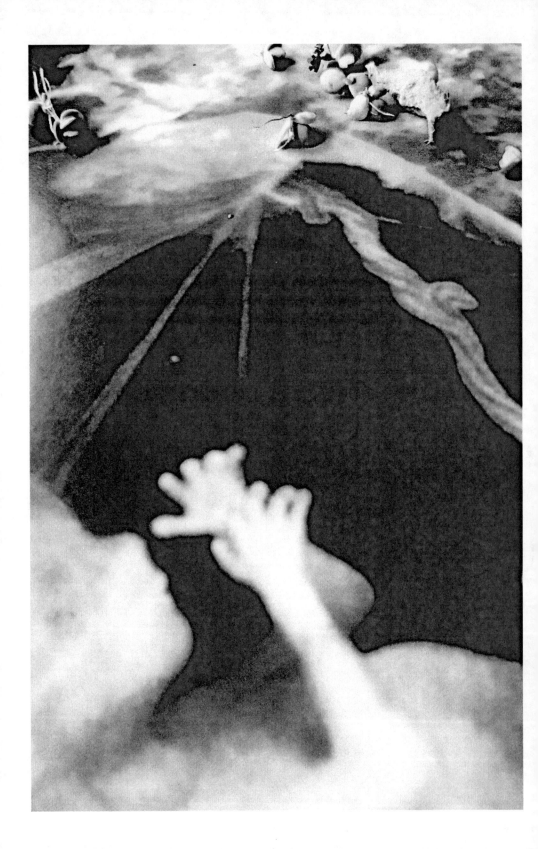

TABLE OF CONTENTS

WE'RE ALL DONORS HERE

Donor	3
Crush	9
Surprise Package	14
Synecdoche	21
The Man I'll Never Love	28
Magical Thinking	34
Progeny	41
Second Thoughts	52
We're All Donors Here	60
More	69

WHOSE LIFE IS IT ANYWAY?

Bloodlines and Babies	91
Whose Life Is It Anyway?	107
The Air You Breathe	117
Lifeboat	139
Sweet Sixteen	175
Target Fixation	187
Feasting with Ghosts	201
Duty Bound	231
It Wasn't Meant to End This Way	253
From the Outside In	271

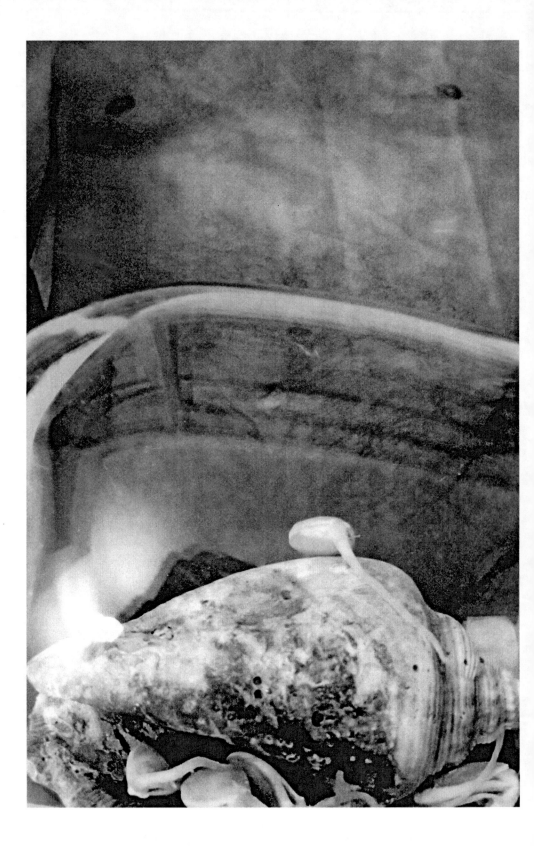

I

WE'RE ALL DONORS HERE

DONOR

They ask you to say why you're doing this—and wait, with their pens poised, like it's a contest or something. Best cum wins was how I went into it—but it's different. Not so anonymous. The interviewers look at this book of movie stars to see who you most resemble. They review your check list and correct it as they see fit. When I hesitated about ethnicity, the woman interviewing suggested I put in everything. "Nobody's pure," she said. "Most of our clients like it that way." She's darker than me by four shades—but I chose to see it for what it was, a dis. I'm mixed, there's no denying it, mixed up, but skin color isn't a big part of it. Ethnicity either. What would it matter here if I listed myself as Pakistani or Sri Lankan? She consulted her book of movie stars again. That's what I put down, with a little Swedish thrown in for good measure.

"You're going to say I look like The Rock?" I asked her. "He's mixed. My brow's as broad, my nose as straight."

She looked me up and down. "I'm thinking more like Gael García Bernal," she said.

"I'm not Hispanic."

"Body type," she said without looking up.

I'm a senior at Emory. Pre-med. My parents would die if they knew I was doing this. It's my way of covering the cost of Victoria's abortion. I guess she'd kill me too if she knew what I was doing.

But I haven't been able to come up with a faster and more private way of getting the money. And, to be honest, I'm curious. I plan to go into an MD/PhD program concentrating on endocrinology and genetics. As far as I know, there's nothing to worry about here. I don't have a brother or sister with Downs or dwarfism or juvenile diabetes or cystic fibrosis or muscular dystrophy. I don't have any sibs, but my extended family is vast. I would probably have heard if there were some really bad genes. I just want to keep track of my own recombinant possibilities, but I don't tell the interviewer that. I'm planning to go to two or three sperm banks under different names. I've read about these gene-pool families, all the women getting together to celebrate their extended families of half-sibs, like a harem. All they're missing is the sulky sultan. And he's missing the headache of all those relationships, all that estrogen, all that PMS mess. Seems like a good deal.

Besides, I can't seem to keep even one girl happy—not Victoria now, or before her Suzanne or Monica or Jessica or Kimberly (I'll spare you the rest of the list). Marriage doesn't seem to be in the cards for me in the foreseeable future, perhaps never, much less a harem. So, along with the need for ready cash, this also seems the only responsible way to satisfy my genetic curiosity. And something more than that. I don't want to be a father yet, but I want a place in the world. I want to know that somewhere out there is someone who would start and look twice if they saw me on the street.

Chances are all these little babies are going to have my far-sightedness, thick dark hair, brown eyes, dimples and full lips. They may be able to stretch their tongues to touch the tips of their noses. If they have two-thirds my IQ, they'll do fine. More than that might be a torment.

No, I tell the woman interviewing me, her name is Donwhanta, I don't have herpes, chlamydia, HIV 1 or 2, HTLV 1 or 2, gonorrhea, syphilis, hepatitis B or C, sickle cell, Tay-Sachs, or cystic fibrosis. They of course won't take my word for it. They'll test anyway. She goes over the medical history, three generations deep. My mother's parents are still living, my father's parents are both dead, of natural causes, well into their eighties. She agrees with me that it is not necessary to list all my aunts and uncles or cousins. She pauses when I tell her I'd like it to be an open donation.

"You sure?" she asks. "You'll be forty, happily married, with a busy medical practice and all these look-alikes are going to start showing up. What is your wife going to say?"

She's testing to see if I'm really straight, I think.

"Who knows. If I do have a wife—and the chances are looking slimmer by the minute—she may have been an egg donor. We may have just as many coming at us from the other side."

Donwhanta smiles but shakes her head. "This is serious, Vikram," she says. "These children, they'll have built up dreams, you know. Fatherless children *be* like that." Her lips purse and flower with that "be." She wants me to know there is another world out there and that she knows about it even if both her parents are lawyers and she went to Spellman. "'It's better for them not to know the scumbag,' is what my grandmother and my aunt would say."

"You think that's what I am?" I ask. "A scumbag?"

"No, I think you're a twenty-one-year-old smart ass. I don't think you're taking the time to really imagine what this means to the woman who chooses your sperm. She's going to be believing what you put down here. You can make this clean. You can make it messy. You came for the cash, just say so. You came because you think you are God's greatest gift to the gene pool, say that. Foolish pride isn't genetic. Neither is self-deception. But they can be harmful in real life. I don't want any baby of mine who makes it to adulthood to go out and try and find the guy who gave him half his genetic information and have the guy say, 'Looking good, kid. See you.' Like he's saluting his own self in the mirror. Here, you know, you can get real. You're doing it for the money, just say it. No one is going to get their feelings hurt. You want to have this fantasy that you're some human Johnny Appleseed, say so. Just don't go getting no child's hope up that there's a heart driving that little wiggly tail."

She hands me a legal pad and a pen. "You're meant to write a personal statement. Describe your personality, your interests and abilities, what movie you'd take with you to a desert island, what you want to tell those babies and their families. Why you decided to donate. Why you think it's worth someone's time to seek out your sorry face when they're eighteen and floundering. Why any mom would want to encourage that. You tell them."

My cheeks burn. She isn't as hard as she seems, I know. I don't think it is just because I'm the right side of brown (that's why all my cousins say I could be in a Bollywood film). Clearly there is something personal back there. Isn't there always?

"I mean it," Victoria had said to me when I told her I couldn't marry her. "I don't ever want to see your sorry face again." It wasn't fair to her, I told her. I was only going to be able to concentrate on my studies for the next decade. I thought she'd understood that. I mean she'd read over my applications, hadn't she? She knew my goals, all printed out there in Times New Roman. She shared them, didn't she? She had her sights set on Harvard, Cornell at the least.

"My mom would help. She told me so." Victoria's mother is a bus driver in Macon. Victoria is her oldest. There are five more and already three grands. Victoria is at Emory on full scholarship, coming in through Oxford College, their feeder two-year college. Two-thirds of our time together, I was tutoring her. I wasn't going to let her slip back like that.

"If you have this baby," I told her, "I will never forgive myself."

"So, your feelings are more important than this child's life?"

"Your *future* is more important than this half-baked *idea*," I told her. "It is just an *idea* at present."

"My future is *your* idea Vikram," she said. "We both know I'm not up to it. Maybe our child will be, but I'm not. I'm just not that smart." She gestured to the biochemistry textbook on her bed. Victoria's this wonderful color, like burnt toast, so you can't see when her blood pressure rises. And she always talks low so you have to move close to hear. But her eyes were red and her breathing was fast.

We looked at each other then. It was the simplest and saddest thing. I could see how much she wanted this baby, and I could see it was the wrong thing. It would mean she was giving up on herself, putting her hope off to the next generation, just like her mother had done for her. Six children and only one of them making it to college and, if Victoria did this, she might not even make it through. She owed them both more.

"Hate me," I told her. "Hate me for life. But this isn't *right*, Vic. It isn't right for you—and it isn't right for me."

"Who's to say I'll ever be able to have another? Abortions can damage you. I know too many women, they're sorry now for what they did before they were twenty. All in the name of something that never came to be. This life, Vik, it's real. It's what God gave me to make up for my disappointment."

"You have to listen to reason," I told her. I had the textbook in my hands, was opening it, trying to get us back on track. "I respect you too much to let you do this to yourself."

"*We* did it," she said. "*We*, Vik."

"I thought we agreed you'd be on Norplant as backup."

She looked away. Slipped her hand under the papers there and straightened the bedspread.

"You'd be a good dad, Vik. I watch how you help me, how patient you are. You would be good with this baby. Your mom and dad would do anything for you. We'd do the same for this baby."

"No," I said. It came out almost like a bark. I was seeing my mom and dad, how tired they were when they came back from the dry cleaners at the end of their twelve-hour days. "I can't stop you if you go ahead and have it. I won't deny paternity. But I will never see this child."

"You're just saying that now."

"You don't want to try me on this, Vic." I was surprised at how clear my voice was, at something very real behind it. Not cold, just certain, absolutely certain.

She looked at me then.

"I'll go with you to the clinic for the D&C," I said softly. "I'll make sure you graduate."

It was an awful moment. I can't describe it—seeing the life go out of someone like that. Like now there was this big dark cave where once there was a meadow, trees. She knew it too and just put her arms around herself as if to contain the emptiness. And it didn't change anything. I meant what I said. My father is one of eleven children, my mother one of ten. They spend their money on two things—my education and supporting all their brothers and sisters in their village in Gujurat. My mother had her tubes tied after I turned three and she knew I'd survive. My father had a vasectomy to make double sure. Everything I do, I do for the three of us—and that beautiful brown horde they left behind. I cannot, I absolutely cannot, add two more to my load.

Why do you want to be a sperm donor?

"I can't afford not to. I think of how much my parents have loved me, what riches that experience of parenthood has given them, and I would like to help someone else have that experience, even when I am not of an age or in an economic or professional position to have it myself," I write in my tidy print. I check the box for anonymity and hand the form back to Donwhanta.

It is my next best reckless gift to the universe that may, yet, in totally unexpected ways return it to me. As I leave, I suggest she put down Shahid Kapoor as my look alike, but she's stuck on *Y Tu Mamá También* and Gael García Bernal.

CRUSH

The same afternoon my friend Tess told me she was doing it with Nathan, I came in and found my mom and her friend Hilary curled over my mom's laptop, giggling like they were my age—which is a little up in the air given the vagaries of the Chinese adoption system, but is close enough to sixteen to make their perimenopausal behavior embarrassing.

"Come join us," Hilary said. "We're looking at donor profiles." This wasn't, I saw as soon as I stepped closer, about fund-raising for charities. It looked like a dating site, but it was worse. It was for a sperm bank.

"Gross," I said. "I'm never having sex."

"My sister Molly isn't either," Hilary said. "But she's decided to have a baby and so far, cloning hasn't panned out for humans. There needs to be a little collusion between the sexes, if only at the level of their DNA."

"If you were looking for an ideal guy," my mom said, "what would he be like, Jessamine?"

Nathan.

It almost popped out of my mouth, but I swallowed it. Just the name got my imagination flashing on what Tess had told me. Just little flashes of skin, the *idea* of them, naked, rubbing, was enough to get my stomach curdling. So I described his opposite.

"White, but with skin that tans, not like white glue paste," I said. "And long straight surfer hair. Blonde. Premed. About five inches taller than me. But muscled. Tutors the disadvantaged, reads for the blind, and builds houses for Habitat for Humanity in his spare time."

Nathan's mom is Jewish, a doctor, *my* pediatrician. His dad is from Ethiopia and teaches world history at the college. Nathan is tall, already over six feet, and thin as a Nuer. His skin is the color of light suede and he has this wild curly hair that is soft and jet black. He made a perfect score on his SATs first time around and raps when he isn't playing violin in the state youth orchestra. He's applied for early admission to Harvard, Stanford, Yale and, as his back-up, the University of Chicago. And when he has nothing else going on, he makes it with my last best friend. Ever.

"Found him," my mom said. "His ancestry is French, Dutch, English, and Danish. He fences. Speaks four languages, including Chinese."

"Let me see." I leaned in over their shoulders. She wasn't kidding.

My mom scrolled down the list. "Then there's this guy who is six foot three who is Dominican and Laotian. That sounds interesting." She opened up the file. I read over her shoulder.

"Oh, he has long curly lashes," I blurted. I was swayed, I admit it. I love long curly lashes. But he wanted to be a dentist. There is something creepy about someone who wants to spend their days with their hands in other people's mouths.

"What about Chinese and Algerian?" my mom asked. She has this thing for Asia—duh.

"Pull up a chair," Hilary said. Maybe her neck was getting hot. "Molly needs as much advice as she can get."

"What does she look like?" I asked.

"Chaste," Hilary said, then shook her head impatiently. "I don't actually know her well. She's my half-sister. Fifteen years younger than me. I don't even know why she asked me to help."

The answer seems fairly obvious. Hilary has two adopted sons, both Korean. She's part of the same foreign adoption group my mom belongs to. It's a pretty big group since this is a college town and lots of women waited until they got tenure to think about having a family. Half of them are single. In general, they look down at people who have biological children. I'm not saying it's conscious, but I have this feeling they think that they've taken the more altruistic path. There are enough babies in the world already who need good homes. Why go manufacture another one just to feed your ego? I think that kind of thing runs through their minds more than they are willing to admit.

I don't know how I feel about that. I think it's fine, what my mom and Hilary did. Certainly I can see how I have benefited. But I don't know how I *feel* about it. It's kind of like sex, which gives me the creeps. I mean, I'm jealous of Tess, but I don't want Nathan pushing himself inside me. It feels really intrusive, a violation of my basic privacy. I'm big into privacy. Always have been I think. I don't want anybody to know me that way—to see things about me that I can't even see myself. Ways I don't even *want* to see myself. I've told my mom that I don't want to use tampons because I'm afraid of toxic shock. She's a health nut, so she's fine with that. But it isn't the reason. I have this thing about being all in one piece. I can't stand cuts, even paper cuts. Their edges are just the scariest thing to me. My mom thinks I tear up because of the blood, but it's the edges. Scrapes I can handle a little better. They scab fast.

Having sex with a woman wouldn't be any better. In sex ed they had us look at anatomical photos, not just drawings. They separated us that day, boys in one room, girls in the other. I could tell my mother was a little shocked when I told her about it. "Is this to encourage abstinence?" she asked, and I could see she was putting on her ruthless avenger face and I told her no, it was just about being accurate, not romantic. I told her that if I'm going to be premed, it's good preparation. I didn't tell her I could begin to understand those African women who claim to like being all stitched up. I don't want the stitches or having something cut away. What I'd like is for us to be all smooth down there, like my baby dolls.

I wonder if I inherited this aversion from my real mother. It feels like it's been there as long as I've been in this world, so it could be genetic. When Tess told me today about her and Nathan, she was real graphic. Especially about the first time. How she had to sneak her sheets down to the laundry room. "It gets better," she said. "But I wouldn't rush into it." She had this heavy-lidded blasé look like she was my older sister or something.

It made me feel angry, which was a relief. Because all the other stuff made me feel like I was suffocating, like I was surrounded by water, trapped in a well or a big sac, like I couldn't breathe, like there wasn't a minute left before I was dead. It made me just want to curl up around myself and kick out at the same time.

My mom says my mother loved me but couldn't keep me, but my mom is a little like Pangloss in *Candide*, you know, "It is all for the best in the best of all possible worlds." I don't think my mother felt that way, otherwise why would she have left me in the market when I was too young to do anything but wobble my head? I think I invaded my mother and I kept taking up more and more space inside her and she couldn't stand it, that it was like a cancer and she just wanted someone to cut me out. I think she wanted to be sewed up tight afterwards, not just across her belly but down there as well, like a perfect plastic doll. I think she had had it with blood and guts. I think when they cut through to me I was crazy with greed for the air and guilty too because of all the space I was taking. I think my mother saw me, stretched out like this gigantic tapeworm, and got the heebie jeebies. I think she couldn't imagine how I got inside her in the first place.

My mom says that when she saw me in the orphanage, I was the most beautiful child she had ever seen—and that when I looked at her, just opened my eyes wide and really looked at her, she had never felt more beautiful, more complete. I believe my mom because that is who she is. She soaks up the world, she expands into it like a sponge. I feel that way too when she looks at me. But I don't feel that way when anyone else looks at me.

"*Yet*," my mom would have said if she had known what I was thinking. "It will change."

But in which way? If my real mother had kept me, I think my look, that same look that made my mom fall in love with me for all time, would have made her feel suffocated. Even today. I don't think it had anything to do with the one-child policy. I think it had to do with me.

I don't know where girlfriends and boyfriends, where sex, enters into all this. I mean, you watch movies and you kind of fall into the actor's eyes—but it's not like that in real life. Life is not like a casting call. It's not like there's a script you're going to recite. It's not like you can write a happy ending, even if you happen at this moment in time to be living one. It's not like you know beforehand what you're going to do to someone just by breathing, just by being.

"Got to study," I told my mom, running my hand across her short gray hair, mussing it just the way she likes.

"What about Thai, German and Argentine?" she was asking Hilary as I left.

"As long as his lashes are long and curly," I called back to them.

SURPRISE PACKAGE

She put so much thought into this. Read every single listing four times over before reducing the number of candidates to ten. Talked each of them over with her friends, her therapists, her brother, her father and me and our spouses. Thorough or obsessive, the two are hard to differentiate with Bridget. It actually brought her father and me closer, a little guiltily. If a tenth of this thought had gone into her conception, would her life have been much different? We never said as much to each other, but it was clear in our glances the evening she brought us all together to announce her final choice.

Clearly, Bridget believed so—even though she always claimed that the first time she became convinced the sun would rise every morning of her life was the day her father and I split for good. "Light and air and quiet. Nothing can compare to it," she consoled me at the time. "There's more room for us, Mom."

"It was as if I'd been living in a thunder cloud since birth," she told me some years later. "And then there was this stillness, this fresh spring air, light. It was the *greatest* kindness, Mom."

That morning, the first day of the rest of our lives, humming, she had arranged her pencils in her slotted pencil bag, slipped it into her knapsack, straightened her dress, bent over and polished her glossy ballet-like shoes, tapped her eyeglasses back on her little snub nose, and headed off to the last day of sixth grade with a little skip to her walk as if reclaiming a childhood she'd never had.

It was a matter of one digit. Somewhere in the middle. Her brother had to go back to the sperm bank and have them check their archives for the date she made her order. The donor list keeps changing. After a year or so, if no one orders, they retire the listing for awhile, then, depending on inventory and demand, may reintroduce it. They had just retired him. They'd carried him for four years. Bridget was the only purchaser. John asked for the profile, but they said they would only release it to Bridget. He was an anonymous donor.

She thought she was ordering a Viking—tall, blonde, green-eyed, broad-shouldered, and genetically humanitarian, like Dag Hammarskjöld or Bono. Nothing like this enchanting little girl, the color of old ivory, with her slanted lids and hazel eyes and tiny fingers the diameter of cocktail skewers, who knows, already knows, what it is to be life's biggest surprise to someone.

Bridget is unassuageable, adamant. "This is not what I planned," she said when they put the baby beside her in the delivery room. "This is not what I ordered."

She refuses to see the baby. Her obstetrician is arranging with the hospital to let her stay another day. She's refused to talk to a chaplain or a psychiatrist. She wants their adoption expert.

"This is not what I ordered," she repeats to everyone.

"But it was," her brother John says quietly. "I've checked the order, B, and those *are* the numbers, the sequence.

My superbly self-controlled and inner-directed daughter puts her hands over her ears and closes her eyes and howls. As the nurse is giving her an injection of valium, we all leave the hospital room and head to the nursery.

I can't keep my hands off the baby, asleep or awake. I'm sixty-two and I feel like I did at eighteen looking one last time into the saucer-wide brown eyes of my other daughter.

"Do you think she'll come around?" John asks us.

I look at my ex-husband James. He looks at our son. We each take a deep breath.

"My travel schedule—" John says. He's two years younger than his sister. Gay, he has shown no desire for any kind of sustained emotional ties, at least as far as we know. His father and I hold ourselves responsible. But he's always there for us. Holidays. Spontaneous visits to San Francisco. He never tells us he's too busy to get together. But he is in high-tech sales and spends much of his time in airplanes, Asian countries.

"Claudia would never—" James says, stops, and both John and I shrug and smile. James is looking ten years older these days. Claudia is about the same age as Bridget and the fertility drugs she took last year resulted in triplets. To James at sixty-three, it must feel like early karma. He looks at me a little mistily, and I wonder if he's had his cataracts attended to.

"You can say no, Mom."

"I know I can," I tell them sharply. "I'm just not sure if my saying yes or no matters. She's Bridget's to do with as she chooses, you know."

The two men, so like each other in height, build, coloring, facial expressions—so like Bridget—shuffle uncomfortably from one foot to the other. They fix their gazes on opposite corners of the nursery. There is a mechanical hum to the room, an antiseptic smell, a chill that slips under your skin, and somewhere behind me, the sound of a woman crying, a man murmuring. "My baby, my *baby*," the woman keeps sobbing.

I lift this perfect being closer to my face. She blinks. When I touch her cheek with my finger, she turns her face and opens her mouth, assured that what she most hungers for is waiting for her.

"Ask the nurse for a bottle," I tell John and begin walking toward one of the rocking chairs. I'm not ready to talk to Rubin, my husband of fifteen years, about this. He has just retired from his job as a high school principal. He's concentrating on his musical ambitions now. He's a songwriter, somewhere between indie and country—"with a Yiddish twist," he likes to joke. He's several times married but childless. By choice he insists. "I couldn't do it if I brought it home with me," he has said of his teaching career. "I leave the little hoodlums where they belong—in an institution."

Rubin has always kept his distance, benevolent but unbridgeable, from John and Bridget. It seems to have worked for all of them. Bridget was already off to college when we married. John, who skipped a grade, was off himself within six months. The three of them have been nothing but kind to one another, but I wouldn't say there's much glue. Although Rubin has actually been the best with Bridget during this baby-planning process, sitting shoulder-to-shoulder with her, talking her through each of the donor essays.

"You want *this* guy showing up when your child is eighteen?" he would ask.

"It's a one-way street," Bridget said. "The kid is the only one who can initiate."

"You want this guy opening his *door* to your kid?" Rubin rephrased it. "What do you think your child is going to see when she or he looks around him to what's inside that house, that life? Is there going to be anything there, inside the guy or around him, that will help her? Looks fade, honey. Aspirations drain away."

Bridget decided to have a closed donation. The agency I gave my daughter Nimbus to called me last year to ask if I wanted to revise my do-not-contact listing. So many people are doing so, they told me. There's so little stigma now, and so much access. But that wasn't why I did it in the first place. I never felt she was mine to keep.

"She hasn't tried to find me has she?" I asked. I knew I shouldn't have asked, knew it just as soon as I said the words.

The woman at the adoption agency told me no, and I felt, once again, as if I had been saved. Everything I had wanted to say to my first born was in the file: *I love you with everything in me. I know you deserve more than I can ever give. I am doing the best I can to provide it for you. Forgive me. Forget everything about me except the love with which I give you up.*

I rock this self-contained, nameless wonder. I could almost swear she winks at me as she guzzles her bottle. I know my daughter Bridget. She can't bear to be reminded of her mistakes, mis-steps. She doesn't keep old lovers as friends. Doesn't keep a blouse with a missing button, a dress with a drooping hem. I've given her needle and thread, but she just looks at me as if I am clueless. "I don't want *mended*," she says.

Why she decided to become a life coach rather than a personal buyer or house organizer is a little beyond me.

"Because I *believe*, Mom," she told me once. "I really *believe* in getting it right. The first time if possible. People pick that up. It's nothing you can fake. They know it matters as much to me as it does to them."

"And if they don't?" I asked her. "If they set their goals too high, if they have wallowed in indecision until the moment of victory has passed, if they just have bad luck?"

"I pass them on," she said briskly. "There are more than enough life coaches. It's a glutted market. That's why I'm so effective. They know they have one chance. There is no tomorrow. I'll back them a thousand percent—I make that clear in everything I do. There is no second best for me. The rest is up to them."

What star did she fall from? I have wondered more than once. Could they have exchanged babies while I was waking up from the anesthetic from the caesarean? If she didn't look so much like James and John, I would have had us tested.

I work in clay. It is a forgiving medium. I concentrate on the human figure, the human face. As a species, we're primed for them. The slightest indication of features—forehead, eye socket, or nose—and we're hooked. I work with clay because it triggers in my body all those feelings I had when the children were small, when my body felt as vital as theirs. Sometimes, if I make a figure that really speaks to me, I'll feel my nipples harden, my sex get wet. I just fold that back into the clay. It's the way I keep Nimbus alive.

"Cirrus," I whisper to my daughter's daughter. "This is going to be my name for you. But no wind is going to whisk you away, no sun is going to dissolve you."

I burp her and put her back in her crib. On my way to my daughter's room, I pull out the piece of paper where John has written the phone number of the sperm bank, the name of the woman he talked to, the true donor's ID.

I push open the door to my daughter's room. The curtains are closed. She is curled up like a fetus with a pillow over her head. I walk over and pull open the curtains. I pull the pillow away. The sun lights up her immaculate Nordic face, those stony blue eyes, those sharp planes to her cheeks and chin, which magnify her flawed, diamond-hard nature. I know she is no match for me, never has been.

"Sit up," I tell her. "Listen. You're right. There is no tomorrow. There are no fresh starts. All this picking and choosing, all this getting it 'right' is a delusion. Always has been. I don't know why I've put up with it for so long. Why we all have."

Bridget looks at me coolly. She leans over and opens the drawer of her bedside table. "I have the papers right here." She looks so weary, my daughter. Wearier than her father after his year of nursing and diapering triplets.

I take the papers from her gently, so gently.

"I am going to make you an offer you cannot refuse," I tell her, "because my life depends on it. Not yours, or hers, mine. I *know* this little one. I know her better than a mother can. There is a space inside me into which she fits exactly, like a key into a lock. She knows it too. We're fused, sweetheart. The two of us are fused. You get rid of her, you get rid of me too. I kid you not."

My daughter looks at me in this room that feels preternaturally still. The scent of narcissus rises from the bouquet I sent her. I reach out my hand to fit that perfect cheek and she instinctively turns into it like a lover, an infant. Her breathing deepens.

"Rubin? What does he think?" she asks.

"The question isn't Rubin. Look behind him through that doorway,

Bridget. What do you see? "

"Tomorrow," Bridget says. "I see Tomorrow. And you, singing her to sleep. There is no room for me."

"Exactly," I say. "You are free to be who you need to be. She is too."

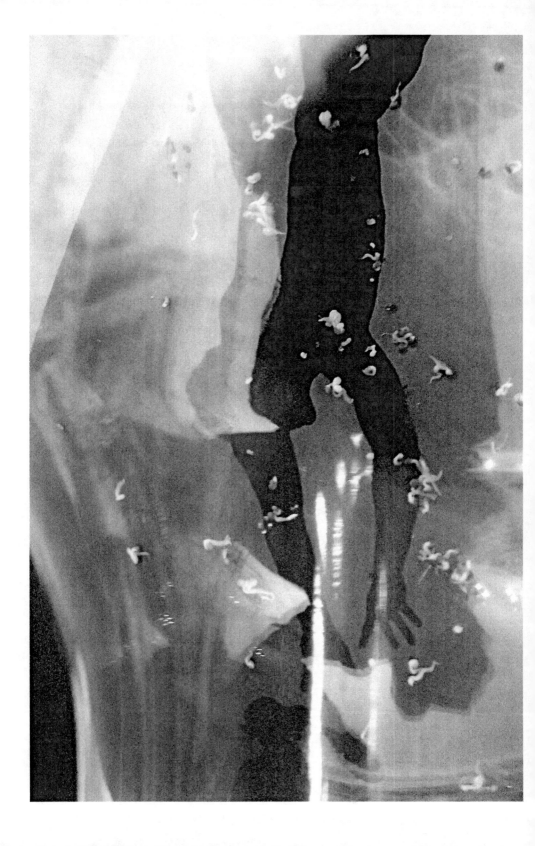

SYNECDOCHE

I told Celeste if she wouldn't change her mind about this, she had to leave the final choice up to me. Unless she wanted to go it alone. I wasn't sure it was a bluff. She wasn't either.

"There's no question of fault here, never is," Dr. Jagerson said to us before he showed us the test results. "There isn't even any question of infertility. Your sperm, Ralph, are mobile and plentiful. Your ovaries respond to Clomid, Celeste."

"Is it just that I have an irritable uterus?" Celeste asked.

"No. Your uterus is normal. I have no doubt with an implanted embryo you could carry to term."

"What is it then?" I asked, eager to get to the point. It's been a rough year what with teaching seven composition classes as an adjunct at two colleges, frantically applying, like thousands of others, for every tenure-track position in the country—and Celeste with that thermometer in her right hand and her phone in her left, with me on speed dial, expected to drop everything when her blood heats up. "You promised as soon as you got your degree it would be my turn," she insisted.

"Bluntly," Dr. Jagerson cleared his throat and looked at the wall chart of a pregnant woman on the opposite wall, "there's a chemical antagonism between your sperm and her egg. They repel rather than attract."

"Like magnets?" I asked, my body filling with giddy air. I could see the little Scottish terriers scooting across the paper. I couldn't keep from smiling.

My wife, who is one of the most lovely beings on earth when things are going her way and a Siberian tiger when they're not, began to lift her upper lip. "This is no laughing matter, Ralph."

"Sorry," I said. "Anxiety. This isn't something a Petri dish could fix? I mean, the problem isn't in the egg or the sperm, really, but the fluids, right?"

"We washed the sperm," Dr. Jagerson said. "No difference."

"You mean," Celeste said, "if we were with other people, there would be no problem?"

Dr. Jagerson, who is about my age, glanced at me then quickly glanced away, but not before I saw the sympathy there—and something grimmer. We both understood that some things once said can never be unsaid.

"In vitro could possibly work. Or artificial insemination. Adoption is also still on the table, I hope," he said, drumming his fingertips on the table as if he were typing a short notice for a medical journal. *Natural Antipathies: Can This Marriage Be Saved?*

"You would deprive me of this experience? Just because of a little male ego," Celeste said in the car. "I've dreamed about it for years, since before I met you. I was *meant* to be a mother."

"And you wouldn't be if you adopted?"

"It wouldn't know me from the inside out. Blood of my blood." That matters for someone whose father, mother, and four generations of grandparents have hung their SAR and DAR certificates over their beds like aphrodisiacs.

I sat in the car staring at her profile, which is, these days, sometimes all that I love about Celeste. But love is too slight a word for the feeling I have. I am uxorious. Or a Tinbergen duck. I took one look at Celeste in our freshman English class, and I've really never looked at anyone since. Celeste has always accepted this as her due.

"The two of you were destined to breed," her father Carl said to me once as we were sitting beside their pool. I may have been a junior then. "Great genes."

Even if my documentable roots only go back two pacifist generations—and only on my mother's side? I wanted to ask him. But he's right. People sometimes mistake us for siblings. We're a few inches different in height, but our faces are both square, our eyes wide-set, our hair on the white side of yellow even in our thirties. Celeste has delicate ears, close set to the head. Mine stand out a little more. My chin has a cleft. But on the surface, the genetics look simple, like two rails converging to a point.

Infinitely far away.

"So let me be clear about what you're proposing," I said.

"It's just like he said. I can be a mother. We just need some other sperm. I don't think it's that big a deal. No one needs to know—and if we choose right, nobody will."

"And the next time, we could plant another egg in your uterus using my sperm?" I asked. "Or perhaps hire a surrogate." I don't know what got into me. It was as if I was the aggressive black Scotty.

"Of course not," Celeste said, scooting away. "It's not the same at all." She didn't even smile.

Indeed, her eyes began to well with tears. I wasn't sure if it was frustration or spring fever. I looked out the car window at the enormous bank of magenta azaleas blossoming under the blooming pines. Already the hood of the car was gilded with pollen. I rolled down the window.

"I've imagined it so many times," she said softly. "You putting your head to my belly to listen to the first heartbeat, feel the first kick. The Lamaze classes. You standing beside me counting while I have the contractions, taking the video during delivery."

She rubbed my right hand, which was still holding onto the steering wheel. "You always said you'd be willing to adopt. You always said it was about nurture, not nature. Why should this be any different?"

"Because you said no. Never," I answered.

"I'm not changing my position."

"I never said I'd be willing to raise your child by another man."

"But that isn't the case here. There is no other man, just a cryovial and some little genetic tadpoles." Celeste turned to face me, exposing thigh right up to her pink panty line. She saw my eyes rest there. She gently prised my hand off the wheel, brought it to her crotch. "Nothing would change, Ralph. Promise. You would just have given me what I want most in the world. How could I not love you even more for that?"

Which is how I ended up at my desk late this evening reviewing donor profiles on a West Coast sperm bank rather than grading blue books.

"Isn't there one for Nobel Prize winners?" Celeste asked as she kissed me on the head and went to bed. As a spa manager, she insists on her beauty rest. As a PhD a thousand dollars from perfect penury, I don't.

I don't even know where to begin. Height, eye color, hair? Or grade averages and education level. I choose a bank in Missoula, Montana. I don't want either of us ever to run into this fellow. I've told Celeste if we're going through with this, his identity will be mine alone to know. I'll leave her immediately if she ever reveals this to anyone—including her mother, her therapist, her best friend. I don't know who I'm kidding. I can't go through with this. And it feels like some awful kind of justice too.

There are things about me Celeste doesn't know. Things nobody knows I know. My mom always told me my dad died in an accident before I was born. She said he was really nice—but just a boy. Nineteen to her twenty-two. "I don't really have any idea who he would have become, Ralph. He was kind and good looking and a bit reckless. That's how he had the accident." It was back on the West Coast, she said. Right after she finished college. It was a fling, nothing serious. I was unplanned but never unwanted, she insisted. Once she found out she was pregnant, she moved to Maryland to be closer to her family. She never told him about the pregnancy. She didn't find out he was dead until a few years later.

I have four aunts and uncles, a really nice step-father and two step-sisters about a decade older than me. I'm not missing anything. That's what my mom would point out whenever I asked about getting in touch with my biological father's family. "What's missing in your life, sweetheart? Let's address that first. Aren't Greg and I enough for you? And what about Susie and Sandra, Auntie Lila, Uncle Bill—"

I don't think she ever noticed when the questions stopped. It was when she and my step-dad were going through a tough time. I think I may have been about thirteen. They're fine now, but I think he was seeing someone then. It might have been a short-lived infatuation, some work crush. But I came in one evening from a friend's roller skating party that had ended early. They were in the den yelling. They didn't hear me. I was so shocked I just stood there. I'd never heard them like that. It was like the floor was shaking. They still had the TV on, so the sound of their own voices came in and out of this canned laughter.

"You are so bound up with that boy," my step-dad was saying as if that was an excuse for whatever he'd been doing. "Who can compete with a ghost? One who never lived long enough to reveal a flaw?"

"*Ghost*," my mother screamed. "What the hell do you know, Greg? What do you know about what it is to compete with the living? It's me who has to compete with you. He thinks the world begins and ends in you. He rolls his eyes if I even ask him to put his dishes in the sink. His biological father doesn't matter to him at all. He doesn't matter to me. Why should he matter to you?"

And then, suddenly, she lowered her voice. So low I had to sneak up closer to the doorway. The whole room had that eerie blue tint from the screen like you were underwater.

"You have no idea," she said. "You have no idea who I am, what I am capable of doing—for him *or* for you."

I didn't want to hear anymore. There was something in my mom's voice that was so tired, bleak. Sort of like Kurtz in *The Heart of Darkness* muttering, "The horror. The horror." But all she said was, "No idea. No idea. No idea. *No* idea."

My step-dad heard it too. "Cathy, can we just step back before we go too far. What I did was wrong. It was only phone calls, emails, a drink or two after work, but it was wrong. I don't want to lose you over it."

"It's time you know. Someone needs to know before I die—and I don't want it to be Ralph, ever."

"What are you talking about?" Greg asked

I could see my mom's reflection in the plate glass window—how she raised her hand to hold him off. My mom doesn't look anything like me. She's little, dark, plump, but she has this really cool, clear voice. If you close your eyes and imagined the person behind the voice you would never in a million years imagine her. You'd imagine someone big, strong, like a Valkyrie—but without the horned helmet.

"What I know best about my son's father is the size of his hand as he held my head down. I remember the feel of the leather on one cheek, concrete on the other. I never saw his face. He wore a ski mask. Rape feels like forever but it is faster than you think. It was my very last night on campus. I'd been partying with friends and was heading back to my dorm. He was smart enough to be methodical—at least about the gloves. The condom was cheap. It leaked. Obviously. We didn't know about it immediately. They never caught him. His breath smelled of raw onion and peppermint. I think I would recognize that. Even today. By the time I knew I was pregnant, it was too late to do anything. I don't know if I would have anyway. I counsel these young women every day now, and I want them to really feel free to choose—but I still don't know what freedom looks like. Except in one way. I chose to never let Ralph know. Unplanned but wanted is what I've always told him—and it wasn't, by the time he arrived, a lie. I will do everything I need to keep the two of us living inside that truth."

"Cathy," my step-dad said.

My mom had that awful flat voice going again. "No idea. No fucking idea. None. None. None."

I slipped back down the hall and opened the front door and slammed it.

"Mom," I called. "Mike and me had a fight and I decided not to sleep over. Anything to eat?"

"You should have called," she said, hands on her hips, drill sergeant mode. More normal than normal. Like I had dreamed all the rest. Sometimes I think I did. "Why does everyone think I'm the keeper of the home-fires here? I could have been out at a movie, having a secret fling." She turned to look at Greg leaning, a little red-eyed, against the doorframe. "I'm putting you both on notice. Ms. Dependable has had a name change to Ms. Dowhatshewannadowhenshewannadoit."

So we sat in the kitchen eating grilled cheese sandwiches, with me telling them about my imaginary fight with Mike, how he kept pushing me into the side rails when we were roller skating.

Before I pack, I make up a list of prospects for Celeste that share some of my best qualities. For fun, I make up a profile for me as well.

Ethnicity: Jewish and your best guess, possibly SAR
Hair Color: Blonde
Hair Texture: Curly
Eye Color: Blue
Complexion: Fair, freckled
Height: feet: 5
Height: inches: 11
Weight: 165
Blood Type: 0+
Education: PhD in American and British Literature, returning to school to study Social Work
Health Status: Liberated
Favorite Hobby: Loving—within reason
Reason for Donating: To continue my mother's genes

I take it with me when I leave, along with my antihistamines.

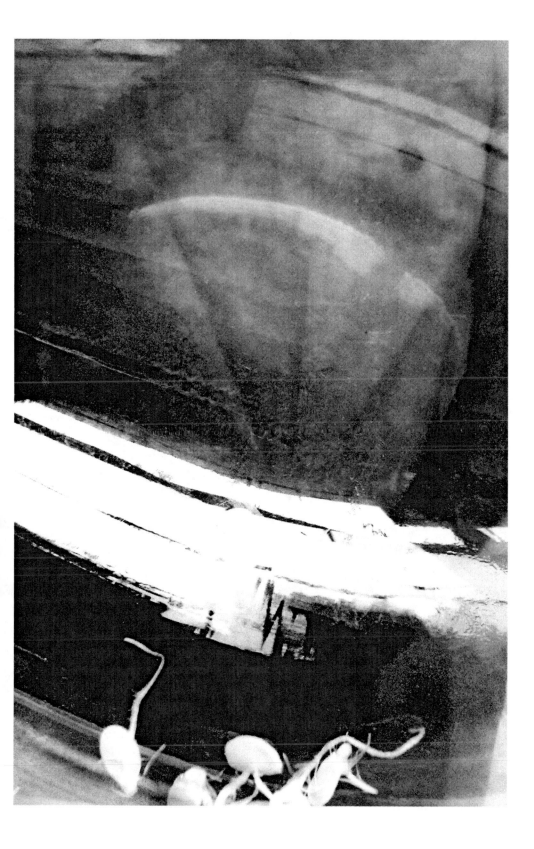

THE MAN I'LL NEVER LOVE

  I bought my first house at twenty-four. It provided a roof for my fourth and fifth boyfriends as well. I've bought two more since then, sold one. The second house I bought to give myself a fresh start, something more appropriate to my actual age. My first house had been way out in the suburbs, in Tucker. My second was in Cabbagetown; it had a third the square footage of the first and was in disrepair, but the location was trendier, near coffee houses and a few music venues. Luckily, my new partner, Kim, belongs on a home remodeling show. I've never seen anyone handier. She had her own house a block away. We moved back and forth as we pleased. It felt great to me. When we decided to get married and put ourselves in the family way, we started looking in Decatur, where lesbian families are more common. We wanted our kids to feel normal. *We* want to feel normal.

  Luckily, all our friends are at the same stage. Four of them are expecting, and another two, like me, are trying. We played with the idea of buying up a block in Cabbagetown, joining our backyards and giving all our kids free rein, but the schools were too bad. Then Anne and Sarah found a townhouse in Decatur. We found a little house with a big backyard in Oakhurst, which would have been out of our reach, especially with the housing market smashed to smithereens here, except that Kim's grandmother died and left her enough for a down payment. Kim sold her house at a loss—but I've held on to mine. I don't know why. Maybe it's just that I don't like loss, and if I can make the mortgage with rent, that's enough for now. Kim's urging me to go ahead and take the hit, mainly because if I do get pregnant, she says she'll be busy enough with our real home that she won't have time to do maintenance on our past lives.

  But there seem to be losses I'm willing to take at this time. Others

I'm not. I don't feel free to talk about this with Kim, or even with my first girlfriends' club. Kim is, I'm clear about this, both my first girlfriend and my last. It took me a long time to come around to the idea of marriage—especially since it doesn't count in this state—but that wasn't because I didn't take marriage as seriously as Kim. If I get married it's for all time—for richer and poorer, sickness and health, 'til death do us part, whether a backward state recognizes it or not.

I hate it when people look at me a little weirdly when I say this, like I don't know what I'm saying. Like I'm a starry-eyed romantic or immature. Shit happens, they seem to be saying. Haven't you heard? Divorce does too. No big.

"We're all decent people here," my father said to me when I went to visit him and his second family in Geneva when I was sixteen. My first and last time. He'd married a woman with a daughter my age. Beautiful in a mindless Paris Hilton kind of way. With a buzzy little French accent, like her mother's. "It's been fourteen years already, lighten up, Laurel."

They'd all been together as a cozy family for twelve years. They weren't a cause of my parents' split, just a sequela. My mom got me, and he was left with whatever else he could round up is the way she sometimes put it. That made sense to me.

Why, after so long, was I there? I wanted to be with my friends back home in Chapel Hill. It was my mother who had decided—dictatorially, I fumed—that it was time for me to reconnect.

"A little dash of cosmopolitanism never hurt anyone," my mom said. "And I need time to concentrate on my research. I have to complete this book contract by October 1st. I don't know how I could have underestimated the time required by so much."

"I can take care of myself," I said. "Take some AP courses at the high school. Go to drama camp."

I don't understand why I didn't see it coming. She'd been dating Steve for about a year, but my mom usually had some guy in the background. I was never close to them. My mom kept her life highly compartmentalized. I didn't visit her office much either, although she'd introduce me to her students or colleagues if we met them on campus or walking down Franklin Street. But the men she saw, her *divertissements* she always called them, had no place in our life. It wasn't just the two of us. We weren't hermits. Her women friends had free run of our house. So did their kids. It was a single moms' mafia. So, I guess it isn't that odd, when I think about it, that I've ended up making the choices I have. What might be more confusing is why I still find them, as I do, both inevitable and shocking. I really didn't see it coming. Until I met Kim, if I ever thought about having a family with someone, there was a papa bear and a mama one. Usually, though, I just assumed I would do it the way my mother had—solo. It was *my* normal. Nothing my mom did later could change it.

My mom didn't break the news to me until we had arrived back at the house from the airport. August 22nd, 1994. While I was sulking in a high rise in Geneva overlooking the lake, she and Steve had gotten married. Without even consulting me, without giving me the slightest hint why. To put it mildly, I wasn't happy.

"It's not going to make that big a change in your life," my mom told me. "It's only one year, and then you'll be off at college. You're already supremely independent. You're out at school events almost every night. Sleep-overs every weekend."

"Can you imagine," a therapist once said to me, "that she might have been doing it for your own good—that she had already received the diagnosis, knew the prognosis? She didn't want it to distort your life."

"She took away the one sure thing in my life."

"She never stopped loving you, did she?" Dr. Watkins asked. She looked at me with *that* look—the one that implied I didn't get it, *life*, that I was wandering dazed in some romantic adolescent haze.

"He wasn't there at the end, was he?"

"Would it have been easier on you if he were? You've said you left the room whenever he entered. Went through that brief Muslim stage so you could be veiled whenever he was around because he wasn't really family." She smiled, inviting me to join her in condescension towards my younger self.

I should never have told her about that. It had all stopped after a few months. It had actually felt like a genuine conversion after my semester abroad in Morocco. That it bugged Steve just made it a little harder to give up.

"What I can't stand is that Steve *acted* like he was there until the bitter end. Like *I* was the one who abandoned her."

"You were in school. You were doing what she wanted you to do—going on living your life to the full."

"I didn't know. I didn't know how sick she was. She didn't tell me."

"Maybe she didn't know." This was another therapist. Dr. Johnson. White-haired, fond of a self-dramatizing beret. "There are a thousand ways to write this story, Laurel. Which one is going to give you the most breathing room?"

"Which one is *true?*" I corrected him.

"For whom?"

He was right. My mom was past caring. My father indifferent. Steve robustly supported by his colleagues, friends, neighbors, even the single moms' mafia.

"I came as soon as she asked me to. I never left her side from that minute until the end."

"And she appreciated every minute, Laurel. She told you so. In person and in writing. She left everything to you. With Steve's blessing. Why can't you let it go?"

The last thing my mom told me was to leave my boyfriend at the time. "He doesn't see your value," she said. "Respect is either there or it's not. It isn't something you grow into. Promise me you won't settle that way, Laurel." I looked at her with blurred eyes. Who was she to talk?

But I saw what she meant at the funeral when my boyfriend Chris asked if it would be all right to leave early, before the burial. He wanted to catch a basketball game with his friends. I just nodded and said, "Don't call me."

I got rid of Louis and Art for similar reasons, one when I was twenty-eight, the other when I was thirty-one. Finally, was all my friends said.

It wasn't until I met Kim that I really understood what my mother was saying. She wanted me to be loved by someone who looked at me the way *she* did.

The way she looked at Steve too.

I thought it was just for me, you know. That it was a mother-daughter, only parent-only child thing—until I saw the two of them together. I never imagined it had anything to do with marriage. Had anything to do with anyone but my mother, really.

That part didn't change, no matter how many questions Dr. Watkins or Dr. Johnson asked me. I think it's something you have to experience to believe. Kim was interested in me for me. No other reason, to begin. And even now, it's always there, this look that says, "Hey you out there, want to orbit a little closer. *I'm interested.*" It's always an invitation, never a demand, but it has real gravitational pull.

So why was it so difficult for me to accept that I'd fallen in love with a woman? Or that I might be lesbian, not just bisexual? I still insist that is what I am—even if I'm not giving myself any more chances to test it.

And it may be true. I think it may be why I'm so confused these days. Kim and I chose a donor who would look like her, shared her mechanical and mathematical talents. But what she doesn't understand is that the man we picked has ended up looking a lot like Steve, or how he would have looked at our age. When I imagine this baby we've just ordered the sperm for, I imagine it being brought into being in the natural way. Natural for my mother. Natural for my father. Natural for me with the young guys who never, my mother insisted, saw my value.

My mother would love Kim. She would not only understand but applaud my choice. But when I imagine this most mechanical of activities, IUI, inter-uterine insemination, the way I ease into it for myself while Dr. Sternberg does what she needs to do with the syringe is not with an image of Kim's beautiful brown eyes holding mine, or memories of how deeply and completely we pleasure each other. I imagine something warm, hot, slowly filling every hollow in me. I fill that void in me with what my mother must have felt when she left me for Steve.

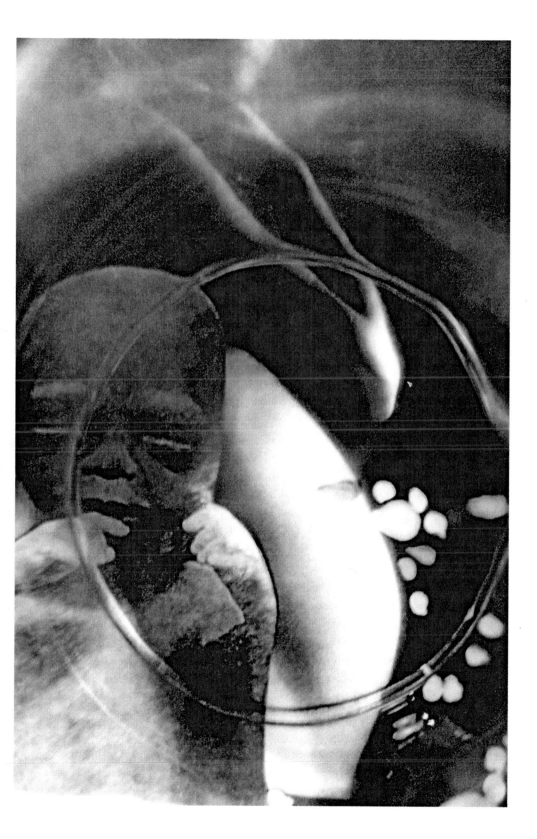

MAGICAL THINKING

I don't know what I feel about it. I mean, I appreciate the concern, but it also made me feel weird. The woman's voice reminded me of this social studies teacher I had in middle school, Mrs. Jefferson, low and calm and clear. Even when we were talking about things like racism, sexism and genocide. I kept waiting for her to laugh like Mrs. Jefferson could, with this deep rumbling laugh that always made me feel safe. But of course the woman from the sperm bank, Melissa, didn't. She wasn't calling to make me feel safe. She was calling to alert me, to let me know that the rate of miscarriage with the donor I'd chosen was unusually high. In the last six months, since they first listed him, seven women had miscarried before seven weeks. I'm not sure if she included me in that number. I did report it, but now that I am sixteen weeks into my first real pregnancy, it feels like miscarriage was too strong a word for what happened back in October one week after my third injection and first implantation.

Now, if I were to lose Cynthia, I don't know how I would handle it. I recognize this feeling isn't going to get all that much better even after she is born. It may be the essence of parenthood. But I've decided I'm not thinking about parenthood, about the baby herself, until I can touch her. Until then it is a special kind of dream and a very precise kind of reality I'm living one day, hour, second at a time. Her name is part of the dream. The cream I rub on my belly is part of the reality. I decided this before I tried again.

But when Melissa from the sperm bank told me about all this—about how they were going to pull this donor until they learned how my pregnancy and that of the other woman who is still in gestation a few weeks ahead of me turn out—I suddenly had this very odd feeling, like I was floating above myself and looking down at myself at the same time and also looking down at all the other women who were carrying or aborting half-brothers and half-sisters to this child who is so privately, so uniquely and only mine. Even if I refuse to imagine her at this time, I experienced a whole different mode and depth of knowing when I saw all these other women carrying babies as close genetically to each other as she was to me.

I mean when you go to a sperm bank, you have to realize that sperm is like money, it gets handled by a lot of people but is essentially impersonal. It's what you use it for that gives it meaning. There was a joke law recently passed in Maryland that defines every egg and sperm as a person, and suggests we make it a crime to waste a single one. And then there are these laws they're wanting to pass with no sense of humor where you force an ultrasound probe up into the vagina of a woman who is already feeling violated by life in the deepest way. Are they going to pass a law that embryos and fetuses can't leave the womb when they damn well please too?

These questions are all easier to think about than those seven women who, *at the very same time as me*, are using the same sperm douche as me, and are waiting, just like me, for something absolutely unique to happen to them. I think of those mass marriages Reverend Moon used to conduct, the aerial views you could see in *National Geographic*, so you were just concentrating on the pattern, like you would a herd of gazelles circling to escape a cheetah. There's a distance at which life looks redemptively orderly. Inhumanly so.

There were only two things I really cared about when I chose the sperm donor. I wanted somebody who seemed resilient, who'd already had some challenges in his life and had been able to bounce back. And I wanted to know he was stone cold sober and chemical free when he jerked off. I called specifically to ask about that. How complete was the drug panel? How often and when was it given? I wonder what the other women were looking for—and whether, when they lost their first dream of motherhood *that* was what they saw themselves as losing: a particular hair color or texture, physical build, an IQ, a curriculum vita, sobriety or can-do-ness. Or was it some barely formed sense of their new self they saw swirling so vividly in the toilet bowl or soaking through their sanitary pads? Someone who finally had exactly what she needed to be the person she wanted to be—and then losing it. When they wrapped themselves in their own arms, crying, or refused to do so—who were they comforting or ordering to buck up and get on with it?

I called my obstetrician after I talked with Melissa from the sperm bank. Dr. Laverne is great. She just suggested I come in for my next regular visit early. "We can do a Doppler just to reassure you, Claudia," she told me. "But I'm not worried about this. Remember at this stage the risk of miscarriage is about one percent."

We listened together to its heartbeat, 150 times per minute. Faster than mine in the middle of my worst anxiety attack, I thought, or a hummingbird high on sugar from the feeder. Dr. Laverne knows I don't want to see the ultrasound images yet. Maybe not until after delivery. She keeps the images in her files in case I change my mind. She knows I want all the tests, including amnio, but I'm saving my eyes for what my hands know first.

"As long as you're eating right, exercising, taking your vitamins, going to therapy and Lamaze classes (when the time comes), I'm fine," she told me. "Every woman has her own way of coping. Her own magic." Dr. Laverne is board certified but also a wiccan. "Pentecostal or pagan," she says, "married or solo, motherhood is the common denominator." But solo is what she focuses on. Most of the women who come to her are lesbian. She runs a support group for single moms out of her office. *From birth to two, we can help you mother yourself as well as your child,* the sign says.

I've heard they do some rebirthing exercises for the moms so they can feel like they're starting anew, just like their babies. Maybe that's what I'm doing by not seeing this baby, not envisioning it at all. Giving it the privacy nature intended.

Maybe that's what I'm doing for myself by not letting anyone, certainly not my family, what's left of it, know what I'm doing. Even at work, they don't have any idea. It's not a big deal, really, since I am my own company of one and can set my own hours and family leave policy. I'm thirty pounds overweight, so I just look like I've been self-medicating general life stress with a little more chocolate than usual. I have some financial flexibility thanks to my grandfather, by way of my prematurely cirrhotic mother—which meant he made trusts for me and my brother she couldn't touch. I could, if I needed to, live frugally off interest for a year. But I've been looking at all my clients and figure I can condense my on-site observations and monitoring to two days a week. I'm an occupational and behavioral therapist for developmentally delayed adults and high-functioning autistics. I do most of my work with small group homes and private clients. I don't think I'll short-change anyone. That's important to me. Win-Win is my middle name.

Dr. Laverne thinks I'm engaging in (white) magical thinking by separating pregnancy from what it results in. Perhaps she's right. But I'm also just doing what I've been trained to do. Breaking any problem down to a series of actions, hierarchical, nested, with a clear goal. Mine is very clear. When I hold that little girl in my hands, I want to know her at that time as mine—and to know myself as unequivocally hers. This is the only way I know to get there.

Until then, I choose to know myself as an inland sea into which she is already pissing and her as an indomitable hummingbird indefatigably treading amnion. Honestly, I'm not sure what's magical in those images. They feel pretty mired in reality to me.

Dr. Laverne says that she isn't worried about the information from the sperm bank because spontaneous abortions (for which they don't probe you with ultrasounds) are so common in the first month, especially with women over thirty-five. Melissa implied most of the women were older than that. At thirty, I'm certainly the youngest. Also, Dr. Laverne said it might be the donor had a congenital defect that would only affect half of his sperm. "So, you're inheriting his good side," she joked.

"Fine with me," I said. "I have enough shadow side for octuplets."

Dr. Laverne, the transducer still in her hand, sat down. She's an attractive woman in her late fifties, earthy. Gray curly hair, long, that keeps falling out of its bun. Brightly colored ruffled skirts under her white coat. With all her briskness, she has a stillness about her that I want to slip into.

"I trust your instincts," she said quietly. "Something in you knew this was the right time—and the right way—to try to have a baby. Has that intuition changed?"

I shook my head. "If anything it's gotten stronger. Until today."

"Why don't you invite us in, then, to rejoice with you? It isn't a choice you have to explain or defend, Claudia. There is no rational reason to bring another life into this world. No rational reason not to either. But there are drives that we can come to trust, become one with. To say yes to a child, to motherhood, is to say yes to everything that life has done and can do to you. Honestly, it doesn't *bear* thinking about."

I could feel those little wings trying so hard to fly in the water. How the water couldn't help but weigh them down.

Pulling the blue paper robe tightly around me, I sat up on the examining table.

"My mother was a very beautiful woman. Vivid. Witty. And a terrible alcoholic. A trust fund dissolute. She died last year. She had two children whose paternity was ambiguous. I was her first, born when she was twenty-one. I'm not sure why she never gave me up. Maybe my grandfather made it a contingency for his support. He liked me. I have a half-brother, Kane, ten years younger than me, with serious fetal alcohol syndrome. My mother never gave him up because I wouldn't let her. *I* made it a contingency. I've always been responsible for his care, even when I was in college. It determined my choice of career. After my mother died, I had Kane moved to a group home here. He loves me, as much as he can love, but he's sometimes violent. I can't manage him on my own. I'll never be able to leave him alone with my own child."

"But he has always been safe with you, hasn't he, Claudia?" Dr. Laverne said. It was, and it wasn't, a rhetorical question.

"I think I just got tired," I said. "Tired of spending my whole life trying to make right what she did."

"Which was?"

"Being at one with herself, with her drives and her instincts, whatever the consequences to those around her."

"You were one of those consequences."

"Happenstance. I was just happenstance. So was my brother."

"To her, maybe. But not to the universe," Dr. Laverne said. "Something in you has opened to that." She sounded like she was talking about taking your daily vitamins, that matter of fact.

"When this woman called, told me about all these women, I can't explain what happened. It was surreal. I could see them, each in a room of her own, one in a bedroom with a partner injecting her by candlelight, one in a doctor's office, the fluorescent light flickering, another with her husband holding her hand. I could see them when the dream ended too, wondering what they could dress their terribly flawed selves in now, what hopes, what destiny, what rationalizations. But what I didn't get, what I can't get out of my head, is this one other woman who is still carrying, that there really is going to be someone out there that this baby may someday somehow meet and look into their eyes the very same way I look into my brother's. I don't *want* her to inherit that. I want her to be the first and the last. I don't know what I was thinking."

I closed my eyes, and when I did, what I saw there was blind as a womb, absolute as my mother's blackouts, indelible as the line I'd drawn between my brother and me with this pregnancy, fungible as the future.

I heard Dr. Laverne stand up and come over to me. She put her hands on my shoulders, so softly I could almost not feel them, just hear the paper rustle.

"Look at me, Claudia," she said. "Something in you knew you were ready. Just imagine that. Something in you knew you were ready for this baby—and for all that comes with her."

So that's my next step, second by second, minute by minute, hour by hour, day by day. Taking that in: Something in *me* knew *I* was ready.

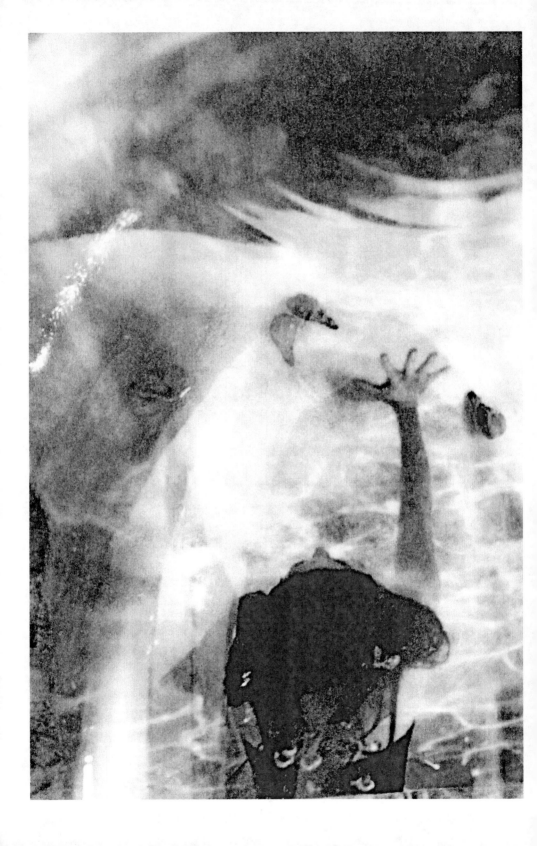

PROGENY

The other day out of the blue my mother asked me if I wanted to know my biological father. Maybe it's because it's my last year home and it's part of her holding on while I'm moving on. Like I couldn't start doing this on my own now that I'm eighteen. Evading, as usual, the *real* issue. She doesn't realize that I'm taking care of that on my own too.

My mom is a psychotherapist and prides herself on her insight, but maybe she should look outside herself more often. I know she feels like she's making this big gesture—acknowledging that there really is a biological father, that it wasn't the immaculate conception and my adoptive father, Bill, isn't Joseph to her Mary. Maybe it is just a natural identification since her own name is Mary. For years she kept insisting that I call Bill "Daddy"—until Bill himself asked her to let up.

I remember exactly when Bill came into our lives: April Fool's Day, 1999, the day after my fifth birthday. We were at the health food store. My mom was buying tea tree oil to see if it would work on my impetigo. Bill was floundering a little after his divorce, trying to decide if he wanted to stay in family law, change specialties, or change careers completely. My mom and I gave him the answer in one package.

The case he won for her, actually for them, was precedent setting. They've both become Christian since then, not evangelical or anything, that would be too hard to reconcile, I think. Episcopalian fits them, acknowledges their history and also holds it at a polite distance. But it's hard for me to get a biblical analogy for my own situation, whatever they feel fits theirs.

You see, I am a sperm bank child that my mother arranged to conceive while she was in a lesbian partnership. The question of whether it was a long-term committed relationship was what brought Bill and my mom together. My mom said no; her partner said yes. My mom says her partner always understood that it was my mother's decision and hers alone to become a mother, and, not to be too crass about it, my mom's cash that paid for the sperm. But the question didn't really come up until I was four and my mom decided to move to Minneapolis for graduate school. It seemed simpler to her to break up than to try to maintain a long-term relationship with no clear plan of return. To my mother, who is nothing if not rational, these decisions had a sense of inevitability about them. *She* knew she was getting more and more dissatisfied with the relationship.

"It was too stereotypical," I heard her say to Bill once. "I wanted someone to share the childcare."

"So you had to turn to a man," he said.

I think part of him enjoyed the irony—on two levels. His own wife had left him because she felt they were too much alike, that there wasn't enough sexual tension for romance. "I feel like I'm living with my best friend," she had said to him. And here was my mother, Mary, looking for exactly what Betty despised.

Jan, my mother's partner, responded badly. She sued for joint custody. Lambda came to her aid, publicizing the case everywhere as a precedent-setting case for gay parental rights. It wasn't exactly that because I'd never been adopted by Jan. Georgia, where they lived at the time, wouldn't allow it. But, just like marriage or long-term commitment, they'd decided (or Jan thought they had) that deed trumped word. She was my second mother, to her mind, in all but name.

My mom and Bill claim they didn't get romantically involved until after the trial, but I could tell that evening in the health food store, the way the color in my mom's face began to rise that something wasn't normal. I mean, who blushes over tea tree oil and impetigo?

The trial took place in September of that year, the same day I started kindergarten. My mom dropped me off and just kissed me once and raced to court. Bill and her pictures were in the paper each day that week, marching side by side down the courthouse steps, the gay rights advocates crowded around microphones. I'm sure the teachers at my school read about it and saw it on television, but no one mentioned it directly, especially not to me. But I remember the last afternoon of the trial, after the verdict in my mom's favor, my mom and Bill came together to get me. The teachers looked at them coming in holding hands, the diamond on my mother's ring finger, and they were super nice to them. Like everything now was right as rain.

Bill leaned down as if he was going to pick me up. I remember that—and how I just shoved my knapsack into his hands and marched ahead of them. Their arms were so tightly wrapped around each other they wobbled a little as they followed me down the hall. "Wait up Madeline," my mother called.

There were flashbulbs popping when I pushed open the school door. Bill and my mom rushed up around me, each taking one of my hands. "For goodness sake," Bill said, "have a little decency. She has nothing to do with this."

I have always liked that line. I've used it with them again and again—for example, when they asked me not to talk about the case after we moved again, this time to Ohio, and nobody knew that I began my life with two mothers. "I had nothing to do with this. Why can't I just be honest?" I asked.

"It's all water under the bridge. Why dredge it up?" my mother said.

What could you expect from her, really, but metaphors as mixed as her messages. By this time, my mom had changed her last name to Bill's, he had adopted me, and they had changed my name too. My mom specializes in family counseling with a Christian emphasis now, and I guess she really believes that what she did before doesn't count somehow, like repentance means that everyone now sees the world the way she does. "Our family," she says at church and school. "Madeline's father and I—"

"You feel true to yourself at last and *I'm* made to feel fraudulent," I tell her.

"What about sensitive and circumspect? Other people may not be as broad-minded as we are. I don't want *you* stigmatized by my behaviors," she answers in that voice that makes me wild, it is such a slick blend of the counselor and church-goer.

What they don't get is I *remember* Jan. I remember being held by her. I remember her voice and how she smelled. She smelled like pine and cigarettes. She was a carpenter and wore overalls with pockets filled with grown-up stuff like hammers, nails, and pliers that she let me play with when my mom wasn't around. She taught me how to climb a tree. When I try to remember how she looks, it's a little fuzzy, but I remember looking at our faces together in the mirror when we were brushing our teeth and her saying, around the foaming bristles, the paste a white ring around her mouth, "Peas in the pod, Madeline, that's us."

So, now you have to understand why when my mother asked me if I wanted to find my biological father I looked at her so blankly. I would think it would be obvious to anyone who has a little insight that my real curiosity is about Jan. I've already made steps in her direction.

My mom and Bill are big into my going to college. Personally, I want to go to a trade school and get a contractor's license. Get out into the real world as soon as I can. Knock down old stuff. Put new stuff up.

"Where on earth did that come from?" Bill wondered when I brought it up. "Your mom and I are all thumbs. And I haven't seen you taking shop or building bookcases, Madeline."

"Or volunteering for Habit for Humanity," my mother said. "Volunteering for anything."

"Don't you want to keep your options open?" Bill went on blandly. "If you went to a school with a good engineering department—"

"And an art department," my mom suggested. "Preferably conceptual art. This desire *is* very imaginative."

I acted as if I was taking Bill seriously. Actually I am. I've looked around to find out where I might go to school that's close enough for Jan and me to see each other. That night I showed them a list of colleges I wanted to visit, and inconspicuously nested in it was one in Asheville. This college tour was all one big circle—from Ohio through West Virginia to Virginia, North Carolina, Georgia, Kentucky, and back.

"It will be my first solo road trip," I said when they start pulling out their calendars. "I need to know how comfortable I would feel in each of these places—and the best way to do that is by going by myself."

"Well, that shows initiative," Bill said.

My mother looked a little less impressed. "It might have been better to do all this thinking last spring. We could have gone with you in the summer." She sounded judgmental but resigned. She really didn't have the time, and I'd already made several long day trips by myself.

"Maybe it didn't feel real to her then," Bill said. "Now she's on a gestational timeline. Nine months and the future is going to pop out, like it or not." Did I mention that Bill is loveable but definitely dorkish if not certifiably Asperger?

"Now my goals are clearer," I agreed. "I'll interview better."

I showed them the itinerary I'd drawn up for fall break. No drive was longer than five hours. In almost every area I would be staying with family friends. I was bringing my best friend, Lisa, with me. Her parents were delighted she was finally showing some interest in higher education. So far she had been threatening them with a cosmetology license as the height of her academic aspirations, which was especially galling to them given her aptitude test scores. I wasn't baiting my parents, just puzzling them.

"Why are you thinking of a Southern college?" my mother asked. "If you're restless here in Ohio, I think you'd be even more so there."

"It's really for Lisa," I said. "She wants to visit Hollins and Sweet Briar and Agnes Scott. But the two state colleges with good engineering programs that are closest to us are in Virginia and Georgia. I thought we'd include those too." I, of course, didn't let them know the reason Lisa was only considering women's colleges, which was also the reason she'd agreed to go along with me.

"Warren Wilson?" my mother asked, looking up from the list.

"A break from the charm schools," I told her. "A little more hands on."

As we get closer to Asheville, I'm feeling more and more nervous and less inclined to talk and Lisa is getting giddy and garrulous.

"I think it is so cool that you're finally going to see your second mother."

I've begun to think maybe this isn't such a hot idea after all. Lisa is interested because she's never seen grown-up gay people, I mean ones who see a future in it with all the things normal grown-ups do—jobs, families, mortgages, divorces. It's not my own sexuality I'm trying to clarify or normalize. I'm hard-wired heterosexual. I don't see this as a virtue—or a vice. I don't see what comes from it as exceptional or particularly exciting.

"Was she surprised when you wrote her?"

"I think so. But she answered right away and sounded willing to meet with me. So however she's living now, my existence isn't a big secret. She did tell me she isn't a carpenter any more. She's a family counselor."

"Irony, my old friend, it's good to see you again," Lisa says. "Maybe she can give me some advice about when to come out."

"Probably not until your dad does," I suggest. When I think *my* family has too many walk-in closets with skeletons, I just have to think about my friends. My friend Carrie found cocaine in her dad's sport jacket pocket when she was looking around one day for change. Laurie's mom embezzled from the PTA fund. Lisa's dad is way too fond of gay porn. Don't get me wrong, we're not troubled. We're Honor Roll, all of us. We're the glistening tip of the meritocracy iceberg. There's not one of our parents, whether they're UCC, Episcopalian, Reform, or Zen, who doesn't actively speak up for suburban family values, especially hard work and professional advancement. It is a cold, paralyzing, but surprisingly buoyant reality—only destructive if you let it hit you broadside.

We arrive at Warren Wilson just in time for the tour. Lisa is smitten. I'm determined to keep my options open. I certainly like it better than Sweet Briar, Hollins, or Virginia Tech, but it feels a little too—something. Self-congratulatory? Privileged in a Whole Foods, my dad's got tenure and I'm just a faculty brat with a trust fund of untapped potential kind of way? I can't say. All I can say it that it doesn't feel like me—which is about as far as I can go in defining either of us. If I imagined it with Lisa in residence, would that change my response in either direction? She's looking more animated than she did at any of the other schools. It was the idea of all those girls together that excited her, she just forgot that most of them would be southern belles far more often into horses, acned and over-sexed boys, and frippery than they were into women.

No one has ever asked me how I feel about my mother's bisexuality. No one has ever asked me how I feel about her denial of it either. They assume I will find the story she tells about her life as true as she does. I'm determined to keep an open mind about it. If she loved a woman once, why shouldn't she love one again? All I'm sure about is that her choices did have consequences—and I am one of them. And because I am, it changes my understanding of all the conditions. I'm just not sure how. Maybe that's what I've come to find out.

By the time we're done with the tour of the college, I'm feeling like I've been stranded in the desert for days, my mouth feels so dry. Jan has invited us to stay at her house (I've not told Lisa that), but I just said Lisa and I needed to leave so early the next morning that it would be better to stay in a motel on the outskirts of town. We don't have anything the next day, I just want to know I'll have something neutral to go back to if this all turns sour.

So we're just going to Jan's home for dinner. She didn't indicate if she had a partner, but when we drive up, there are two cars in the driveway. We park on the street. Asheville is all hills and gullies and cul de sacs and towering trees that now are turning colors. They live on the side of town where people hang prayer flags and decorate their lawns with teddy bears and bowling balls and frequent vegan ice cream parlors, without being troubled by the oxymoron.

"Cool," Lisa says. Then turns to me and puts her hand on my arm. "Breathe," she tells me. "If it's too bad, just rub your nose and close your eyes and we'll leave."

We both laugh since this is an uncontrollable tic of mine.

The woman waiting at the front door for us as we walk up doesn't look anything like what I remember. She's tall, almost six feet, and thin. She's dressed in her work clothes, an elegant gray suit and expensive red leather flats.

"Catherine," she introduces herself, shaking my hand. "You must be Madeline. Jan is running behind and asked me to make you comfortable." Catherine, it turns out, lives next door. She is an administrator at the University of North Carolina-Asheville, a high up one I gather from her clothes. The second car is for Jan's client. She has a home office downstairs. Catherine gets Lisa a coke and me a glass of ice tea and excuses herself so she can go home and change into something more comfortable. She'll be joining us for dinner.

While we're waiting, Lisa and I take turns playing lookout and private investigator. The house is very clean and simple. From the front it looks like a nondescript bungalow, but when you walk in, you realize that's camouflage. The whole back of the house is made of windows. All the rooms open into one another, so there's no place you can't see trees and sky. There's a big deck as deep and wide as the house that extends out over the steep sloping back yard. It's gorgeous and nonsensical. Why keep the front the way it is when it doesn't fit anything inside? Or maybe that's just the point. Why not?

Lisa returns from her trip to the bathroom, the only walled space on this floor, pausing here and there. The conversation nook, the sleeping corner, the kitchen-dining area, the study, and the craft space are divided by etched glass screens. Nothing is out of place. The walls on either side of the house are decorated with large quilts, all of them bright. It feels warm, unusual, open and imperturbable. I, on the other hand, feel cold, dull, and a little defensive. Lisa and I look at each other but don't say anything. I don't know why.

We can hear voices downstairs. A man, then a woman. He sounds angry. She sounds tearful. A third voice comes in, and I do feel something then, something that makes me sad and excited. We can hear a door opening and footsteps around the house. A car door slams, then another door closes. It is a softer sound, but a little more ominous.

"Families," Lisa says. She smiles but she looks really bleak.

"Begotten, not made, being of one substance with—" I recite, not knowing exactly where I'm going.

"Shit, heaven and everything in between," a voice says behind us and both Lisa and I spin around. The woman standing there is nothing like what I remember. Her hands are manicured. She wears a quilted jacket in many colors and a long black dress underneath. She has long silver earrings but no other jewelry. Her hair is short, expensively angled, graying. Her voice, though, sounds like something straight from my dreams.

Even though Lisa and I are sometimes mistaken for sisters, Jan knows immediately which one of us is me. She nods and smiles warmly at Lisa but comes over to me and just stands there, holding one of my hands in each of hers, tilting a little backwards. "Let me look at you, Madeline."

It's not like her eyes travel, it's like she's just taking me in, all of a piece, like a sunrise or a sunset. I don't feel like I have to say anything—which as you may have gathered by now is very unusual for me.

"What is that line from Wordsworth, the child is mother to herself? You feel *just right*, Madeline. Surprising and just right. Tell me about yourself—and your friend. What are you up to these days?"

Catherine joins us a little later and we sit out on the porch sipping ice tea in the late afternoon sun and then go inside and have dinner. Catherine is interested in the colleges we've been visiting and suggests that we tour her university too if we have time. "This is a comfortable city for young people finding their direction," she says.

"Or giving up on that and just going with the flow, which is slow and eddying here, lots of chances to revisit the same place floating on a completely different current every time," Jan says with a smile.

"Did you build this house?" I asked her. "Rebuild it, I mean?"

"You mean the craftsmanship? No. My back protested at the very thought. I designed it with the help of a friend who is an architect. I made all the material choices. The realization was done by others."

"Sort of like therapy," Catherine teased her.

"I'm still living my way into it," Jan said with a smile. And then she looked at me. "When I was a young woman, I wanted to be a carpenter. Wood felt safer to me. Dependable. If I could get the angles right, the supports right, the structure would hold. If I could just get the outside right, everything else would take care of itself. When your mother left, when I lost you, I realized I had been trying to build a shelter from the storm and what I really needed to build was a *life*. Your mother had had it right. I didn't."

I looked at her, shocked, and then out those plate glass windows at the dark sky, our faces reflected so clearly in it. Our eyes met there. Had she just invited me back into another closet, a live in closet?

"She pretends you never happened. It's a matter of public record, scandal even, and she acts as if it never happened. She wants me to go along with that."

"And maybe that is true for her," Jan says in a voice that sounds like the one I heard reading me to sleep as a little girl. "Maybe she didn't know what love was until she had you. Maybe what she feels for Bill is the same stuff as what she feels for you."

"But you, what about you?"

"No," Jan said. "What about you, Madeline? What is the story of your life that feels as true as you can make it at this time?" Her voice is warm, steady. I see Catherine reach out and put her hand on Jan's.

I keep my eyes fixed on the darkest part of the windows as I talk. "There were nights when I was little when the two of you would sing me to sleep together. I remember. You sang "Mockingbird" and "Summertime" and "On Top of Old Smokey" and I would listen to your voices with my eyes closed, how they became something different when they came together, and what it was they became together, *that* was exactly like what it felt like inside me, there wasn't any inside or outside anymore, there weren't three of us anymore, there was just me and it was a good thing. It was a very good thing and I was it and it was me." I looked out at that dark sky, that wall of black, and it was like there was no holding it off anymore. I closed my eyes and it was so still and full inside, I felt like I might be drowning and that it was all right. There was no need to fight it. The life passing before my eyes was already in me. Permanently.

I felt Jan's hand in mine. I heard her say, in a voice that sounded like it could have been the wind in the trees or my own breathing, "You can't know how happy it makes me to hear that. To know that you experienced me as part of that. The question for you, Madeline, is what do *you* need to do to be true to that feeling in you."

"Poet, priest or family counselor," Catherine said briskly. "Definitely not an engineer. Come to career counseling and we'll give you the whole inventory."

"Or hit the road with your best friend. Let the sunshine in." Jan stood up, putting her hands lightly on my shoulders. "It's off to bed with you."

When we hugged, I knew, we both did, that we might see each other again or we might not, but that it wouldn't make any difference. We were both closed books and open questions, *neither made, nor begotten, but proceeding.*

SECOND THOUGHTS

Was it Einstein who said that the definition of madness was doing the same thing in exactly the same way and continuing to expect a different outcome?

But variation, especially intentional variation, brings its own kind of madness. Or a logic searing in its implications.

I have just made two choices that may one day come to haunt me. First, I'm going to bear a baby by a father of my own choosing. Second, I am going to keep this secret from everyone I know—except, in time, the child. This includes my first child—and her mother, who is the love of my life, and with whom I share a home, a marriage license from another state, and an intention, not legally binding, to share a sperm donor.

I don't take these decisions lightly. I don't make any pretense of being in charge of their consequences.

But let's be clear about one thing: the love I feel for Serena and Hazel is real and lasting. We went into all this with such good faith—and hubris. As soon as Serena and I married, she was thirty-four and I was thirty-one, we enrolled in the sperm bank. Our intention has always been to create a nuclear family as like the ones our parent's *didn't* create for us as possible. Two doting parents, two accomplished and accommodating kids.

Why exactly we thought the sperm of a handsome, multi-talented, hyperactive dyslexic high-wire gymnast was perfect for two bookish women of fairly sedentary disposition escapes me at present. I've gone back and reread the donor description to try and reconstruct our reasoning. Was it the height, the hair or eye color—or some idea that we needed some effervescence in our relationship, more fizz than a child who shared our own fairly similar temperaments could reasonably be expected to provide? I think we overlooked some obvious challenges out of, we see now, misplaced confidence. We are both educators, so the dyslexic history felt interesting, manageable—and also provided a healthy dollop of laissez-faire to a rather surreally intentional process. This isn't about eugenics after all. How much control do heterosexual couples have about attraction, recombinant possibilities?

Well we certainly got what we asked for. Hazel is a gorgeous, whizz bang handful. Charismatic, headstrong, and heedless, bright as tacks, able at three to climb thirty feet up into our neighbor's magnolia without once wondering how she'll get down. I adore her. Although she bears no genetic relation at all to me, I feel she's a direct expression of everything precious and hitherto unseen in me. How else, for example, would I know that I too could scale a magnolia tree in two minutes flat and capture this little smudged-face dervish, swinging there by one arm, and descend again without a thought in my head until my feet touched ground and Serena grabbed her. At which point, true to what I generally understand to be my character, I just started shaking and leaned over and vomited.

Serena and I had been sunbathing on the lawn, deep in conversation about our work schedules and daycare fees and trying to decide when was the best time for me to start my own insemination cycle. Hazel was playing with the neighbor's puppy. (We're all around the same age here and haven't gotten into fences yet.) We were deep into our back yard so we weren't worried about Hazel and the cars on the street. Our chairs blocked her way to the creek, the other major danger. But we got lost in this conversation the way we haven't ever let ourselves get lost before in Hazel's waking presence.

"It's the level of attention," my mother blurted out to me after she'd kept Hazel for a weekend. "This is no criticism, honey. But I'd forgotten how much attention babies take." It was clear to us that it would be a good six months before my parents, both in their seventies, would offer to take Hazel for an overnight again. We've never left Hazel with Serena's parents. Serena's father lives in California with his third family, and her mother is a high-powered business executive who I've never seen in flat shoes or without a perfect manicure. (She also drinks a little more pinot grigio than is good for her.)

Serena and I lost our sense of time because the conversation between us was getting heated. My thirty-fifth birthday is fast approaching. I don't feel like there's a clock ticking in me, there's a bomb. We'd said originally I'd start trying when Hazel was fifteen months old at the latest. But at that point I was starting a new job (I'm an elementary school principal), we were still trying to find a daycare for Hazel that made adequate allowance for her energy and also provided her with gentle, steadfast focus. Two years later, our quandary about what's best for Hazel has intensified. Serena is up for tenure at the university and can think of little else. I'm clearly better at responding to Hazel—as evidenced by my faster-than-thought clamber up the magnolia tree—but also because I have a more playful streak and deflection is far more effective with Hazel than reason at this age, and probably always will be. So Serena feels we shouldn't mess with whatever modicum of balance we have now. We know what we're getting ourselves in for and, honestly, two Hazels at this stage would probably require four mommies.

"A year or two more," Serena murmured.

I had just gotten up from my lounge chair, the flare of anger so high it shocked me. "This isn't just about what's best for the two of you—" I had begun. Furious, trying to control myself, I had looked away from Serena, aware of the stretch marks on her too pale belly, the baby weight that was now hardening into middle-aged spread, that professional pinch to her lips—and then I'd registered Hazel, or rather Hazel's bright red dress, flashing up there amid the deep green leaves and wide white flowers of the magnolia. I hissed, "Shut up. Don't say a single word." Then I set off running.

But alone there under the dark arch and swag of the magnolia, Serena and Hazel now safely in the house, the air now redolent with my own vomit, something happened to me. It wasn't an insight, rather a visceral certainty. I wasn't going to let anyone or anything stand in the way of my having the baby that was right for me—and all I knew so far is that it needed to have different DNA from the one that Serena and I had originally chosen *and* that I couldn't trust Serena to help me with this selection. I couldn't trust anyone but myself.

We were both very quiet, even for us, that evening. Hazel was imperious—and impervious to the tension between us.

"Momtoo," she said to me, coming out of her bedroom for the third time clutching our favorite book, *The Island of the Skog*. "Read."

She handed the book to me and I turned it right side up. She stood before me, happily studying the inverted pictures. She may end up a mechanic or a printmaker. She has phenomenal spatial perception and the ability to effortlessly rotate form mentally. It augurs well for life in the jungle, but poorly for school where we want our letters firmly oriented up and down, right and left.

I turned the page and read, "I'm tired of living in a hole."

"Let's sail away instead," Hazel said, jumping ahead a few lines. "Let's find a peaceful island."

She smiled that irresistible smile of hers and improvised, "Filled with momoms, momtoos and Hazels." She sighed with contentment as she edged around the book and settled into my lap. I leaned down and sniffed the smell of shampoo, soap, and pure Hazelness. With the brush of her skin, the synchrony of our breaths, the fear of the afternoon finally dissolved. She would live until tomorrow. But the dark conviction remained. *My* time. *My* choice. *Not* this.

I imagined what it would be like perhaps some time the following year to have this book or Hazel's next favorite balanced on my belly, the book jostled by the impatient movements of my own child.

My own child. I found the thought, the words, chilling and thrilling. We had been so careful from sperm selection on to refer to Hazel as our daughter. "*We're* pregnant," we said to friends and family. It is no more foolish an expression for us than it is for heterosexual couples and, after the first three months, no more confusing in person. Actually, Serena said that. I never did. *Expecting*, is the word I preferred and finally asked Serena to use too. That felt true. We were both expecting.

But I should have listened more closely. Between ourselves, we had been clear from the beginning that we both wanted to become biological mothers, we each wanted that primal experience. Hadn't we? It never occurred to me that Serena, raised as an only child herself, might have really thought that once we had one child we'd both realize it was enough. It put a whole new inflection on her decision to go first. As if her experience really would be *our* only pregnancy. As if she'd chosen me to be her live-in nanny.

I didn't like where my thoughts were taking me at all. What troubled me most was my own naiveté. I *bought* it, you know. Bought that Serena was going first just because of the few years between us. Bought that this child was going to be as much mine as hers. Bought that the choice of donor was mutual. But was I swayed far more than I realized, all the way through, by

Serena's needs, Serena's desires, Serena's drives?

Hazel and I were, I thought, indissolubly bonded emotionally. But as long as we lived where we did, I would have no legal claims to her at all. I would never be able to claim biological primacy. And the truth was I *wanted* that. I wanted to know my own body as life-bearing. I wanted a child the world saw as indisputably *of* me. *And* I wanted that child to be as indisputably different from Hazel as I was from Serena. I wanted that for us *as a family*. I couldn't explain why. I wanted those to be the real terms I was always operating under—and that Serena was too, whether she knew it or not.

I told Serena I had a special grant I was working on and that she had to do the evening daycare runs that week, perhaps the next week too. I spent the time in my office at school reviewing donor profiles on my personal laptop. It's all intuitive, this decision process. It was clear I was not willing to push the envelope in some directions—like race—but would on height and hair texture. Day after day, reviewing the donors, I kept choosing tall, rake thin, and brown-eyed with unruly black curls. Usually with a scientific or musical disposition. One day a biologist, the next day a math major, the next day a jazz musician.

At dinner, as we ate our tomato and spinach pizza (with Hazel dropping the spinach on the table, sometimes the floor, with a sprightly grimace), I imagined him, quiet and musical, tapping out complicated rhythms with his fingers and his feet, his black hair shivering wildly in response. *Alton.* As he did so, Hazel would begin to dance, her silky blonde hair swinging out in a single smooth wave. Serena and I would look at each other and smile.

"Who could imagine a better fit?" Serena would say. "But who could imagine the extent of the variation too."

Years later, to explain the difference between our two children, I planned to 'discover' through well-timed testing that the sperm bank had made an error—and we were its beneficiaries.

But there were the other evenings when I read through all these donor descriptions and I couldn't get my mind around what we'd already done, the lunatic good faith of it, the crazy illusion of control. Would we be any worse off if we had just closed our eyes and clicked? Would we, truly, have any more, or less, control of the outcome?

I thought of the heterosexual couples I knew. My parents. My decades older brother and sister and their spouses. My best friend from high school and his wife. What would they do if their loves were as crazy fluid as ours? My mother didn't, looking at my father, imagine what their genes melded would look like. They didn't say, like they were making their own sundae at Haagen Dazs, I'll take freckles and artistic talent and a dry sense of humor with a stammer and a tendency to sties. I wondered what my mother must have felt like pregnant with me, her ominously late in life child (at least for that time, she was forty-two), for whom she had refused amniocentesis.

Alone at my computer, I tried to get a feel for what I was bringing into being with this choice of mine. What I was refusing. I realized that there wasn't a single thing I'd change about Hazel. I liked the challenges she posed for us—and for the world around her. I felt ready to meet them. Who says we all have to be mild, amenable, conciliatory?

I just wanted out next child to lead us somewhere different. I wanted this with an intensity that was shocking to me. So was its secrecy. *I* wanted to be the surprise element in this marriage, this family. *And* the glue. I wanted to create the difficulties and to embrace them.

The night that I thought I had made my decision (a doctoral student in mathematics and a concert violinist with both an Arab and Jewish background), I decided to sit on it for a night before I ordered my vials of washed sperm and called and made an appointment with a new fertility expert. I think I both wanted to be sure I had made the right choice and to get a real feel for the secrecy I was committing myself to, what it might do to us, for us. I brought flowers and Thai take-out home. I told Serena the grant ordeal was over and that I was now available to take up my fair share of the daycare runs. She looked relieved. Hazel, sneering at the curry, insisted on peanut butter and jelly, made by Momtoo's own hands. I opened a bottle of wine for dinner.

After we put Hazel down, and both of us took our turns reading to her, we went into the bedroom.

"Have I ever told you how beautiful you are?" Serena told me as she watched me brushing my hair. "How much I'd love to have a daughter who looks just like you." She smiled.

I looked at the photo of us with Hazel we took at the zoo last year, which was slipped into the mirror. The resemblance between Hazel and me is startling. Serena, with her wild black hair, her deep set brown eyes, looks like a passer-by. Why had I never noticed?

"Lola, what I said to you the other day was wrong," Serena said quietly. "I don't know if you'll ever forgive me. The timing of our next child is yours to decide. It's just, you know, you're so much better than I am with her. A natural. I just don't want to feel any more marginalized than I do now."

"Marginalized?"

"I chose a donor who looked as much like you as I could. I was so worried that you might feel left out, I think I left myself out. I've never called Hazel my child—always ours. Even when you're not around. Even alone with her."

I looked at Serena's reflection in the mirror. She was sitting on the edge of the bed, her hands in her lap, looking intently at my reflection as well. She was lovely in her long-limbed, sensuous way, with that wild black hair of hers tumbling over her shoulders. Her brown eyes were tired and beginning to tear.

"I adore Hazel. I just can't imagine keeping up with another like her. I'm so sorry." She began to shake and whatever had been condensed so tightly in me expanded, became translucent, fluid.

I put down my brush and turned to her.

She was staring at her hands. "I can't ask you not to—"

"You're right about that," I said. "And I would never forgive you if you tried. So you're not going to do that."

I went to my briefcase and pulled out a sheaf of papers. "We're going to learn from experience, change what we can and accept the rest. Key terms to look for here are tall, dark-haired, academically gifted, introverted, kind, imaginative.

"Brown skin?" Serena asked with a smile, then got serious again.

"And Hazel?"

"Will be, like the next one, *sui generis* and loved for it. Like us."

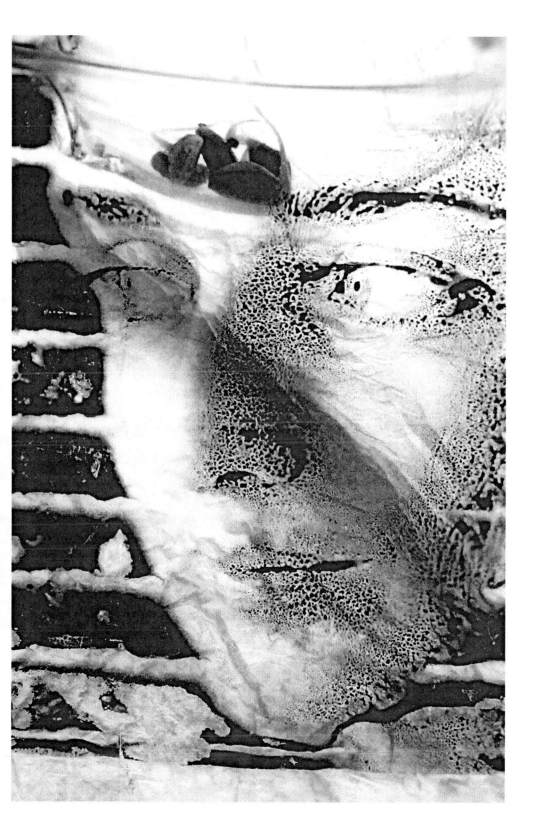

WE'RE ALL DONORS HERE

"You are essential to our success," they told us in the training course. "We're a non-profit, sure, but we need to break even. We provide a service that is half animal science, half romance. The romance is the clincher for everyone concerned. We need these guys to keep coming back—and much as they think it's for the cash, and tell anyone who asks the same, they're bound to experience some push back, some remorse. It's your job to make them seem attractive, genuine, a little noble."

Noble for jerking off twice a week to a porn video or a porn magazine in an empty room? I think.

"For jerking off all by their lonesome for a full year. Don't think it doesn't get to them. They feel virile at first. After awhile they can feel perverted, exploited. Your job is to write them up so they, and our clients, see them as loveable, *dateable*."

"Three-quarters of our clients are lesbians," a woman in army fatigues and a buzz cut, whose first name is Lacey but who prefers to be known as Wilson, protested.

"They're pretty adept by now at making gender translations," Delores said. She's our trainer. Delores is gorgeous. Long curly black hair down to mid-back, brown skin, tight jeans and a tight sequined T-shirt. She's a performance poet in her real life—but her poems are all stories, she emphasizes. She has an MFA from San Francisco State. She's here because her boyfriend has a three-year post-doc at Emory. He's in neuroscience and is going to be their financial bulwark and ballast, she says.

"And they're susceptible. You'd be surprised. We were. Our sales went up dramatically when we began including the interviews. The donors' own narratives weren't half as effective. The guys came out, well, like you might expect. Like guys. Self-absorbed and a little boastful, or terse and flat. But when *we* described their physical appearance (muscular or tall, thin or broad shouldered, dimples, long lashes, a little tattoo showing under a neat blue shirt, a swagger or contagious laugh) or their attitude (withdrawn but slowly warming up, especially when talking about a beloved mother, grandmother, or younger sister; or brash but also self-aware with a keen sense of humor) something changed all around. The orders came rushing in. The guys completed their contracts and brought in referrals.

"And we, my dears, all of us starving writers, became indispensable," Delores said with a broad inclusive gesture to the four of us, which set her sixteen glittering bangles ringing. "But this is the course they don't give you in college or grad school, the one that puts a transforming gloss on real life. I need to tell you before we begin, it's contagious. It begins to infiltrate your whole life and, I'm sorry to say, your writing. Bid adieu to MFA angst and arid superiority—as if the meaninglessness of the universe is your own private secret. Think *juicy*. Two adjectives where once you used none. Think cute, adorable, charming, magnetic. Think women's romance fiction. Think prepubescent girls gushing over Justin Bieber."

We began to look at our hands, the door.

Delores, who knew her audience, looked at us with a gentle smile. "It's not *that* bad."

It was primarily a writing class. We were paired off in twos and asked to write a description of each other, from wide forehead and widow's peak to heart-shaped mouth and sensuous lips, arched or straight brows, strong or pointed chins. Hair texture, not just color. Touchable was a texture. Clothes, hipster or Green Peace, Occupy Wall Street or Goizueta Business School wasn't enough. Black pants, tight, with a beige metrosexual cardigan or green zippered hiker's pants and a plaid shirt.

We also had an interviewing class. We were taught how to create a comfortable interview environment, even in a fairly sterile office. A plant on a window sill—lucky bamboo or a flower without much scent, like carnations or daisies. Kleenex. A water heater, tea, real cups. Cookies on a plate. A warm but neutral expression.

We were told to tell them right off that our job was to get to know them so we could write a warm and positive description of them that would help interested clients know why *we* thought they would be a good choice for progenitor of that client's son or daughter.

"Be careful not to use the word father," Delores said, "except with the ones who are willing to be identified. Even then, it is best to use the word donor. Emphasize the other family relationships. Do they have a favorite brother or sister? What do they like about the relationship?"

She sat down in front of us and pulled her chair up. She had added a black sweater, still low cut. She leaned over so we could see the effects of her push-up bra. "The real secret here is that you have to let yourself be, for that hour, the person, the sensibility that *needs* them, their particular gifts, *their* quirks. So, honestly, we're looking for people as whole-hearted and promiscuous with their affections as labradors. In other words, fiction writers or playwrights. No poets. Or memoirists. They're inveterate solipsists."

"This isn't about you," Delores scolded us more than once. "You are just a conduit, a match maker. But to do this, you have to be in touch with what is most seductive and susceptible in yourself."

We left the two-day course as jazzed and confident as we were supposed to leave our interviewees.

"I can't believe your good luck, *mijita*," my mother told me. "So many young people these days, even with these college degrees, there is no employment. And here are you, your first week out of school, already helping to pay the rent. Using your *mind*, not your hands."

My mother is a maid, has been as long as I can remember, but her hours at the Hilton have been cut with the recession. My dad recently returned to Chiapas because he was worried about the new law they've passed here. I was born here, so I can still go to school but my two older brothers are undocumented and have left Georgia with their families. So I'm all Mamí has now.

We've rented out two of the rooms in the house, but the five guys who are staying here don't feel like family. It's like *we're* the renters. We come in at night and they're all sitting in the living room watching TV, filling the chairs where my dad and brothers used to sit. My nieces and nephews aren't around. It's just Univision, Telefutura, and occasional laughter. Everybody's in bed by nine, except on weekends, and out of the house by six. They're an intrusion, but they're also seasonal workers, and when they leave, I'm not sure how we'll make it. I almost told Mamí that I'm paid on an emission basis, but that made me feel creepy. If I were it would be about 20% of what each of the guys I am interviewing gets for "active" ejaculate. I wish they had told me that when I took my GREs.

I think about these guys in our living room quietly watching a telenovela and consider suggesting that they participate. I could get a referral fee. I could do the interviews. You're supposed to be in college or technical school, but I could fake that for them, claim they all received degrees back home. It's not like they make people bring in their diplomas. But you have to be able to work legally in the state, and I'm not sure any of them qualify. They're braver than my brothers, or more desperate. And not as tied down. Both my brothers have legal wives and kids. So they stand to lose everything if they're deported. By the time they get back in, their kids will have forgotten them. That matters to us. Families stay together. It hurts my mom to think of my dad all alone in Mexico. As soon as I can stand on my own two feet, for example, my mom is going to join him. That's a joke. You'd get it immediately if you saw me.

I know they're experimenting now with injecting stem cells in your spinal column, but I am in a wheelchair for life. When I was fourteen, my dad and I were driving to Walmart and there was an accident. It wasn't anyone's fault. A car had a blowout and the driver lost control and steered into our truck and then we rammed into a semi in the next lane. My dad will never forgive himself. He feels he should have swerved the other way—but if you just try and imagine it, I mean in reality, the physics of the whole thing, there wasn't anything he could have done. It's just that he came out in one functioning piece and his beloved daughter did not. It broke his heart and even I can't mend it for him. It's one of the times when the fatalistic reflexive makes sense: *Mi espina se rompió. El corazón de mi papa se quebró.* My spine broke itself. My dad's heart shattered itself.

It was as good an injury as you could hope for, I suppose. The break is pretty low, T-11, and incomplete. So I can feel below that even though I can't walk. My pelvis wasn't shattered like Frida Kahlo's (although she was able to walk). I don't get to wear those fancy plaster casts she decorated so dramatically or to keep a mirror over my bed.

It's odd, since I'm the one who got hurt, but it's clear to all of us that it is my job to make this better, bearable, for everyone. I've taken my role seriously, and it's helped me. It means that I'm the only member of my family to finish high school, let alone college—or a masters. They are *all* so proud of me. My brothers came back for my last graduation ceremony. They left their wives and kids in Illinois, but they were here, cheering. My dad left for Chiapas the day after. I offered him my diploma, but he said he wanted me to keep it here. It was safer. None of them know they supported me in getting what must be one of the most worthless degrees on earth. So it's my job to make sure that the cost isn't too high, that my mother gets reunited with my dad as soon as possible. They're good with each other, my parents. It's what I'd call a murmuring love. Not lots of *mi amor, mi reina* or *mi cielo*. Just this constant undercurrent, as much tone as actual words, *"¿Tortillas?" "Sí." "¿Huevos?" "Gracias." "Aquí es la renta."*

When I wrote stories in grad school, I wrote about all of them. What it was like for my dad at twenty to leave his village in Chiapas for the first time. What it was like for my mom to follow him eight years later—bringing my brothers, they were seven and nine, in through the desert. How my brothers met their wives. I could see everyone in the class was waiting for me to describe why I was in a wheelchair, but I never did. It just isn't that interesting to me. I'd rather write about them, their prurient curiosity, what they imagine might have happened. I've introduced myself into this story more than in any other I've written. It's my try at experimental fiction (which mainly means lost in the *ombligo*) and is quickly boring me. I want more options than this one body, this one life offer me. I think I wanted this as intensely at twelve as I do now, so in the most profound way my character hasn't changed because of the accident, if anything it has become more itself.

My thesis advisor, Antonio Rosario, was also Hispanic, but third generation, all of them educated, which he complained was not so good for his writing. "Now you," he said, "have primary source material." He kept fondling my stories in a way that made me feel he was touching something else.

He told me that if I sequenced my stories right, added one or two more, I'd have a novel-in-stories, which would be more marketable than short stories. "Once you have 200 or 250 solid pages, just send it out. Contests. Publishers. Agents. Be promiscuous, polymorphous perverse. The worst that can happen is that it will be rejected. Don't do it, though, until you're two-thirds of the way through your next book," he warned me.

His first book had been published to quite a bit of small press hoopla about eight years ago. He was too busy to write another, he said. He regularly applied for one hundred writing jobs a year. His wife Karen worked as a librarian at Georgia State. He was the primary care-giver for their two-year-old daughter. Karen, beautiful, blonde, with a little of the reserve of Catherine Deneuve, was jealous of me. I could feel it when I ran into them on campus together. But I'm not sure whether it was because of my relationship with Antonio or with their daughter, Cielo, who loved to climb up on my wheelchair and take a ride with me—and had learned to smother me with kisses as petition, bribe, and payment all rolled into one. Cielo was adopted. From Guatemala. She looked a little like me. My family is Mayan, like her.

Karen was the one who couldn't conceive. Antonio told me they had gone through her whole trust fund trying to find out what was wrong. They were thinking of an egg donor so she could have the experience of pregnancy. He looked at me a long time after he said that. I was glad Karen wasn't there. There are romantics who gloss reality like Delores said, and there are romantics who deny it entirely. I could see clearly into which category Antonio fell—and I wanted to be in another. When I graduated, I lied and told him I was returning to Mexico with my parents, that I'd be gone at least a year. Atlanta is a big, sprawling city. As long as I avoid the campus, it could be years, perhaps decades before our paths cross again.

I suppose that experience *is* what made me apply for the job at the sperm bank. That unvoiced suggestion about being an egg donor. What use, Antonio implied by his silence, were those eggs to me? He has no idea. The doctors have said that there is no reason why I can't, with adequate medical supervision, conceive and carry a baby to term—or care for it. This has always been a most secret source of hope for me. It is, along with consoling my family, why I have studied so long and so hard.

I think there was something about Antonio's silence, the rapaciousness of it, that was as decisive to me as the moment in the hospital when the doctor told me that I would not be able to walk again. I mean, I *knew* I wasn't going to be able to walk, but there was something in the saying of it, in all that would be set in motion once it was out in the air like that, that created a brave new world for me. One that brought out the best in me. One that let me claim my strength. Antonio's implying that my whole life was destined to be one of all give and no take, the write-off in it, did something similar. What had been a secret source of hope for me was now going to be an open one.

When I interview those young men, I *am* going to be one of those potential mothers. More than that, I am going to have those mothers see the world through *my* eyes for a moment. I am going to write about how these young men walk, when they pause to reflect, when they make eye contact, when they stare at the door, what they probably looked like as babies, as boys of three or nine or thirteen. And these young men, having lost themselves in my attention like Narcissus in a pond, will when they read what I've written be surprised into an image of themselves that is a little tougher, more sharply focused, more robust.

I can't wait to start. I decide I'm going to practice on our boarders and roll my wheelchair into the living room, station it in front of the television. "*Caballeros*," I begin, "*necesito su ayuda.*" I gesture for them to turn off the television. "If we are to make the rent this month, I need to practice my interview skills," I tell them.

I explain the sperm bank to them. They are stunned. Only in America. But they want me, like a sister, a daughter, to succeed. They don't know I have an ulterior motive. I am harvesting their stories as Antonio wanted to harvest me. But unlike him, I want to give them something in return.

"I need to have you tell me why you think any woman should choose you to father her child." The bright bangles on my wrist clatter as I arrange my long red skirt. My earrings glitter. My long black hair flows like water over my full breasts. I have their full attention. I have degrees. Citizenship. English. And the power to raise others up like me.

"Roberto?" I ask. He is the oldest, the leader. He is in his late forties, but looks ten years older. He comes from Guerrero. He has six children. His oldest son, Dionisio, is with him this trip. Roberto is a gentle man, his hands worn from work in the peach orchards and tomato fields. He is missing the first joint on his right ring finger. He has built a house of cement with his own hands. He can't read but he can recite all the psalms from memory, and many Juan Gabriel songs as well. When he smiles, it's as if the light is falling in saints' rays through dark clouds.

"*Soy honesto,*" he tells me. "*Leal, cariñoso.*"

His son Dionisio nods. "*Humilde,*" he adds.

"And determined and intelligent," I add. Roberto smiles, blushes.

When he starts telling me about his childhood, the dirt floor, the smell of pine smoke from the fire, the sweetness of his mother's tamales, a silence circles us. I can hear my pen moving over the paper.

"And as a father, what is your *don*, Don Roberto?" I ask.

Dionisio laughs. "He loves and leaves. Loves and leaves. Nobody ever gets tired of him."

And sends money home, Roberto adds. Every week. *Por la leche y el techo.*

My mother comes in, settles herself in a chair at the table. There is a gentle glow from the summer twilight lighting us both, a dignity to our separateness. She can see, finally, that it is safe to leave, that I too, have a *don*, a gift, that can't be taken from me, that replenishes itself through its giving, like a fountain, and that is as visible to others as it is to her, as it will be to my own daughter. I have *room* for the world—and the world has room for me.

MORE

    I just can't get enough of her—my first child, a girl who we've finally decided to name Pearl because her skin is such a luminous ivory and she is, clearly, without price. I'm taking paternity leave because there were complications in the delivery. We were going to stagger our leave: Lily first, then me. But Pearl was born two weeks late and was so big she required an emergency caesarean after twenty-four hours of pitocin-induced dry labor. My wife Lily is still recovering. They're a mismatched pair, Pearl at a robust ten pounds and twenty-two inches, Lily at a scant one hundred and five pounds (now that she is relieved of Pearl and placenta) and five foot one if she holds herself very straight, which she usually does. (Lily teaches dance and martial arts.)

    All Lily wants to do right now is sleep. She's very upset that the obstetrician who delivered her wasn't the one she regularly saw during her pregnancy and somehow in the danger of the moment her preference for a bikini incision (expressed in the quiet of the doctor's office in what to both of them seemed at that point the exceedingly remote chance of caesarean) went disregarded. If she catches sight of herself undressed in a mirror, sees the long longitudinal slash, she starts sobbing loud enough to tear the stitches.

    "Think of it as a battle scar," I tell her. "Proof of your heroism."

    I don't tell her I love her more for it. I couldn't love her more if I tried. She's given us the most amazing, life-transforming gift. What I feel for her is the sweetest devotion, deepest love—and phenomenal exasperation. It's three weeks now and my hardy warrior wife is still a basket case. The doctors are beginning to talk anti-depressants, perhaps hospitalization. But Lily doesn't believe in allopathic medicine. So I encourage mental homeopathy, suggesting she sit by herself for fifteen minutes every morning and night and meditate on world sorrows, on every personal wrong and slight she's ever endured. Anything to get her mind off those stitches, the loss of integrity, fundamental integrity, they symbolize to her. Anything to change the way she looks at our truly beautiful, totally blameless little girl with her wide brow and black curls and rosebud mouth. This sadness of Lily's came from somewhere else. Not Pearl. Never Pearl. She has to understand that. Fast.

I turned forty the day before Pearl was delivered. Lily is thirty-eight (however rapidly she seems to be regressing to an inconsolable three). Our baby was much anticipated. We've been together for eight years now, the first five of which were devoted to my playing academic catch up after a globe-trotting, off-the-beaten-track twenties in which I taught English in China and South Korea, tended bar in Thailand and Barcelona, meditated in Buddhist retreats in central Massachusetts and northern California, earned money as a juggler in Key West and an acrobat on the Santa Monica Pier.

Now, with my Masters in Environmental Policy, I'm working at NIEHS in the Research Triangle. We live on the outskirts of Chapel Hill in a house we bought with some help from Lily's parents. Lily has her own dance and martial arts studio in the mall, near Whole Foods, so it draws in aggressively ecological academics as well as more mellow counter-culture artisans and artists and the chronically under-employed. My mom and two sisters live in Hillsboro, Durham, and Cary. The six boxes of photos and memorabilia I have stored down in the basement—and the masks that are hung all over the house—are the only proof that I ever left the area and lived so peripatetically for a decade.

Lily has never expressed much curiosity about my earlier life. I at first understood this as part of her Zen approach to life: what you see is all there is. Now, when I hear her sobbing about those stitches, I wonder if for Lily anything but her own experience exists. Period.

Lily is the only child of older, immigrant parents, both academics. They both come from the Netherlands, her mother from Delft, her father from The Hague. This is an important distinction to them. They are both full professors of statistics, retired over fifteen years now. They speak a completely unaccented English, look like identical twins, are imperturbably up-to-date on current events, fond of walking, birdwatching, and talking their own version of shop. They still attend the annual American Statistical Association meetings religiously.

From what I can gather, Lily was an unexpected but wanted child born when her mother was forty-three. Lily is convinced that she was adopted, how else explain her black hair and faintly Asiatic features, but her parents both insist they must be throw-backs to great-grandparents who were born in the East Indies. What is clear is that, with benevolent detachment, she was allowed, indeed encouraged, to be a world unto herself. Slow to speak, dyslexic, she mastered body language early and seemed to have spent her childhood in tutus, princess dresses, and ninja costumes. Her parents enrolled her in Montessori, where she learned to wash and put away dishes, identify those tasks she wanted to complete and those for which she had no affinity, and feel no anxiety about restricting herself to the former. She liked to dance her words, finding ways to fold herself into N's and O's. As a teenager, she became obsessed with ballet, making it as far as tryouts for American Ballet Theatre. She was disqualified when she improved on the choreography she was asked to perform. She didn't see this as self-sabotage, only common sense. Her version was more beautiful and more challenging.

She went to Bennington and majored in dance, leaving her junior year to join a deaf dance troupe as its lone hearing member. In her twenties, she lived with the troupe's director, twenty-five years her senior, and became fully fluent in sign language, translation skills she still uses in courts and hospitals to augment her income when enrollment is down at the studio. She also offers a weekly mixed martial arts class for the deaf. When I asked her how that was, leaving it vague whether I meant living with the director or working with the troupe, she said, "I could turn my back and say anything I wanted at the top of my lungs. It simplified things."

She left the director because he began pressuring her to get pregnant and she wasn't sure she was willing to raise a deaf child. Besides, the sex was getting too routine. Her next lover was a heavily tattooed, husky-voiced lead vocalist for a rock band who left her for an extended stay in rehab and a complete life make-over.

I met her some months later through aikido. I'd gone in to her studio to ask if they had room for another instructor and another form of martial arts. They already offered classes in karate, tai kwan do, qui gong, and tai chi, along with ballet, modern, and tribal belly dancing. I needed to bring in some extra income to supplement my scholarship.

"Show me," she said, getting up from her desk. I had thought she was the receptionist.

Aikido is all about balance, using your opponent's natural momentum against them. It depends on close observation, accurate prediction, and surprise. Lily was a natural. We could both feel it. It intrigued her, so she opened up a time slot for me, took a third of my class fees for overhead, and received free private lessons as well. I thought I had a great deal going. Still do. We moved in together six months later.

When Lily turned thirty-five, her fertility clock belatedly started ticking. I think we're primed for these urges in ways we can't understand. Both my sisters had their first babies at the same age my mother was when she had each of them. And they each birthed three, just like our mother. I flipped it a little. My dad died at forty of a heart attack. At the same age, I welcomed in new life, my beautiful girl, Pearl. It all sounds so foreordained, but it was pure chance, great luck. Symbolic only in retrospect.

Lily felt all she had to do once she decided to have a baby was spread her legs. We were never shy about sex, nor low in libido, so we just figured we'd go on the way we had been only leaving out the Norplant. After six months, we realized it wasn't so simple anymore. It was a wake-up call for both of us. Because we're fit and look younger than our ages, we believed the mirrors. It was more flattering, easier. But we *really* believed them. So when the fertility expert floated the idea of tired eggs and low motility we both felt shamed in ways that went beyond the biological normality of our situation. Indeed, its normality was what shocked us. We had never seen ourselves as like those tired men and women coming into our classes hoping for a zest-me-up. *I* didn't see myself as similar to my colleagues at NIEHS who had circles under their eyes, twenty extra pounds around their waists, and were always racing off to hockey or soccer or dance classes muttering, like the White Rabbit, "I'm late. I'm late."

At first Lily wanted to ignore the doctor and just do what we were already doing more often, longer, harder. Then she went to various naturopaths, taking all kinds of supplements meant to increase fertility. Then she went high tech. She assumed the problem was with my sperm and had them spun to increase the count. Then she went to Clomid to ripen her eggs. I went along, but at that point I wasn't avid the way she was. I have five nieces and three nephews, after all. I mentioned adoption, once, and quickly backed off. Lily wanted her *own* baby. *Our* baby. And she wanted it now.

Those were a very dour two years. My mother and my sisters didn't help, all three so thoughtlessly earth-mother fertile and irritatingly laissez-faire. "If it is meant to be, it will happen," my sister Bess said. "It's dangerous to fool with mother nature." She teaches special ed and went on to tell us about some of her students whose difficulties, she believes, are the product of fertility drugs, multiple fetuses crowded in a womb and born too soon.

"Trust," my mother would interrupt. "Look at your own mother. She was six years older than you are now when she conceived you."

"Adoption is always an option," my sister YoYo said. Her fourth and fifth came from China and Ethiopia respectively.

It was a relief to all of us when Lily began to throw up constantly and dropped ten pounds and was diagnosed as definitively pregnant. As soon as she had what she wanted, Lily, although gaunt, lost her haunted look. She became the woman I'd married—beautiful, imperturbable, hyperactive, so unintrospective there should be a special word for it. She didn't stop teaching until she was full term, although she stopped flipping students in karate or demonstrating grand jêtés in ballet by the seventh month. When the baby still hadn't appeared a week beyond the due date, she threatened to dance it loose.

I realize now there was something I should have been paying attention to here. Something about Lily's relationship to her body. Something about what happens to Lily when something—anything—steps between her and her goal. I don't know what I've been thinking. Truly. It didn't hit me until they put Pearl in my hands, still a little bloody around the ears and nostrils and I just wanted, with all my being, to pull her inside me. I walked over to Lily, but she had her eyes shut. They'd had to give her general anesthetic she'd become so distraught during labor and they needed to be able to act quickly. (Was she trying to remind them of the bikini incision?)

As I approached her with our daughter, Lily looked so beautiful and tired, her eyes closed, her breath clouding the oxygen mask. I looked at Pearl and held her closer.

"Your mother would love to share this moment with you," I whispered. "She's going to be the happiest woman in the world when she can hold you for the first time." Did I know, even at that moment, I was lying? My first words to my perfect girl and they were untrue.

"Oh my god, oh my god," my mother said when I called to tell her. "We'll be right there. There's no high in the world like your first child."

But Pearl isn't my first child. She is, I learned a month ago, my ninetieth conceived, my sixty-eighth live-birthed. Lily has no idea. No one does. I mean, how can you get your mind around that? I hold Pearl, her big steel-blue eyes staring up at me blankly, her beautiful full mouth, just like my mom's, pursing and relaxing, and I think my heart will break, my mind will explode with the enormity of it. I have never imagined, let alone known, love like this. So pure. Complete.

In the last twenty years, sixty-seven times a woman, perhaps a man too on occasion, has had this experience staring down at a baby who has just as much in common with me as this terrifyingly perfect being, and I had no idea. Truly, I had no idea what that really meant.

Honestly, what healthy red-blooded twenty to twenty-two year old eager for travel funds, more than willing to jerk off regularly to get them, really does. But *ninety* conceptions, *sixty-seven* live births. I would have guessed, oh, ten, twenty at the most. But I have as many progeny as a Saudi sheik, with more women and in a much shorter time. They used up all my sperm allotment, even those set aside for families, by the time I was thirty-two. I know that because I called at that point to ask if they could withdraw them. It was my secret wedding gift to Lily. But they told me not to worry, nature had already run its course. They did tell me I'd been one of their most popular donors, that mothers liked the sperm's high motility and even more the babies themselves, found them bright, adventurous and easy-tempered and shared this news with their friends, along with my donor number. At that point, the sperm bank didn't offer numbers of conceptions and I didn't think to ask. Anymore than I thought to ask where the mothers were located. Why for years did I imagine those no-more-than-twenty babies scattered equitably across the whole globe?

When the sperm bank called last month it was to let me know that although I'd been an anonymous donor there was a high probability that at least one of those babies, now nearing the age when I jerked out my minimal but essential contribution to their existence, might be contacting me despite my expressed desire for anonymity. Recently, their computer files had been expertly hacked and the donor files stolen. Since there already was an active family group organized around my donor number, there would be a lot of curiosity about my identity and these days news travels faster than sound so they thought I should know and prepare myself for the eventuality.

The woman I talked to, her name was Soledad, seemed astonishingly blasé. "With all the genotyping today and increased openness, it is becoming more and more likely that donors will be identified. We always include that possibility in our forms now. When young people write us, we relay the request to donors even if the donor originally indicated he wanted anonymity. We change as we age. Some of our donors are gay and now, in middle age, are delighted to welcome these kids into their lives.

"In your case," she said bluntly, "it's probably safer to know. Now we restrict how many women in a geographic area have access to a particular donor, however popular he may be, as well as how many women can buy in overall. It's not great, you know, to have sixty-seven half siblings in a three state area who have no idea of each other's existence."

"What three states?" I asked.

"North Carolina, Virginia, and Georgia. For some reason our donor bank wasn't as attractive to women in South Carolina or Tennessee. Neither were you. Your profile appealed to urban women. Mainly lesbian."

"Do you have a state by state breakdown?" I asked. In my mind's eye I could see the GIS map I was going to generate as soon as I got to work. All the places Lily and I wouldn't even stop for lunch anymore.

"My suggestion is don't stress yourself," Soledad said, her voice warming. "The support group organized around your number has about fifty members, ten families with two children and thirty single moms. From what I gather, they meet annually. Some who live closer to each other visit together more frequently. They have a Facebook page listed by donor number. If they're responsible, once you're outed they will probably send a single representative and then choose to meet with you as a group. You're free to refuse. But if you do meet with them, mention how young you were. Talk about the importance of nurture over nature—that will play well with the moms."

What Soledad of the Good Seed Bank didn't know and I still didn't come clean about was my family medical history. In particular, the death of not only my father but also my grandfather and great-grandfather of heart disease by the time they reached fifty. I had told Lily about my dad of course, because if I didn't my mother and sisters certainly would. Somehow, my mother and sisters hadn't put that together with the early deaths of my grandfather and great-grandfather, perhaps because their wives were so lively and long-lived and had been such a sustaining part of our family system. It's like they didn't notice the absence. Only I, as the last remaining male, did.

My mother and sisters were oblivious, but I didn't have that excuse. I had lied to the Good Seed Bank. A year after my father's death, I swore he was alive and well, with nothing more worrying in his medical history than childhood asthma. My own doctor, a new first year resident at the college health center, gave me a clean bill of health—great blood pressure, cholesterol, no heart murmurs—and convincingly relayed back to the sperm bank the same family medical history that I'd already given them myself. If you'd asked me then why I did it, I'd have said I really needed the money. But now it is clear to me that I needed the lie. And I needed it in that particular context. I mean, there certainly were other ways, at that age, to earn more cash. Working construction, for example. I could have embezzled if it was only deceit that appealed to me. No, I needed to lie about my own suitability as a potential father.

I wasn't going to be around for these children any more than my father was for me, but I was *worth* something, my genes, *his* genes, were *worth* something.

Now, I wonder if I'm vulnerable to a class action suit. I listen to Lily sobbing over her stitches and I think of all those sixty-seven mothers standing over ICU beds, their children's chests sawed open, huge stitches embroidering their bisected sternums.

This last month I've been visiting the medical libraries at both UNC and Duke reading everything I can on congenital heart defects and genetics. There is one question I didn't ask, couldn't ask Soledad. I still can't. How many of those sixty-seven are boys?

I felt such a sense of relief when we could tell Pearl's sex. I'd sworn to myself I'd let Lily know the full history of my family if it came back XY, that I'd take sole responsibility for whatever might follow: abortion, divorce, every genetic test and medical procedure on earth. When we were told we were having a girl, I felt absolved in some profound way. But I want to make it clear, my concerns were all for *my* daughter, not for anonymous spawn. Even in my wildest dreams I never imagined there were more than I could count on my fingers and toes three times over and that they weren't, as I had so conveniently although improbably imagined, scattered sparsely across the whole country and various foreign lands.

But they are all in Virginia, North Carolina and Georgia. They have annual family reunions in the Smokey Mountains in the summer. For all I know, there could be as many as thirty of them in the Research Triangle. There might be one living right down the street. I know it doesn't pay to think about it, but as I dress Pearl up in her little green fleece onesie and pull a knit cap over her hair, tuck the blanket around her in the carriage, I can't help myself. The oldest could be a junior in college now, the youngest eight years old.

"I'm taking Pearl out," I whisper to Lily who, exhausted by her tears, lies in a light doze. She flips her hand gently to register she's heard me. My heart goes out to her. She looks so small, so demoralized. I go over and kneel by the bed and put my hand on her back. "It's going to be all right, honey," I tell her. "These hormones are going to subside and it will be all right."

"I don't know what I imagined," Lily says softly. She doesn't resist my touch. She doesn't respond to it either. She could be talking to a stranger. "I don't know what I imagined, but it wasn't this. It wasn't *her*. She doesn't look like anyone I know. She's as different from me as I am from my parents."

At this point she turns over and looks at me. "I think they gave us the wrong baby, Caleb. I want a DNA test." Her thick black hair is tangled. The light from the windows glints off her near black eyes.

"If it will ease your mind, we'll do it, honey. But I have no doubt. She has my mom's mouth. She has your ears and will probably have your beautiful hair. Her eyes will turn brown."

"I'm sure," Lily says, meeting my eyes. "I'm sure she's not mine. If she were, I would feel something for her, Caleb—and I don't."

I have always enjoyed Lily's sometimes brutal honesty. I know it has made her enemies, but to me it has felt as impersonal and thoughtless as a child's—driven by a need to get the world right whatever the cost to the feelings of those around her. Usually I've responded in kind and she doesn't mind. This time I can't stop myself. I know it's wrong before I even open my mouth, but I feel she just slammed her whole weight into my chest with a karate grunt kick and drove the words out.

"Who *do* you feel something for, Lily? Truly. I mean, other than whether they're meeting your immediate needs. Is there anyone you love just for being themselves, completely independent of you?"

Lily's forehead creases. "Why would I do that, Caleb?"

Her face is so open, so nonplussed, all the energy dissipates. It's like arguing with a cat.

"I'll be back," I tell her. "*We'll* be back."

"No hurry," Lily says, turning over, wrapping her arms protectively over her stitched, still puffy stomach. "We can do the test tomorrow. Return her as soon as we get the results." She takes a deep breath, relaxes. By the time I'm on my feet and closing the door, she is snoring lightly.

When I go on our walk, I take my cell with me, relieved we've never had a common landline. I don't want anyone from Donor 1324 Family Circle announcing themselves to Lily.

As we walk, I murmur to Pearl trying to see if her eyes will turn in my direction. They don't. I lean close but her eyes wander as they will. Her hands thrash happily until she hears a crow caw loudly from a tall pine, when they still as she listens. I inspect her earlobes, still visible under the purple cap my mother knit for her. They *are* like Lily's. It's a warm afternoon, the light is that special autumn one that seems to have something spacious to it. Pearl's skin has an otherworldly glow. She can't smile yet (honestly she can't do much except breathe, suckle, piss, shit, and cry) and her natural expression because of her small, round, faintly receding chin is a mild scowl, but she seems like a happy baby to me. I don't care what any test tells us. I'm never going to let her go. Lily's right, she *isn't* like us. She is her own self—and I want to get to know her. I *need* to know her. I'm not going to let Lily get in my way. *Our* way.

I call Lily's obstetrician and talk to her about Lily's crying bouts, about her belief, which I clearly label a delusion, that Pearl isn't our own flesh and blood. The obstetrician suggests a psychiatrist who could, if necessary, recommend hospitalization.

"Do you think she is a danger to herself?" Dr. Campbell asks me.

"No," I answer immediately. "Lily turns her anger outward."

"Is she a danger to the baby?" Dr. Campbell asks.

I pause, aware of what impression that pause makes, but I am also considering the question.

"As long as Lily gets what she wants, no."

"And what does Lily want?" Dr. Campbell prompts.

"To send her back and get the right baby. The one that she can identify with."

"Do you have any doubts?"

"No. I feel I can see traces of both of us in her. I saw the nurse in the operating room put the bracelet on her. Lily didn't. She just has my word." *For what it's worth.*

I lift my head and look at the bright white clouds whipping across the clear blue sky. I smile at Mrs. Williams, a widow in her seventies, who has put down her trowel and is coming over to admire Pearl. I smile and point to the phone in my ear. She waves and returns to transplanting her pots of bright yellow chrysanthemums. Pearl lets out a mewing sound, half complaint, half exploration. I jiggle the stroller to distract her.

"Lily will never agree to see a psychiatrist," I say.

"Then do the DNA test," Dr. Campbell tells me. "She needs to be reassured. Once she knows the baby is really hers, the other issues can be addressed."

I thank her and hang up. It's an expensive way to reassure Lily. Besides I don't think it will work. Lily doesn't believe her parents are her biologic parents, no matter what they've said to her. As a girl they introduced her to the obstetrician who delivered her. They pointed to her blood type, which comes from her mother's Type A and her father's Type B. If DNA tests had been available then, they might have had one done. When she stopped openly contesting them, they felt that they'd convinced her. But she is as sure now at thirty-eight as was she was at three. However many tests we do with Pearl, I'm sure Lily will remain equally convinced that Pearl has as little to do with her as her parents do. Lily looks at her parents and does not *see* herself. She looks at Pearl, two weeks and three days on this earth, and feels equally little visual or emotional connection with her.

I wonder if the general anesthetic is to blame—I mean there is a gap in Lily's memory, a blackout, that she doesn't trust anyone to fill in for her. There were the feelings Lily had about a baby kicking and squirming inside her. There are the feelings Lily has about this little creature out in the open air thrashing and crying and snuffling and nursing. They bear no relation to each other. Lily has no doubt which sensations and emotions she preferred. She wants those feelings back and knows in a way that no one will ever change that she can't attach them to this little being who is her own justification.

The process for me is nearly the opposite. I mean, I would listen at Lily's belly at night, but it was an almost scientific interest, as if I were a deep sea diver trying to detect what was moving in some very dark ocean cavern. But when I *saw* Pearl, touched her, something in me *knew* her in a way I don't even know myself. I *latched* to her the way her mouth latched to Lily's breast. Pure instinct with something absurdly holy in it.

As Pearl and I are walking, I put in a call to my mother, who is out, then to my sisters, who are also unavailable. "Family consult," I say to each of them. "As soon as possible."

I call work and arrange to take a week's family medical leave on top of my paternity leave. I cite Lily's postpartum depression. I consider pretending to arrange a DNA test—going as far as to get out cotton swabs—and then reject it. Faking the results feels like too much work. Lily brings it up again after dinner and we fight about it, but in the middle of the argument, Pearl cries and I go to feed her and Lily falls asleep.

I'm always the one to feed Pearl. By the time Lily had breast fed Pearl three times, she'd had enough. It hurt her stitches. But it was more than that. "She's like a little vampire," Lily had said to me handing Pearl back. "But it's not just my life blood she's sucking away, its my *Chi*."

"Let me explain it to the lactation nurse," I said. I didn't want the nurse to get the wrong idea about Lily. I just told her that I was hopeful Lily might have a change of heart after she was feeling a little better.

"It's much better to start right away. What about a pump? Just to make sure she's producing."

"Let me see," I said. But a breast pump was even less acceptable to Lily than Pearl's mouth. Lily kept her hands on her contracting uterus, weeping, while the kindly lactation nurse, forty pounds overweight and with ponderous breasts of her own, told Lily she mustn't despair, that if she kept at it she would be able to give her daughter the nutrition she needed.

I stepped in, "There are also wonderful babies raised on formula, Lily. You, for example. I'll check with my mom, but I believe I was too."

The nurse looked at me disapprovingly. Lily turned her face away from both of us.

"Hush," she said. "I don't want that baby to wake up."

The next morning when I wake, Lily is on the phone with her parents. They offer to pay for the test and be tested themselves. I refuse to go along.

"You're the ones with the questions," I tell them as they head off with Lily to the obstetrician's. "Pearl is already as much mine as any child can be."

"You'll see," Lily says. She is animated, happy. The truth, her truth, is going to be verified. Justice will be served. We'll see. Her father, Hans, has the back door to the car open and the child seat secured. Lily tells her mother to sit back there with Pearl and takes the front seat. Hans looks at me and I can see he is a little frightened, probably always has been, of this raw force he and his equally mild-mannered wife, Anna, brought into the world. He looks older than his eighty-three years. He won't live to see Pearl through elementary school.

My mom and my sisters arrive shortly after they leave. We sit in the living room looking through the floor to ceiling glass windows at the changing leaves pulsing in the wind. Occasionally one loses its grip and swoops slowly to the ground. All our eyes follow its flight. Everyone is drinking pomegranate green tea. My mom has brought fresh scones.

"I need to come clean about something," I tell them. I close my eyes. I have no idea where to begin.

It's at that moment, my phone, off in the study, begins to ring. I shrug and go off to get it. I'm buying time, that's all I'm doing. I expect it to be one of the exasperating robo calls we've been receiving lately.

"Caleb Crusoe," I say waiting for the pause and click before the voice starts in: *The FBI reports an increase in break ins—*

"Caleb Crusoe," a man's voice repeats. "Am I speaking to Caleb Crusoe?"

When I affirm my identity, he continues, "My name is Paul Stewart. I am a student at Davidson." *Not yet*, I think. *Not yet.* "I'm working for the Obama campaign," he continues. "We are calling to encourage you to vote this year."

"Thank you. I plan to."

"Barack is encouraging people to vote early. He has. The nearest voting location for you is on Estes Drive. Could you tell me if you plan to vote for President Obama?" When I say yes, he says, "Can you tell me if you plan to vote early this year?"

I tell him, yes, I'm voting Democrat, but no, I'll probably vote on election day. I tell him I'm taking my newborn daughter with me.

"Cool," he says after a slight hesitation. That's not part of his script but he rises to the occasion. "You have other children?" he asks. "You bringing them too?"

"Just this one," I tell him. Openly testing now.

"President Obama and Michelle appreciate your vote, sir," he says. "And congratulations on your baby and the good civic model you are setting for her." He laughs and I do too.

I end the call, turn the phone off, snap it shut and slip it in my pocket. I can't stop laughing, the relief is so great. My mother and sisters look at me quizzically when I come back into the living room. I don't even try to explain. "An old friend," I choke out. "Congratulations."

"Stress," my mother says calmly. "You're having a very normal stress reaction, Caleb. Very normal. All of this is normal, darling."

I haven't told them, yet, about where Lily and her parents are. An outing, I'd said, suggesting through my tone either a mall or a leisurely stroll.

"No," I say. "It's not normal at all. It's crazy as hell. All of it. And I bear a lot of the responsibility. But I don't know what to do with it."

Mom and Bess and YoYo turn equally motherly faces towards me. How did we all get this old without noticing?

"There are things you need to know." They look nervously at each other. I forge on. "One. Lily doesn't believe Pearl is our baby. She believes we were given the wrong baby, that somewhere between the operating room and the recovery room, she was switched on us."

"A DNA test will take care of that, right?" YoYo is a paralegal.

My mom and Bess exchange glances. They know Lily.

"Lily and her parents have all gone out for DNA testing this morning. But Lily is only going to trust results that confirm what she already knows—she feels no *bond* with this baby. She believes there is another baby out there for whom she will have that feeling."

My mom is about to say something but I go on. "I feel like I need to protect Lily. She is no different from me, really. I *feel* an equally irrational bond with Pearl. No DNA test is going to take that away."

Bess cuts to the chase. "Is the baby safe with Lily, Caleb? Given what she's feeling?"

"*Alone* with the baby?" I ask. And suddenly it hits me in a way it didn't talking to Dr. Campbell. My girl, my perfect little Pearl, is not safe alone with her own mother. The only way either of them is going to be safe is if *I* separate them. I can see that my mother and my sisters have already gotten there.

"For the short run," my mom says, her eyes filling with tears, helping me to voice what I can't bear to hear. "Only for the short run. You know we'll all do what needs to be done." She looks at each of my sisters who don't even hesitate, just nod and reach out to each other. It's a lovely tableau, the three of them, Mom and YoYo on the couch facing me, Bess on the chair, all holding hands, then reaching out to me to close the circle. But I can't. I know them, I know that their minds are whirring, juggling schedules, deciding what to tell their husbands and kids. They haven't noticed, but they're automatically relieving me of responsibility.

"Lily is going to need someone to stay with for awhile," I say.

"Lily?" YoYo asks.

"She has her parents," Bess says.

The baby, it is clear, they would take in a heartbeat. Me too, with perhaps a minute's hesitation. Lily never.

I realize I have had this crazy idea that if Lily is near them, any of them, some of their kindness will rub off, some of their ease with babies. But in the eight years of our marriage, Lily has never expressed interest in them, their children, or their spouses—except to teach them martial moves at family gatherings, and collect and rinse dishes after meals. They've never complained to me, never objected. But they will never willingly bring Lily into their intimate family circles knowing what they already know of her. Even less so now that they know, even vaguely, how she feels about Pearl.

Who does Lily have, except me, to protect her in her fierce, instrumental purity? Lily *needs* to be inviolable with the same intensity that my mother and sisters *need* to flow continually in and out of each other. Maybe the Leeuwens understood Lily best, having grown up with water and dikes, they understood what it might mean to a dike to be breached, so they flowed gently around her borders, generous in their indifference.

I look around the room, appreciating the spaciousness the huge uncurtained windows give it. I realize I'm saying good-bye. Lily needs as little change as possible, especially of place. Pearl has no preconceptions. I've always lived light, as if in five minutes I can be ready for my next jaunt abroad.

"I know the commute is longer," my mom volunteers, "but there is plenty of room at home. And my schedule is flexible. I can cut my hours back if necessary. " My mom is a visiting hospice nurse.

Different scenarios flash through my head. Taking Pearl and moving to Seoul or Buenos Aires or Amsterdam. Staying here and enrolling her as an honorary member in the Donor 1324 Family Circle, for she has more in common with those sixty-seven half-sibs than she does with anyone besides Lily and me. She would have the added distinction of being the only motherless child among them. There is, of course, the little problem of potential class action. Would it be more likely or less if they had a face, a name, a life history as complicated as their own to hang their demands on.

"There's something else you need to know," I say slowly. The neighbor's cat, a black Persian, has wandered into our yard and is crouched to pounce on a yellow leaf as it twists and turns toward the grass as if it were a falling fledgling.

They get stuck on the number, just like I did.

"Sixty-*seven* more grandchildren," my mother says dreamily. "It's like I've inherited a kingdom."

"Queendom," my sister Bess says dryly.

"More likely something with far more of a pioneer flavor," YoYo says. "Remember, most of them are only children."

They all nod gravely. *Like Lily.* Why hadn't *I* put that together? Why would I expose Pearl to that, sixty-seven times over?

"Do you think you are going to be outed?" YoYo asks. I can see that she's making a mental note to talk to one of the partners at her firm.

"Inevitably, if he stays in the area," Bess says.

"Unless he changes his name," my mother chimes in.

For a second I think about that. It would free me from the problem of family history, for one thing. I take a deep breath. "There's more."

My sisters both look at my mother. I'm not sure if they're feeling protective of her or wanting her to protect them. Sixty-seven nephews and nieces. It's no small thing. I realize that I'm protective of Lily and protective of Pearl, but it never occurs to me to be protective of my sisters and mom. I didn't tell them about the donations in the first place only because I felt it was my own business, that it expressed a rage that distinguished me from them, one that I felt towards all those men who had died so unseemly young and left me to face the same destiny, unready, unsteady, abysmally bereft.

"I lied," I tell them. "I lied about my medical history. I pretended Dad was still alive. I said his dad died of diabetes. That his grandfather died of pneumonia. I added ten years to each of their lives."

"Why?" my mom asks.

"I wanted Dad back. I wanted a decent chance."

"Your grandfather did die of diabetes," my mom says. "Why was that a lie?"

"You told me a heart attack. I know you did."

"Brought on by diabetes. He was a man of excess, your grandfather. And your great-grandfather *did* die of pneumonia—brought on by congestive heart failure," my mom says. "Which was brought on by having scarlet fever when he was a child, which damaged his heart valves, which led to congestive heart failure, which made him more vulnerable to infection. It was before there were artificial valves, dear."

"And Dad?"

"No one knows. There was a big thromboembolus. No one knows exactly why. He'd taken two long air flights for work in the past month—one to Tokyo, one to Rome. They didn't know about aspirin then. He was so young and he took his health for granted. He assumed he'd live to ninety, honey. He didn't see himself as having a history of disease." My mom pauses, reaches out her hand to me. "I'm so sorry you've been carrying this alone all this time."

The cat is rolling around the lawn, batting leaves, biting into them. I feel dizzy. Furious. I walk to the plate glass window, tug it open, walk out onto the stone patio and yell at her to stop, to get back where she belongs. She pauses, rolls over, stares at me with her mesmerizingly malevolent yellow eyes, then stretches and saunters off.

As I pull the door shut, I see leaves have scattered across the floor. My mother and sisters are caught still frame in a stranger's home video. After a second's pause, a deep breath that brings with it a faint smell of earth, mold, pomegranate and the perfumes my sisters are wearing, patchouli and lily of the valley, I nod and the movie begins to roll again.

"Aside from denying dad's death, nothing you said was untrue," YoYo says. She pulls her long graying brown hair back up into its clip.

"And your father's death was a fluke," my mother adds firmly. "You can't generalize from it—and neither can they."

Those sixty-seven mothers. Those sixty-seven boys and girls.

"And you're only half the story in every instance. *Less* than that if you take in nurture and environment," Bess says. "Do you think we received a three generation medical history when we adopted Lucien and Hilda?"

At this point the doorbell rings. I shrug and go to answer it. A young woman stands there gripping a clipboard. She is tall, blonde, with a scattering of freckles. She smiles.

"My name is Carol. I'm canvassing for the Romney campaign. We know you're a registered Democrat, but in this election, we know everyone harbors some doubts. We just want to be sure you're fully informed in your choice."

"I'm sorry," I tell her. "We're having a family emergency at present."

She instinctively glances past me into the living room.

"If you want to leave some materials with me—" I extend my hand and step back to block her view.

"Of course," she says. As she is reaching into her canvas bag, I hear a car coming up the drive. Lily and her parents are returning. I pull the door firmly closed behind me as I move out to greet them. Carol begins to hand me the circulars as I'm passing, then hesitates. She's already taken in the age of the driver of the car and is obviously thinking he might be more promising. I move around her and head down the stone walk, past our overgrown lotus pond, to the gravel drive.

Lily again is riding shotgun to her father. Her mother leans over Pearl murmuring softly. Lily looks out at me with a radiant smile as Hans turns off the ignition.

I open the door for Anna, my eyes on Pearl. Lily opens her door and stands wedged between the doors for a second.

"We'll have the results in two weeks. Then it will all be settled. Dr. Campbell said she would notify the hospital that we're contesting, so when the proof comes in they will be ready to act immediately."

She heads up the walk as I lean in to help her mother. Anna, whose complexion, even at her age, has the same luminosity as her granddaughter's, gives me a tired smile. "We have done what Lily wanted," she says softly. "I hope it will have the effect you desire." Her eyes are bright with tears.

"You did what you could."

"She is *so* sure." Anna shakes her head. "It has never worked to argue with her, you know. Reason is not much better. She is not crazy, Caleb. She is not cruel."

She turns and puts her hand on Pearl's little face. "She was so very beautiful, Lily, when she was born. We were so awed, Hans and I. We had many years before stopped dreaming of children. And then there she was, as shocked to be born to us as we were to receive her. I wonder, you know. I never stop wondering. If we had been younger, would things have been different for her?"

"Worse."

"We did not regret the way she was," Anna says, fumbling with the lock on Pearl's seatbelt. "We did not challenge it. To us she was a miracle of nature. We were content with that."

"Here, let me." I put my hand on Anna's shoulder, and she leans into it slightly, then turns and slowly shifts her weight to leave the car. I give her my arm, and she rests on it heavily. I hand her her cane. She stands there as I reach in and unclasp Pearl and pull her out. As Pearl opens her mouth to cry, I slip my index finger between her lips and she begins to suck greedily.

Hans has come around the car and stands there with his hand on Anna's shoulder. "We are too old, Caleb. We would take them both if we could."

They look so tired, so lost, like children in a fairy tale with no trail of crumbs to lead them home.

Pearl continues to suck vigorously on my finger. Lily and the tall blonde canvasser are in animated, not necessarily amicable conversation. My mother and sisters have come to the door and are watching, ready to intervene if necessary. A crow cries out from the pine. A cardinal swoops down to peck in the grass at the edge of the lotus pond. I feel a spring in my feet, unreasonably lifted.

"This is all going to work out," I say. "In a way that works for *all* of us. I don't exactly how, yet, but I know it will. I really do. And I want the two of you to be part of it."

Anna and Hans both smile. Tired, so tired, and also, in that cool autumn breeze, quick with hope. "If your Pearl makes you as happy as our Lily has made us, Caleb," Hans says softly, "you will have a very full life."

"It is our wish," Anna says. "Our deepest wish."

"And I think it has already been granted," I say, pulling Pearl close.

"Come by and see us when this is all over," Lily is saying to Carol as she hands her a business card. "We have self-defense classes too. Just leave the slogans at home." With a smile, Carol pockets the card.

We all stand and watch her walk down the drive. Then Lily ushers her parents into the house. My mom, at my side, cooes over Pearl. As we turn to go back in, she whispers, "Did you notice that girl's lips, Caleb? I thought they looked like your father's."

"And her walk," YoYo adds. "It has a lot in common with yours, bro."

"Gestures have more to do with nurture," Bess demurs.

"We may never know," I say, then stop.

I feel electric. Has Pearl just turned her head, however slightly, at the sound of my voice? Have those eyes that I am peering so deeply into truly registered me, her daddy, for the very first time?

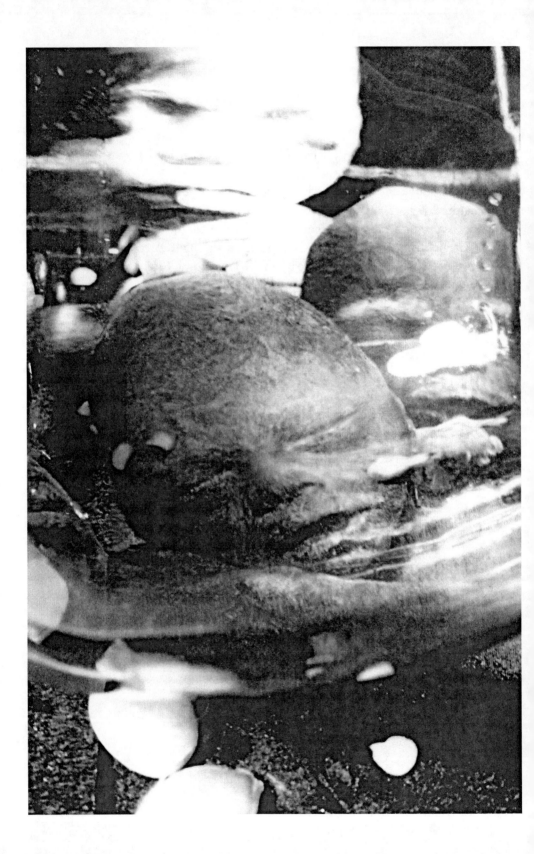

II

WHOSE LIFE IS IT ANYWAY?

BLOODLINES AND BABIES

Diane

He's our first grandchild. Andy and I were so excited when we heard. We'd had our concerns about the marriage, which we did our very best to hide. It happened so fast and there was a child on her side. And Dylan, at twenty-four, was five years younger. Honestly, we expected to learn within months that they were expecting, that that was what had precipitated the visit to Asheville City Hall in September when they had only met in May. But we didn't get that call for a full twelve months. By then, we'd all come into some kind of new balance, or so Andy and I thought. Certainly the start hadn't been smooth.

No one was being invited to the wedding we were told at the time. Sparrow said she thought it was enough change for her daughter Sam just to have Dylan as part of their household. She didn't want to burden her with extra personalities. Andy and I were a little taken aback. We're mild-mannered people, so it made us wonder how Dylan had described us to her. But, like I said, we thought the marriage expedient and we thought Sparrow had a point if they had, as we assumed, another baby on the way only five months after the two of them had met.

So, we invited them all to join us up here at Thanksgiving instead. But Sparrow, who taught fifth grade, said Maryland was too long a drive for a short visit and she didn't have the time for a longer one.

Christmas, we suggested. Dylan's sister would be home from Seattle with her boyfriend, and both Andy's parents and mine would be coming over from their retirement homes. We've always been a close family. Andy and I are both only children, so it has been a joy to us that our parents have enjoyed each other so much that we've all always celebrated holidays together.

But Christmas belonged to Sparrow's family, Dylan told us. Sam had always done this. She counted on it. They couldn't change this—certainly not this year.

So, Andy and I drove down to Asheville right after Christmas intending to spend three or four days with them. It was only as we pulled into Asheville that Andy told me that Dylan had called him to say he'd made a reservation for us at a motel in the middle of town. Andy said he hadn't told me because he wanted us to have a good time on the road trip and not to spend it analyzing. "Besides," he said with a smile, "I decided we could treat it as our own romantic get-away."

When we met her at last, Sparrow was polite and hospitable. She was clearly not pregnant, indeed, if anything, looked anorexic. She was wearing her spandex running gear when we arrived. She told us she was off for her run—but that she had made sure we would be well-attended in her absence, nodding at Dylan and a rather rotund and very pretty girl of six who was wearing a long pink dress and a princess tiara. On the counter, Sparrow had set out cups, a plate of ginger snaps, a bowl of orange and apple slices. Green tea was steeping.

She slid by us out the door and, with a wave, pounded off down the steep road like a super hero in hot pursuit, her long curly blonde hair spreading and coiling as she strode.

Dylan, who had been slouching against the wall, straightened and came over and gave us warm hugs. "She'll be more relaxed when she gets back," he murmured. "It's just that she wants everything to go well. She really wants you to like Sam."

"And why wouldn't we?" I asked him.

Dylan stepped back a moment to look at us, this searching expression on his face. Dylan is a wonderful surprise to us. Andy and I are attractive but not striking. Dylan, though, seems to have inherited only our best features, and we are a little awed by these unforeseen possibilities. His sister Allie, two years older, feels periodically peeved. "Beauty is as beauty does," she has warned her less ambitious brother for years. She has just joined a high pressure law practice in Seattle. Marriage, should it ever take place, obviously won't happen before she is made partner. Too distracting.

Dylan's eyes, which are the most forgiving of colors, something like sandstone, softened even more as he smiled and hugged us again. "I'm so glad you made the trip. Next time we'll have you stay with us."

"Everything in its time," Andy said.

I turned to Sam, slipping down to my knees so we would be more on the level. "Now who is this beautiful princess?" I asked her.

"I am a fairy," Sam said, "not a princess." And then a little mischievous smile crossed her face. "What story do you think I come from?"

"Peter Pan?" I asked. "Are you Tinkerbell?"

She shook her head.

"The one who turns pumpkins into coaches in Cinderella?"

"No, the one in Sleeping Beauty who gets even because she didn't get invited to the birthday party."

"Oh," I said. "Were you not invited to a birthday party?"

"No one would dare do that," Sam said seriously. "I've told everyone at school all about my powers."

Were these the powers, I wondered, that had kept us out of the wedding—for it turned out that it was only Dylan's side of the family that wasn't invited. People Sam already knew were welcome—all Sparrow's vast extended family (I believe each parent had been married three times, all the grandparents twice, with children from every union), all her colleagues from the elementary school where she taught, and, since she had grown up in the area and stayed on, friends from elementary school through college. Even Sam's paternal grandmother, one of Sam's nine grandparents (if you count all the steps). We learned this because there were wedding photos in frames on the mantel, a photo album on the coffee table, and Sam, over the next hour, walked us through the whole cast of characters.

"There's me cutting the cake. There's my daddy's mom getting the first slice," Sam said.

"And your daddy?"

"He's with God. That's what my grandma says. My mom says no one can prove any different since God is a matter of belief not science. He is where I get my fire power."

"That sounds pretty impressive," Andy said. "What do you do with it? Explode buildings or provide heat to homeless people?" Andy is an accountant but is the more fanciful of the two of us.

I just kept looking from the album back to Dylan, who shrugged and went into the kitchen and started pouring us tea.

I patted Sam on the head and went in to join him.

"It was the only time in her life Sparrow had her family's full attention," he said. "You have no idea what this meant to her. She and Sam's dad never married. She's the second child of both her parents' second marriages. She wanted Sam and her to have pride of place—just once."

"And you were just a glamorous means to this end? Would a cut-out have served as well?" I asked him bluntly. Both of us took a quick, shocked breath. I can't remember ever speaking to my charming, amenable son so harshly.

"I knew I had to explain it in person," Dylan said.

"You can't." Then I reached out and touched him gently. "And you don't need to. We love you and trust you—and we want you to be happy."

And to be part of our life, I told Andy as we drove away a day and a half later, during which time somehow Sparrow had scheduled the three of them in for a family therapy session and a family yoga class. Dinner was gluten-free and vegan and in a restaurant downtown near our motel. "To save you the drive back and forth," Dylan told us, looking at Sparrow like she was a teleprompter.

"Why?" I asked Andy as we drove home. We had been listening to Maeve Binchy without comment for three hours at that point. "Why is he doing this to us?"

"It will be easier if you think of it as his doing something *for* them, not *against* us. I do believe he thinks nothing can change the love we feel for him or the love he feels for us," Andy said quietly, his eyes on the snow beginning to fall. "Give it all some time. She's like a mama bear with her cub. Her world as she knows it is her lair, it's where she can keep Sam safe."

Truly, I tried. But it's very strange if you have always known yourself as tolerant and welcoming to be treated like a dangerous intruder.

"I predict when they have children of their own, things will change. She'll feel more sure of Dylan, of the relationship, of Sam's well-being," Andy said, putting his wipers and lights on and moving into the slow lane.

I was surprised at the feelings that surged in me as I remembered Sam's fat little hands opening the wedding album, that smug little look on her freckled, pudgy face. Or Sparrow's practiced school teacher murmur of greeting as she rose from the table at the vegan bistro. "Mrs. Lamar, Mr. Lamar, so pleased you could join us." When she sat down again, I expected her to open a file, discuss Dylan's reading level, his social relations with his peers as I sat submissively in a chair a third my size.

Quietly, Andy and Dylan worked something out so Dylan would visit us on his lonesome twice a year. Never on holidays—and only for two nights. We paid. Dylan always spent a good third of the time fielding calls from Sparrow or Sam, always beaming at us after he said good-bye and telling us they said hello or sent their love.

I actually liked watching Dylan on the phone. More accurately, listening to him. He had, I could hear, modeled himself on Andy—that warm calm. I heard it as he listened to concerns about Sam's homework or a broken ice-maker or something one of Sparrow's myriad halves or steps had said to send her into a trilling fury. "Have her start over from the beginning," Dylan would say about Sam and her homework frustration. "Let her reward herself with what she's already learned." "I have the repair man's number here. I can call if you want." "They were just being thoughtless, Sparrow. They don't realize how sensitive you are. But you have your own home now. Nothing they say or do can take that away."

It made perfect sense to me when Dylan called in May and asked Andy and me if we would help him finance a degree in social work with a focus on clinical counseling. We said yes immediately.

He applied and was admitted to an MSW program designed for working students and arranged things with the restaurant where he waited to take one day off a week. He said Sparrow was relieved he was going to join the professional class, that his future earnings and improved social status would make up for the time it would require. He and Sam were bracketing off father-daughter time on weekend mornings—so Sparrow could sleep in.

He told us this as we all sat in our kitchen over coffee in late July. We were celebrating his twenty-fifth birthday a few weeks late. His grandparents were all coming within the hour, and we were going out to brunch so he could catch an afternoon flight back to Charlotte—in time to have a late dinner with Sparrow and Sam at home in Asheville.

"You haven't even had time to unpack," my mother said a little petulantly at brunch.

"He's a family man now," my father said with a proud, understanding smile.

Dutifully Dylan handed around photos of him with Sparrow in her running lycra clinging to one arm and Sam, now dressed as a ninja, hanging from the other. He didn't show the wedding photos.

"We'll see you all at Christmas this year," Andy's mom said innocently. "We can't wait to meet them, honey." Somehow this whole interchange felt worse than what it had felt like last December when we visited. Dylan, to his credit, blushed.

"It may be a little longer," he said. "I'll come for sure somewhere in there. But the Christmas period is reserved for Sparrow's family."

Two years in a row, we all understood, would make it a tradition. His grandmothers each looked at the photos he'd given them and dutifully handed them to their husbands. The clatter of cutlery on the surrounding tables was brisk.

In the silence which went on so long no one could break it, I realized we had created this little bubble, Andy and I and our parents and our two children. No one had meant to. It was just such a joy for all of us no longer to be so triangulated. There is such a thing as too much attention, as any beloved only child knows. And we came from two generations worth. Perhaps Dylan and Alison had felt smothered by all that adult attention all those years. Maybe they felt exposed rather than embraced by it. Maybe that was why Dylan had agreed to realize Sparrow's vision of what rightful family was—and what his part in it was (tallest, dead center, both backdrop and material support).

To be honest, whenever Dylan called that fall I expected him to tell us that he and Sparrow were divorcing. *Anticipated* his telling us.

Instead he was filled with stories about his friends in the social work class. There were several guys in their early thirties, all with young families, and women making mid or late career changes (he was the youngest in the group by four or five years). He was finding his counseling class, especially the unit on family therapy, fascinating.

"Do you think our family would have met the definition of enmeshed, Mom?" he asked me once.

"You tell me," I said, having a vision of minnows thrashing brilliant silver in a net.

"Sparrow says so."

"And how would you describe her family?"

"She says she doesn't have one, just a jigsaw puzzle with lots of missing pieces."

"I asked what *you* see, Dylan." I sounded like the high school English teacher I am.

"Everything," he said with a loud, genuine laugh. "Chaos, hardening of the boundaries, enmeshment, neglect, over-protectiveness, substance abuse, in-breeding, delinquency, emotional cut-off. It's great. I'm acing all my papers. I've started sharing my riches with my classmates. We're thinking of making them up into a book of case studies: 'What You're Liable to Find in Any Appalachian Hollow.'"

"Sparrow approves?"

"Of course. She wants to out them all for being the neglectful, self-absorbed, fatalistic SOBs they are and ever will be."

I couldn't read his tone at all. I think at that moment I began to be afraid for him in a way I had not been before.

Sparrow

Sam's as close to a clone of her daddy as any child can be—boy or girl. Round-cheeked, pig-eyed, and bull-headed. Hair so pale it looks like rice noodles. To die for in a uniform—although hers are restricted to brownie uniforms and school T-shirts, ninja costumes and princess gowns. Possessiveness I expect she inherited from both of us. In spades.

All of which goes to say, there's no chance I'm going to be forgetting the lessons I learned when the three of us failed to make a family.

"How can you generalize from there?" Dylan asks me. "You were sixteen when you met, pregnant when you split, two days post-partum when he died. You never married. Never even lived together for more than two months at a stretch."

"Death intervened—but that doesn't mean I didn't see where it was all leading."

"And where *was* that exactly?" Dylan asked. A year ago, he would have asked anxiously. He wasn't at the eye-rolling stage—yet. But coming closer than I liked. "Was he looking around at other women? Spending too much time at work? At his parents? With his buddies? Or were you afraid he was spending too much time at your belly listening for Sam, leaving you on the outside yet again?"

Dylan's tone was actually kind, as were his eyes. They were large, accepting, a strange tawny color that went well with his red hair, which he used to pull back into a ponytail but which now, cut short for grad school, curled boyishly over his still boyish face, emphasizing our age difference. There were dark circles under his eyes, testimony to how much he was trying to cover all the bases—work, school, time with Sam, time with me, preparing for the coming baby.

Dylan was turning his wedding ring (silver and turquoise, I insisted we save gold for our tenth anniversary) round and round his finger, a gesture he would need to relinquish when he became a counselor: it made him seem nervous and indecisive. Which he isn't. He's actually pretty determined. Strategic. He was choosing his words now.

"I am going to do my utmost to make a strong resilient family with you, Sparrow. I'm doing so now. But it needs two of us. Patterns are inherited, adopted, fallen into—but they are all learned, Sparrow. They're not hard wired. They are not biblical curses. Fate. Your mom and dad are both in solid marriages now, so are your grandparents. *They* learned."

"You're wrong," I said. "They just wore out."

He laughed. It was such a simple, genuine sound it made my eyes water. One of the most amazing things about Dylan is that just being myself I can make him laugh. Not at or with me—just because I am who I am and he likes that.

I wish I could say he felt the same for Sam. But he doesn't. Whether that is a can't or a won't, I'm not sure. It is just a fact. One that Sam wakes with every day. We're over a year into this marriage, and it hasn't really changed. It's not like Dylan isn't trying. It's not like Sam is helping. I can *see* that. Whatever it might look like, I'm not blaming anyone—including myself. And if there weren't another baby on the way, I might have just accepted it. Up until now Sam has had no basis of comparison. The constant pausing and reorienting, that deep patience-inducing breath are just what Dylan *is* to Sam. But bring his own baby into the picture and she'll feel the difference. I can swear to it, many times over. If there was one thing I promised myself, it was this was never going to happen to my little girl. She was never going to feel second best.

Dylan's righter than he thinks. I never married Sam Jewell because I *did* feel he loved the Army and his own mama most and that his attention was destined to slipslide to someone in the Army, someone who could look at him with his mama's eyes.

But I always had a *hope*, you know, a hope that we might pull it off.

In the letters he sent me from Afghanistan, he was sounding the same way. He was imagining himself as a family man. Of course, he was imagining a son—and I didn't let him know different. I've never regretted that the news never reached him, although I do think, if he'd seen Sam, he'd have been just as proud to have a daughter. It wasn't true of his mother. She came to the apartment the day after I brought Sam home, and she looked at her and just started crying.

"My *boy*," she sobbed. "Where is my beautiful boy?" She's a big woman, Darla Jewell, and she just rocked back and forth on the sofa wanting some man to make it right. Sam got real quiet, so did I, and we rocked in our rocking chair as the sun slipped behind the trees, sending this sad cold glow, like a shawl, over Darla's shoulders.

Darla has come round somewhat since Sam is really all she has left of her husband or son. I take Sam over there once or twice a month, and she and Darla go to the cemetery, and Darla tells her what a brave man her daddy was, how he killed those wicked Taliban and Al Quaeda Muslims to keep her safe, how if he were alive now the two of them would be going hunting or fishing. Then they go back to the house and eat Snickers cheesecake and look through Darla's picture albums and open up the box with the Purple Heart and Bronze Star. Your name would have been Jewell, Darla will tell her—more often now that I've married Dylan and changed our names to his. (I was just so tired of Crabtree. I liked the idea that people here would have to wait a minute or two before they placed me.)

When Sam comes back from her afternoons with Darla are the worst evenings for Dylan. Sam goads him. "What kind of star do you have, Dylan?"

"There are different ways to be brave, Sam," he answers. "One of them is conscientious objection."

"Conceited is having a swelled head," Sam says.

"*Conscience*, Sam. Knowing right from wrong." And then Dylan pauses, kicking himself.

"My dad was right," Sam says, her voice wobbling a little.

Dead right, I think. Sam went into the Army because he couldn't find a job and he wouldn't have graduated high school except for the special football dispensation. But he was a good soldier, a good follower, and, in time, a good leader. He made sergeant. He died pulling two of his men out of enemy fire.

"Bath time," I say as Sam opens her mouth tonight to prod Dylan again. Her dad liked to pick at people too. I'd forgotten.

"I haven't had dessert," she complains.

"Snickers cheesecake doesn't count?" I ask, hugging her firmly as I march her down the hall. I can *hear* Dylan exhale.

I ache inside. My beloved child truly isn't loveable. And then I rage—at Sam for her six year old's peevishness, her crazy belief that she can do anything and still be loved, at Darla who doesn't give a shit if Sam and Dylan and I connect, at Dylan because he can't see, will never see, what I see in Sam, at me for having gotten us all into this mess. The only one I leave out, because at present he's incapable of speaking in his own defense, is this son who has five months more of amnesty.

"Ouch," Sam cries. "You're rubbing my skin off, Mom." I stop scrubbing off the chocolate on the back of her neck, under her chin. I stand up.

Did we fall into this pattern, like Dylan says? Was it forced upon us? It feels like a rack to me—and I'm strung on it. The only time I feel I'm free is when I'm running. I can't imagine what's going to happen when I stop.

Dylan

I've always adhered to the water theory of life. It seeks the vast. It follows the path of least resistance. It isn't afraid to change forms. Lately, though, I've become more aware of the other ten percent of our make up. How fucking ungiving it is.

My mother didn't take the news lying down. I don't know why she should really, except that she and my dad have never chosen to be a rock when I've been pressed up against a hard place. Honestly, I haven't tested it much. There was the marijuana smoking at senior prom—but no one got busted. And having to repeat a math course my freshman year in college at their expense (and to my sister Allie's scorn). But other than that, they've not had much of a challenge from me. I've always been there at holidays, worked summers to help with college expenses, found a job within a month of graduating. Not, at least, until this marriage. What has hurt most is seeing their hopefulness dissolve.

They had been so positive when I told them about the pregnancy.

"What good news, Dylan. You'll be a great dad. We can't wait to hold the little one in our arms. Our first grandchild," my mom crooned.

"Timing's a little off," my dad agreed, "but stick with the program. You'll be solid as a provider once you get the degree. We'll do whatever is needed to see you through."

Honestly, I don't know how it happened. Sparrow has been on the pill since our first scare. Besides, she been running so much she's not having periods. But something messed up. Maybe it was, like she said, because of the antibiotic she took for that sinus infection at Christmas. The timing isn't good. She's due around our second anniversary. I'll have just started the second year of my program.

I know Sparrow wants me to say I'll drop out for a year, but I'm not going to. I've told her that the first semester, when I'm commuting down to Chapel Hill for two days of classes, I'll do all the daytime babycare on the five days I'm in town—and night feedings after I get off my evening shift at the restaurant. Second semester, when I have the full-time internship, I'll do everything needed when I get home in the evening. We can supplement for anything else.

It's not just that I don't want to waste my parent's money, I want this degree. I want to go out and fix problems for people who have it worse than me. Shell-shocked guys who see a flash of white fabric turning the corner and are on their knees, aiming. Men the age of our fathers with Korsakoff's who keep reliving their first day in Nam rather than the first time they got laid.

Sparrow's voice when I told her was as hard as my mom's. "That takes care of the new one, catch as catch can. But what about Sam?"

I was amazed at what came to mind. "Maybe she'll learn to read." "Maybe she could pick up after herself." "Maybe she will discover some inner resources."

Instead, I said, "Sam's routines aren't going to change. She will still be going to the same school. She'll have her days with her Grandma Jewell. Maybe she'd like to have a few more. Or have play dates with some of her cousins. Who knows, Sparrow, maybe having a baby brother or sister is just what she needs." *They take orders better than parents*, I thought but had the grace (at least that day) not to say.

The truth is the ice we're skating on is thawing fast, cracking like thrown plates.

"Honestly," Sparrow said, "you haven't given her a thought." She looked at her protruding stomach with the all-consuming sorrow of a child. She turns thirty tomorrow. It isn't, hasn't been from the first breath she drew, the world she wanted for herself. And there's not a goddamn thing in the world I can do to change that.

"My parents could come down for a couple of weeks to help," I said. "They could do it more than once. They both have a lot of vacation time. My mom says she can't imagine a better use of it."

"You talked to them about it before mentioning it to me?" Sparrow said. Oh, at that moment, her eyes were as small as Sam's, but they weren't even mammalian. She twisted her head back and forth like the bird she's named for, but I'd make her for a larger, darker family. Crow.

"I didn't want you disappointed," I said. "I didn't know if they would be open to it." And why should they be? I thought, remembering their only visit here, how Sparrow wouldn't even let them stay in the house. *Her* house.

The truth is, there are times I imagine getting my MSW and applying for a divorce and custody the very next day. For a child whose sex its mother won't even divulge to me. Either way, it's going to be too much competition for Sam.

"Clearly, we're going to need back-up, Sparrow. We need a village, like everyone else," I told her. "Would you rather ask your mom or your stepmom to come help?"

This was a low blow. Sparrow's two sisters from her mom's first marriage were pregnant (older) and divorcing (younger), her full brother had just lost his job and had moved back in with his father (with three kids and a wife with a drinking problem), her full sister in full throttle sibling rivalry had announced her own pregnancy a month after Sparrow and had promptly snapped up promises of assistance from both grandmothers. I could go on, but it would be more of the same. Besides, everyone, quite reasonably, expects reciprocity—and how many kids can I babysit for and still study?

"My parents don't require a lot of attention," I said. "My dad cooks, my mom *likes* to clean. They're excited as can be at the idea of their first grandchild." I shouldn't have said it, of course. And since I did, I should have stopped there, but couldn't, of course.

"And I, Sparrow, am very excited about the idea of *my* first child."

"Which makes me *what*, Dylan. Surrogate? Breed cow?"

"Let it go, Sparrow. For god's sake, let it go. You have this really kind, undemanding family ready to take you in, ready to love you if you'd let it happen, ready to help us be the parents we both want to be. Why do you insist on having all of us living under your own shadow as if it's not you causing it by standing in the way of the sun?"

"Sam," Sparrow said, pushing herself off the sofa. She was dangerously thin, brittle. The obstetrician had told her she needed to put on at least thirty pounds, fifteen for herself and fifteen for the baby. After her first trimester and the extra weight she lost with morning, noon, and night sickness, the obstetrician had upped the needed weight gain to forty. It was *my* baby she was starving.

"Would you mind watching Sam while I go out for a walk? I have to clear my head." Sparrow looked at me, her large blue eyes welling. "I have to get a handle on this."

I stood at the picture window watching her start down the hill, shoulders curling around the load inside her that she couldn't carry and couldn't release. She looked older than my own grandmothers. Like someone in a story Sam would tell—about a beautiful queen changed by a wicked fairy's curse into a frail old witch.

"What do you mean you don't want us to come, Dylan?" My mom's voice echoed with Sparrow's slow steps. "It's our first grandchild. The first *great*-grandchild on both sides. What you're asking is unnatural. We are not giving up so easily, believe me."

I don't know where I went. It was like time slowed, spread out. Every slow step Sparrow took was like a year together. I began to count them. At three I was breathless, damned as Sisyphus.

Sam's hand on my arm brought me out of myself.

"If I went to stay with Grandma Jewell, would you and mom stop fighting? Would there be room for this new baby?" she asked quietly.

There was something in Sam's voice, something clear and sad and generous and yearning and true and tough, really tough, the way we can be at that age before we've decided what will break us. I understood she would do that for us, and for her own, her very own.

"It's going to be a boy," she said. "I heard mom telling Aunt Kathy that Grandma Darla would be mad to hear it. Grandma Darla wanted me to be a boy, you know."

"I don't," I told her, putting my arm around her. "I want you to be exactly who you are, Sam." And, for the first time, I meant it. I could tell she could feel that too—and it surprised her, and she moved into the space that had mysteriously opened up for her.

"Your mom, does she want a girl or a boy?" Then I turned and grinned at Sam. "It doesn't matter. She doesn't have to choose, does she?"

"No, she has me and Alex, right."

"Alex?"

"Yes. It's like Sam. Girls and boys can both use it. That way we don't have to let Mom know we know what's coming—but we can plan."

I smiled. We stood there, the two of us, holding hands, breathing quietly, looking out at the empty street, the daffodils lilting in the spring breeze, the scatter of dogwood petals on the overgrown lawn, feeling the world curving protectively around us, so much space, so much space.

I wondered if something similar was happening to Sparrow out there alone in the big world, remembering what I had said, feeling it stretching her from the inside out, just like our quickening son, and feeling the fragrant and welcoming spring air folding around her body, so small, so wanted, so worn—making it all more than bearable, making it buoyant, home for herself and everything in her.

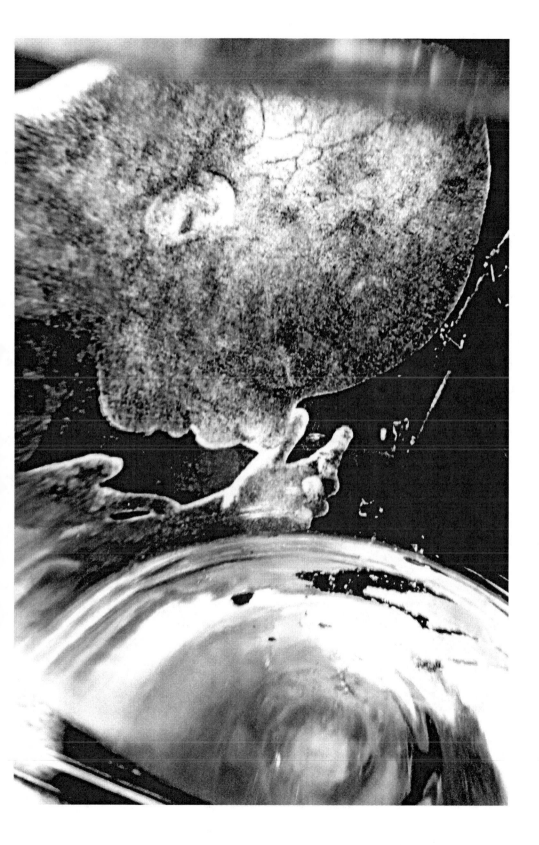

WHOSE LIFE IS IT ANYWAY?

"Is it any wonder?" my wife Suzie said when I told her my parents' plans. "Given the circumstances, it makes perfect sense to me, honey."

She rubbed her belly, at this point the size of a bowling ball. The gesture was already so habitual, I was wondering what she would do when it wasn't there anymore. Would she be making these little expansive circular gestures to the baby and me?

"Perfect sense. To *them*. For *them*," I said. "But what about us?"

"What *about* us?" Suzie asked. "We could use the help, especially the first few months. It's not like they're planning to be here permanently."

"You mean constantly. No. We're going to have bouts of them permanently—like incurable malaria," I said glumly.

"It's not like they're going to be in the house—or even next door," Suzie said, turning to go back to her study.

It's not like the baby's even safely born yet, I wanted to say but didn't dare.

What I hated most about my parents' response to Suzie's pregnancy was their unreserved joy—like there was no margin of error here because no error was conceivable. In one unplanned swoop, all their hopes had been restored. The pregnancy was going to be unproblematic, the birth a breeze, the baby's future assured.

I went back to stripping the wallpaper from the second bedroom, which I had been using as a study. Since I had an office at the university now, Suzie had decided my study was the one to go. Once she'd finished her master's thesis and was gainfully employed, we could share it. Until then, she was going to need a room all her own.

I thought I'd lay claim to the basement den, but she said that it should be a family room—so it would be easy to have play groups over. I'd gone over to Home Depot to price sheds and then had refused to go farther, feeling sullen. Why was I the only one here who couldn't have personal space under the roof *I* was paying for?

"Your parents are going to have a second bedroom in their condo," Suzie said when I tried to talk to her about it.

"Right. That's just what I need," I said. "A return to dependent adolescence."

"From what I heard, you were pretty independent," Suzie said.

As if I had a choice back then.

As if I have one now.

It's true that my parents feel that their world has cracked open like an egg and new life is spreading its wings, while I feel that destiny is closing down around me like a fist. It has nothing to do with becoming a father. It has to do with becoming a son again. I don't want that experience anywhere near my own child.

"You're a great guy," Suzie told me. "Funny, generous, talented, iconoclastic *and* hard-working. Surely they had something to do with it."

Probably the most important thing to know about me and my parents is that twenty years ago my beautiful, brilliant, hard-working, talented and compliant younger sister Isabelle died of acute lymphoblastic leukemia. She was fifteen. She died in the fall, a month into my freshman year at Penn. She had a miserable year and a half before that, which included two months of isolation during a last ditch bone marrow transplant. I was the closest match, so I provided the marrow. I don't remember anyone asking me if I wanted to. I mean, how could you not? There was no choice. For any of us.

But it means that when she died, my parents were completely devastated, and *I* was the reason why. My rebellious cells couldn't come through for her. Their perfect girl.

I don't talk about this with anyone because the heart is a senseless place, impervious to logic. *Post hoc, propter hoc.* After my cells, because of my cells. Because I gave, she died. You couldn't pry it apart if you tried.

Which is why, when Suzie told me that she was pregnant, that our so carefully sequenced plan to complete both our graduate degrees and then look into foreign adoptions had been shot to naught, I wept. Had the doxycycline she'd been taking for a staph infection she'd picked up working in the church nursery (she believes, I don't) interfered with her birth control pills? Maybe it was the St. John's Wort tea she had been drinking to help her with test anxiety? she wondered aloud as she went to get a box of tissues and pulled one out and handed it to me.

"Not yet," was all I could say.

Only one week into it, that little aggregation of cells barely implanted, her hands still went to her belly. I do believe in a woman's right to choose, so when she did that, I knew the choice had already been made and it wasn't in me to question it.

"Your job is solid, isn't it, Chris?"

I'd graduated in June, and because of the lousy job market for historians, and the fact Suzie was still in school, I had taken a job with the university press editing books in my discipline, to hell with the country or the century. Between my job and my gigs as a musician, we were more economically solid than any of our friends.

Especially if you added in my parents' gift of a sizeable down payment on our house as a wedding present—which was, they told me, also a present from Isabelle since it was her college fund applied to a purpose she'd thoroughly approve.

"It means they've moved on," Suzie said. "It's a good sign."

When I finally returned to school at twenty-eight, I never used a penny of my parents' money. Never considered it. Never imagined that they might have had a fund with my name on it. It wasn't something we discussed when I was applying the first time. In fact, I think they didn't realize I had applied anywhere until I brought them the acceptance letter from Penn—with a full scholarship. This was just after the bone marrow transplant, which hadn't been covered by insurance because of Isabelle's prognosis. I'd written my college essay about Isabelle's illness, how we were all giving everything we had to keep her alive.

"They haven't moved on," I said to Suzie. "They've displaced. They did not need to bring her into this. If they had a college fund for Isabelle, they had one for me. The down payment—which we never asked for—could have come from that, from all the money I saved them by dropping out and by taking it all on again by myself later. But no, they wanted to insert her into *my* life, *my* home."

"It would be easier on us to have the down payment. If they want to help us, I for one want to be helped," Suzie said back then. "I want us to have a home. Even if it means thanking Isabelle in absentia."

"We have room for Isabelle in this marriage, in this family, Chris," she added quietly.

I might have agreed, if my parents' generosity (according to Suzie) or intrusion (me on bad days) had stopped with a down payment on a house for us. I never expected it to extend the way it just has.

"Let's just define her as an angel, not a ghost, Chris," Suzie had said two years ago when we grudgingly (on my part) accepted the down payment from my parents. As if, with a simple shift in perspective, the world was righted. What I adore—and detest with equal strength—is my wife's ineradicable optimism.

Here she was doing it again about the baby. "This baby is a gift, Chris. We have to accept it. We can *do* it."

Easy for her to say, with her parents and grandparents and two older brothers and their wives and their children all alive. But I looked at her and it was clear to me that I had just as much choice about this as I had had about the bone marrow.

I smiled, took her in my arms. "Of course we can. When's the first doctor's visit? Let's go out and get you some prenatal vitamins right now."

All I asked her was to let me decide when—and how—to tell my parents. Even in my worst speculations, I didn't expect something like this before the baby was even out of utero.

I don't want to imply my parents don't have full lives. They do. They live out on the Main Line. My dad was a popular professor of history at Haverford. He retired this year. My mom still works as a hospice nurse. Until Isabelle died, she worked in pediatrics. They have many old and dear friends in Haverford. Which is what makes it all the more surprising that they decided, without consulting us, to buy a townhouse condo in our small college town—"so we can be a regular presence in our grandchild's life." They intend to come for two months at a time, three times a year.

"Not so long that we'll be intrusive, honey," my mother said, "but long enough that you can rely on us." She and Suzie are already talking about how to space the visits, for example during the time the baby is transitioning to daycare after Suzie's semester leave is up—and when Suzie takes her comprehensive exam, or in the last frantic days of thesis preparation.

All of this only a month after I told them. No wonder I held the news back for six months. Told them only because they were coming for a three-day visit and it would be impossible to conceal.

"You've known for six months," my mother said. "We're not a family with secrets, dear. We told you about Isabelle's diagnosis as soon as we heard. Is it going to be a boy or a girl?"

"We've decided we don't want to know until the birth," I told my mother. About this I'd played hardball with Suzie, told her if she let them know the sex of our child before the birth, I'd put the house up for sale and return them their down payment.

We're going to have a girl. There is no way in hell I am going to name her Isabelle—or even hear someone suggest it. The very idea provokes a rage in me as intense as the one I felt when my parents called to tell me Isabelle had died. They hadn't let me know the end was that close. I wouldn't have gone to school if I'd known. I thought the transplant was working. I'd have taken a leave of absence, or dropped out (as I did the following semester). *My cells were dying in there with her own, and they didn't feel I had a right to know?*

Oh, at that time in my life I had rage flying in *every* direction. When my mother's friend Annette, Isabelle's godmother, hugged me at the funeral and said, "Be strong. You're all they have," I pushed her away saying, "They're really down to the dregs now, aren't they?"

She looked at me, red flowing up into her cheeks. "Jealousy kills as surely as cancer, Chris."

How could I, tall, athletic, smart and cancer-free possibly be jealous of that frail, hopeful girl, balder than a newborn from her last round of chemo, who, even the last time I talked with her fully intended to beat me on the SATs if it was the last thing she did in life. "Luckily I have all this time to study," she joked with me. "You set the bar really high."

"You can do it," I said.

"Or die trying," she said, and then made this sound between a cough and a laugh. I will never be able to describe what that sound did to me—still does to me whenever I hear it in my dreams.

The only person in my family who saw me as someone worthy of emulation was Isabelle. Did I return the favor? Certainly, I tempted death many times in the decade after her death. I binged, injected, sliced, over-dosed, drove down deserted highways clocking 120, teetered on bridge railings—and built up this dynamite rock band that sounded like people screaming in the middle of indiscriminate shelling and the triggering of roadside bombs.

Then, one day, I just stopped. My own conversion experience. I was alone in a field the night of my twenty-seventh birthday, thinking of doing myself in yet again, and I heard Isabelle, clear as if she were right beside me. "I set a bar so high, you can't beat me. Give in. I win." There was that laugh and cough, that horrible mix, but also something so clean and sweet, so eagerly Isabelle, I'd know it anywhere. "Let it go, Chris. Not for them, for me. Please."

All she had to do was ask. I still can't believe it was that simple, but it's true. I dismantled the band. Took the SATs again, scoring lower than a decade before but still undeservedly well, then fed from a community college into the University of North Carolina at Wilmington, where I happened to be living at the time. Moved to acoustic and put all the crazy stories of those years into rhyme and melody that appealed to bookish undergraduates—like Suzie.

All I told my parents was that I'd found a good, regular gig with a new band in a college town and was staying put for awhile. I'd go up to Pennsylvania to see them. They didn't ask questions. I didn't volunteer—not until I was graduating with my BA and had already been accepted into graduate school. I invited them to the graduation, that was it.

My dad was obviously proud of me, but all he said when I told him I was going on in history was, "You don't need to fill anyone's footsteps, Chris. Just keep making your own tracks."

It was my mom, of course, who implied I had done this for them, for Isabelle. "Our angel is smiling down on all of us today," she said as she hugged me in my black robe. I held my diploma scrolled and out of her reach as she squeezed. She knew, I could feel, that she'd said the wrong thing and also knew she couldn't take it back—and wouldn't if she could.

I stepped back, smiled. "Do we have time for lunch before I drive you to the airport?"

I saw the look she exchanged with my dad. I don't know what they thought, that we'd all hang together for a day or two, spend quality time. At our ages? With our histories?

Once I'd moved in with Suzie, the idea became, just barely, tolerable. Luckily we only had one bedroom in our apartment so there was no question of their staying with us. Which may have been why, when we said we were marrying, they weighed in for a house with several bedrooms. If only they hadn't tainted the gift by linking it with Isabelle.

"Your taint, their bless," Suzie translates. But I'm the one who lives there. The impact on me is mine, and mine alone, to define.

"It's true," Suzie says with imperturbable lightness. "They're pouring everything they would have given to Isabelle into you and you alone. That's why we're so lucky—and you're so lucky—to be having a baby, and a girl at that. It relieves you of expectations."

Then why, I want to know, do I feel I'm ready to blow, just like I did at eighteen?

As I strip off the wallpaper, I imagine welcoming my daughter into a large sunlit room whose only decoration is the changing leaves of the poplar tree outside. Those large pale green flowers with their orange stamens opening in the spring, the rich green leaves shivering in the wind all summer, the clean yellow against the cloudless blue sky in the fall, the bare branches with their bobbing flower husks in the winter. There will be bright toys scattered over the floor, plenty of room to roll and crawl, walls against which her parents can rest their backs as they sit quietly and watch her as she explores her world. Parents who don't imagine they know her better than she knows herself. It's an expression I've caught now and then on my own dad's face.

But have you ever *listened* to women with babies. They never stop, seriously. Their voices rise and they're always cooing and crooning at them. I've seen it already with Suzie and the babies in the church nursery. They can't leave them alone. They just can't.

Look, honey, see that bird? Hear that train? Watch that cloud! Clap your hands! Let's sing A-B-C-D-E-F-G. Old MacDonald had a farm. Eeyi, Eeyi, OH. Wave to Mama! Are you hungry? Wet? Don't you think it's time for bed? Oh, give us a little smile. Shhhh. Shhhh. That dog isn't going to hurt you. That disease that's devouring your blood cells, darling, it's never going to win. There are always cells you can borrow from your brother. There's always hope, sweetheart. There's always help.

"You have to take over, Chris," Isabelle said to me that last time we talked. "She won't let go. I have. Dad has too. But she won't. I can't die feeling she's going to die too."

"It's Mom's choice to live through you," I told her, eighteen and so damned stupid. "Only she can stop it."

It's like a cancer, this all-consuming love. It's been lying in remission in all of us for twenty years. What life can possibly be strong enough to withstand it?

"I'm thinking a honey gold for the walls and brick red for the molding. Winnie the Pooh decals for the motif," Suzie announces from the doorway.

"Sweet," I say. When I realize I mean it, I laugh and cough at the same time, I can't help it, releasing from my own chest the exact sound that has haunted my dreams for so very, very long.

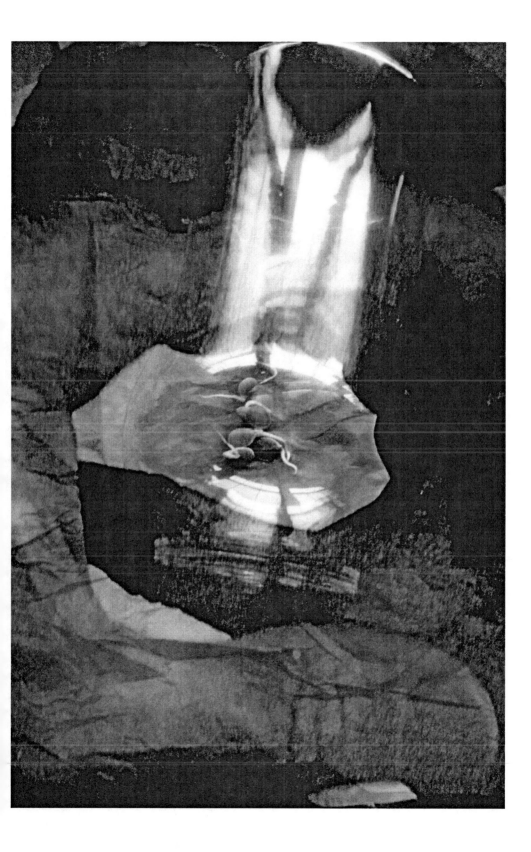

THE AIR YOU BREATHE

I know many people disapproved of my parents' choices. The psychiatrists and psychologists I was sent to regularly in my teens to treat my severe agoraphobia and social anxiety all made it clear—explicitly or implicitly—that they did and that they found in those choices of my parents sufficient cause for all my symptoms. My last three lovers might concur. I myself am not so sure.

Consequently, I've found it is generally wiser not to share the particulars of my upbringing anymore. This isn't denial. It just doesn't help me clarify my own responses. Certainly, I know I was shaped, permanently, by the events of my late childhood and prepubescence. I believe I would have been whatever choices my parents made. I'm not sure I see that formation as negatively as did Drs. Robinson, Freed, Smith, Dalton, and Ellis.

But it came up this afternoon in the conference about Sophia Greene. I found myself taking her side—to the surprise of everyone at the table. Sophia is fifteen. Her sister Chloe is seventeen and in severe heart failure. She is on a transplant list, but is very low on it because of uncontrollable pulmonary hypertension. Chloe is eligible for hospice, to her mother's great distress, but that only involves a weekly nurse's visit and monthly social worker's visit. She doesn't like staying home alone, and it also worries her mother if she does. Chloe isn't eligible for home health because she is mobile and able to care for herself. She is in virtual school. Her mother wants Sophia to go to virtual school with her sister Chloe this year so they can have as much time together as possible.

The girls are close and Sophia is fine with this plan. Sophia is a smart girl, extroverted and generous, and her homeroom and English teacher Annie Hughes's pet. Annie Hughes is the one who has insisted on calling in

DFACS—and me.

"It isn't forever," I said. "Chloe's already in hospice. That gives you a time range. Six months, a year at most."

"Her mother's going to continue working because she's used up all her leave. There's no adult oversight," Annie protested.

"Virtual school is all computerized. You've said Sophia is disciplined. If you're worried, you can call her periodically or stop by once a week to review her work."

"They're locking her up in a sick room just so her *sister* doesn't feel isolated. They're sacrificing *her* life."

"It isn't forever," I said.

"It was Sophia's suggestion," Julia Greene, Sophia's mother, said when Annie called her to object. She repeated it in the conference. "Sophia says she thinks it will help everyone. I won't have to worry about getting her to and from school. We'll save on fees. Chloe and she will have fun. She will be able to go at her own pace, maybe skip a grade."

"What do you think Sophia will gain from the experience?" I asked Julia before Annie could say anything.

"What she would say herself: that she hasn't missed a minute of her sister's precious life. And that however tough things are, she can always care for others, make their lives a little better. That's not a small thing, you know." Julia Greene, a thin woman in her late forties with blonde hair going dark at the roots, spoke to her crossed hands, then looked up at Annie with a look beyond grief or contempt.

Annie opened her mouth to protest. I shook my head. We had talked to Sophia earlier—and she had said pretty much the same thing. Although the person she saw herself helping was her mother.

"They need me and I want to do it," Sophia had said to us. She shook her bangs from her eyes briskly as if to wake us all up. This was common sense to her. "Chloe wants to stay home. She doesn't like the hospital. She can't stay home alone—and mom has to work."

"Legally, you have to go to school," the social worker said.

"If you're worried about my slacking off, two thirds of my work needs to be done on computer for virtual school. It can be checked on every day. But look, I spend a lot of my time at school just hanging out. I'd rather spend that time with Chloe. *I* will feel better." Sophia sounded calm, sure of herself. She made eye contact with each of us as she spoke, a gentle smile lighting her face.

"Who came up with this idea?" the social worker, Andrea Moran, asked Sophia.

"Honestly, I can't remember," Sophia answered. Again, she flashed that wonderful smile, and her interesting dark blue eyes weren't hesitant to peer into our own. There's something straightforward and good about her—which makes me understand Annie's protectiveness. But she also projects a self-assurance that she may well feel. "Does it really matter whose idea it was? It *feels* right to all of us. Whatever happens, we'll know we've done the best for Chloe. Mom and I can be at rest about that."

"And *you*," Annie Hughes said. "Will *we* have done the best for you, Sophia?"

"If *we* haven't, we have longer to get it right," Sophia said. "The decisions for Chloe, those are probably lasting."

"Are you making Sophia pay for her good health?" Annie bluntly asked Julia Greene in the conference we held alone with her. "Is Chloe?"

"Chloe loves Sophia. The girls have always been good friends. They're even closer now. Sophia can make Chloe laugh like no one else."

"I can see how this might be the best choice for Chloe, Mrs. Greene. But are you sure it is the best choice for Sophia?" Andrea Moran asked, backing Annie up. She was a robust red head with a permanently flushed face but a deep, comforting voice.

Julia Greene stared at her hands for a second, then turned her own stormy blue eyes on me. "Best is a ludicrous word in these circumstances. Almost obscene—"

"Death happens," I said to the far window, the tree branches tossing in the wind.

The three women looked at me.

"Dr. Bellamy?" Andrea Moran asked.

"Josh?" Annie added.

"Death happens," I repeated. "It's a fact. In itself it's neither a tragedy or a blessing, obscene or pure. It's a fact that leaves an astonishing void at the center of most of our meaning systems. Most likely Chloe is going to die by the end of this year. All the love in the world isn't going to stop that. Neither is medical science. Neither is Sophia's personal sacrifice, if it is that. Chloe has to live with the knowledge that the world as she knows it and she as she knows herself are going to stop existing."

I took a deep breath and looked directly at Julia Greene, who looked away. I looked at Annie and Andrea and continued. "Mrs. Greene has to live with the loss of her child, with the knowledge that she brought Chloe into this world to experience an inescapable early death and that another child, no more or less worthy than Chloe, is going to live a longer life whatever her relative affection for the two might be."

I could see Julia Greene open her mouth to protest but went on. "She has to live with the reality that, because Chloe needs health care now and she and Sophia need a future, she must keep working, can't spend every minute with her beloved first born. And Sophia" I began to conclude staring at my hands, "has to live with the gift of her own good health, the weight of her sister's irremediable illness, the injustice of this difference, her love for her sister and her mother, and the reality of a future with her mother that extends beyond Chloe's."

"Care to apply this, Josh?" Annie asked. "It's like you're reading from a script here."

"To the extent that *anyone's* choices are based on denying rather than accepting that— independent of our will or wisdom or actions—*death happens*, those choices are probably distorted. Why *should* Sophia's life go on 'as normal,' meaning as if death, especially the death of a beloved sister very close to her in age, isn't happening? Why *should* Chloe feel that she can ask Sophia to give up her social world if death happens, it just happens? Why should she ask Sophia's life to stop too?"

I have a nice voice, people often remark on it, ask me if I've ever considered radio. I could see all the women relax as I spoke. But my own right leg was doing its bouncing thing, and then my fingers began their tapping.

Annie was looking at my hand with a little smile, both sad and satisfied. "It makes you as uncomfortable as it does us, Josh."

But I know, I wanted to tell her, exactly what I'm talking about. It's just that there are no words there, never have been.

"Death happens," I said again. "When it does, it makes mockery of our law of averages."

My father died at seventy, leaving two families, six children, four adult, two not, and the impact was exactly like Chloe's death here. Astounding to everyone concerned. Should it have been? That's the question I have been asking myself for years now.

The women all looked at each other. Was Annie rolling her eyes at the social worker to say, *Just like a man. Making it all abstract. Law of averages. Death happens. What crap.*

I don't know what happened. My hands got still, my leg stopped jiggling. I stood up to my full height of six feet. I'm thin and hold myself straight, so I can appear taller or smaller depending on people's focus.

"Let me tell you where I'm coming from. When I was nine my father was diagnosed with ALS and given a year at most to live. He was sixty-eight. He had retired two years earlier and was looking forward to spending more time with me and my older sister. My mother, twenty-four years his junior, a social worker, had recently retooled for a career in public administration and had just started a new job. My father had been a college professor. They were all analytic types—my father, mother, sister. Their responses were pragmatic. They learned about voice storing and Hoyer lifts. I was the one who freaked. I was afraid to leave my dad alone, afraid that something might happen to him. I couldn't concentrate at school. I began to fail. The solution they came up with was for me to stay home with my father and be schooled by him. As he became more incapacitated but didn't die, questions were asked about my parents' choices, especially toward the end, by well-intentioned people like you. My parents persuaded everyone they were doing it for my good. At the time, I agreed. I felt both responsible and very privileged."

"And now?" Annie asked softly.

"Look at me," I said, smiling broadly. "I have a doctorate in child psychology. I've made a career of wondering, exploring all sides. There isn't a choice we make when young, or that is made for us when young, that doesn't shape us, perhaps permanently. But many of these choices are inescapable. Death happens. Illness happens. Poverty and wealth and disability and general weirdness *happen*. Who is to say they shouldn't?"

The trees and I nodded to each other.

"Point, Josh?" This is one reason Annie and I stopped seeing each other. There was too much explaining involved.

"If they stop enjoying each other's company, separate them. Until then, find the choices that enrich Chloe's present and safeguard Sophia's future as much as possible. It seems as if the family may have come up with a good working solution."

Annie looked at me like a disappointed lover, which she is. "You're satisficing, Josh. And in this case, it really is the same as sacrificing."

"Egotistical bastard," is what Annie said about my own father. "Thinking he was the only one who could help you. Using you as an excuse to keep hanging on at any cost."

Annie's the blackest of Irish with a redhead's skin—the thick white kind that doesn't flush and bright yellow-green eyes whose perceptiveness I actually find restful although other people can experience it as scornful. The oldest of six, with two alcoholic parents, she is enraged by parental lapses, or what she perceives as them. She is five years older than me, thirty-seven, and without, as far as I can tell, a functioning fertility clock. Perhaps it was replaced by her ten nephews and nieces, her affection for her students, her passion for teaching, the care she generously but caustically distributes equally to her divorced, ailing parents.

We weren't involved for very long: three months soon after I came to work at Greenwood Academy. She was uncomfortable with my open bisexuality, but more so by what she said was my lack of resistance.

"I *need* strong personalities," she told me. "With you, Josh, I keep looking for the wall, and all I get is foam pillow. I *need* the push back."

This might have bothered someone else, but I know the calls I've been able to make in my life. I don't feel I need to share that knowledge with the world. The question that engages me is could I, if necessary, make those choices again. I doubt I'll ever be able to be really intimate with anyone until I'm sure.

Annie and I decided it was best just to be friends—and for the last three years we've considered ourselves good ones. I've seen her through a serious relationship with a married man. She's seen me through my mother's death, my sister's wedding, and four short trysts, three with men, one with a woman. She called me into this conference because it is my job as school counselor—and also because she was counting on me to be the cushioning between her rock and Andrea's hard place.

Annie called me into the conference knowing my own story and assuming that it would naturally mean I would support her. Instead I provided a door out of the either/or cage she keeps building as compulsively as bees build hives. She didn't expect me to find my grounding in the *and*—or to stand there so openly. Truly, Annie who is so busy defending the helpless and the hopeless has far less knowledge about how to protect herself than me.

After my father died when I was eleven, I was forced to go back to school because I was too young to stay home by myself. Not too young to stay home, mind you, with a man who couldn't speak or breathe or eat or piss without mechanical assistance. And they were right, however much I protested, however unbearable the alternative felt to me then. For how can a boy of eleven possibly describe the rarified existence I experienced for a year and a half as my father's primary caregiver?

I understand that my sister and my mother never saw it that way. Honestly, I don't know what planet they were living on. Of course, I do. They were seeing it as my father did. My mother lifted my father into his chair, attached his catheter and diapered him for the day. She poured a can of nutritional supplement into a plastic glass and fed it to him through a straw. I did the same at noon. She returned religiously at five-thirty, the first year with my sister Sabrina, who was a junior in high school. My mother and I made dinner while Sabrina filled my father in about her day. My mother interrogated my father and me about ours at dinner. She talked to us in the same voice she used for her welfare clients. It's hard to describe but easy to recognize, and it's one I'm careful never to use myself. It grates on me like you wouldn't believe. All that faux respect, that pretence of 'can do-ness,' that bonhomie. At least my father had genuine hopes for me—and for himself. I was the son who was going to know him in sum. I was the one whose gifts, as yet invisible to the larger world, he would identify, protect and nourish.

I keep trying to see what the world saw in me back then—both positive and negative. I know afterwards my therapists saw me as vulnerable, isolated, exploited. But I think *I* saw myself as in the thick of it, as remarkably indulged, treasured, crucial. That's a wonderful thing to feel at any age: *crucial.*

It was happenstance that learning about my father's illness, experiencing the existential vertigo of his imminent (or so they said then) death, and the fourth grade agony of having Miss Mary Lovejoy as my language arts teacher coincided. Miss Mary Lovejoy, you had to use both her names, was more than contrary, she was cruel. She read aloud the names of anyone who failed a test, "These are today's big losers, class." Then she passed our tests back with a smile that made me cringe. Our school straddled an economic divide, so it didn't help that she was also drawing a color line. In solidarity, my own scores in spelling and grammar began to fall by Christmas, but it wasn't until I returned in January that things fell apart.

My father's diagnosis had been delivered over our Christmas break, and my mother spent her nights in the garage heroically muffling her sobs. My sister obsessively ran laps around the block when she wasn't practicing her violin or researching at the library or talking compulsively with my dad about her college plans as if nothing had shifted.

"Don't look so sad, Josh," my mom would say coming in from the garage, red-eyed. "We'll all help your daddy. It's going to be all right."

It was so obviously not going to be all right, all I could do was pat her arm, at which she grabbed me and pulled me to her and wept into my hair until my scalp began to crawl, a poignant form of water torture. Since escape wasn't possible, I hugged her closer.

Within those two weeks, I discovered my own indispensability and what it consisted of. Whenever anyone else looked like they would break, it was my job to break first—not into tears, but into activity of one kind or another. For example, I used my savings to buy my mom food for Christmas—sausages and cheese and crackers and cake so she wouldn't have to cook. I had Sabrina practice with the Hoyer lift my parents had immediately ordered, lifting me from the bed and dumping me on the floor with a rapidity and force that soon blotched my buttocks and back with bruises. When my mother put a stop to that, I had Sabrina try to teach me the violin until the parakeet's horrified shrieks put a stop to that as well. With my dad, I read through all the information the doctor had given us about ALS, asking really simple questions, hundreds of them, so he could use his quiet teacher's voice. I held his hand after he said, "I'm so sorry, Josh. I was counting on our having another decade together. I've been so looking forward to this time with you and Sabrina."

My father was a small man and at that age I looked as if I was going to take after him. My sister, at sixteen, had obviously inherited my mother's more statuesque genes and at five ten with a well-rounded figure looked as if she were already in college. She almost was, for she had inherited more than her fair share of the smart genes in the family and was already getting A's in all her advanced placement classes. She had scored a perfect score on her math SATs and was now feverishly trying to get a matching score on the verbal.

By the end of that vacation, Sabrina too understood the role she was to play. Family star. Nothing was to disrupt her practice or study schedules or her prep for the retake of her SATs. Colleges were already writing her. She and my mom and dad would laugh about it, but leave the letters lying around like get well cards. Which they were. They said there was light at the end of the tunnel. Sabrina ended up graduating early after taking an extra English course over the summer and then heading off to Swarthmore a month shy of seventeen. "Don't you worry about us," our parents said to her. "You go on out there and do what only you can do."

I, on the other hand, was to be the light *in* the tunnel, hesitant, wavering, and real as the line between life and death.

But to return to language arts and Miss Mary Lovejoy. It wasn't what she did to me that drove me to act (it rarely is). It is what she did to my best friend Jesse. Jesse was a thin, funny boy with a hyperactive bladder. When he asked to go to the bathroom, Miss Mary Lovejoy would make him wait so long he'd have his whole desk bouncing up and down, then he wouldn't make it in time and when he returned to class with his pants wet, she would order him down to the office to call his mother to bring a change of clothes because of his lack of self-control. I can still hear her say that. She made it sound more serious than being a serial killer. Jessie's mom worked two jobs, his grandma, who watched him, had arthritis so bad she didn't leave the house, and his dad wasn't expected out of jail until Jessie was twenty-one. No one had time to bring him dry pants. Miss Mary Lovejoy knew that, knew that Jesse was going to have to parade down the hall to the office in his wet pants—and parade back in borrowed clothes from the lost and found. Girls' clothes sometimes. I had thought about this over the Christmas break and with my mom I'd come up with a solution, which was to bring some extra pants and underwear in my knapsack and let Jesse use them, but I hadn't had time to give them to him yet.

So when Jesse asked if he could go to the bathroom and Miss Mary Lovejoy gave him that sneer of hers and said, "All in due time, Jesse. Try and control yourself," something took possession of me and I stood up.

"Yes, Josh?"

"I need to go too."

"Fine," she said. Even though my grades were falling, at that time my mom was on the PTA board.

"Not unt-t-t-il Jesse," I said. "He asked first."

"Are you t-t-telling me how to run my classroom, young man?" she asked.

"You just look like a person," I said. I was looking around the class as I spoke. I can still remember the looks on the other children's faces. Little Kayla's eyes opening wide, Dynetta bending her head to hide her smile, her beads clattering together. Emboldened, I looked back at Miss Mary Lovejoy. "But you're really a witch," I continued. "A wicked one. And I wish you were dead. Dead. Dead. Dead. Dead. Dead."

"Ohhh boy," Jesse whispered. "Ohhh boy. She goin to get you, boy. Shit hitting the fan now."

"Are you threatening me, Josh?"

"No," I said with a smile, channeling my sister Sabrina's precocious know-it-all voice. "I am expressing a heartfelt, well-considered opinion. I am exercising my right to free speech in a democracy."

And then I picked up my knapsack and opened it and just had time to pull out the bag of extra clothes and hand them to Jesse as Miss Mary, all contrary, grabbed me by the shoulder with her pincer fingers.

"Dead, dead, dead, dead," I sang as we walked down the hall. "I wish, I wish, I wish you were dead."

"He should be institutionalized," Miss Mary Lovejoy, her face as red and moist as a raw steak, told the principal, then the guidance counselor, and then my mother.

"And you should be fired," said my mother, her face as white as Miss Mary's was red.

"Just try it," Miss Mary Lovejoy said with a smirk.

"If I could, I would," the principal confided in my mother after abruptly escorting Miss Mary Lovejoy from the room. "She retires in June. Let's just find a solution for Josh until then."

Which is how I began attending home school, with my father taking the role of beneficent mentor. I can't tell you what bliss it was not to have to sit in a desk for hours at a time, not having someone always criticize my handwriting, not having to watch all the petty cruelties Miss Mary Lovejoy exulted in dealing out, being able to read about Prince Caspian and the Dawn Treader at any time in the day as long as I finished whatever my father assigned me by the end of the day. My stutter disappeared. My mom, who saw my dad's spirits rise with my presence, the demands of my education, stopped crying. My sister looked at me with respect because I was doing something she didn't dare—spend hours with our increasingly feeble father.

Neither my dad nor I were really big talkers, so what I remember of those hours are mainly the singing of our parakeets, the hum of the refrigerator and the air conditioner or heater, the occasional sounds of cars on the back streets, the sounds of my basketball hitting the wall of the garage when I took a recess, coached by my dad from his wheelchair stationed on the deck.

While I completed my reading or my math exercises or practiced my typing (we all agreed my handwriting was a lost cause), my father was busy recording short all-purpose phrases in his own voice so when the time came when he couldn't talk anymore, we could still continue our work together. I heard him saying, "How was your day?" "Tell me more." "Could you repeat that?" "Great job." "Try again." "I love you." "Thank you." "I'm sad." "I'm happy." "Water, if you could." "I'm hungry." "The joke is on me." "It's time to end this." "Tomorrow is another day."

I enjoyed my reading and writing lessons without the anxiety of Miss Lovejoy. The farther I got from her, the easier it was to contract her name, although I couldn't go as far as my father who called her Mean Old Mary All Contrary. I loved having the freedom to reward myself with a chapter of a favorite book whenever I tired of the formal assignments. My dad wasn't a task master. I just wanted to earn his smiles, which came most readily when we were on task and on time.

The first year, Mrs. Deal, my math and science teacher, came to the house once a week. She kept saying she looked forward to seeing me back in school next year. I liked Mrs. Deal and she liked me, but she looked at my dad in a way that made me nervous and protective. "My dad already checked that," I'd tell her as she looked over my math assignments. "He checks everything I do." Already, even though my father was still able to get up out of his wheelchair unaided and his voice was clear, I felt somehow we were doing something a little shady, a little under the table. It was too good to be true. The two of us on perennial hooky. Appearances were important, so I was always nodding at Mrs. Deal, looking as shy and withdrawn as I thought suited someone whose mother claimed he was too vulnerable to be in school.

My dad seemed oblivious to the threats I intuited, chatting with Mrs. Deal just like he would have before he was sick, always a little punctilious, with practiced charm.

"Josh and I are having a fine old time here," he said. "We've worked out our daily routines like two old bachelors. No surprises." He briskly wheeled his big new motorized chair around the living room, escorting Mrs.

Deal in and through the house to the sunny back room we used as a shared study. "We have everything we need at our fingertips. Curiosity, peanut butter and jelly, pencils, erasers, spit balls."

But he knew what he was doing, he knew what to say to reel Mrs. Deal into our conspiracy. He looked up at her as she was leaving and said with a wave of his better hand, "You do know that my son's well-being comes first with me. Let there be no mistake about that. To the extent that I am the cause of his anxiety, it is my responsibility to relieve it."

Mrs. Deal was in her late twenties and pregnant with her first child. My father was older than her grandfather. You could see how she was torn in her responses. He was talking like a man in the middle of his life, and part of her wanted to respond to the parental authority of that voice, but her natural response when she looked at him was to humor him like she would her grandfather with his harmless delusions of control and influence. And when she looked at me, her response was too much like my mom's for me to feel comfortable. I felt she wanted to pull me right up against that bulging belly and start the water torture.

"I like being able to read at my own pace," I told her. "Every morning I get up and read some on my library book, then have breakfast and start in on my schoolwork. I can do my classes in whatever order I want. Dad lets me choose. But I have to do all that subject before I go on to the next. Dad makes our lunch." (Already this was white lie.) I took a deep breath and hurried on. "Then we have discussion hour after lunch. We talk about world events. After that I play basketball or run around the block five times and then practice my recorder. Then my mom comes back with my sister and she takes over."

I would smile my biggest smile and close with, "Dad says he wishes he had been home schooled. He says it is made to order for a shy kid like me."

Mrs. Deal would smile at me gently. She had this thick blonde hair filled with curls and skin that looked very soft. "It always seemed to me that the other kids liked you, Josh, and you liked them. I wouldn't have described you as shy—just someone who needed to have his private thoughts from time to time. You always seemed to be having a good time when you were playing with Jesse and Louis and Dynetta. Don't you remember?"

"Do you want to meet my parakeet?" I asked her. "I'm trying to teach him to talk. His name is Jeremiah and when he learns to talk he can utter a jeremiad. And here's my dog, Jove, who you can see is very jovial. Look, he's smiling at you. He shakes hands too."

The truth was I couldn't remember the faces of any of those children. I couldn't remember what it had felt like to play with any of them. When I thought of school all I could remember was Miss Mary Lovejoy's wrinkled, spiteful face, her red mouth opening: "Are you t-t-telling me how to run my classroom, young man?" And then that merciful wave, equally hot and cold, of nausea, rage, oblivion. Honestly, I didn't remember what followed those words until I began writing here. I always assumed I'd just blacked out.

With Mrs. Deal, the situation was more delicate. I needed her to trust us. I needed to protect my father. I needed to project the same kind of have-it-all-under-control, can-do energy my father, sister and mother did and, with the crafty ingeniousness of a child, I did my best. The only problem was that the real resilience I did have, my essential optimism, began to feel fraudulent, as severed from real feeling as the responses of my highly cerebral parents and older sister.

Mrs. Deal, the last day she visited, slipped a piece of paper with her home phone number into my hand as she was leaving. "I'm not going to be teaching next fall," she said, patting her ballooning stomach. "I'll be on maternity leave. That means you can call me whenever you want to, Josh." She had just learned that my parents had decided it was best for me to spend another year being home schooled by my father, until middle school.

"Josh asked for that?" Mrs. Deal asked my father with more force than I thought polite.

"He didn't need to," my father said. "Many things here don't need to be put into words."

Truly, my parents saw themselves as making near super-human efforts to meet the special needs of their bright, distractible, adored, anxious, maladaptively shy, youngest child—all in the face of the deepest tragedy the family would ever know. My mother had been my father's student and she remained willingly in that position with him. "If it were only me," I heard her tell an old friend, "I would choose to go at the same time Bill does—but I have the children to think about."

That feeling of hers, I'm sure, changed over time, but it guided many of my responses. If it weren't for me, I often thought, *both* my parents would die.

"Bill is determined to do everything he can for Josh so that Josh knows, he'll always know, how much he is loved." I heard my mother saying over and over again, to everyone who asked how my father was doing, how we were all holding up, most especially to anyone who looked the least bit quizzical when informed that I was being home schooled.

That everything that my father did for me required certain things of me in return—one of which was that I should never imagine being anything but the family linchpin—we all knew but never mentioned.

Originally, I think my parents just imagined keeping me out of Miss Mary Lovejoy's malicious clutches for the rest of the school year. I think they thought that was all the time my Dad had left. It was our relationship, the strength of it, that might have contributed to Dad's extended survival. Certainly that was the unspoken understanding between us.

I was the one, keying in on it, who insisted I stay home for fifth grade too. My grades on the standardized tests were improving dramatically and, although I had no dreams of matching Sabrina's achievements, I began to imagine that I might come in a presentable second.

As I said, Sabrina, after my dad's diagnosis, had gone into overdrive and, combining AP course credit, summer school, and a little administrative legerdemain, had graduated a year early. She was busily packing when I made my request. Mom, who had been acting on the assumption that I was going back to school, was trying to talk Dad, who now could not drive, not even with our new van with a lift, into accepting a home health aide.

"I'm a private man, Melanie," I heard him tell her. (Closed doors were as rare as psychological boundaries in our house.) "Dying is as intimate as love. I don't want a threesome."

Unless, of course, that threesome included me. At that point, my dad couldn't walk at all, but he still had some function in his arms and his voice was getting husky but was still clear. He was a high-spirited man, curious. He didn't make light of the limitations, but he never sentimentalized them either. He really was only asking for privacy.

"Look," he said. "Why don't we put in a feeding tube now. That way you can just hook it up when you leave in the morning, pour in a can or two of Ensure, unhook it when you get home. I have you on easy dial on my phone."

My mother began to cry. "That's no kind of life, Bill."

"It's a hell of a lot better than a hospice, for which I still don't qualify. We said we weren't going to let this go on long enough for me to become a burden, Melanie. I have nearly seventy years of a very rich life to review. I have the riches of my library. And my memory. The other kids call me while you're out."

My mother wouldn't have it. "Let me see how much sick leave I qualify for."

My father barked at her, "I never want to see you sitting here just waiting for me to die—that's moral suicide for you, honey. You can't stop your life. Remember, we said quality of life would determine our choices. No trach. It can also include no feeding tube."

That's when I broke down and broke in, sobbing, acting as if I had heard none of the preceding, was totally engulfed in my own ten-year old misery. I couldn't stand going back to school, I told them. I wanted to stay here with my dad and Jeremiah and Jove. I wanted to keep on making 98th percentile on the standardized tests. I couldn't remember the names of the kids in my class anymore. It would be like starting all over again. Why couldn't I wait until middle school when it really would be a different group?

It only occurs to me now that none of us thought of suggesting that Sabrina might delay college for a year—or just go somewhere closer to home. I think the two of us had been given separate responsibilities for living out the two kinds of normal—life as it should be ideally and life as it is. I don't know what to make of the fact that Sabrina dropped out of college a few months after Dad died, moved to Colorado and worked at a ski resort as a ski instructor and member of a jazz band. She returned to live near my mother in her late twenties, earning a degree in physical therapy from the local branch of the state university. She works with young spinal cord victims, takes them deep sea diving and on wheel chair marathons. A year before my mother died, Sabrina married a physician, neither particularly wealthy nor handsome, a widower twenty years her senior with two sullen teenage children. My mother wept through the whole wedding although Sabrina looked radiant. But that was far in the unforeseeable future that day.

I was both plaintive and practical as I tried to persuade my parents. Dad could still review my work, answer my questions. I could heat his soup (he could still swallow though it was slow) and make myself a sandwich, staving off the need for a feeding tube for some more months.

It's a strange disease, ALS. Deeply debilitating, rapidly so in some ways, very slowly in others. Your mind stays clear, just all volitional movement deserts you—and then the involuntary ones, like swallowing, breathing. My dad had the slower kind that starts in your limbs. At first, when his legs went so fast, they thought he was going to be one of the ones who went quickly. But then, when the weakness went so slowly in his arms, they began to talk as if he were one of the outliers, maybe as much so as Stephen Hawking. Oh, we could only hope. Or dread.

Alone together the next year, my dad and I just took the changes on one by one. We stopped predicting or comparing. We just moved on. My father liked to write—and as long as his voice held out, he continued dictating letters to his friends (and to my mother, a love letter a day), which I would transcribe on email and send. He regularly wrote Sabrina. I never felt jealous, of course, because nothing was withheld from me. Indeed, my father made our days sound adventurous and happy. It was the background music of my days, my dad describing vivid moments in his courtship with my mother, or, when writing to his older children, with theirs. I knew the sweet victories of their childhoods as well as I did my own, felt his pride in their accomplishments, his gratitude for their being. My dad, you have to understand, was a very sweet and loving man. He was an amazing—inimitable—model, rather like my sister.

I got better and better at deciphering the sounds he made, translating so smoothly for my mother as we sat at dinner every evening that she was shocked when old friends visited and acted as if my father, no longer able to lift a finger to feed himself, were uttering gibberish.

I still can't identify when it was that I quietly, unnoticed, began to refuse to leave the house at all. Because we had a large backyard and I ran Jove there, a basketball hoop on the back of the garage, and, later, a trampoline, there wasn't a decrease in my level of physical activity. I had been going out with my mom to do errands on the weekend, or to church on Sundays—but I always avoided other kids, said I thought Sunday School was a waste of time and that I would rather maximize my mother's and my time together. It was true. My mom was working longer and longer hours. It seemed like it was always audit time or grant time or program review time at her agency. So our weekends were compressed, intense, sweet. But too nerve wracking.

Years later, she told me, "I began to imagine telling your dad I'd change places with him if only because it meant I could finally get a full night's sleep. Paralysis would be a small price to pay for adequate REM."

We never settled in, you see. For the first year, after the lifts were put in the bedroom to help get my dad in and out of bed, my mom slept on the couch. After Sabrina left for college, I made her sleep in Sabrina's room, but she always pretended it was on a night by night basis. She never moved a single thing around in Sabrina's room—the trophies, the stuffed animals, the movie posters.

I took the same approach to my self-imposed house arrest. "Maybe next time," I would say when my mom would suggest a walk in the park, a quick trip to the grocery store. "I have this chapter I really want to finish." And she never pushed me because the fact was she was as anxious as I was about leaving my father alone. And she was never *refusing* me anything, you see. She was offering, and I was thanking her and passing up the opportunity *just this time.*

By the end of that school year, my dad was on a feeding tube, even soup was too hard for him to swallow. His voice had gone and the taped voice was laborious to use, haunting and limited if he did. The voice was his with all the life taken out of it. So, most of our time together, my dad and I just communicated with our eyes, my gestures. I wrote to him rather than speaking. I'm not sure why I decided to match his silence. I think it made me too sad to hear my own voice echoing alone there in the air between us.

Sabrina came for a few weeks that summer but it freaked her. I heard her talking to my mother. "He's like a zombie, can't you see? They both are."

I think it wasn't like that you know, whatever it looked like from the outside. We were like each other's seeing eye or PTSD dogs. It was all visceral, what we were exchanging. Shared gazes, smiles, silent laughter. I'd bring my book over and point to a page I especially liked and my dad would read it and then smile or just blink his eyes twice. When my mom was around, I did the voice over. But with Sabrina when she visited, I didn't. I don't know whether I just forgot or I just wanted to leave her out.

"It won't be long now," my mom told Sabrina whenever she complained.

Oh, I can't tell you how much I hated them both at that moment. There they were, sitting out on the lawn in the long summer twilight, their own bright worldly unit. My dad couldn't leave his wheelchair, but that also meant he couldn't leave me, who couldn't, at that point, cross the threshold of our house even to get the paper.

"They're able to give each other something no one else in the world can give either of them," my mother said softly.

"But what about you?" Sabrina asked. "I thought he said he wasn't going to prolong things, that he wasn't going to deplete the family."

"He doesn't think he is. He's doing this for Josh, all for Josh."

"You really believe that?" Sabrina asked. She was pacing the lawn, her voice low. My dad was asleep with his external ventilator, so he couldn't hear them.

"He does," my mother answered. "Josh does too. That's what counts."

"What's this talk about a trach tube? I thought that was ruled out from the beginning," Sabrina said.

"He says it is Josh's idea. That Josh isn't ready for him to leave yet," my mother answered. "Who am I to make that decision?"

"Who is he?" Their voices were so alike it was hard to distinguish them. It wasn't clear whether that *he* referred to my father or me.

That was the moment when I assumed full responsibility for my father's next breath. If it was a trach tube he wanted, it was a trach tube he would get. Only I knew that I had never asked for it.

The next day, as I blew out the eleven candles on my birthday cake, my mom asked if I had made a wish and I said yes. When she looked at me quizzically, I tapped my throat. "For Dad."

Strapped in his chair, my father blinked and nodded his head. Sabrina let out a huge, harsh breath and stood up.

"You *promised*," she said to my small, motionless father, to my overwhelmed mother. "You *promised*."

"What does it matter to you?" I said quietly as I began to pull the candles off the cake. "It won't make any difference in your life."

"But it will in yours," she said. She put her hand on my mom's shoulder. "And what about her? Just because you don't dare leave the house doesn't mean Dad has to go on like this, that Mom has to live for years in this kind of purgatory. What kind of life is this for *any* of you?"

I could see my dad was getting really upset, his eyes blinking and tearing, the oxygen mask fogging up. My mother was in tears. But inside me it was really quiet, you know that kind of stillness you can experience in the middle of a car accident just before the impact.

"He is *eleven* years old," Sabrina said. "You *cannot* put this on his shoulders."

When I think back on that scene now, I'm both amazed and amused. There was my sister tall as a Valkyrie, filled with righteous fury, and there was me, still small for my age, not even up to her shoulder yet—but we were a perfect match for each other and I knew it. We both did. Sabrina was the only one there young enough to respond to me as an equal, to put the consequences of my actions squarely on my shoulders, whatever she had said to my mother. Even as she spoke, I could see she was right. Who *was* I to make this choice? Who was my father to foist it on me? My mother to accede to that? And who was Sabrina, soon off to Interlochen, to object?

What Sabrina didn't understand was that, more than prolonging life, the trach gave us, we thought, control of the inevitable. Once in, life stopped rapidly when we removed it. There would be none of the soul-hollowing unpredictability we experienced now. Soul *hallowing* unpredictability. The two months that followed, in my memory, have no language.

My dad indicated that night, after Sabrina's outburst, that he wanted to go to bed. Sabrina and my mom used the lift to get him in and my mom diapered him. I went in to see him and stood there holding his hand. He held my eyes for a long time, and there was such kindness there and such defeat. I expect he read the same in me. *That* was the minute, you know, when the choice was made. I could have sobbed, begged him to reconsider. I could have badgered my mother. But I didn't. I stood there staring into my dad's eyes feeling the weight of the last year and a half lifting from my shoulders, all our determination, all our can-do. I also began to feel how *real* our lives were, that this was *our* air, my father and I, *our* trach, and we were both, at this moment, taking it out.

That was the moment my childhood died. But as I write about it now I wonder if it meant, as I always thought it did, the death of my manhood as well. I felt, at that moment that I was committing a terrible betrayal, one that deeply invalidated everything I might have hoped to become—but perhaps, it occurred to me today, I was keeping faith with something larger than either of us. *Death happens. Life does too.*

The last two months of my father's life were completely silent except for the oxygen mask, the involuntary sounds he made when we turned him to wash him. He made no more efforts to get up after that night, to use his voice, or even his eyes. My mom called hospice in. The social worker wanted to send me to friends but I went wild at the suggestion.

"He will never recover if you do that," my mother said. "His fear of death is devouring his life. And mine. His father's too. He needs to touch it, know it intimately, so it has no mystery for him anymore."

Or more— the kind of wonder that lifts us up like a tornado and sets us down unscathed in a completely new state.

"You do not know," I told Annie this evening when she called to scold me about my scandalous performance in the conference. "Seriously, you do not know what is best for them."

"Neither do you," she snapped.

"I don't dispute that. But I believe, Annie, I really do believe, they are taking their next best step to find it—and they will know when they get there. Sophia, Chloe, and their mom too. Each of them. *All* of them."

"Like you?" she asked and then began to cry. "I really hate what they did to you, Josh. And what I hate most, truly, is that you don't see it. It's such a loss, to all of us."

"But I do," I said. "I do see what *we* gave, what *we* received. It's you who can't. I was in on this too. I had choices. I don't want to be saved from the enormity of it all, Annie. I just want to claim its beauty. It's the very air I breathe, it is what defines me. And it's sweet, Annie, it's really so sweet with possibility."

I took a deep breath. She did too. And we slowly let them go, in unison.

"Dinner?" I asked.

Annie laughed. "My place. Eight."

As I walked to the car, my step was heavier and quicker than usual. Turning the key in the lock as I was leaving my apartment to meet Annie, I realized that for the first time since I was nine leaving home didn't set off an ache that seemed to reverberate into infinity, an absence that was its own form of presence. For I knew now, I really knew, that what mattered was inside me, always had been, and would be until death.

And there was no way, never would be, to hang on to it. I had to let it go. Hope. Let it back in again. Ad finitum.

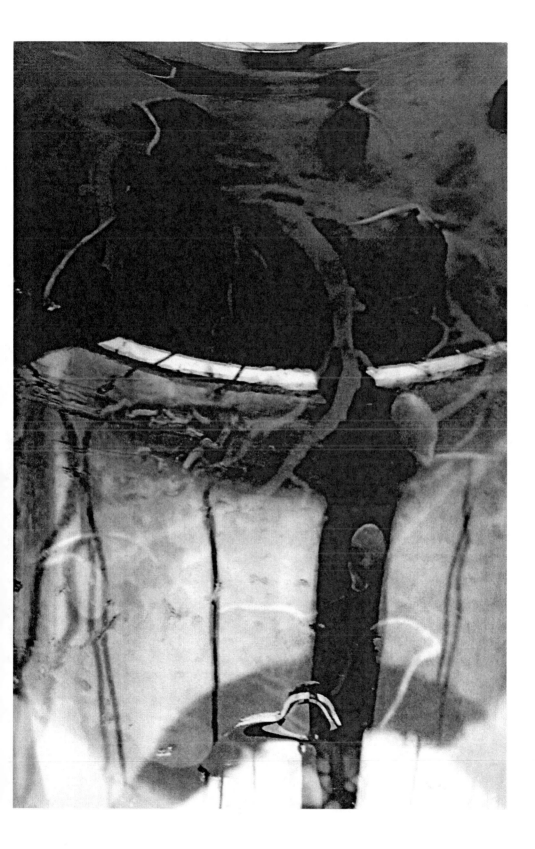

LIFEBOAT

"No big," I say when my mom calls to tell me my father died. "I never knew the guy."

She pauses, and I can feel her wanting to probe but deciding it's my lost tooth, my choice to explore that emptiness—or not.

"His sister called me," my mom goes on. "She started talking to me as if thirty-eight years haven't passed since I last saw them all. It was surreal. She talked about his wife and his other children as if I knew them. Finally I told her that all I could really remember about him was that he used to walk from our apartment to his work through a meadow growing under the electrical lines thinking, *I'm a free man among serfs*. That always stuck in my mind—what it meant about how he saw the world. I expected him to start brewing mead or something."

I'm on my pedicab. I have a delivery to drop off at the homeless shelter on 33rd and a donation to pick up at Mort's Bagels. I keep telling the dispatchers it would be more efficient for me to pick up the donations first, but they don't mind. Some of the other drivers take them home with them, sell them to their friends. I don't think that's right—and not because I'm white, although the other drivers think so. I'm a week shy of forty, college educated, and the only incorruptible delivery boy for Seasoned Giving, a high-end charity that redistributes uneaten food from fancy restaurants, corporate cafeterias, and bakeries to the homeless, flea-infested, and meth-raddled of this city. I may be the only person in the whole organization who really believes in the mission. I have to. Otherwise how can I explain how I've chosen to spend the last four years? Why shouldn't the destitute nibble on nouveau cuisine, complex reductions, hand-fed beef?

If I weren't biking for my livelihood, I think I'd be a chef. My mother told me my father was a good cook—so maybe it's a genetic predisposition. If so, it's the only good thing I've heard about him so far. How do you mourn a man you've never seen since you were two and about whom you've never heard a good word—even from his own father?

"I feel sorry for his wife and kids," my mom says. "It was so unexpected. She woke up and he was lying there dead right beside her. No warning." My mom sounds kind of dreamy, like she's watching the opening scene in a movie.

"Sorry. I've got this run I need to do. I'll call you later." It takes a little longer to get off, but I persist.

As I bike, my mind rapidly settles into its familiar grooves like the call never happened. The better groove is just a sense of flow, the movement of my muscles responding to differences in terrain, rough asphalt or slight incline, this sense of the people moving by me like water, gathering in little eddies, surging forward again, or, occasionally, a single face, some indefinable expression that will surface again in my wayward dreams months later.

The worse groove is my obsession with Selwyn, with the moral dilemma he keeps putting me in—falsifying his delivery sheets, selling off the best donations, bribing the dispatchers to give him the lightest routes. Look, I *get* it. He feels the world owes him. He never went to college, probably never even imagined it. I'm not sure he ever finished high school. He's forty-eight. He has, like most of the drivers, kids by several women. (He does for them what he can, shoes here, a knapsack there, daycare fees, sandwiches or quiche.) The job has union benefits, so he's bringing in his friends and relatives. He sees me as having options he doesn't. He thinks that my position here is easy pickings for me, a luxury, that I'm really living off some trust fund and am doing this out of anthropological curiosity—or just slumming. He believes that what he's doing is normal, that if I were in his situation, I mean really in his situation, I'd do exactly the same as he does. All the other guys do. I can see his reasoning, but I don't know if he's right. I think that the very least we can say about morality is that it is what it is only when it frees itself from necessity.

All I know is it makes me crazy angry that he puts me in this impossible position. I don't want to hurt the guy by reporting him—but he's hurting the whole enterprise. "Yo, man, I *am* feeding the hungry," he's told me when I've tried to call him on it. "And one of them hungry is me."

We have a month vacation a year. Health care. Education benefits.

Brute strength. Time to have our thoughts revolve as often and as freely as these wheels. What more does he expect?

"Your aunt said she and her daughters have talked about you for years," my mom said as I was trying to hang up. "Whenever they see a red-headed man, they wonder if it might be you. She sounds kind of nice, honey. A bit of a dry drunk, maybe. I mean, this way she had of settling into the conversation like we were the closest of friends. But the daughters sound interesting. They all live an hour's train ride from you at most. I didn't tell her where you lived, of course, but I took down her phone number and address."

I didn't have to tell her to toss them. My mom and I communicate in a way that amuses my wife, Phuong. Phuong's Vietnamese and she gets it, the indirectness. As my mom talks, she listens to my silences, their length and intensity, as if they were speech. I listen for everything my mom *doesn't* say, the fears and truths that shelter behind her steady flow of words. Like, *What is going to happen when I'm gone and you have no family to your name? I'm so sorry I couldn't provide you with more than just me. You're almost forty and a delivery boy. You could still be anything you want to be. Why are you choosing to throw it away?*

I'm heading down to the UCC mission, which is located improbably near the financial district. I like the minister there. His name is Sutton. He doesn't believe in titles although he collects degrees. He's in his early sixties. I think this may be his third career. In the one before he was a social worker. He says he's dealing with the same clientele, he just finds the work load lighter when everyone, him included, knows it isn't all up to him to fix it. There are higher powers here we can all appeal to, curse when they let us down. He looks at me with this quirky little twist of the lips. It's kinder than a smirk, but it's clear he wants me to lighten up. He gets what makes me mad about Selwyn—but it doesn't seem to trouble him. Any more than when management dressed up all the drivers in tuxes for their annual fundraising gala, then restricted them all to a table in the back where they were forbidden to drink or to speak with donors—like they were infectious. It's funny how social diseases go in only one direction, isn't it?

"You're a brooder," Sutton has told me more than once. "And an idealist. Nothing wrong with that, Derek. Unless it blinds you to the good in yourself and those around you." He looks me up and down in a way that I'm used to but that still disappoints me. Looks are something you're born with, nothing you've earned. He's gay and a lonely guy, has to be. I mean, look at it: I'm the high point of his day, cycling up with William James in my front basket, gourmet comestibles in the back. I'm always careful to gesture with my left hand, have the wedding ring flash, mention my wife by name, make some little comment that shows we're close, it's a good marriage.

Today, I imagine telling him about the call from my mom but when I go into the church, I find he's in his office talking with a woman, well-dressed but in tears. He looks up and smiles and waves but then turns right back to the woman. Maybe she's one of his real parishioners, one of the complex derivatives that enter through the front door on Sundays. One of Seasoned Giving's donors. Maybe she's lost a job, a husband, an exercise coach, an odd million or two, or her cat. I'm surprised at my bitterness, but it's because of how disappointed I feel not to be able to speak to Sutton, even though I know it's just transference from Dr. Berlioz. I can hear Dr. Berlioz's voice as I turn away, "It's just a feeling, Derek. *It passes.* There's no emotion we have that's intrinsically good or bad. It's what we do with it that defines us."

As I'm closing the door, Sutton calls out to me, "No more portabellas, Derek. The guys think they're getting meat and then they bite in and they freak."

Last week he complained that the lettuce was limp.

One reason I like my job—and I do (whatever my mother thinks about it) is that I keep getting these glimpses of lives I will never lead. Before I had this job, I made deliveries for a florist. Mother's Day was the saddest day on earth. I spent all my time going to the twenty-first or forty-third floors of these tall apartment buildings and nursing homes with bouquets of daisies, roses, daffodils or sweet peas. And there would be this lonely old woman opening the door, sometimes pushing a walker before her. They all searched for a note, any word, true or not, that proved . . . I always smiled, hoping to ease their disappointment. They almost all invited me in. I drank so much tea and coffee that day I had to hit each and every one of my usual pit stops. All night, the scenes would keep repeating, those wrinkled faces, the hopeful look, the disappointment of seeing *my* face behind the flowers. The brave smile that quickly concealed it.

Finally, I couldn't take it. Now I lounge at the back door of these busy kitchens, the line workers all speaking Spanish or Chinese, the chefs murmuring in French, yelling in English. Nobody knows how to place me at first. But by the second visit, I'm invisible. Someone will gesture over to a box that is filled with coq au vin, broiled or braised vegetables, baked salmon. I'll refrigerate what I can, check my delivery route. Trundle on—with a stop at a coffee house to read James or Damasio or Kahneman or, if it is a free day at one of the art museums, I might go there.

And then I bring these crazy luxuries to men and women who abandoned their children for crack, robbed their mommas for heroin, keep constant company with hallucinations as vivid to them as my own thoughts are to me. My mother fears, even though I've never used any drugs but nicotine and caffeine, that that is where I'm headed—for reasons neither of us are able to fathom or change. But, for reasons I'm also not able to fathom or change, however much I may share my mother's fears, grant their realistic basis, I am just as sure that madness and destitutions are *not* my final destination. Just as sure as I am that this job that brings me up against them daily *is* exactly what I need to be doing right now. There's something I'm learning here with all this cycling, both physical and social, that I cannot, given who I am, learn in any other way.

If I could, I'd take a more direct route. Who wouldn't? That look of disappointment, I've seen it all my life. The old woman looking up at me from her bouquet of flowers with the bravest smile of all is my mom. Actually, my mom's not that old. She had me at twenty-one. She's my biggest supporter and always will be, and I am an endless source of disappointment to her—and probably always will be.

"*Always*, Derek?" I hear Dr. Berlioz asking. "And why do you need your Mommy's approval at your age?" This was five years ago now he asked me. He's been dead for several months, and for all this time I've been trying to give him an honest answer. Still am. His point was—*is*, because he is still very much alive in me—that my mom's sense of disappointment and what happens inside me when I see it, *feel* it, are just feelings. They're as real as stratus and cumulus clouds but no more lasting. It's a question of weathering them.

Images are interesting. You think of rain, the worst of thunderstorms, and you can imagine holding fast, seeking shelter under a very tall tree, pulling in like a turtle and letting the hard rain drum on your bony spine, your muscles. But imagine a lightning strike, all that energy lighting you up from the inside out. Or an earthquake, the ground giving under your feet, huge buildings crumbling to dust around you, on top of you. Or an avalanche. There is weather and there is cataclysm, onslaught. Like this storm they say is coming any day now.

"Tell me about your mother," Dr. Berlioz would say. "Let's de-mythologize her, shall we? How tall is she? What color is her hair? What does she do for a living? Who is her best friend? What does she look for in men?"

The answer to the last is simple. For as long as I've known her, my mom has been looking for a man who could love me the way she does—and my own father couldn't.

"You mean she always felt you deserved more, Derek? That life had short-changed you? There was a lack here that needed filling? Or is it just that she thinks you are fantastic just the way you are and doesn't trust anyone who can't see that? Does she believe if you receive this confirmation of your value from a man as well as a woman, something essential in you is going to change—you're finally going to become the man she wants you to be? Or is she just so controlling she can't trust anyone who doesn't see the world exactly the way she does—you included?"

I don't know why, but I got angry then. There was something about the way Dr. Berlioz was talking about my mom, like she was this stereotyped Freudian image in his head, like she really was the cause of my problems. "Look," I said. "I *am* a disappointment to her—but just because she wants me to feel free inside and to stop being my own worst enemy. She sees in me a potential I cannot for the life of me truly see in myself. She's one of the strongest people I know but there are two realities she cannot change. She cannot stop me from sabotaging myself and she cannot *make* anyone else love me even if they love her with all their heart, even if she feels her love for me is the most essential thing that *she* is."

"So it all hangs on you, Derek. Whether a man loves her or not? Whether she's happy?"

Dr. Berlioz was in his eighties when I saw him. Eighty-nine by the time he died. I think I may have owed him eighty thousand dollars, possibly a hundred thousand by the end. He never treated me for free, he just never collected on my debt. It was an essential part of our relationship. I used to anguish over it. He told me, like my mom did when I had to borrow money from her once after I broke up with Karen, my first long-term girlfriend, that I could repay him with paintings. Which, now that I think about it, is when I gave up painting.

"Face it, Derek. The truth is you are never going to pay me—*and* that I am going to continue to see you. Just like your mom. And you are definitely never going to pay us in your paintings, that would be like paying us in blood. Your paintings are to you what you are to your mother; they are your *raison d'être*."

I pause on my bike. I can see Dr. Berlioz, that smile he had, the deep creases around his eyes, which were so large and milky blue behind his glasses, the way his cheeks hung so heavy with age and understanding. What he was giving me was never lost on me—on either of us—but I feel the reality of it today more keenly than I did three months ago when his wife called me from the Cape to tell me he had died in his sleep and wouldn't be keeping his weekly phone session with me. (Even in summer, he never lost touch.)

"You are not going to cry?" my wife Phuong asked me when I told her. "This old man who loved you like a father? Your eyes are going to stay dry?"

What I like about Phuong is that this really was an open question. And it was about appearance rather than essence. She doesn't have so may preconceptions about how we should show what we feel. *Do* Americans cry at funerals? Do they touch people they do not know on first meeting? Why *should* our feelings and our actions match?

"I'm so sorry to tell you this," Dr. Berlioz's wife said to me. I think she must have been his age, but she sounded like a young woman. "You were in his calendar. I wanted you to hear the news from me personally."

I seem to have found my way on to a number of old men's calendars these last few years. This same aunt we haven't seen in thirty-eight years wrote my mother two years ago to let her know that as she was cleaning up her father's house after he died, she found that my name and my birthday were the only listing on his calendar for the coming year. He had seven other grandchildren he saw regularly, but my name was the only one on there. This grandfather had written my mom a year before that. He had found her name on the internet. (She's a fiber artist and sells over the internet.) He told her he wondered often what had happened to us and would like to know how we were doing, especially me. He would like to be in touch.

My mom let me know about that too. "No," I said immediately. "He had over thirty-five years to find me. They all did."

"I'll write to thank him for his concern," my mom said. "He and his wife were kind to me when I was eighteen. I told him you might not want to see or talk to him if it meant you were going to be in contact with your father. He said, 'You don't have to explain that to me. I know my son.'"

Your own father saying something like that about you. It gave me a chill, I mean something worse than panic, a paralyzing dread. *What if I am just like him?* This man for whom no one, even his own father, had a good word?

That is the question I never asked Dr. Berlioz, although I can hear how he'd answer. "Well, what exactly would that *mean*, Derek? To have half his traits combined with half of your mother's—all jumbled up in a way that is peculiarly your own?"

William James says that our sense of self is just the unbroken flow of thoughts, sensations, emotions—but what if it comes to a dead stop, what happens to us? He also says that we may have numerous consciousnesses. So at a point like that, do we just jump into another flow? Do we have as many selves as we have consciousnesses?

I stop at a bistro on Second Avenue, a pizzeria on Third, and then make my way over to a women's shelter nearby. A woman four inches taller than me, in other words over six and a half feet, and easily two hundred pounds heavier, opens the door and bars it with her body. I don't think she's tran, just Amazonian.

"Tofu and spinach pizza and salad. Spring greens with candied pecans and cranberries," I tell her. "Raspberry vinaigrette on the side."

A little girl peers around her vast right thigh.

"I want chocolate," she whines. "Frosted Flakes."

"And a slap on the head," the woman says, hoisting the boxes up, stepping backwards into the hall, her eyes still fixed on me. "Leave the rest right there. Don't take one step more. This here is sanctuary, bro."

I look at her enormous body, bigger than any Botero figure. I think of all that weight as silence. How deep are the sanctuaries people need these days? Just look around you—people can hardly move with the weight of the comfort they're seeking.

The woman looks at me, smiles. "You sure you don't want to take one of them boxes with you? Don't look like you have an ounce to spare."

I shake my head. "It's all for you." As I get on my pedicab my spirits soar, I can't help it. It's a great city, a beautiful day, and here I am shuttling the meager portions of our wealthiest neurasthenics to our morbidly obese poor. Who, truly, could ask for more?

When I get home that evening, having met up with Phuong after her rehearsal and stopping off for falafel and spanakopita on the way back to our apartment, I find my mom has forwarded an email from my dead father's wife. Her name is Sandy Masterson. My father's name was David Michael Masterson III. Don't be misled. The first David Michael Masterson, Sr. was a clerk in a dry goods store in Kansas. His son, the one who had me inscribed in his calendar when he died, David Michael Masterson, Jr., was a line-supervisor in a rubber factory. My own father, the first college graduate, worked as a lab tech in a research lab where the most important thing about him was probably his suffix. When my mom married him, he was hitting rabbits on the head with a hammer to study shock, but his boss decided to study learned helplessness, so he shifted to shocking dogs with electricity instead. Later, he moved to North Carolina and went to work for a pharmaceutical company testing chemo agents. I think this just involved injecting mice and monkeys.

Sandy Masterson wants to send me some papers. Actually, as one of my father's legal progeny, she can't do otherwise. It turns out she is going to have to have me sign off if she is going to be the executor. She tells my mom she understands I may want to keep my privacy and that I can just correspond directly and confidentially with her lawyer if I prefer.

Call me to discuss, my mom writes.

It's already eleven. I decide to call her in the morning. I close my account and hand the laptop to Phuong. She's creating a new performance piece and is still trying to secure space to present it next week. She hasn't told me what her latest show is about. I'm fine with that. Nothing she does surprises me—or more exactly, everything she does surprises me but none of it, as yet, has bothered me. We've been together eight years now, so that is saying something. She has already performed nude, tarred and feathered, sequined, and demurely dressed in her old Catholic school uniform. They each seemed appropriate for the occasion. No one can understand our glue. But I think that is part of it. Phuong is a force of nature, kind of like my mom, and I accept that. I don't try to channel or block it. I just ride it like surf.

I don't tell Phuong about my father. I tell her instead about this interesting essay by James I've been reading—about what he calls percepts and concepts. There are lines from James that echo for me: *Concepts are secondary formations, inadequate, and only ministerial . . . . They falsify as well as omit, and make the flux impossible to understand.*

Phuong lies with her head on my chest, listening as I talk. She likes the sound of my voice, especially if her ear is pressed close to my ribs. The bones make the sound more mysterious, she says. I like the pressure of her cheek bones on my skin, the feel of her soft, silky hair. I feel that some understanding moves between us by osmosis, chemicals naturally seeking to establish their own equilibrium between us as if, for a moment, we were a single organism.

What James is saying, I tell her, is that perceptual life is all about flow but concepts are static and if we use them too much we begin to misunderstand the nature of reality and of ourselves. We become discontinuous to ourselves, because what we really know as 'I' is just that unbroken perceptual flow of consciousness. I is that which experiences. But when we replace that flow with the concept 'I', we lose that perceptual dynamism. Our 'I' is frozen, fragile.

"*Concepts are essentially static—and what we do is confuse the relations between concepts, which is only comparative, with the dynamism and fluid transmutation by association that is our natural stream of consciousness. We take the map to be the world,*" I read aloud to her.

Phuong is an accountant by day, a performance artist by night, so she knows a lot about abstraction and flow. She generally prefers gestures to words, but she gets the point, any point, pretty quickly.

"Like a balance sheet," Phuong says. "It tells you nothing about taste buds and smells, chapped hands, the weight of knives, the cool feel of coins or softness of paper money, how loud the voices of the cooks on one side of the door and the customers on the other, the heat of the steam collecting on your cheek or fogging your glasses as you're serving, or how raw the desperation, how deep the exhaustion day after day after day." Phuong's parents have a little phô restaurant in a small town outside Atlanta and she draws a lot of her examples from it.

In the morning as she is dressing for work, Phuong says, "Your mother called me, Derek. She asked me how you felt about your father's death. I told her you hadn't told me about his dying yet, but when you did I would ask you how you felt."

"He wasn't," I said. "He wasn't my father."

"In fact, yes. In feel, no." Phuong is trying on shoes, of which she has many, trying to see if she prefers the shape of her dress with boots or with high heels. She works for a firm that specializes in accounting for small businesses and non-profits—and she dresses for her clients. Another form of performance art, she says. The firm's name is Creative Accounting, which all its members, artists of different sorts themselves, like—even when they get the occasional shyster as a client. Their slogan, written to clarify is, "We're on the up and up. We help you monetize your dreams." English, obviously, is everyone's second language. Their firsts are Russian, Amharic, Vietnamese, Mandarin, Hebrew and French.

Today Phuong is wearing a bright red skirt, short and swishy, and a black and red tapestry jacket, rather boxy.

"Boots," I say without even asking who she's meeting.

Phuong shakes her head, her long black hair flashing, and puts the boots back.

"It's a dingy little coffee shop. They're trying to go boutique."

She chooses red shoes with silver stiletto heels and puts them in her bag. She puts on sequined tennis shoes for the walk to the subway.

"I have never been to an American funeral," she says as she is leaving the bedroom.

"And you're not going to start now," I say turning on my side to look out the window.

"Do you dress as you do for an art opening—all black?" Phuong goes on as if I haven't answered. I can already tell she's not going to let this drop. Phuong is irreverent in her art, but she has this thing about respect for elders. It upsets her sometimes how I talk to my mom—or don't. (That's why my mom calls Phuong when she doesn't get the response she wants from me. Phuong never puts her off, never cold shoulders her.)

"Like, dislike mean nothing. You owe her everything," she tells me. "To turn your back on your mother is to turn your back on your own life."

Phuong never turns her back on life. That's another part of our glue. Wherever I hesitate, Phuong says yes, and plunges right in, while I stand stock still on the bank anxiously planning ways to save her. James asks, *Who can decide offhand which is absolutely better, to live or to understand life? We must do both alternately, and a man can no more limit himself to either than a pair of scissors can cut with a single one of its blades.*

Phuong is still standing there in the doorway. I can feel her. I don't turn, but I know she is waiting until she has my full attention.

"You are number one son," she says. "Much depends on number one son. Number one son is a fact, not a feeling, Derek."

"So is dead."

"Yes." Her tennis shoes stick a little on the floor as she leaves. I can smell her perfume, it has something a little soft, rounded, like sandalwood and something sharp, astringent, maybe pine.

I listen to her descend the wooden stairs, all three flights.

I can't define what I am feeling. It isn't in me, it is rolling over me in waves, salt as the ocean, hot as flame. *I am not going to sign.*

I'm working the one to nine shift this week, so I have time to call my mom, but I don't. I go down to my favorite coffee shop with my journal instead. My mom thinks I lead this really irregular, downward trending life, but I don't. Here in the city, I fit seamlessly into the flow just by *being* here, walking these streets, struggling to make ends meet. Not only artists starve here. Most people here are more than what they do for a living. If I don't speak, and I often don't, nobody gives me a second glance, a second thought. I like that. I spend way too much time as it is trying to explain myself to myself, I don't need to try to do it for someone else as well.

Phuong early in our relationship created a performance piece called The Power of Silence, where she and five friends played twenty-five different people, all coming up and trying to engage me in conversation as I sat cross-legged and in my customary silence in the center of the stage. Some sidled, some strode, some minced, some sneaked, some glided, some hobbled. They were dressed in business suits, jeans, swimsuits, ball gowns, anoraks, sweats, and clown suits. They spoke in Vietnamese, English, Basque, Tagalog, Swedish, and sign. They looked down at me from a distance, stared me in the eye, whispered in my ear, spoke over my head. Some left flattered, others furious, others wept. At the end, tiny Phuong hauled me upright, then, standing behind me on a chair, she moved my arms and head like a puppeteer, and in a deep voice said, "For it to mean anything, I need to make the first move."

Then she edged around me, her face expressing delight and astonishment, her arms still circling my waist. She winked at the audience as she circled, then when she was directly in front of me, she leaned precariously far back on her heels to bring me into focus.

"Can you define IT?"

At which point I smiled warmly, leaned down, grabbed her by the waist, slung her over my shoulder and strode off the stage, whistling a song from *The King and I* that my mother taught me as a child, while Phuong waved and prattled happily to the audience, "Sometimes we don't need a willing ear, all we really need is a platform."

But to return to my mom and why I don't call her. I don't *want* us to be in this together. I don't want to be in this alone. I don't want to be in this at all. The man was nothing to me and still I have more feelings than I would ever have imagined and nothing human to attach them to. When I was very small, when I heard the kids at daycare talk about their fathers, I made, or retrieved, something that was more feeling and kinesthesia than image. There wasn't really a face attached to it, just this sense of great height, something safe and also foreboding. When the other kids asked me about my father, I'd bring this feeling to mind. I told them, and myself, he was coming to get me sometime soon. At *his* house I wouldn't have a bedtime, I wouldn't have to eat my vegetables, I would be able to watch television every day, all day, there would be no limit on candy or cake.

When I was five, he sent me a birthday package. I think it was a puzzle, maybe a toolkit. He had included a card for me. I opened it and there was a piece of paper inside but because I couldn't read yet, my mother took it and began to read it to me. After a few words, her face got really still and she stopped. "He says he hopes you have a good and special day, honey," she said quietly, folding the card closed.

"It's mine."

"Of course." She handed the card to me, but kept the paper. The card was blue with a big 5 on it and five balloons and five cats gamboling with five puppies. Inside there was a signature, a scrawl I couldn't read yet. It could have said Santa or Euripides for all I knew. The printed words, Happy Birthday, I did recognize. I looked up and saw my mom reading the sheet of paper. There was a photo tucked in there as well. When I reached for it, she held it up higher.

"These are for me. Boring grown-up stuff."

That night I heard her yelling at someone on the telephone. "What business did you have putting that in his *birthday* card? 'Now I have two children, you and a daughter two years older than you.' On his *birthday*. You haven't seen or spoken to him in years. Who are you trying to fool?

Luckily he can't read yet. How would you feel if you were his age and a father who hasn't shown any interest in you for as long as you can remember sent something like that to you? What do you *mean* it was my job to explain the divorce to him—like you had no hand in it?"

And then she was on the phone with her best friends for hours, crying, raging.

The next night, while taking my bath, was the first and last time I brought my father up as a child.

"Why don't you let my daddy see me?"

Oh, the look on her face. Dr. Berlioz says that feelings pass, but I can tell you images stay. I bring that one to mind and a silence so deep and freezing descends, I feel there is no beginning or end to it.

There *were* words, first.

She stared at the soap bar she was rubbing against the wash cloth.

"I don't keep him from seeing you, sweetheart. That's his choice."

"He doesn't want to see me." Even as I spoke, I could feel the towering figure begin to dissolve, then the thick roughness of denim shifting into pure color, like a deepening twilight, nothing solid, just air, then the color and the vague musky smell that usually accompanied it dissolved too and were replaced by the clean white of the bathtub, the white of the suds floating on the water, the brisk, unequivocal smell of Ivory soap. I ran my fingers through the suds, making channels, inlets, estuaries.

"Maybe he treats his daughter the same way."

My mom looked startled, then resigned. She realized I had heard her the night before.

"What do you mean?"

"He never sees her either."

"Oh honey," my mom said and reached over to hug me but I grabbed my blue tugboat and slipped under the water and began to run it vigorously over my face blowing bubbles to make a wake. Vroom. Vroom. Vroom. I know I was making sound, but neither of us, I was sure, heard anything. When I sat up, the silence was so thick around each of us it was surreal.

That unanswerable silence is at the core of my relationship with my mother. We're both powerless to break it. I mean, what can you say? It happens every day? It's not the end of the world?

I never talked with her about my father again until I was sixteen and age-appropriately alienated. Then I suggested to her I go visit my father and the three other men who had played important quasi-paternal roles in my life: a scientist, Rolf; a musician, Larry; and a lawyer, Henry. We had moved a number of times in my life, so they were scattered all across the country, and this was really an excuse for a cross-country trip, couched in terms I thought my mom would find hard to refuse. They certainly did that. I was age-appropriately alienated but not a sadist, and as soon as I saw the look on her face, I backed off.

"Maybe I'll wait until I'm in college to see my father," I said. She promptly arranged for me to fly to Houston (Rolf), San Francisco (Larry), and Chicago (Henry).

After that, we only talked about my father once more at my initiative. I was in my late twenties and in my first serious relationship—with Karen, a law student. Two months earlier, we had decided to abort an unplanned pregnancy, which I didn't tell my mom. It was more Karen's decision than mine, but afterward I was having a hard time with it. I kept making paintings that looked like fire storms, or—if you knew the back story—suctioned wombs. I'd moved here by then. My mom was visiting. Even she could feel the tension. We were taking the subway up to a museum. I remember that. The clatter and blur of motion outside the train. How we were seated side by side kind of talking out into the car, like none of this was particularly private or personal.

"You were born into an existing relationship," my mom insisted. "You were *planned*—as much as someone twenty can know what they're planning. I've never regretted it for a minute. In many ways you were the making of me, Derek. I had strength to do things for the two of us I couldn't do for myself alone."

"I know *your* story, Mom," I cut in, already feeling that wild impatience that only my mom brings up in me. Constantly.

"Why did he leave?"

"I left. I felt you were unsafe with him. Now, when I think about it, I wonder if he was just too young. I mean, he was five years older than me, but you know men, they lag developmentally by about a decade."

Old shtick. I stopped it, stuck with the important stuff.

"What do you mean unsafe?"

I could feel my mom pull into herself, trying to focus, be clear with herself almost more than me. "It was so big to me at the time. Mostly it was small stuff. Leaving poisonous plants on the floor where you could get to them. You were teething. And stuff that wasn't that little. Like taking the screen off the window on our ground floor apartment to run an electric cord outside to the lawn where he was working with power tools. I think he was making a table or a flower box. He watched you crawl out that window and head out into that busy parking lot and didn't lift a finger to stop you. He walked all the way around the building into the apartment and yelled at me, 'Your son just took off across the parking lot.' Not even 'our,' *your*. That was the final straw for me. You were this little *baby*, honey. A toddler. Sixteen months. And he was so into his own little project he would endanger your life. For a table, a flower box. It still makes me angry."

I could see it did. Her face was flushed and her voice had risen in pitch, so sharp now that people at the back of the subway car were glancing over at us. A young mother reached out to pat the hand of her baby in a stroller. A drunk guy in a knit cap, sitting a little closer to us, rocked back and forth with his eyes closed saying, "It's cool. It's all cool. Let's just keep it cool."

I didn't necessarily agree. Usually I try to be the cap for my mom's feelings because otherwise my own threaten to blow, but this time I felt oddly detached from both of us. Her voice could go higher, everyone could get a little more anxious. I didn't really care. I needed to know, but it also felt old.

I kept seeing Karen gathering up her law books, smiling at me, waving good-bye, the day after the abortion—like nothing out of the ordinary had happened to her. To us. *That* still felt hot to me. Raw. I'm not saying that I felt Karen had done the wrong thing, or that *we* had done the wrong thing having the abortion. We could both feel our paths were beginning to diverge. I wasn't making it with my painting. She was doing well in law school, setting her sights higher with every A she earned. I didn't think she'd stay—or take a baby with her when she left. I didn't want a kid who was always wondering why they didn't merit the time of day from someone. Anyone. Who would ever have to ask what I did when I was five of either father *or* mother. Who would have to hear the answer.

"Afterwards, though. Why didn't he ever see me?"

"He saw you once. On your second birthday. He took you out by yourself and brought you home hours early. Your diaper was dirty—so were you. He confided that he hadn't enjoyed it. It wasn't fun. You'd cried, been demanding. And I looked at him and I couldn't understand how I'd managed to live with him for three years. A two-year-old baby on his birthday—and all he could think about was whether *he* enjoyed it. I couldn't believe the selfishness. He did pay child support for a number of years. He wasn't a monster—he just wasn't ready to be a dad. Your dad." She stopped. Even after all the years, you could see what it cost her to say it flat out.

"I also didn't make it easy for him to see you, remember. I moved away. He could have made an attempt, I guess, but he never did. He was an out of sight, out of mind kind of guy. A few years later, he married someone with a child and had babies a little compulsively, I think there were three, maybe four, until he had another son."

"David Michael Masterson IV?" I was joking.

"Exactly. I refused the legacy on your behalf."

I went through most of my childhood informally using my mother's name, Carpenter, which she returned to after her divorce, shifting to my legal name, Masterson, at seventeen—as a way of distancing myself from her, not of getting closer to him. The name felt like I'd pulled it at random from a phonebook. The benefit was that I didn't have to pay to change it. Listening to my mother that afternoon, I was tempted to shift back—or choose a new one.

My mother patted my hand. "There were good things about him, honey. Later in life he may have made someone a good partner. He was tall and handsome. He was very smart, even if he didn't like to perform to other people's expectations." My mom looked at me and quickly looked away, her concern evident. She was aware of the tensions between Karen and me, just not the reasons for them. "I think your artistic talent may have come from him. He was constructive. He liked to build stuff. Tables—"

"Flower boxes."

"He even thought about building a boat. Later, he lived out in the country, built a house, I think. With indoor toilets finally." She laughed. "I discouraged you from seeing him earlier, Derek, but it might be a good idea to go see him now. Experience him for yourself. People change, you know. And you'd have a ready-made family. He has a number of other children."

Including David Michael Masterson IV. At twenty-eight, I was terrified I was destined to be like him. I kept hearing Karen saying, "What does it take to get your attention, Derek? You honestly think you would be able to focus on a baby? Get real. You can't even focus on me, let alone making a living."

As we got off at our stop, my mom touched my arm gently. "I wish you'd *say* something, Derek." When I didn't answer, she went on. "You're a wonderful man. You're going to make a great father some day." She talked about it as she might have when I was sixteen, as a remote but pleasant possibility, like becoming president. I was, I realized as she spoke, the same age my father was when he brought me home from our last outing. We aborted so early, Karen and I never learned the sex of our child, but that day I knew with irrefutable certainty that it was a boy and if he had been born, I would have named him after me.

My mom calls me as I'm walking to the subway to get to work. No preliminaries, just, "She wrote me again asking if I had a copy of our divorce agreement."

"You trying to mess with my inheritance, Mom?"

"Never. Do you want me to give her your address so you can take it from here?"

There are a group of guys out playing soccer in the park. The sky is perfectly clear except for five high white clouds. The temperature is warm for September.

"Send it to the lawyer," I tell her. I figure if I'm going to jam the works, I need a buffer zone. I'm feeling very energetic, almost gleeful, at the prospect. "I'll take it from there."

In his essay "The Will to Believe," James says that a genuine option is one where we have two live hypotheses, the choice is forced, and the consequences are momentous to us. I wonder if this is a genuine option.

In general, I am extremely bad about choices.

"Not choosing is a choice," Dr. Berlioz would tell me constantly. "Not submitting your work to galleries, not paying me, not speaking—those are all acts, Derek. They are all choices even if you don't experience them that way. They have consequences that are just as decisive as doing the opposite."

I'm not sure I agree with Dr. Berlioz, but I am sure that I am very sad we can't argue about it anymore.

"I'm sending you a copy of our divorce settlement as well, Derek," my mom says. "There's something she said in that letter that made me see red. I wrote back and told her so. I'm sending a copy of that letter to you too."

This is very unlike my mother, whose given name is Hope and whose middle name could be Too-much-information. She loves to talk through everything. FYIs are not her style.

"Spill," I say. "I have two blocks left."

Hope wastes a block. A full block. I wait her out, easily. "I just feel I've gone at this wrong all these years. Your father had obligations he never met. I was so focused on proving to both of us that we were fine, honey, I never gave you the space to be angry with him, to hold him accountable. I never gave you the language, the frame. I never gave you the freedom to expect."

"So I have your permission now?" I ask, and my anger at her is crazy, really crazy. She honestly thinks it's that easy. One day you wake up and decide you've approached this wrong and you just change it. Black magic. White magic. Everyone falls right in line, unhesitatingly, with your new version of reality.

James says that we cannot will belief. Or disbelief. We can desire to believe something, but that is not the same thing as doing so. In fact, belief is distinctive because it is independent of will—for better or worse. Except there are some social conditions where our openness to the hypothesis, the *live* hypothesis, is what allows a certain condition to exist. So an openness, however hesitant, to the state we desire to believe in helps create that state. He uses trust as an example. If we can't grant the possibility of trust, we can't experience it towards others, and they can't experience it with us. The act itself is necessary to its own validation. You trust me because I trust my *own* desire to trust enough to let it show.

"Phuong says that first son is a fact not a feeling," I say to my mother. "Abandoned son is too. Got to go," I add.

I hang up as she is asking, "What are you going to do for your fortieth?"

I can't bear the sadness in her voice. It is, my fortieth, whatever I want to say about it, a forced choice. Momentous in its own way. And I do have two very live hypotheses about it, but they have little to do with either my mother or my father, whatever Dr. Berlioz might say. They have to do with the adequacy or the inadequacy of my gifts *as I experience them* in relation to the equally real but invisible forces that block them *as I experience them*. I am not, as my father once claimed of himself, a free man among serfs. I am either bound or cocooned. Either way, I am fully encased at present. Incapable of action, however assiduously I keep moving.

James says that part of the experience of life is of directionality—

but that conceptually we can't define direction until the action is completed. Forty is a completion of sorts. Is it also a judgment? A prediction?

I do know that bound is how my mother has seen me these last ten years. Perhaps the whole world (except Phuong) sees me so. I don't know that I have always or usually experienced my own life that way. I know it matters what I believe, and I know that will can't create belief. I know sure as hell it isn't all as simple as my mother makes it sound.

Is it any wonder I have fallen in love with a woman whose name means phoenix? Who comes from a country where the whole population derives from one hundred ancestors who, the human progeny of a dragon and a fairy, battered their most human skulls, pulsing fontanel and unfired synapse, against egg shells to emerge, for all they could tell, self-generated?

Phuong is the only living child of five. Her parents lost their other four children during the war and the tortuous journey that led them to the U.S. by way of several refugee camps. Phuong was born in the U.S. several years after their arrival. Her mother thought she was menopausal, then mortally ill. When she finally went to a gynecologist at the refugee health clinic, her belly pathologically distended, her arms and legs wasting, she expected a diagnosis of cancer—not a fetus already six greedy months into gestation.

I think it might have been easier for her mother if it had been cancer. Phuong says all Asian mothers are harsh with their children as a way of preparing them for an even harsher world, but I feel that her mother, whose third name is Thúy (which is pronounced Twee and means friendly), was even by these standards extreme. It wasn't that she was physically abusive. She just kept criticizing her unexpected and unexpectedly gifted daughter.

"She named me Phuong because I rose up out of the ashes of her other children. She talks like that to me to heap more ashes, remind me where I came from," Phuong explains. "To remind me to keep rising."

Mrs. Thúy always introduced Phuong as her third daughter, fifth child. "Others better," she assured Phuong's teachers.

On the other hand, she took Phuong to the library from the age of two to listen at every reading hour and had her listening to tapes of people reading in English, so Phuong was reading fluently in English by the time she was four, even though her mother's own grasp of English was and remains minimal. By the time she was six, Phuong was the family translator. An unreliable translator, but a reliable narrator.

"I made a special world for them. I told them exactly what they wanted to hear—that I was obedient, quiet, industrious. That all the children were my friends."

Phuong actually did have many friends, but not necessarily ones her parents would approve. They were the boys who couldn't sit still or the ones who daydreamed, the girls who towered, fought, and talked back with the vocabulary of drill sergeants. The English she learned at school was black and southern, and even now she will slip back into it when she feels crowded, aggressive. "You dissing me, Derek?" she'll ask, her chin jutting, her eyes nearly closed, her fists clenching like there's a switchblade hidden inside them. Even at my height, I step back. As I said, Phuong is a performance artist.

But it wasn't through force that Phuong prevailed. In reality slight and studious, she brought everyone into line with her stories. She created a back story for herself filled with such exotic tragedy and privilege no one on the playground could compete. She told them her father had been a wealthy landowner, the first son of a wealthy Frenchman and a Vietnamese woman. He wrote books in French and Vietnamese that are revered to this day (but unavailable in the United States). But during the war, he was captured and imprisoned, his teeth were all pulled out one by one, his body was engraved with whiplashes. After he escaped from the Viet Cong through a tunnel he spent ten years building, he was found half-drowned, naked and mute, in a rice paddy by her mother, the beautiful, brilliant but illiterate daughter of a simple farmer. She had had her foot broken at the ankle by a soldier, an American one, so she walked with an ugly limp. Even so, she hauled Phuong's father back to her village, her family house, and nursed him back to health. Her mother lived in the village alone since everyone had been massacred by American soldiers, like in Mai Lai. But her mother had a touch of magic to her, so she was able to become invisible when the soldiers stabbed through the corpses, set fire to the houses. But her foot would never be straight again.

The two of them decided it was their job to repopulate the village. Phuong's father never spoke again until his first son was born. A demon had set up residence between his tongue and his heart. During that time of silence, Phuong's parents developed their own sign language that only they could understand. They used it later when, trapped in a refugee camp with vicious guards, they planned how they would escape. They made their way out of the refugee camp and found passage for themselves and their remaining children on an old trawler. But four days out to sea, the boat began to leak. They heard the captain and crew plotting to abandon them, so one night they lowered the only life boat with their two remaining children inside (their second daughter had died of diphtheria at three, their first son of malnutrition and pneumonia at one). Her parents had just gotten into the boat when a big storm came up and they were washed farther away from land. They weren't picked up for three weeks, by which time their last two children had become, like the ones before them, hungry ghosts, insatiable and indestructible. Her parents spent all their time making offerings to them, but they were unappeasable. When Phuong was born, they gathered around the delivery table. They made a bargain with Phuong's mother not to consume their sister, but only if she fed them daily with a diet of story and song.

"That's why I have to keep changing my story," Phuong told her friends, "so they won't get bored and turn on me and my mother."

I've never asked Phuong to ground her playground myths in reality. Never saw the need, still don't. My own hungry ghost, William, says, *Whether our concepts live by returning to the perceptual world or not, they live by having come from it. It is the nourishing ground from which their sap is drawn.*

Phuong is not out of touch with reality. Far from it. In some of her performances, Phuong uses video of her parents at work—her mother in the kitchen of their restaurant, her father setting up tables, taking orders. She ages the film, fills it with scratches, leeches the color, so they look, her stout, energetic, caustic mother with her game leg and twisted foot, her slim, silent father with his patrician features, like ghosts of themselves. She inserts herself, vividly dressed, fully fleshed, into their flow of activity pulling a red wagon filled with diplomas, flowers, fruits, burial urns, incense sticks, statues of Buddha, which she offers them as they, oblivious to her three dimensionality, scour pots, ladle out phô, work the cash register. At the end of her performances, sometimes Phuong takes all her offerings back, turns away from her oblivious parents, and offers her gifts to the audience, who embarrassedly accept or reject them. Sometimes she carefully stacks them back into her wagon, bows to it, and pulls it off the stage. Sometimes she kicks her offerings around, then climbs into the wagon herself and sits there in the lotus position, her arms lifted, a long lit match pinched between the thumb and index finger of either hand. Sometimes she stands in the wagon and pulls her hair and wails, "I'm hungry. I'm *so* hungry. Why won't someone feed me. Why won't anyone ever feed me?"

 I think of Phuong as I am biking with the flow of traffic this afternoon. I have my pickup and delivery schedule, and it is the usual pellmell scatter shot our lazy dispatchers hand out. It has nothing to do with efficiency, just who's bribing whom. It takes me up to 58th Street and Tenth Avenue, down to 30th Street, then up and over to Second Avenue and 78th. Ten food collections, three drops. I usually entertain myself as I bike, have done so whether I was free-lancing with my own pedicab or working more steadily for that florist or Seasoned Giving, by making different maps of the city in my head. Each of them is an abstract design of some kind. Once I find one that appeals to me, I enact it. It makes the day more interesting—the tension between that inner design and the sweat and flesh, clamor and grit, color and flurry of the real world. As I move into the design I have made, I am filled with a sense of direction, a desire to bring these two experiences together, make them one with my own actions. But today, I don't do that. Instead I decide to enact my list in the crazy, random sequence I was given. I pick up macaroni and cheese, fruit salad, steamed vegetables and chocolate cake from a law firm cafeteria; hoagie and kaiser rolls from a bakery; stir fry and dim sum from an Asian fusion bistro. I bike them over to a shelter for street kids. It's on the twenty-second floor. I ring them. The girl who answers sounds like she's ten and still having trouble with her 'r's. She also sounds addled. She asks me if I can bring the delivery up. She's alone at the moment. She has no idea who I am. I feel a need to protect her from herself. I tell her I'll go park my bike and ring again.

 I look around for a place to lock the pedicab up and then figure out what I'm willing to leave as offerings to the city's hungry ghosts, since the wagon doesn't lock. I take all the carbs—macaroni and cheese, rolls, chocolate cake. Leave the stir fry.

 The woman who opens the door looks to be in her late forties and as if she has vigorously lived each one of those years. But hers is the voice I heard. I'm fascinated by it, not just the 'r's but the clarity of the pitch, and it has this weird lisping quality like the words are perpetually new to her tongue. I ask her some questions just to keep her talking. How many kids usually visit? How much food do they need?

She tells me they feed about twenty kids a day, usually in the late afternoon—before their art program. She gestures to a large meeting room that has about ten easels set up. Its walls are papered with drawings, some of which, at first glance, show real talent. I want to go over and look—and want to get out of there as fast as I can without giving them a second glance.

"Where do you want me to put this?" I ask.

She points to the large table in the center of the room.

"The macaroni and cheese is probably better heated."

She nods. "They know where the microwave is."

I put the box down, then move over to look at some of the drawings. They've been working from a live model. A young girl with a blue mohawk and a tattoo of a knife on the side of her neck, just under the ear. They all have the tattoo down.

"It makes me anxious, just thinking of those needles, the carotid artery," I say.

"They aw awl immohtaw, evey single one," she says.

I'm surprised at all the practical questions I want to ask her. Where do the kids come from? Is this a way to lure them back into civilized society? Where's the funding coming from? Where do they go from here? *Is there room for another teacher?*

Instead I talk about color and composition, line and shading. I'm trying to make points before a total stranger in an empty intake office for street kids. It makes me sick.

"The class stawts at foh. Five aftehnoons a week. Come and wohk with us," she says. "Bwing a sketch book."

When I just nod, she says, "You have a good vibe. I think they would wespond to you. Owah last teachuh found a paying gig. We'uh looking for a weplacement."

By the time I get back to the street, the adrenaline is surging. I too have a hungry ghost and what makes it most ravenous, most insatiable, is any thought of putting brush to canvas, pen to paper again. I am starving us both into submission.

No one has touched the stir fry, but a sparrow is pecking at the paper bag with the rest of the rolls. I shoo it away, grab my random list, and jab at it with my eyes closed and go exactly where it lands, no questions asked, no personal preferences considered.

I say I gave up painting when my mom and Dr. Berlioz both suggested I use my paintings to repay them. When they gave them a cash value. In some way it should have been flattering that the two of them really found them of value. Instead I experienced it as condescending, invalidating at levels I had—and still have—no language for. I also felt it was a violation of what little autonomy, jobless and for the moment homeless, I had left.

But that isn't why I stopped painting. It isn't, actually, when. I stopped when Karen and I split. What I love about Phuong is that she never knew me then. My talent as a painter, such as it was, isn't what her love for me is based on. For me, no longer being a painter was inconceivable, something that had to be lived to be believed. In my mind, my paintings were, perhaps they still are, indistinguishable from me, or all that distinguishes me. Two live hypotheses. Aborted.

I stopped painting when it no longer gave me what I most hungered for—a feeling of possibility. *Real* possibility. I can't explain this well, so I usually don't try. Dr. Berlioz always thought it was a question of narcissism, that if I couldn't meet my ideal of being an artist, I didn't want any part of it.

He was wrong. I wanted to paint, I *did* paint, because it opened a door into the flow of life for me. The *only* door. Inside that flow, thinking was tactile, the world was vivid, warm, *essentially* mutable, responsive. I could dissolve into the activity, emerge changed.

That stopped for me, I realize now, when I agreed with Karen, when I let her idea of me replace my own experience of myself. My paintings stopped with those red tumultuous ones, the ones that dissolved all illusions I had about being able to be a father, even a father to myself. The silence that surrounds me when I look at a blank canvas is as absolute as the one I knew at five but far more terrible for I, and I alone, am responsible for it. It is, that decision I never consciously made and that is beyond my will to change, both momentous and forced, but was it a genuine option? Were there two equally live hypotheses I was capable of believing? Or was there only this one that I kept fighting, with all that was in me, to keep from devouring me?

When I get home, there are five emails waiting for me. Three from my mother, two from the lawyer. The lawyer, as expected, has sent a form for me to sign that gives my father's widow Sandy permission to become executor of his estate. The other includes a list of my father's individually owned worldly goods that are to be executed, I assume, in some way that the joint possessions are not. They include a fifteen-year-old wooden fishing scow with outboard motor and boat trailer, a five-year-old tractor, a two-year-old car, a power saw, sander, and bread machine. The oxygen mask he used to treat the sleep apnea that I assume killed him is missing from the list. Perhaps he just leased it. I feel queasy at the brevity of the list and realize if I died tomorrow my list of worldly goods would be even shorter.

The first of my mother's emails includes the copy of her divorce decree. The second includes the email from Sandy that sent Hope through the roof and her response to it. The third explains what set my mother off, the offending three letter word in Sandy's message brightly highlighted.

"If she hadn't used 'the'," my mother wrote.

As my mom already told me, Sandy had written asking if my mom still had a copy of her divorce decree and settlement. My mother had responded promptly, saying again how sorry she was for Sandy and her family and that she did have her copy and had just been reviewing it to share it with me and could send a copy along to her as well. Sandy responded to thank her and to add, "I can understand if Derek might not want to do so, but the children and I would be happy to meet him at any time."

My mom wrote back to her an hour later saying, "Any relationship with my son needs to be based on the understanding that a real moral, financial and legal wrong with lasting consequences has been done to him. His father had responsibilities to him that he never met. Anyone living with his father had to be aware, and complicit, in his failure to honor those legal and moral obligations. I was wrong not to hold him to them. That Derek does not bear any ill will says much about his generosity—and mine. I was so focused all Derek's childhood on assuring my son that he was wanted that we chose not to focus on this very genuine question of accountability. I feel I have done Derek wrong by not clearly holding his father responsible for his failures toward his first child. Derek deserved better. He deserved more."

The last email from my mother tells me to read through the divorce decree, to see what it was my father had failed to do—what was owed me—as his child first or last. She closed it saying, "I should have said this years ago. Sorry it took so long. Do whatever you want from here on out."

"Hope's right," Phuong says, looking over the divorce settlement. "He owed you child support, medical care, and a college education. He could have visited you and had you visit him twice a month during the school year and a month in the summers."

"How close to breaking even do we come if I add the bread machine to the tractor, the boat, and outboard?" I ask. Phuong has had her calculator out as she's been reading through the divorce settlement.

"Nowhere near," she says.

"Add the boat trailer."

My mother is right. She did do me a disservice. She didn't give me a space, a frame, a larynx for anger. I close my eyes and I see those red canvases of mine, carefully wrapped in brown paper and tucked away in the back of the closet. I see the profile of the young girl with the blue mohawk and the dripping knife so dangerously tattooed over her carotid. All those easels with variations on a single theme in an empty room. I see that boat, peeling red paint, battered, probably home-made, heavy as sin, and I imagine towing it all over the city filled with my hungry ghosts. I hear Dr. Berlioz saying, "Why do you need anyone's approval at your age?"

"I want that boat," I tell Phuong.

She looks up at me, her dark eyes, her delicate face unreadable.

"Go for it," she says quietly.

She's kidding. She's not kidding. I can't tell. It doesn't matter. I'm not going to do anything about it and we both know it.

I also don't do anything about the other emails. I don't print out and sign the agreement allowing Sandy to be executor. I don't write my mother. I don't tell her the lawyer has included my email address on his group mailings, ignoring my request for privacy.

Phuong has taken the laptop and is busy sending out evites to her performance. She has found a large garage near several new art galleries. She's already apologized that the only date she could get was my birthday.

"It's just a day," I tell her. "No big."

But it is and we both know it. Watching a performance by Phuong seems as good a way to spend it as any other. I'm curious to see what she has come up with this time.

"I'll think of this as my own private command performance," I tell her, but then need to explain what this means.

"So you are the king—or the first son of the king?" she asks mischievously.

"Hope's one and only heir."

"Lowely. Vey lowely tew mee you, Mizuh King. My dawer no bes." Phuong imitates her mother's accent. "My bes is det."

"Couldn't have said it better myself," I agree.

We find each other in bed, hungry and angry and passionate. Satiable. Completely satiable.

I wake at around three dreaming about that boat. I have the boat trailer hooked to my pedicab and I'm towing it all around the city. Dr. Berlioz sits in the front, where he can talk to me. At the back are four men of graduated ages and heights, arranged smallest to largest like Russian dolls—all the David Michael Mastersons from Sr. to IV. They have curly black hair, crooked noses, thin lips set in a variety of expressions, big ears. They're all clearly related. Each one holds a large rectangular package wrapped in brown paper. They're looking obediently at Dr. Berlioz and he is lifting his arms like a conductor.

"Keep pedaling," Dr. Berlioz tells me. "Don't look back."

They are going to sing Happy Birthday to me, but it's the wrong day. They all have the wrong day. For some reason this feels unbearable. I turn around and say, "Wait. Just wait, can't you?"

Dr. Berlioz looks at me with a grave, sad expression. "I gave you so much, Derek, and this is how you repay me?"

The men in the back of the boat begin tearing at the paper. I know what's in the packages. It's like my own skin is being torn off. I turn back. I begin pedaling like crazy. The traffic is thick. The boat is so heavy that I can't get any traction, any momentum. The sound of the paper tearing is unbearable, really unbearable.

"It's just a feeling," Dr. Berlioz whispers. "All that matters is what you make of it."

I have to move, even remembering the dream I'm back in it. I get up and go out to the living room and into our storage closet. I don't turn the light on. I walk to the back of it and prepare to pull my paintings out from behind our winter coats. I painted them twelve years ago. They are devouring me, I know it, and I still can't let them go. No one needs to tell me that's crazy.

I wonder if he ever wondered about me, ever asked himself even once who I had become?

But the paintings aren't there. I go and turn on the closet light. This is a set of nine paintings, each six feet by four. Three triptychs. They're impossible to miss. Phuong is very orderly. All her winter clothes, and mine, are neatly arranged on racks, all our linens on shelves, our suitcases on the floor. But the paintings are gone. I can't believe this of Phuong. In a material way, they're all I brought into this marriage. She never objected to their being there. She never asked to see them. Never, as far as I know, tried to unwrap them. She accepted as a sufficient response to her questions about them that they were both necessary and taboo. My baggage, I told her as I lugged them in. She's never since then expressed any curiosity about them. She moves them in spring and fall to dust behind them. That's it.

I don't think I realized how necessary they were to me until now. I feel wild, really wild. *How long have they been missing?*

I go in and wake Phuong who, after our love-making is sleeping naked. She greets me with a slow smile, which fades when I turn on the bedside lamp and she reads my expression. She doesn't pretend to misunderstand.

"When?" I ask her. "Why?"

"Long time," she answers. "We needed the space."

For shoes? I wonder, enraged.

"Where are they?" I ask her. My hands are drumming on the bed. I'm frantic, really frantic. Frightened too in a way I can't ever remember being.

I hear people jeering. *Raison d'être. Raison d'être. Derek's lost his raison d'être.*

"Did you send them to Dr. Berlioz?" I ask Phuong, taking her by the shoulders. "To my mom? *They were mine.*"

"Why are you so worried? They're safe," Phuong says, sitting up sleepily. She pulls the sheet up over her breasts, yawns. She is completely indifferent to my anxiety. It's making me feel even more crazy.

"You can always make more."

"That's not the way it works. You don't understand."

"You're forty years old," Phuong says looking at me steadily. "You have to decide. Every day. Am I going to live? Am I going to die? Am I going to seize this day and paint? Am I going to ride?"

"That's not the way it works," I said. There is such a blackness, such a darkness in the back of that closet where once there had been fire. I can't see how we can live here anymore.

Is *this* a genuine option, I wonder. Are there two equally credible hypotheses—I can paint, I can ride—is the choice forced, do the stakes really matter?

"You can make more, Derek," Phuong repeats. "That's what it boils down to. You believe that or you don't."

Cocooned or entombed. What does *choosing* have to do with this?

"What did you *do* with them?" I whisper.

"It's the *experience* of painting you miss," Phuong says. "Not the tracks it left."

It's odd what we believe and what we don't. I look at Phuong and am enraged and afraid and I want to shake out of her where she's taken my paintings. But I believe her when she says that they are safe—and that there are choices before me that I cannot escape.

"Whenever people praised me as a child," Phuong says quietly, "my mother always said, 'She not the bes of my children. The best all det.' I had an answer for her, Derek. I still do: *I am the best that's left.*"

"I want to spend my life with you. But not on that basis. Do you understand me?" Phuong stares at me intently until I nod. Then she makes a space for me on the bed, opens her arms.

In the morning, she wakes me as she's leaving with a kiss on my cheek. She slips an invitation to her show between my fingers.

"I have a part for you."

"No."

"Yes," she answers. "A good one."

All day at work I have this crazy feeling that I'm towing that battered red boat, Dr. Berlioz riding in the bow, the four Mastersons seated in the transom. Everyone is chatting. I'm not, as usual, saying anything.

"If you squeezed something out of them, do you think you'd end up paying me?" Dr. Berlioz asks.

"Would you accept it?"

"Sure," he says promptly. "How many times are you going to try to evade the truth, Derek. You stiffed me. I didn't choose to stop you—but *you* stiffed me."

"You *loved* me," I said. "You didn't do it for the money. You did it because you loved me."

"How many years has it taken you to see that, Derek?" Dr. Berlioz asks. "Couldn't you have said it once while I was still breathing?" But he puts his hand on my shoulder, and when I smile, my eyes tearing, he follows suit.

"Space to earth, Derek," Sutton says to me. I've pulled up to the mission, and I'm so lost in this conversation I don't register his presence.

"No portobello," I tell him. "No limp lettuce." I look at the empty rear basket. I have no recall of where I've been, if anywhere. I don't even remember logging in at the garage to get the pedicab or receiving my route for the day, but I must have because here I am and the paper is folded and tucked into my shirt pocket.

"Nothing but the pleasure of my company." I burst out laughing.

"You OK?"

"I'm forty. Happily married. I bike for a living. My wife quietly removed all traces of my higher aspirations without my noticing. My father just died and I find I couldn't care less and my analyst died three months ago and it just hit me that I was, truly, like a son to him. I've decided to claim both legacies. My lifeboat is filled with squatters, hungry ghosts. But rather than evict them, I've decided to cut them all adrift and stick to land myself."

"You still have our friend William along for the ride?" Sutton asks.

"I left him behind today, but I'm on to *The Varieties of Religious Experience* next," I tell him. "Can I trouble you for a cup of tea?"

"Gunpowder or Zen?"

"Why is it when time moves in only one direction, we still believe we are free to revisit our pasts and revise them at will?" Phuong asks.

She has set up folding chairs on either side of the large garage—in between the car bays, the cans of grease, the hydraulic lifts. In the space in the middle of the room she has run a long, undulant white scrim about twelve feet high. There are bright floodlights lighting it from either side.

On one side of the scrim is a pedicab, two skeletons are seated on its bench, one wearing a bridal dress, the other a funeral suit. They are both fully toothed, grinning. On the other side of the scrim, at the opposite end of the garage is another pedicab pulling a boat trailer with a bright silver boat on it.

"Choose," Phuong says to me. "If you drive the pedicab with the skeletons, you must give away whatever is put into the cab. If you drive the one with the boat, you must accept what you're given. Whichever you drive,

I'll ride in the other."

"My only choice is which one I drive, not whether I drive?"

She nods. She is dressed in a slim red tunic dress with a high neckline. She looks demurely Vietnamese. She's drawn a large crowd. Standing room only. It's not just politeness that brings them. There's something about Phuong that is irresistible to many, not just me. It crosses all social strata. There's the old man, César, from our favorite pizza joint, people from her tai chi class, neighbors, her partners from work and their networks too. She warns everyone about the grease.

"Stay within the lines I've marked or suffer the consequences," she says. She has everyone sign a liability disclaimer. The garage insisted, she tells them. But I expect it's Phuong. She's not about to feel responsible for the living as well as the dead.

There is nothing in the basket behind the skeletons. The boat is already as loaded as Santa's sleigh. It doesn't feel like there's much of a choice here. I'm just doing this to please her. So I choose the lighter load. Phuong's friend Lucas, a burly bodybuilder, gets on the pedicab that will pull the boat. We're going to be traveling in opposite directions.

Once I'm in place, Phuong puts a blindfold over my eyes. When I protest, she says, "I've put a guide rail on the floor, just keep your eyes down and don't go too fast." She loosens the lower edge of the blindfold so I can peek. I feel her filling the basket in the back of the cab.

"Don't look back," she tells me. "Don't look ahead. If you get too anxious just look at the lights on the floor."

The pedicab is heavier than I expected with whatever she has added. Phuong isn't riding there but someone is. I can feel the mystery rider leaning out of the back of the cab, throwing the balance off right and left without any warning. He or she is distributing something. I can hear paper tearing. I have a really terrible feeling that I have chosen without knowing what I was really choosing, and that I have chosen wrong and am going to pay for it forever in ways I can't foresee or bear.

The sound of water, slowly flowing, building, running over rapids, receding, surging and falling like ocean tide fills the garage. Somewhere in the space there are Chinese gongs resounding, large drums thrumming. A flute. A singer whose voice simultaneously high and low, like Virginia Rodrigues, melds them all.

I want to take the blindfold off, but I don't. Somehow I settle into the flow, the way I can see the lights flickering just below me, hear the audience laughing at something Phuong is doing or inviting them to do. I use my own weight to counter balance the movements of the unknown rider. My pedicab gets heavier and heavier, then suddenly lighter. I begin to feel people gathering on either side of it, jostling as they move, like another kind of river, flowing against me. I can see the guide rails, but I don't stop. I have no idea what this looks like from the outside. I have no idea what point Phuong is making, and I don't really care. I realize I like being part of it, I like not knowing, I like the resistance I'm encountering, find it reassuring—all these people with their eyes open pushing back at me, oblivious to my intentions.

"Great artist, lousy one," Dr. Berlioz asks. "What's the difference, truly? From the *inside*, Derek, what's the difference?"

"Now those who participated watch and those who watched participate," Phuong says as she climbs up on the bike to undo my blindfold.

Together we wander up and down both sides of the scrim, the shadows cast by people on one side towering, suggestively abstract and ghostly, melding with and diverging from equally magnified shadows cast by people on the other side, and all of us, so solid and so much smaller, sweltering with color. On either side of the scrim the flow of life moves inexorably in opposite directions.

Phuong whispers in my ear, "In the words of your good friend William, *Intellectualism draws the dynamic continuity out of nature as you draw the thread out of a string of beads.* Just remember that you *chose* me, Derek. It's the choosing that matters. It doesn't matter why."

People are passing my paintings around—along with inflatable toys, glass vases, expensive porcelain figurines of Kwan Yin and Buddha, fresh flowers and silk ones, two live chickens, a miniature pig, a goldfish in a bowl, oranges, apples, kites, stiletto heels, financial printouts, DVDs, blankets, baskets, an empty bird cage, a child's casket, a frisbee, a fragment of a Greek frieze, poker chips, a kazoo, a tenor sax, a violin with a broken string, a burka, a bikini, a stuffed ram's head, a wet cat.

Phuong touches my arm. "Choose," she says. She holds one of my paintings up with her right hand, steps behind it, extends her left in which there is just a paintbrush.

"I don't have to," I say. "Remember, I chose you. They're both inherent in that choice. I've just been slow to realize it. But the boat. I'm sticking with that. And its trailer. And the outboard. And shipping costs."

"We can use it as an art installation," Phuong says.

"A portable studio." The minute I say it, I can seeing it sitting on the grass in the center of the park, five easels, with five kids—with blue and red mohawks, dreads, shaved heads, pierced eyebrows and navels, grills on their teeth, tattoos peeking out from their low riding pants and skimpy tops and snaking around their wrists and ankles—facing that blankness, as skeptical as they are trusting.

I'm sitting in the stern and they glance over at me, expecting something. "Don't look at me, I tell them." Look around you. Listen. Smell. Taste. Get out there and touch. Trust what you are experiencing. Everything that finds it way onto or through those canvases has its origin in moments like this and, if it is worth a damn, returns us to a moment like this."

I pull out my well-worn copy of James.

"As an old and dear friend once told me," I continue, "*the deeper features of reality are found only in perceptual experience. Here alone do we acquaint ourselves with continuity, or the immersion of one thing in another, here along with self, with substance, with qualities, with activity in its various modes, with time, with cause, with change, with novelty, with tendency, and with freedom.*"

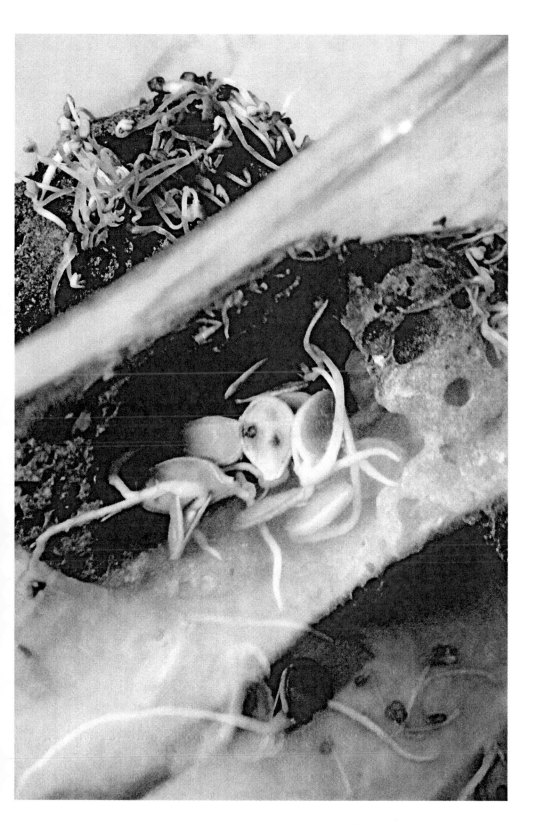

SWEET SIXTEEN

It started five years ago with my niece, the oldest of my sister Helen's children. My niece (my only one) and I had a good relationship and I wanted to mark it by doing something special to celebrate her turning sixteen. To mark as well, I guess, that at forty-eight I was relinquishing all hopes, however vague, I had ever had of motherhood myself and that these five nephews and one niece of mine were my only live connection with the future. It was time, I decided, for me to know them and for them to know me as real people, not roles.

My sister Helen was delighted by the suggestion. "God, yes," she said immediately. "Take her to the moon for all I care. I'll even understand if you leave her there." I think they had been fighting over driving privileges—or was it dishes?

My niece Barley (a family name on her father's side) and I decided on Paris instead of outer space. We talked for months beforehand about it—where she wanted to go (the Louvre, Les Halles, the Eiffel Tower, a fashion show, a barge on the Seine and a bookstall beside it, the Folies Bergère). She came back with a trendy haircut, an expensive scarf, a new platonically long-distance boyfriend of Algerian descent, and a delightful aspiration to follow my own career path into high stakes consulting, even if it would require a major preliminary investment in time and hard labor to raise her grade point average, which she did. She's now at Boston University, graduating magna cum laude next month. "Not summa, Aunt Holly," she says apologetically.

"I couldn't be prouder if you were my own daughter," I assure her. And for all I know, it's true. "What's your next step?"

A job search from the luxury of my Milwaukee apartment, if my partner Larissa agrees to keep a detached but benevolent eye on her. I will be off on the third of my birthday trips, this one with the second of my five nephews, Dan, the oldest son of my other sister, Honey. Fair is fair. But adolescent males are, well, *really* adolescent. I've called in my brother Henry, who hasn't developed much beyond that in the intervening thirty years, to help. He's in relationship rebound right now, so it is good for him too.

But the truth is, this is now a good idea gone stale, a good intention soured. We're soldiering on, though, a metaphor which Honey and her boys, all militarily inclined, should appreciate. Soldiering on with Obama stickers pasted on all my suitcases as well as my bumper. When I visit, they all look at them as if they're seeing the antichrist. But I'm their aunt, their superior officer, at least for these eight days, so what can they do?

Whatever my sisters' views are now, the military wasn't really the guiding metaphor of our own childhood. My brother and sisters called us the 4-H club (Holly, Helen, Honey and Henry) when we were growing up—thinking it might bring me back into the fold. It wasn't age difference that separated me (we're one of those stair-step families, each of us about eighteen months older than the following one), or my homosexuality (since Henry too is gay), or even my introversion (although they are all, in their own ways, extroverts). From as early as I can remember, I wanted to be free to define myself. I didn't want to have all those imprinted ducklings following me, imitating every move I made. I did not find it flattering. I found it distracting. How could I decide if what I was doing was true to me or not if every step I took, every move I made, was slavishly copied and amplified as soon as I attempted it?

It is ironic to me that I've developed a very successful career with large businesses as a leadership and organizational creativity consultant. I always begin my gigs by saying, "Whatever you do, *don't* describe yourselves as a family—functional or dysfunctional. Everyone in this organization from president to janitor is free to leave. That fact underlies everything I am going to say to you."

"All they ever wanted was to be close to you," Larissa said to me of the 3-H's early on in our relationship. Larissa's an only child of a single mother and the idea of being part of a brood or a litter appealed to her. The reality, she soon saw, was different. I tried to warn her.

"There's close and there's fused," I said.

I guess the major difference between me and my sibs is that I knew a world without them. I knew a brief, romantic time when I was the one and only of my kind and I measure everything against that. *My* Camelot. Always have. It's not restricted to them. This need of mine to stand apart has been a bone of contention, a thorn in the side, in every relationship I've ever had.

"You really don't *care*," Julia, Katrina, Zelda and Nina each said as they stood at the door to my apartment, their bags packed, ultimatum delivered, waiting for me to repent my ways and ask them to stay. I never did. Perhaps my relationship with Larissa has lasted as long as it has (we celebrated our fifteenth anniversary two months ago) because we have never moved in together. We're monogamous, committed, spend frequent overnights, but each of us keeps our own space. I know this is a calculated move on Larissa's part, that she believes as long as I feel I don't have her undivided attention, I'll want her, that the minute I'm sure of her she'll lose her allure. She may also genuinely prefer things this way. She shares her own condo, has for a decade now, with an old friend, Colin—whose own romantic life consists of passionate infatuations that last, at most, a month. "The next is best," is his motto. But he enjoys domesticity as well, and he and Larissa chatter and gossip constantly, like my sisters used to.

I'm struck with how we reconstruct our childhoods without knowing it. My two sisters both have created these tightly fused nuclear families that do everything, I mean everything, together. My sister Helen and her husband Scott and her kids Barley and Brett move as one from vacation cottage to suburban McMansion. My sister Honey and her husband and her four boys hike, camp, and run marathons in perfect synchrony.

Henry's been less lucky in love, but he treats his employees as family, lunches with them daily and takes them all on frequent retreats, or did before the recession. "It's not what we share or what we accomplish, it's just the time together that matters," he insists. He can't bear to let anyone go. Recently he's been calling me to help with payroll. "The thought of losing them is worse than losing Louis," he tells me. Louis was his partner for twelve years, who left him for a younger man of pre-Hispanic descent with shoulder length hair and an unquestioning, single-minded devotion to the source of a potential green card. Louis couldn't resist. "We all want to be worshipped," Henry said philosophically at the time, but I notice he's drinking more, secluding himself, checking the mirror.

Given all this, everyone is surprised by my newfound interest in my sisters' kids. On visits, each of them has taken me aside to check.

"You and Larissa splitting?" Henry asked.

"Is everything all right with your work?" Helen wondered.

"How is your health?" Honey probed when I saw her two months ago. "You look thinner than I remember, Holly." Honey looked both worried and envious as she said it. She has always been a butterball. Giving birth four times and the steady diet of carbs of her all male enclave don't help.

"Nothing menopause won't take care of," I said. I have an appointment for a hysterectomy scheduled for two weeks after I return from France. (Even Larissa doesn't know.) I am going to France because my nephew Dan, a military history buff, wants to tour the major battlefields of World War II, beginning with the beach at Normandy. He only wants to see the sites of successful battles and I'm restricting it to scenic ones: Normandy (D-Day)—where I hope to slip in a trip to Mont Saint Michel, the Dardennes forest (Battle of the Bulge), Marseilles and Toulouse and the Vosges mountains (Operation Dragoon).

"Surely you can do this one alone," Henry said with a yawn when I informed him.

"No way. I have nothing to talk to him about. I never played football or considered going to a military college, hung out with the right wing, or believed in papal infallibility."

"I'm sure you did the last, if only for five minutes when you were three," Henry said. "All children believe in infallibility, papal, parental, personal. What makes you think I could do any better with him?"

"Balls," I said. "That's all they respect. That's all you need to be respected."

"Do I hear a little misandry there?"

"Fear. Eight days feels like forever. How did I get into this?"

"You're checking for the gay gene."

I don't know why Henry saying it aloud shocked me. Of course, that *is* what I've been doing. In part. It seems like common sense if two out of the four of us are gay. But both my fertile sisters deny any possibility that any of their kids could have a genetic predisposition. They've never brought it up even once, at least in Henry or my hearing. Honey who is still seriously Catholic is especially stout in her resistance, even though she and her boys pray every night to St. Michael to help them fight off Satan (who may have other pseudonyms and acronyms, like LGBT). Even our parents are more relaxed about the issue than our sisters. If anything, they prefer Henry's and my company because it keeps the focus on them, their arthritis, gout, and osteoporosis, their golf swings and the score card for their marriage that, even in their early eighties, they are still acrimoniously tallying.

But we are all bundles of contradictions, often good ones. Even though Honey wouldn't allow me to be godmother to any of her boys ("You know, because of how the Pope feels about your lifestyle choices—"), she has no objection to my being a fairy one. Both of my sisters are more than willing to have me take their children off on globe-trotting trips, all expenses paid, no questions asked.

It was my idea of course. They just fell effortlessly in line, as was their custom. Ducklings.

Actually, it wasn't my idea. It was Larissa's. "You stand apart from your family, Holly, especially your sibs, but they are still your primary frame of reference. They're the only people in your life who can't be replaced."

"They're blood," I said.

"That doesn't make them *fate*, Holly. Actually you are the most loyal of all. Each of them has been able to make another fulfilling primary commitment."

"Not that again."

Which is how Henry ended up joining me in this project five years ago instead of it becoming an experience that created an extended, surrogate family for Larissa and me.

So maybe it isn't the gay gene I'm exploring here, rather the family one. Why won't I let them go? Why won't I let them close?

"There's a difference," I tell my clients, "between invention, discovery, and creation."

We invent because we can, because it's useful. It's all about novelty and doing. Discovery is about the hunt, the unknown. It's mental and possessive. It looks like it is about something aside from us, something out there—a gene sequence, a new element, a deep sea cave no one has ever seen before, the dust and ice on Mars, an historical fact unearthed, reconfirmed. But its importance is based on our mutual frames, what *exceeds* them, what challenges or supports them. It's about what we did not *know* before. It's about buying into our own mental force field, our systems of meaning—as individuals or groups. It's about getting there first.

With creativity, we often have to step aside, appreciate, stretch to understand, participate as a willing incubator while something prepared for but mysterious takes place in us, *through* us.

At this point, everyone is restless, crossing or uncrossing legs, glancing more or less pointedly at their watches, checking for new texts.

"You're looking at me as if I'm some New Ager, but I'm not. I'm an accountant by training," I tell them. "One who got tired of watching what happens in an organization when we forget that people aren't balance sheets, that we are not common currency, we each have minds, and gifts, of our own. Ignoring this can be calculated as hours of productivity lost, employee turnover, customer dissatisfaction, bureaucratic rigidity.

"When you go back to work today, I invite you to look around and discover where inventiveness would be helpful, where creativity is called for. (When you go home to your families, I invite you to do the same thing.) Ask yourself, is what I am responding to a creation, an invention, a discovery? What difference would it make, one way or the other?"

This, really, is what I want to ask my nieces and nephews when I take them off to discover a new country or continent. Are *you* an invention, a discovery, or a creation? When the time comes, will you invent, discover or create a family? *What place will I have in it?*

In preparation for my trip with Dan (who precedes brothers Dave, Dale, and Dean), I've been watching World War II movies. So far, I've seen *Saving Private Ryan, Schindler's List, The Great Escape,* and *Ike: Countdown to D-Day.* I've printed out a list of battlefields from the internet and am mapping out our route. I've suggested to Dan we might read biographies of George Marshall, Dwight Eisenhower, and Charles DeGaulle, but I don't know if I have the stamina. Our conversations are polite, tamped. I can see he has no real desire to go but doesn't feel free to refuse. Like me.

That he's so focused on battles and leadership I find poignant. Anyone who spends time with Dan can see he's a shy, unimaginative, obedient young man who feels impelled by birth order to recreate himself as a bold commander. By reading everything he can on military history. By loyally warming a bench all football season. By making his way into the higher echelons of the homophobic Boy Scouts. He talks for hours every night with his best friend, Lance. He's never dated or expressed any interest in doing so, which sets off no alarms in his mother.

"Take him to graveyards, Holly, lots of graveyards," Dan's father, Donald, surprised me by saying when I made an overnight stay with them on one of my business trips.

For Dan does have areas of genuine persistence. He is applying to

West Point over the strong objections of his father, who was in the National Guard in what he thought was a sinecure position, but ended up serving tours in both Iraq and Afghanistan. Donald came back disillusioned with our foreign policy, and guilty about the time he had spent away from his growing boys, who in his absence had glamorized his stop-loss tours as choices, ones they intended to make as well.

I'm trying to suggest to Dan that he might like to teach military history instead of live it.

But to do that, I am going to have to show some more discipline. So far all I've done—besides watching movies, mapping routes that include as many other points of more general cultural interest as possible, and finding hotels with generous amenities—is print out Wikipedia World War II entries, not read them. To help me stay on task, Larissa has come over this evening with a movie, *Aimée and Jaguar,* that she claims is about World War II. We're watching it when Honey calls.

"I've sent Dan all the information on flights," I tell her, putting the movie on mute.

"It's not that."

"He doesn't want to go?"

"It's not that."

"Has Donald been called up again? I thought they promised they wouldn't deploy him again. The guy's approaching sixty for God's sake."

"I wish you wouldn't—"

It took me a second to see what Holly was objecting to. Donald wanted to stay in until he made lieutenant colonel—the pension would help with college tuitions—but they'd made the same promise about no deployment when he was staying on to make major, and had reneged, twice.

"Donald is out for sure next month. The papers are being processed now."

"The other boys?" I'm getting a little tired of this. Larissa is looking at me curiously. I shrug. She gets up to make us a pot of tea. I decide to wait my sister out.

She sighs. I breathe in deeply.

"This is uncomfortable for me," she says finally. "To say this, I mean. I've been talking to Helen about Brett's trip."

Henry and I took Brett to Cuzco, his choice. But he was horrified when we chewed coca leaves on our hike up to Macchu Pichu, and pissed when we pulled him out of a bar. I'm not sure why he chose Peru. It wasn't to his liking. The mountains were too cold, the accommodations too austere, the shamans too flaky. Lima, with its dire poverty, even worse. And he kept baiting Henry and me about Obama, gay marriage, the Tea Party, insidious socialism, guns, and women's rights. You'd think, with his dad out of work for two years, he might have reconsidered, even briefly, the need for a safety net. Not Brett.

I thought Henry and I had shown great restraint—except late at night when we started imitating him, the conversations that must take place around their family dinner table. "If that fancy ass, Ivy League, labor monger, pro-life, pro-gay, anti-war black guy without a valid birth certificate hadn't gotten into the White House, had just stayed in Kenya where he belongs, there'd be no mortgage crisis, no financial chicanery, no lay-offs." Even at the time I was upset with us, but even more upset with Brett.

"Brett was at a difficult stage. And Peru was a bit of a shock. But I can't see the same thing happening with Dan. For one thing, Dan's too polite."

"But you need to be too," Holly said. "I mean, can you just agree not to bring up sex, religion, or politics?"

"Brett said *we* brought them up?"

"He said you were ragging him all the time about his beliefs."

"I was on *him*? He said that?"

"I'm not worried about Brett. He can stand up for himself. He's like you that way. But Dan is different. So could you just stay off those subjects?"

"What about war?" I asked. "I mean, we're touring battlefields."

"Don't talk about Iraq and Afghanistan. Not Vietnam." Honey paused. "I think Korea is OK. Let me check with Donald. And the Pope. I want you to stay away from the Pope, Holly."

"I've done so for years. I won't go anywhere he goes. I make it a matter of principle."

"There's that as well. Dan wants to go to mass when he's with you."

"Confession too?"

"I don't think it would work, would it? I mean the priests over there speak French, not English. I think he can miss a week."

"All duly noted," I said. I was ready to call in sick.

"I appreciate your doing this," Honey said, her voice thick. "It's so nice to have someone in our family care about our kids. Mom and Dad, well, you know. And with Helen, it's always about comparing. But I can't see that, you know. They're all so different. Just like we were. It's like mangoes, coconuts, and—

"Heirloom tomatoes."

"Soybeans." She stopped. "That's not really why I'm calling. None of this is. I mean, it needed to be said. I promised Donald I would. And I did, but—" Honey's voice broke.

Again, I waited her out. Henry said I was looking for the gay gene, but you know, at that point, I felt terrible for her. Worse than I ever felt for myself or Henry. Dan was a follower, a believer. All he ever wanted to do was be the son he thought his father and mother wanted. Gayness had no part in it. They had given themselves no room here. The military may have abandoned Don't Ask, Don't Tell—and Henry and I may never have considered it at all. But Honey and her family—oh, I tell you at that moment I wished that doddering, homophobic Pope, that whole ancient, pompous, rigid and cruel male hierarchy dead and buried, with stakes through their hearts. The old words came to me, *Ubi caritas et amor, Deus ibi est.* When the hell were we all going to get it?

"I'm pregnant," Honey said. "I can't believe it. I turn fifty in three months and I'm pregnant."

I took a deep breath. Different situation. Same damn constraints.

"What are you going to do?"

"I haven't told anyone. I don't dare."

Honey had her first child, Dan, at thirty-three. Her youngest, Dean, is seven. Everyone was worried then, but he's fine. He may be the brightest of the bunch. Honey refused amniocentesis because it wasn't going to change the outcome. Maybe she wanted to do things differently this time. Why else would she be calling me?

"Whatever you decide, I'll stand by you."

"It's just that with the breast cancer, you know. It's five years now, so I'm pretty sure I'm in the clear. But they say the last pregnancy may have contributed."

"You have four healthy boys. No one could question your commitment to life, Honey, if you decided—"

"Stop. That's not what I'm calling about. Of course I have to go through with it. That's not in question."

"What is then?" I asked softly. I was angry at her, sure, but she was my baby sister. "You want to know if I'll make the same offer when this one turns sixteen? The answer is yes—just as long as she doesn't want to scale Mt. Everest." I said she on principle. We both knew that with four boys, Honey had about a one percent chance of having a girl.

"It's more than that. I need to know, if something, God forbid, should happen to both Donald and me—would you be her guardian? You know, if she is a special needs child."

"Like me?" I asked. "Why don't you ask Henry? He's just as special as I am." The answer, of course, was I had greater assets.

"The thing is," she went on hurriedly, "you'd have to promise to bring her up in the faith. Donald would never agree otherwise."

"What did you say then?" Larissa asked when I filled her in after I hung up.

Larissa was drinking tea. I was sipping bourbon. The wind whipped up white caps on Lake Michigan twenty stories below.

"But before you answer, I have to tell you Colin and I wanted to ask something similar of you, but with different conditions."

"What do you mean? Take the two of you on a free trip? Make sure we never talk about sex, religion, or politics?"

"We decided we both wanted to become parents," Larissa said. "But we thought it might be more fun as a threesome. Whoever said three's a crowd never had a baby."

"No."

Larissa smiled at me warmly, cupping her hands around her own special Obama birth certificate mug, bringing it close to her face to breathe the steam. "I've started taking Clomid. The first injection is tomorrow. Ten o'clock. I'd like you to be there."

"You're forty-three," I told her. "I'm fifty-three with a uterus solid with fibroids, scheduled for a hysterectomy in a month. You'll be eligible for Social Security when they're graduating from college."

"I'm so glad you're making some allowance for multiples," Larissa said. "That's always a possibility."

"I'll be in assisted living," I said. But I discovered I was excited, elated really. "When she's sixteen—"

"Oh, you're backing off," Larissa said, but she was smiling.

"And I'm seventy—"

"Where will you be going?"

"Depends on whether I'm using a walker or a wheelchair."

"It's a lifetime commitment, Holly. Not to me, necessarily, but to her."

"I want a proper christening—by a witch, a warlock, and a goddess if you can. I want Henry to be godfather. I want her to carry all our surnames."

"Waters-White-Stone," Larissa started.

"Stone-White-Waters," I tried.

"White-Stone-Waters." They all sounded fine, but this last sounded right. I could see that stone skipping across a lake, an ocean.

"Marry me," I said. I stopped, startled but not shocked. I hadn't seen it coming, but I meant it.

Larissa took another sip of her tea and said gently, "You don't have to do that for me, Holly. I'm not asking you to change."

"I don't intend to. I'm not asking you to move in. I don't want to change our set up. It works for us. But I do want to claim what you mean to me—baby or no baby. I'm asking for *me*, Lar. Besides there's an irresistible window of opportunity here—after I return from storming the beaches at Normandy and before the hysterectomy."

"I could be feeling queasy," Larissa warned.

"I'll snag a few bags from Air France," I said. "I'll come prepared."

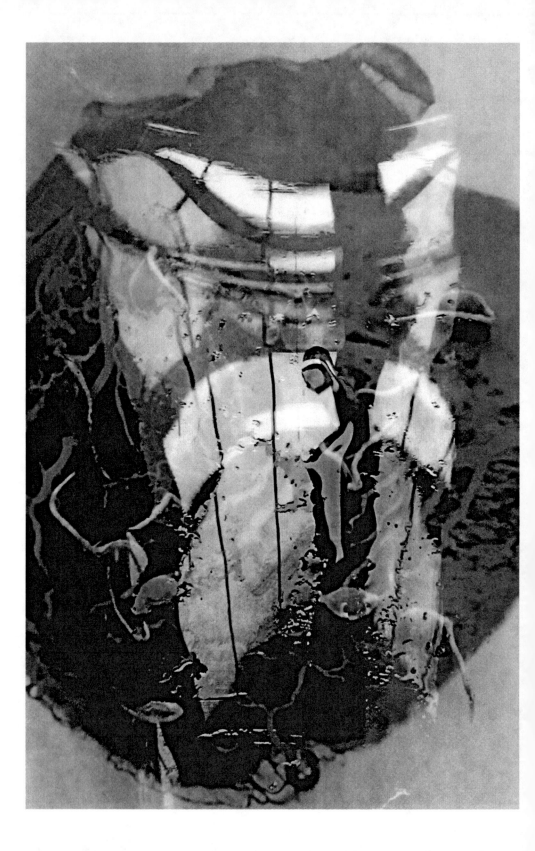

TARGET FIXATION

If there's one thing I've taught my son that will serve him really well in life, it's keep your eye on where you want to end up, not on what's in your way. I've seen too many guys crash when they don't. I taught him this for dirt biking and stock car racing, but I think it applies to life as well. We aim for what we're looking at. It's called target fixation. It's a physical response. You're racing around a track and the car next to you spins out and crashes and if you look at it, before you can think your own car is slamming into the metal, the wall, bursting into flames. *Keep your eye where you want to be.* If I've told my son once, I've told him a thousand times.

People were surprised when I had my son on his own dirt bike by the time he was five. He'd been riding a two-wheeler since he was three; he was ready. I explained this to my wife's family, but they still thought I was crazy. Life's dangerous, that's just a fact. It's how you take it on that makes the difference. You're never too young to learn that.

I should know. I came here from Tamaulipas by myself across the desert when I was twelve years old. My mom had six more kids to raise and my dad was dead. I was the oldest, so it was up to me to help her. My goal was really clear. I had my eye on more food for all of us. I worked in the fields, then construction. I still remember looking at the food on my shelf in that first apartment in Rio Grande, my amazement at what I'd been able to do: Feed myself until I was full. But I knew I had to do more. I joined the military when I was eighteen. Served in Vietnam. Got my green card. Got my GED. Became a citizen. Sponsored every one of my brothers and two of my sisters and paid their way. Now I work for the Border Patrol, fixing their motorcycles and jeeps so they can go out and catch people like me. Go figure.

You ask what I've kept my eye on through my life? I mean, after I was sure I could keep a refrigerator full and once I'd brought my family up here? The answer is my kids, especially my son. I've tried to teach him everything I know. Fast as I could because you never know how life is going to turn out. I taught him how to hunt, fish, rebuild an engine, detail a car, race a dirt bike and a stock car, box as hard with his left as with his right, how to flip a guy in a fight.

How much of that he's going to be able to use at MIT is not so clear to me. But it's what I have to give—and I have to say this for Jordan (his mother's choice of a name not mine), he's learned all of it. I have no fears for him in that way. He can take care of himself. He can also (and I think this isn't so usual with engineers) hear beneath the words, with his heart and his gut. He's not going to get took.

I've taught my son all I know so he can do better than me. I remember when he was thirteen and he passed me on his dirt bike during an off-road race, just sailing out over a rock, riding on one wheel then settling back in, not giving me a glance, keeping his eye where *he* wanted to be—at the head of the whole goddamn pack. Near blinded me, the feeling I had. It wasn't pride. I taught him what I know, but he was the one who knew how to use it. I think what I felt at that moment was full—like life at that moment held more than I had ever imagined, all I could possibly want.

I wonder if my dad, if he'd lived, would feel that way looking at me. I remember so little about him. He was dead by the time I was ten and at least half that time he was off working somewhere else—first in Mexico, then in the States. All I can remember about him is he had this really sweet voice, deep but sweet, so when he said, "*Mi hijo*," it slipped right into you, dark and rich and warm as chocolate. And he was tired, he had the most tired eyes I've seen in someone ever. Tireder even than my mom's her last year when she was dying of cancer. Tireder than my wife's, who feels more weighed down than she'll ever admit by the life she's chosen to live for me and the kids. The one that feels so rich to me, given where and what I come from.

My wife is college educated. She's an epidemiologist with the county board of health. If there's an outbreak of hanta or Nile virus or food poisoning, she's meant to investigate. She does that using numbers. *Chance, bias, confounding*—those are the three things to look out for she warns our son—like the words don't just apply to diseases, they apply to love, friendship, schooling, road races. These words are red flags to her. They are things that can distort. They can invalidate your findings.

I'm not so book smart, but the words never stop meaning, least as far as I can see, what they always did. Chance is what brought us together. If I hadn't stopped into that college bar that evening in April thirty-five years ago, if Candace hadn't just been dumped by her boyfriend of three years because she "wasn't the one he needed to ensure his advantage in the corporate world"—well, Jordan and Juana (my choice) wouldn't be here, that's for sure. You can say higher—or lower—forces were at work. You can say there was a divine plan. Or that two total strangers, after shipwreck, clung to each other on the off chance either of them could swim.

Does it explain why we're together now? Does it need to?

"What's the glue?" Juana asked me right after she got engaged last year. I almost said fear of drowning, but instead I said what I always do to Jordan: *target fixation*. "We never took our eyes off where we wanted to be, honey. We never took our eyes off family."

In other words, we looked out over each other's shoulders, at our own private and wide stretch of desert sky, our bodies doing what a man and a woman's body do best. And then we both kept our eyes on the very best there was in our shared, chance destiny, these two great kids who just fell from heaven into our laps and looked up at us as if we were, each of us, something unbelievably special. They were biased, maybe. Maybe completely biased in our favor, like we were in theirs. Who wouldn't want to aim there?

These days I think about why Candace and I are still together after thirty-five years because both my kids are marrying young too. Jordan's marrying up, like I did. Juana's marrying down, like her mother. I feel like Candace failed her daughter, but I don't like saying *I* failed my wife. It's like Candace knows the reality of target fixation from the other side, the helpless crash and burn side. She feels it's pointless to try to reason with Juana.

"Juana's heart's made up, Julio," Candace has told me several times. "You want to try to change it, try. Just leave me out of it. She knows I'm going to stick by her whatever her choices."

Candace's not saying I won't. She's talking about her own family up in Phoenix, how they act like the distance between Phoenix and Las Cruces is greater than between New York City and LA, Mexico City and Seattle. They have the kids up to see them there, Candace too, but not a one of them will set foot in our house. It's like they're afraid they'll catch something. Spanish flu maybe, although neither of my kids speaks Spanish like it's natural to them. When their attitude isn't pissing me off, I think it's kind of funny because the one place Candace has been a real hard ass is our house. She wants it to look just as good as the one she grew up in. Better, actually, since I'm handy with repair and remodeling. If her parents and her three sisters were to come, they'd think they were in their own homes. Except for the number—and color—of the people living in it.

It's not like we're isolated here. Two of my brothers and one of my sisters live in the area and we're in and out of each other's houses constantly. Holidays, the rest of the family drive down from Chicago, over from LA. It's crazy and good. At those times, Candace stands out here just as much as I would in Phoenix. Our kids have her height. In the right context, like school, they can pass for white. Juana especially when she dyes her hair, which she used to do before she met Vicente. It's not just their looks, it's also their accents and the way they carry themselves and their mother's book learning that help. But they fit right in with their cousins too. That's never going to be true for Candace, anymore than it would be for me with her people. I never thought she minded though I've never asked her straight out. It seemed that maybe the difference felt good to her somehow, that without having to work at it, she was a standout. I have always liked looking at her from across a room, so tall and white skinned with her straight blonde hair brushing against her shoulders, her blue eyes always so serious, her mouth lifting a little at the edges as she surveys the room to make sure no one is feeling left out or drowned out. What I see is not happiness exactly, but tranquility, some pressure on her heart easing momentarily.

For there are pressures on Candace's heart, real pressures. It's not just her way of getting to me, letting me know what she feels about the drinking, the other women, me being me. I'm shamed to say it wasn't me but Jordan who took her seriously and made her see a doctor. She's got something wrong with one of her valves, the mitral, and that means half the time her blood's washing back instead of forward, a turbulence that robs her muscles of oxygen and leaves her breathless, tired. They can fix it. Give her a mechanical valve or take one from a pig. Being a mechanic, I know which one I'd pick. Troubles me to think of my wife's heart fixed with used parts from a pig. For one thing, there's no warranty.

But here Candace isn't taking anyone's advice except the doctors, and sometimes not even theirs. They want her to do this soon as possible.

But she says, "I've survived with this for fifty-four years, I can survive a year more." It's the weddings. She's focused on the weddings. She's not going to take her eye off them for a moment. Which is why the kids decided, without consulting either of us, to have a joint wedding earlier than either of them planned. They have told their mother to schedule her surgery for a week to the day after the ceremony, so they'll both be back from their honeymoons.

"What's the hurry?" I asked Jordan and Juana. "Your mother's health comes first, doesn't it?"

Juana and Jordan looked at each other uncomfortably.

"It's what *she* wants," Jordan said finally.

"Why?"

"She doesn't want to stand in the way of our happiness."

"That's what you told her? Postponing the weddings would make you unhappy?"

Jordan stood up. He's thinner than me but five inches taller. Tough.

"Of course not, Dad. But if it's going to make her happy, we'll do it."

Juana shook her head, her face reddening a little. "It's not that, Dad. It's Vicente. She's worried about his status. She thinks the faster we marry the more likely it is he'll get a green card."

Jordan smiled. "And she's afraid Marisol, if she's given a few more months to think, will decide she can do better." Marisol graduated summa cum laude to Jordan's magna and is going to Harvard Law in the fall, married or not. Jordan is an add-on to her life plans, not the focus.

We're good parents, both of us, but it is breaking our hearts to see our children following in our footsteps, and, at the same time, we're doing our best to encourage it—including double weddings. I'm having a hard time getting my mind around that and I can't, hard as I try, look beyond it either.

I'm thinking about it today because of the bachelor party tonight, which I see as my last time to prepare either of these young men for what's facing them. Then comes the wedding, where I've got to say something to everyone, but to Juana in particular, about setting your sights high, staying focused. I just wish for her I could have said it earlier. But what am I going to say, "I don't want to see you making your mother's mistake?" She wouldn't listen to me anyway. Candace and I divided the children between us real early. Juana loves me but she looks up to her mother. Jordan, it's the other way around. Where one sees strength, the other sees weakness. So, it's only her mom has a chance of changing Juana's thinking, but Candace doesn't seem to have the interest.

I don't think the boys are making mistakes in who they're choosing, so tonight feels easier. It's a full moon and we're dirt biking off-road in the desert: Jordan and his two best friends and three cousins, Vicente and his two brothers, me and my brother Rafael. I've borrowed bikes from my buddies, checked them all out and filled their tanks, tested their headlights. They're all loaded on my truck and Rafael's.

Candace and Juana and Marisol are having a spa day, then going to an evening praise service, then a night out at a very fancy restaurant, compliments of Marisol's wealthy divorced mother, flying in for the occasion from her second home in Miami (her first is in Caracas). Marisol's father, equally wealthy, now located in New York, flies in tomorrow with his third wife, who is five years older than Marisol—and also a graduate of Harvard Law. They are going to be joined by Vicente's mother, who is illiterate and comes from the highlands of Guatemala, three nieces from my side and Juana's best friend Alison who, like her, teaches ESL to immigrants, illegal or legal makes no difference.

"I wouldn't trade places with you," I tell Candace.

"Ah, but you haven't seen the masseuses, Julio," she says. She laughs genuinely. Something has happened with Candace since the diagnosis. You can see it in her eyes, hear it in her laugh. It's like some weight has been lifted from her spirit that we thought was just part of her basic nature, a sadness, a heaviness, a fatality. It's like she has no worries now.

I can't help feeling this is a bad sign, which is strange because for years I've told her not to worry so much, it just makes you grow old, doesn't change what's going to happen one way or the other. Candace calls that my "culturally foreshortened risk horizon." I call it keep your eye where you want to be.

But I don't like this shift in my wife. It's like nothing bad can happen to her, she's free of something, she's feeling so light if she didn't have the kids she'd float up above the mountains like one of those hot air balloons, just a bright red dot slowly disappearing into the clean, cloudless blue.

As we're driving in the truck, I try to explain this to Jordan. Vicente and his brothers are riding with Jordan's friends Sam and Ernesto, and Rafael's sons are riding with him.

"You think Mom has a mood disorder?" Jordan asks. "You think she can't just be feeling happy that finally what is bothering her has been diagnosed and something can be done about it? That her kids are getting settled at the same time? That they're going to experience the same joys that have made her own life so worthwhile?"

I look over at him. He smiles—and it gets to me, everything he's saying and not saying.

When we get to the pull-off, Rafael and I open up the backs of the trucks and set up ramps and the boys wheel all the bikes down. I'm working on a Bud and so is Rafael. I offer them around. Rafael's sons take them, so do Jordan's friends Sam and Ernesto. Jordan looks like he's going to say something, but doesn't, just bends down and double checks the height on his bike. Vicente and his brothers refuse. They're church goers like Candace and Juana (that's where Vicente met Juana, through the church's ESL tutoring program where Juana was volunteering), so they're going to act like they have no vices—at least in places where it might get back to the powers that be. I respect this. Vicente is keeping his eye on where he wants to be—and he's bringing his brothers along.

I offer a beer to Jordan again, and he shakes his head and smiles. Marisol probably said something—or Candace. He's not going to pass it on, but he's going to respect their wishes, be the guy they wish I would be. My son is a good-looking guy. I look around and think, damn, we are a fine sight, every one of us.

I hand around reflective vests. I borrowed them from work, so they have the Homeland Security logo. "Everybody keep them on at all times," I say, looking directly at Vicente and his brothers so there's no confusion. "Jordan's going to take the lead," I go on. "I'm bringing up the rear. We're heading away from the mountains, so if they're in front of you, stop and turn around. Everyone keep your lights on. Don't look down at the ground right in front of you, if you see it then, it's too late. Look out a good twenty, thirty feet, where the light first hits, so you have a better chance of responding. If you've not done this before, take it slow, get a feel for your bike, your own center of balance before you accelerate, pay attention to the changing levels of traction with sand, grass, gravel, rock. Aim between the prickly pears and the agaves—not at them. It should take us a half hour to get where we want to be. There'll be a truck there with supplies. A bonfire ready to light."

Rafael and I've been working days to get this all to flow smooth. I look at all these handsome young men. In the glare of the headlights their faces are shadowed and over-exposed at the same, and for a second it feels like the first day in boot camp and it gets to me, it really does, how young we were, and how at some level it is no different now, we're just as ignorant of what we're getting ourselves into, Rafael and me, in this new stage in life when our kids have grown and left us, just as unaware as we were back then. I don't think that is something you can teach anyone, what real relation the past has to the future. It's changing, it's always changing and we're always its turning point.

The group naturally sorts out, with Jordan and his friends, who've ridden with him for years, in the lead, then Rafael and his sons, then Vicente and his brothers, then me. 3-4-3. 3-4-3. I keep scanning as the groups fan out wider and wider, each rider finding his own path through the creosote, yucca and ocotillo, wanting some feeling of freedom, the illusion that it's just between them and a moon so bright it's thinking it's really the sun and the stars stabbing through the sky like light from a tin lantern.

I can see something has come up minutes before I get there—all the lights converging, lighting up the metallic sides of the trailer of a large semi. Somehow it's gotten itself straddling a wide arroyo, the rear wheels of the cab on the rim of one bank, the rear wheels of the trailer on the rim of the other. The arroyo is about four feet deep. It looks unnatural, how exactly it is balanced, like it was picked up and carefully set down just so. What the fuck, I think. I immediately start trying to imagine how to move it, that's just the way my mind works, I'm a fixer.

Jordan and Rafael are over at the cab talking to the driver. It isn't until I came up to them that I realize the driver is a woman. She's laughing and crying at the same time.

"She was following her GPS," Jordan tells me, his voice kindly, expressionless. The highway is miles back, she's been driving all this time and never registered she was off the road? How can you be so clueless? I wonder. We all wonder. But nobody is saying because it's a woman and she's crying more than she's laughing. A guy, he'd be cussing himself out so loud he'd have no room for advice.

"A miracle of balance," I tell her, putting my hand up to shake hers. "You want to come and see for yourself? I'm Julio. I'm sure my son and my brother have introduced themselves."

The guys are staggered along the length of the trailer, marveling. I can see Vicente, like me, is playing various scenarios through in his mind. You go forward, the trailer might flip. You go back, you'll up end the cab.

The woman we help down is blonde as Candace, tall as her too. She looks, by moonlight, to be in her early twenties. She's thin. Big boobs. "We could hire her," I hear Sam whisper to Ernesto.

"Mind yourself," I tell them. I'm busy thinking what we need to do. The boys need their night out. She obviously needs a tow, and it isn't coming from eleven dirt bikes.

"You're going to need it craned up," I say.

"I don't know what I was thinking." She puts her hand to her forehead. "I mean, I saw this stretch was different, but I didn't register it as deeper. I just kept telling myself that the GPS had a better sense of direction than me. I thought I was on a dirt road, that I just couldn't quite make it out in the dark. I was just scanning everywhere for asphalt, and that voice kept saying turn left, go straight ahead for one mile. "

"Your daddy never teach you not to believe everything you hear?" I ask.

"From men, sure. But this was a woman. She sounds like my mother on her good days. Once I felt myself going down I gunned as hard as I could but it was too late. I made it all worse. Worst. They don't teach you about this in driving school." The young woman shook her head, the tears gleaming on her cheekbones. She had a thin straight nose, thin lips that made her look tough until they trembled. "Don't mind me, I'm losing it. I tried my dispatcher. I tried 911. There's no reception out here. Just cactus and coyotes." *And eleven strange men on dirt bikes out for a good time.*

"But the air is clear," I pat her arm the way I might Marisol's. "Take a deep breath. We'll get you out of this."

"Shit, Valerie, you're a real idiot. Your first big job—and your last." She made to hit her forehead, but wiped her cheeks instead.

"Where are you coming from?"

"Ohio."

"Know what's in here?"

"Household appliances. Refrigerators, dryers, dishwashers, and washing machines."

"Ouch." They'd have to empty the trailer before they lifted it, but who wanted to be the one doing the heavy lifting if it came unbalanced. Death by Bosch or Kenmore. There are better ways.

"At least it isn't flat screens," I say.

She smiles, drawing her breath in with a trembling sound, like a little girl getting over a tantrum.

"Dad—" Jordan begins.

"Anyone have reception?" I call out although I know the answer. We chose this location so we'd have a real night out, no one able to reach us.

"I'm off schedule. I was supposed to deliver this evening. They're going to dock me," Valerie says.

Oh honey, I think, that's just the beginning.

"Nothing's missing. So far as you know, nothing's broke. They're not going to bring heavy equipment out in the middle of the night. Why don't we have someone drive you back to town, find you a motel. You can organize things from there."

"I can't leave." She's standing in the arroyo now, her hand over her mouth, tears streaming. "I can't believe I did this to myself."

"You're going to sue GPS, Google maps," Sam tells her. He's just been accepted into law school. He is looking Valerie up and down with appreciation. "If I was farther along in my studies, I'd help you. Pro bono."

"I'm sure you would," Ernesto hoots. "Pro boner."

I tip my head at Jordan and walk aside. "Someone's got to drive out and call for her since she won't leave the truck—you know, for fear of illegals. Someone has to stay with her, of course, because she can't get back in that cab. You and Vicente, it's your last night of freedom. Take everyone on to the campsite, enjoy yourselves."

"You planning to stay with her, Dad?" Jordan asks, his voice too relaxed, even.

"Rafael just came to please me. He's complaining about his back. He'd be happy to spend the night in his own bed."

"We could leave the guys here and drive out and get the other truck and drive it back. They could party in the meanwhile."

"It's not a good idea," I say. "So many men and one woman. Anything happens, we'll have a lot of problems."

"Same goes for one on one," Jordan says. "And this isn't the time to raise such questions."

"What do you suggest?" I ask. Something happens at that moment, as different as can be from the feeling I had when Jordan passed me at thirteen never looking back. This feeling hollows me out. *My own son does not trust me.*

"Whatever your mother thinks, the women in those bars were just that. Women in bars. No one to take home. It never went too far. I let her think so because I was tired of the suspicion, the accusations."

"Those hang ups at the house? The women asking for Julio? You *planted* them, Dad?"

I straighten up then, furious. "I don't have to answer to you."

"But I'm going to have to answer to Mom, Juana and Marisol tomorrow," Jordan says.

"And what are you going to say? We left a woman all by herself in the desert?"

"We offered help but she refused it. She's an adult, capable of deciding for herself."

"She's not refusing help. She's refusing to leave the mess she made."

The moon lights up the silver sides of the trailer. It has a picture of Rosie the Riveter on it. *We do more for less. Put us to the test.* Like *sin papeles*, I think. Talk about selling yourself short.

Valerie is heading back to the cab. "I wouldn't do that, sweetheart," I call out. "Too unstable."

She looks back at me, suddenly insecure. Her cab is home. She's even bought floral seat covers. She ignores me and goes back to the cab and opens the door.

"I have to write down the GPS readings."

"Right," Jordan mutters. "They're what got you here."

"She needs to feel in control," I say.

"Be careful. Move slow. Get everything you need," I coach. "Have a blanket, water, food? A flashlight? Hand them out here."

"And a book," she says, handing things down to Rafael.

After some discussion among the boys, the upshot is they all ride back together on their bikes to the trucks we left at the pull out. The bonfire goes unlit. The booze in the other truck will be added to the bar at the wedding reception.

Rafael and I sit out under the moon and the stars talking quietly, while Valerie, wrapped in her red flannel blanket reads and weeps, weeps and reads. She is reading *The 7 Habits of Highly Effective People,* which she picked up used at one of the truck stops. Obviously she hasn't gotten very far into it and given how hard she's crying, I don't think she's going to take in what she does read.

"You don't have a romance or nothing?" I ask. "My wife's a scientist but she likes Nora Roberts."

"I think I need all the reality checks I can get," she answers. "This is surreal."

So Rafael and I lie on our backs and stare up at the sky that is a deep blue under the April moon. Whatever wisdom I had to share with my brother, I shared years ago. My son and Vicente, they will have to learn for themselves. For the first time, I let myself think about Candace's operation, how dangerous it is, how unready I am for the consequences in either direction.

"You think she regrets it?" I ask my brother.

"Not looking at what's right before her eyes?" Rafael answers, misunderstanding me. "Believe me, it's not a mistake you make twice."

The next morning when I walk into the house, dusty and tired and sore, the first tow truck has already radioed out for a tall crane, just like I thought. Candace was the one got them out there at dawn. After Jordon stopped at the house and filled his mother in on the situation and gave her all Valerie's information, Candace immediately started making calls—while Jordan and his friends and Vicente and his brothers went to a bar and drank beer and sang rancheros until dawn. Now Juana's accusing her brother of corrupting Vicente, who has a terrible hangover. She's afraid Vicente is going to stumble over his vows—maybe forget his English completely. His Spanish too.

Candace, when she hears the whole story from Rafael and me, gets herself patched through and invites Valerie to the weddings.

"Two for one," she tells Valerie. "Think of it as a favor to me. From what I hear, it sounds like you could pass for a member of my family. Since they're not coming, I'd welcome a stand-in. You can pretend you're my long lost cousin."

"Sounds like she'll clean up nice," Candace says when she gets off the radio.

The sun pouring in the window is not kind to either of us, but it is fair.

"You'll clean up well too," Candace says to me. Then she pauses, straightening the papers on which she'd been writing notes about the operation, the wedding, the calls she'd been making for Valerie. "It was kind of you and Rafael to stay there with her."

"We're sore as hell. I feel fifty-eight going on eighty. But we would be feeling this way in any case. What the hell were we thinking, Rafael and me?"

She brushes my hair back from my face, what's left of it, and studies me. "Whatever the kids like to think, I knew what I was getting myself into when I chose you, Julio. Whatever happens, I want you to remember that. I have no regrets."

"Enough of that," I say. "I have my eyes fixed on our future and you should too."

That's what I say, but I am also thinking as I kiss her how a marriage can be just like my wife's heart, with that valve whose leaflets don't always close tight, that contraction that is meant to send the blood and oxygen out to the body but instead sends some of it back so we come up short of breath and of the hope that comes with it, how sometimes we can fix that and sometimes we can't, about what it would be like if I told my kids that today: Keep your eye on the goal, but sometimes the goal floods back in on you. I'm thinking maybe they already know. Know they are both true. We need to keep our eyes on where we want to be—and nature can push back, reverse our momentum whenever it damn well pleases. You got to be prepared for both.

When we get to the hotel, we're looking good. I'm in a tux with a red rose on the lapel. Candace is in a red silk dress, looking fresh, like she just woke up from a long nap. But I take Jordan aside and tell him I'm going to escort Candace up the aisle myself.

"You walk too quick for us. It's your age, you can't help it. She walks with me, your mother's going to look like she's the stronger one."

Jordan just nods. He has other things on his mind. Marisol's mom and dad are arguing about where the step-mother is going to sit. While the parents' voices get louder and louder, Jordan puts his arms around Marisol and she clings to him like a little girl. Juana is giving Vicente the silent treatment. I give that marriage a year at the most, but people did the same with us.

As we walk up the aisle, Candace whispers, "Oh, if only my family could see us now." She squeezes my hand whenever her breath gets too short, and I slow down. The give and take, it is as good as it has always been between us in the bedroom. By the time we get to the altar, we've both worked up a sweet sweat.

FEASTING WITH GHOSTS

This fall I relaxed my fierce resistance to meat and conventional familial bonhomie and suggested we all congregate, for a day, under the same roof. I'd chosen Thanksgiving for its time constraints. No point in pushing things. Seth looked at me astonished. He had given up any expectations that I would assume the role of hostess to our far from blended brood. After a few disastrous attempts early in our relationship, I had tried my best to keep our families out from under the same roof. It always felt too explosive.

Isn't this too little too late? Seth's expression said. But I repeated my suggestion. Sometimes I receive clear guidings (from above or beneath isn't the question, rather the existence of something larger than my own often petty consciousness), and this invitation, just like my previous resistance, was one. We had, after all, celebrated our fifth anniversary in May. My daughter Serendipity's having had a baby recently may have also helped tip the scale.

"Do what you want," Seth said. Then his face softened. "Grace, I've waited so long for this. I'll do everything I can to help." Although Seth sees his family of origin rarely because they are on the West Coast, it is a large one, and he has warm memories of holidays, of being swept up in the sheer tribalness of thirty people squashed into a dining room. As the only child, unplanned and unwanted, of a single mother, now mercifully deceased, I do not.

Seth scoured the internet for cheap flights from Seattle (my daughter, Serendipity, and her six-month-old son, Keith), Topeka (his daughter, Chérie and her husband Tom), Gainesville (his other twin daughter, Rêvé and her husband Tyler), and New York (his son Jason, a recent law school graduate, and my son, Solomon, a starving artist). I called local hotels for rates, then went to the library and checked out an armload of seasonal cookbooks.

I was surprised at how quickly they all agreed to come. I would have thought someone would have begged off, citing other family responsibilities, peeve.

"Glad you've come around, Mom. Means you think this one is a keeper," my son Solomon said. I could see him, in my mind's eye, shaking out his wild mane of black hair and binding it back up into a ponytail.

"I have my hopes," I said, laughing.

"I'm driving," he added. "Can't face something like this if I don't have the means to beat a quick retreat. If you're nice, Mom, I'll take you with me. Leave our ghosts back there in the dust."

"Waving wildly. I can see it now," I laughed, deeply relieved. He is my son. We share a take on the world, a similarity of response I find deeply soothing.

But I wouldn't need to take him up on his offer. I had decided to seat our ghosts openly so they wouldn't lurk behind our every word, every gesture, leaving us breathless, dizzy with rancor.

It is about time, as Solomon said, that we all get acquainted—living, dead, and absconded.

I stood in our sweet little dining room hearing Solomon's offer to take me with him. How were we going to seat nineteen? I had decided to limit the ghosts to one each. Serendipity's son Keith, at six months, hadn't had enough time to accrue his own following, but he would need a high chair. If I moved in my work desk, we would have the right expanse. Chairs were a bit of a challenge—but then inspiration came so quickly an observer might mistake it for hyperventilation. I would paint a named chair for each of us and our favorite ghost. I imagined being able to set them out in the backyard in the summer, home to a convocation of ghosts who could socialize together under full, new, waxing and waning moons unimpeded by our dross vitality. Already I could hear the unexpected alliances, the fights, like the high murmur of cicadas humming through the summer nights. The beginning of a shared supernatural history, one that didn't depend on any of us acting as conscious or unconscious mediums.

It is like me to set up a seemingly deflectionary activity, like painting chairs, when I should have been concentrating on hotel reservations and menus. I liked the challenge of matching colors to personalities, deciding on designs for the seats of each chair. It calmed me because I felt I was honing in on the essence of things. I am an artist after all and my imagination is what attaches me to the human condition, however obliquely.

So, while Seth was on the phone, I took our van and headed off to the unfinished furniture store. I ended up buying nine bar stools. Ghosts, I decided, preferred to perch and peer over the shoulders of the living. I stopped at Home Depot and bought a full spectrum of paints. By the time I returned, I was hot on this new project, filled with a blitheness almost fierce in its vigor.

When I walked in, Seth was on the phone with his daughter Rêvé, confirming her flight times. Even from the kitchen door, I could tell she was whining. It was something about Seth's determined but cajoling tone. Rêvé was his baby, even if only by twenty minutes. She seemed to lag a good five years behind Chérie, her identical twin, in maturity. As I said, I was an only child myself, taught at an early age to be self-sufficient, which may be why I had so little sympathy.

I busied myself with unloading the van and carrying all the stools out to my studio. It made the whole space feel a little close, premonitory, which was as it should be. I arranged eight of them in a semi-circle facing my latest newly primed and invitingly blank canvas. The ninth I set in front of the canvas and perched there, elbows on knees, chin in hands, contemplating what I'd just set in motion. My elation surprised me. It was so like what I feel when I'm starting a new painting—and so unlike my responses to all these obstreperous adults I had held firmly at arm's length since we married.

I expected, as I sat there, to feel the old anguish start building up again. It had been such a core, centripetal force for the first years of our marriage—more like a black hole, actually. The roles we found ourselves in, with each other and with our children, were an astonishment, an outrage. Here I, who had held open house throughout most of Solomon and Serendipity's childhood and adolescence, not only with their friends but with my own as well, found myself determinedly walling out Seth's family—and trying to keep mine away too so they wouldn't see the chaos into which I was thrown by this new hardness of heart. For most of that time, I gave up painting as well. I guess I didn't dare read the writing on the wall—and the only way to avoid it was not to make the marks themselves. But there is a world of anguish in a blank canvas so intense it is like the whole brain screaming.

I don't know exactly what it was that made Seth and me stop

hammering at each other. Perhaps it was just that our kids had spread out across the continent and made their own lives, and Seth and my expectations of each other in relation to them began to seem more and more irrelevant, even to ourselves. Crossing the threshold into our second half-century also created in each of us an aching awareness of our own mortality and made us ever more acutely aware of our need for each other.

When Seth knocked on my studio door and came in, I had just decided, rather perversely, to paint Rêvé's chair a hot tropical pink with a stag on the chair seat. (She favored blanched pastels, small floral prints, and treacly images of fawns and baby chicks.) He looked surprised at the plethora of stools, and then, smiling, took his seat in the center of the semi-circle and raised his hand.

I stood up and gestured professorially at the blank canvas as if it were a blackboard. "As we all know, there really is no tabula rasa at fifty (if there ever was)—just a fog waiting to dissolve so we can finally see what has been calling to us all our lives, deep to deep."

"And what would that be?"

"Today?"

"What else do we have?"

"You're sure you're up for this?" he asked.

"What on earth will they have in common?"

"Me," Seth said. "You."

But would they? Isn't that what had been the problem all along? What Seth's twin daughters and his son Jason agreed on when they saw me had nothing in common with what Solomon and Serendipity saw.

Seth leaned forward and smiled expectantly. "I can't wait to see what's coming."

He loves my imagination—the surprise of it. I love his acceptance, and in our time together, have grown into it, making works of greater sureness and larger scale. Once, that is, I got over the devastating artist's block that defined our first years together—when all our life was whirling around us and there was no room left for what might come in out of my imagination, my blessed left field.

Why is it, then, that the same qualities that attract Seth to me here in my studio have, in our daily life, run us into such difficulties? For they are the same qualities—my need to focus on the ambiguous, the discordant, and bring it into high relief; my insistence that form accommodate to feeling, not the other way around. What is there in my nature that would have led either of us to expect that I could or would slip, easily or at all, into any ready-made role—especially one so pernicious to my soul as that of (wicked) step-mother? I shook my head, trying to wake up. That was all past now—the expectations, the disappointment, the terror of losing each other.

"I'm thinking we should buy a better video camera. High definition, to better record this for posterity."

"The Last Supper?" Seth caught himself. "Don't get me wrong, I'm glad we're trying this." I looked at the sweet fatigue lining his face and felt such love for him.

"I am too. But just for our sanity, let's assume that whatever can go wrong will." As soon as I spoke, I knew I'd said the wrong thing. Isn't that how we played those first terrible years—in constant violent mourning and rage at the transpositions and repetitions that felt like confirmations of our deepest fears?

"And something better," I continued, crossing the room to embrace him, "will come to take its place. Let's just be open to it—grace in chaos."

Which is what I was the next month, Grace in chaos—as I prepared the stools, sketched out several new paintings playing with Seth's suggestion of the Last Supper, made the hotel reservations and developed a menu that would work for bon vivants and teetotalers, vegans and primal man dieters. When Seth got on the phone with his own kids, I always told him I was too busy to talk—which was just my way of glossing the reality that, although his kids were coming, they still did not voluntarily exchange a word with me. My own progeny (who didn't interact a great deal with Seth either, but without, I insisted, such an unforgiving subtext) and I, by some osmotic decision, didn't even discuss the coming festivities, at least not directly. Solomon and I discussed my latest work, his, and the angst of artistic rejections. Serendipity and I discussed formula, mastitis, colic, food stamps, resumes, and recording sessions.

In early November, delighted with my stools, which I now kept mysteriously shrouded, I asked, expansively, "Do you think we should do an early morning brunch too?"

Everyone was flying in late Wednesday evening. Seth and I, without discussion, had divided the airport runs biogenetically. I knew Seth's three—

or five, going on seven, actually—were a little peeved at being put up in a nice hotel in the center of town a mile or two from our little house. My three were delighted, of course, at having a private place to fade out in. Their motel was even farther out, on the beltway. Solomon had asked that we put Serendipity and Keith and him in a separate hotel, even a fleabag or a trucker's stop. "The only time I saw Seth's kids was at your wedding. Not exactly a stellar encounter. I've repressed it as best I can. What if I don't recognize them in the halls when we get in?" Solomon would be a little easier to remember, with his long, black ponytail and the ring in his eyebrow.

"Brunch?" Seth cleared his throat, looking weirdly embarrassed. "I've been meaning to bring this up with you. Rêvé thought it would be a good idea to visit her mother's grave."

"On Thanksgiving? Everyone?"

"No. She thought it should just be the family. She and Chérie would leave Tyler and Tom at the hotel."

"*The* family?"

"You know what I mean."

We stared at each other across the abyss.

"It's a two hour drive to get there, Seth." Lila, Seth's ex-wife, was buried in their old home town.

" Rêvé was wondering if we could do an evening meal rather than an afternoon one."

"We're flying them in for a day so they can spend most of it driving out to their mother's grave?" I shrugged. We were beyond all that now. "Are you lending them your car or should I reserve one?"

Seth cleared his throat again. "Rêvé wants me to come with them."

"And you said—" I waited. I knew Seth was squirming, waiting for the explosion as soon as he got the words out.

"I said I'd check with you."

"You want to go then?"

"I don't want to disappoint them."

"I know. Do what you think best." I was as astonished as he was to hear the tenderness and acquiescence in my tone.

When I met Seth, he told me he'd been divorced for two years. He still lived in their family home in the small town in north Georgia where he taught, his wife having moved to Birmingham four years before, while the girls were still in high school, to find herself. Since our courtship took place in torrid weekends primarily on my turf in Highlands, North Carolina, it took me some months to realize that the divorce was in name only. His ex-wife, Lila, returned whenever the girls came back from college, leaving her lover working at his bank in Birmingham. That meant she was in residence throughout the summers. Seth would move, he assured me, from the bedroom to his home office when the time came. He had looked quite pleased with his sensitivity.

"I'm sorry," I told him. "I can't date someone who still shares a roof with his ex-wife."

"But the girls," he said. "Their sense of security."

"They're twenty years old, sweetheart. You've been separated for four years, divorced for two. They're halfway through college. She has another relationship. Can't they go to stay with her in Birmingham if they need to see her?"

"Chérie doesn't mind, but Rêvé does. She says it doesn't feel like home if we're not all there together. Besides, she's a little afraid of her mother."

"What about Lila's lover, does he think this is a good idea?"

"I don't see why he would have any say in the matter."

"You don't?"

Seth's face reddened with anger. He had, he insisted, wanted the divorce. Demanded it, actually, after having gone on a surprise visit to see Lila in her new digs in Birmingham (where she claimed to be broadening her horizons with steady therapy and episodic stints as an activity director in a retirement home) and discovered a smaller man's clothes filling her bureau drawers.

But Lila had a strong, if crazy, sense of what was owed her—for all those dreary years in a small town, the tedium of her husband's dependability, the breakdowns.

"For the children," she would say, or so I gathered. "I am still their mother after all."

"What children?" I asked Seth. The one time I had met his daughters, I had seen two smart, capable, attractive and rather petulant young women, sophomores in college.

"I'll be driving over to be with you almost every weekend," he said. "Or you can come up here."

"And bunk with your ex?"

"We could stay in a motel."

"I think we may need to think about relocating." I said. "Both of us. But until then, if you want to keep seeing me, you need to stop cohabiting."

"I don't know how I'm going to explain this to any of them," he said.

"Say you're serious about me and you need the freedom to establish new commitments, just like their mother has done."

"That doesn't mean things have to change for them."

"Why not? Isn't that what the divorce meant—the two of you split up?"

What the divorce seemed to mean in "the" family was that Seth wasn't going to be financially liable for Lila's increasingly wild swings between mania and depression. Or the borderline disorder that drove her to increasingly debilitating attempts at suicide when she was disappointed by failures of attention—by Seth, her new lover, or her increasingly independent and distant daughters. Or the alcoholism and drug addictions that led to more than a baker's dozen of rehab stays. Other than that, she came in and out of their lives as she pleased.

"I don't how I will be able to explain to anyone that I'm seeing a man who lets his crazy ex-wife define all our lives."

"She isn't responsible—"

"If that's the case, you need to be responsible—and stop the damage she is doing."

"What damage is that? She's just coming to visit. My being there makes it feel safer for the girls."

Seth took me in his arms, buried his face in my neck. "I love you so much," he said. "I can't imagine life without you."

"I am marrying you," I told him. "Not this convoluted system."

Easier said than done. I was so outnumbered, for one thing. So were my children, should we bring them all together, which I was careful we didn't. Keeping them out, though, only made me feel more beleaguered even though Seth heeded my ultimatum and announced to his distraught and disbelieving family that he was selling the family home, giving the proceeds to Lila in lieu of alimony, and setting up a new life with me. We married in June. I guess I felt that marriage would serve, like a surgeon's scalpel, to make the separations clean, precise. Hah!

The wedding itself was a maelstrom of competing energies. Seth's daughters, enraged at their father's perfidy—they had depended on his life staying the same whatever their mother chose to do—sulked, wept, sulked again. Their mother, enraged at their disloyalty in coming, called fifteen times a day, shifting to our home phone once Jason had taken his sisters' cellphones into protective custody.

I made the mistake of answering once, only to hear, "They're *my* daughters, let me speak to them, you goddamn bitch."

I handed that phone over to Solomon, who listened, said gently, "And she's *my* mother, so just mind your fucking tongue." Then he unplugged all the phones and insisted Seth tell everyone to turn off their cellphones for the duration of the ceremony and reception.

That day, as our small audience assembled in the little house I'd moved into after my children were on their own, Solomon and Serendipity focused on being helpful. They walked around with trays of canapés and flutes of champagne. I heard them both giving their last name, which differs from mine, and not clarifying their relationship to me, giving the impression they were there in a purely professional capacity. "And would you prefer tofu and black mushroom turnovers or goat cheese and truffle?"

Only in the bedroom, as I was adjusting my dress and make-up before the ceremony, did they say anything.

"You sure about this, Mom?" Solomon asked.

All through dinner the night before, Seth's three had looked through my two like newly cleaned window panes. Rêvé and Chérie had talked about their disrupted plans for the summer, the inconvenience of having to move out of "the" family home. Jason had talked about his LSATs, his internship in a law office in New Haven. Solomon had sketched. Serendipity had hummed quietly to herself, working on a new song she was composing. (It's lyrics, I learned later, were obscene.)

But it wasn't until Solomon asked me directly that it truly hit me what I was doing, what I had already done. It wasn't the father they never saw who hurt my children, it was the men who, throughout their childhood, enamored of me, looked through them as heedlessly as if they were the clearest of glass, just as Seth's children were doing now. *The way I put up with that.* Taught them, through my tolerance, that it was normal. Worse than that, that we were invulnerable to it, that we needed no more, the three of us, than our own warmth, the vivid world we made unto ourselves. If you had asked us, we would probably have said those occasional visitors were irrelevant. For one thing, they were outnumbered, three to one. It was *our* home. But it is also true that I never remarried, never even considered living with anyone, until Solomon and Serendipity were both safely on their own. But I had put them now, through my own actions, in exactly the same situation I had tried to protect them from before—made invisible not just by an individual but a whole group, "the" family.

My kids got it all, my delayed reaction, the guilt, the helplessness, without my saying anything.

"Is this really the life you want for *yourself*, Mom?" Serendipity asked. "I mean, we're fine. We have our own lives. You can come and visit us whenever you want."

"With Seth if you like," Solomon said. "He seems like a good guy."

My beautiful, implicated children, so adult, so severed from me—and for what?

"Hell, it's worth a try, Mom," Solomon said, handing me a tissue.

I could not give up Seth, this wonderful man who saw me, truly saw me, saw me from the inside out, saw the effort and cost and commitment of all those years as a single parent. And I knew, looking at Solomon and Serendipity that afternoon, that without a doubt I could not accept these terms—and so far it didn't look like there were any alternatives.

"The worst that can happen is you decide to get divorced," Serendipity said, wiping away the mascara that had run down my cheek. "We'll be there for you either way."

That day, I recited the vows Seth and I had so optimistically written with a sense of profound futility, bottomless remorse. All I knew was that I never again wanted my own children to see me like this, or be seen themselves in this way, especially within my own home.

I expect in the guestroom Jason might have been saying something similar to Seth before the ceremony, with Rêvé and Chérie serving as Greek chorus, their muted cellphones buzzing like a hornets with calls from Lila.

I lasted less than a year in the little college town where Seth had lived for nearly a quarter century, unable finally even to walk to the post office without looking over my shoulder to see the ghost of marriage past. Seth's marriage. That town had no room for my ghosts, or for me. I had never felt so unreal, so stripped of my own life, my own dear chaos—since everyone there only knew me as a function in Seth's life story. "So nice for him," his colleagues murmured. "It couldn't have happened to a better man."

It meant, I assumed, me. "I am not an *it*," I screamed at Seth. "I am not a *she* either." For that made me feel even more unreal, the way I would hear Rêvé and Chérie on their tense but frequent visits that summer (now scrupulously divided between Lila and her lover in Birmingham and us), asking their father if *she* would be around, what *she* wanted, why *she* didn't seem up to having their friends drop in unexpectedly to hang out, giggling, until all hours of the night as had been their habit in the past. They never spoke to me, that was why. They just marched in, a horde of young adults, and made themselves comfortable in Seth's and my home as if I was the one who didn't belong there. I felt just as blank as one of my untouched canvases.

By April I had announced my plans to relocate our marriage. It wasn't Seth I wanted to leave, just his context—and before another summer with his girls. I was sure I wouldn't make it through it, *we* wouldn't. Every day I woke haunted by the canvases that stayed so implacably blank. People looked through me, but I could not see an inch into my own future. I couldn't see what was coming from behind, just felt its hot breath on my neck. *I*, who had once been such a source of security for myself and my own children, was now the most dangerous thing in my universe. There was a tigress in me more terrible than the ghost of my own mother. She could, in a single bound, grab the neck of any one of us here, Seth and myself included, and with a single snap of her teeth and a twist of her head sever our spines. Without thinking. Without remorse.

"They're adults now," I told Seth. "All our children are adults now. Go visit them where they are. It's healthier for them to forge out on their own rather than hang around resenting me."

I rented a one bedroom apartment in Highlands. Seth joined me as soon as his classes were over. The twins, faced with the prospect of spending the entire summer with their mother, decided to tour Europe before returning to college for their senior year. Seth and Jason visited with them in London, while I went to New York to visit Solomon and Seattle to visit Serendipity. From then on, we visited our children separately, sometimes as a couple, sometimes to each our own.

Seth and I found jobs in Atlanta, a hundred miles from his little college town. We settled into a bungalow in Decatur near his current teaching job at a small women's college. I worked part-time for the county arts commission and tried to keep up my relations with galleries in North Carolina while trying to break into the Atlanta art scene. Things began to feel sane, but strange. It was still difficult to share our tumultuous history with strangers. I had trouble talking about myself as I, that *she* having gotten into all my thoughts, except when I was painting.

So, now, finally having a house and city unencumbered with history, getting our act together as a couple, Seth's girls several years out of college and married like good bourgeoisie, Lila dead of an overdose, my creative muse having returned and now speaking to me faithfully every day—why did I decide to open the doors to all our chaotically milling ghosts? Maybe because at fifty I had decided I couldn't face my Maker—or more to the point my own mortality—feeling I was still running from something.

"Running and keeping a healthy distance are two different things," my oldest and dearest friend, Rose-Ellen, a therapist, told me.

But the distance I had been keeping from our children wasn't healthy. It was desperate and draining and I wanted to put an end to it, out of love for Seth as much as for myself. I intended to live with him until one of us died. Honestly, I didn't have the energy to think of twenty-five more years (God willing) of this intense discomfort. Something had to give.

But the conversation about the pilgrimage to Lila's grave set me back, no doubt about it.

"Fine," I told Seth. "*The* family will wait for you until five. Serendipity's flying out at ten, if you remember."

Oh, I was in a fine fury, whatever my intentions. The next day, I could barely recall that sweet voice that had said, "I know," and did. That said, "Do what you think best," and meant it. I decided to scratch the turkey from the menu, which I was cooking just for the benefit of Seth's carnivorous brood. I decided I would make drumsticks out of tempeh instead, concealing their fleshless reality under a liquid smoke and soy flavored gravy. I could see the looks of surprise and disappointment on their faces already. I saw myself gesturing hospitably at the whole carp, the tempeh sculptures, the carrots carved into butterflies and swans. "Help yourself."

But when the time came, I ended up making the turkey. Seth had bought one, which I had promptly tucked away in the freezer, knowing he couldn't ask a lifelong vegetarian and current wife to baste it while he was on a pilgrimage to his ex-wife's grave. But when Solomon and Serendipity showed up around nine in the morning, my son insisted we defrost it.

"They're off to their mother's graveside," I told them as soon as they walked in. "Welcome to your own mother's hearth."

"Hmm," Solomon said, patting me on the shoulder in greeting, "I can smell it from here—domestic shit."

"I think that's Keith's diaper," Serendipity said. She handed me my malodorous grandson, whom I gratefully received, cooing into his dear brown face with its look of proud accomplishment. Serendipity handed me the bag of diapers. Keith gurgled and kicked his feet in the air as alone together in our bedroom, I wiped and talced his rosy bottom and taped him into a new diaper.

When my grandson and I came back, thoroughly bonded, Solomon and Serendipity had pulled the turkey out of the freezer and had put it in a sink of hot water to defrost.

"I think you forgot this," Solomon said. "Serendipity has foregone her gatherer and reclaimed her hunter. She needs the protein."

So we spent the morning concocting a strange stuffing from delicacies tucked into forgotten corners of the pantry. A small can of truffles given to me by an old, peripatetic beau ten years ago—the weekend he returned from Paris and broke off our relationship in favor of a woman, younger of course, he had met there—and which I had been unable to either open or discard. A can of pureed chestnuts with no personal history that Solomon had brought from New York. Bread crumbs Serendipity grated from several freezer-stale loaves of bread. Fresh cranberries and red onions. Plenty of sage and marjoram.

By the time we had put the turkey in the oven, we were looking flushed and feeling extraordinarily pleased with our inventiveness. There is nothing that feeds the imagination like actual constraints.

"You think we should call those by-laws and invite them over?" Solomon asked about two o'clock. "They're probably getting bored holed up in their hotel."

"Nap," Serendipity pleaded. "This breast-feeding seems to be sapping me of all my essential nutrients, especially blood sugar."

Before leaving to get the by-laws, Tyler and Tom, Solomon helped me bring in all the stools, which he duly admired, especially his own, done in a deep dioxazine purple, with a Rodin-like thinker in gold on the seat.

Serendipity's had a hot air balloon with a little gondola attached, from which she and Keith, in a snuggly, waved down at the adoring crowd on the ground. Mine had a tiger with its mouth shut; Seth's, two hands, bronze on a phthalocyanine green background, opening like a book. Rêvé had her stag, and Chérie a fierce Kali-derived goddess, while Jason's had a sea otter cracking a sea urchin open on its chest, an image that had come out of nowhere. What it had to do with an ambitious new Columbia Law School graduate, I didn't know. The image just came to mind and wouldn't leave until I made it real. Rêvé's husband, Tyler, also a law student, had a gavel; while Chérie's husband, Tom, a psychiatric resident at the Menninger clinic, had a head in profile with a winding staircase inside.

"Doing some scripting?" Solomon asked as he set the chairs up around the table, alternating, to the extent possible, the families.

"With more than enough space for improv," I said, setting a stool a foot behind and between each chair. Along the edge of each seat I had stenciled *Ghost Gnosis* in gold along with the name of its owner.

"Tyler," Solomon read out. "Tom. Those French ticklers, Rêvé and Chérie, and the straight man, Jason. And Seth, your best bet yet. They're works of art, Grace, but don't you think they're also rather blatantly leading questions?"

"Sometimes you just have to channel the flow rather than damming it completely."

"What is it, exactly, that you have against them?"

I looked at my tall son, betrayed by his gently ironic expression. I thought I was doing such a good job, whenever I talked to him, of putting a good face on things. I thought it bad form for him to call me on my incompetence of heart right now.

"I feel they wish I didn't exist. That they'd like to have me and Lila change places."

"Sounds pretty natural to me. I'd rather have you here than her, of course, because you are my progenitor. You think that's what Seth wants too?"

"No. He wants me just as I am—and he wants me to fit into his past, rewrite all those manic episodes, all those crazy fights. He wants us to have been, or to become, one big happy family."

"It's normal," Solomon said, touching the ring in his eyebrow gently, no longer able to wink.

"No," I said. "It's not. Anymore than my reaction to it is normal. I just can't feel that way towards people I didn't raise, situations I didn't create."

"You're not a stranger to craziness, Mom."

"Don't I know it. But it had my name all over it. I put the pieces together when things shattered and I could see someone familiar, however scarred, looking back at me from the shards. I don't know myself in their responses."

"Well, you know yourself in ours." Serendipity said, pausing on her way to the bedroom.

My two children, so indubitably adult, looked at me with their familiar, assessing gazes. I took a deep, comfortable breath.

"At least with the two of you I have impact—for better or worse. It's this mild but intractable depreciation that seems to erode the ground right out from under me. I feel completely helpless against it."

"Think hate then," Solomon suggested. "Think that they hate you and see if that makes you feel any more solid."

I started laughing. My son has always had a gift for naming my fears. But this relief bordered on hysteria. I couldn't stop the laughing, or the tears.

Keith, sleeping on a little mat we had made for him on the living room rug, began to fret at the ruckus, so I picked him up, quieting us both. I carried him in to nap a little longer with his mother.

Solomon headed out to fetch the by-laws.

"He isn't very preppie looking," I told Tom and Tyler when I called to let them know Solomon was on his way. "He'll meet you outside. His van is the one where you can see through the paneling, it is rusted so badly in places. It's a vile navy blue."

"You're right, it is vile," Tom, the shrink to be, said when he came in. "I peeked in the back expecting to see spare body parts—but all I saw were rags and buckets and a long ladder."

"To be honest, it kind of gives me the creeps too, but it establishes street cred with my biker clientele." Solomon shrugged. He supported his art with a side practice as a tattoo artist. His serious work involved large, eerie installations where strange black and white scenarios played on the walls, and suddenly you might find yourself up there too when a live video tucked in the scaffolding picked you out of the milling crowd and displayed you, leeched of color, on a screen imbedded in the wall where the other images were already playing. I think it is important to Solomon's art that he can never attend his own openings because he needs to be behind the scenes, weaving the present back into whatever scripts he has written and recorded. Not me. I wanted the present played out before me in vivid color and a single take. I wanted our past scripts set, at last, to rest.

"And you," I asked Tom, "how do you establish credibility with your patients?"

"Unconditional positive regard," Tom answered with a smile. "But I think we call them clients now, not patients." He really was impossible not to like, a big blonde farm boy who had met Chérie when he was an intern in Birmingham and she was making one of the last few trips to the emergency room with her mother. Lila's behavior, as her daughters approached their graduation, had grown increasingly erratic. She had managed to time most of her lithium 'oversights' with their vacations—so it was increasingly difficult to sort out the histrionic from the intentional—leaving all sorts of uncomfortable room for interpretation when she died (surfeited with xanax, oxycodone, and alcohol, depleted of lithium) just before their final exams their senior year. They missed their graduation for her funeral, spent the summer making up their courses and preparing for their twin August wedding.

Tom had been the only one among us at the funeral able to shed easy tears. "I just think about how I'd feel if my own Mom had died," he said. "This grief is pretty universal. It would be crazy to fight it."

"What is *she* doing here?" I could hear Rêvé and Chérie whispering to Seth during those uncomfortable days. "*She* didn't know Mommy."

"She's my wife," Seth would answer, shrugging apologetically.

"Mom wouldn't like Grace looking down at her like this. Can you forbid her to look into the casket?" Jason asked his father.

Lila had actually left a husband behind, the banker, whom she had married three months earlier. For the first time, Jason and Rêvé and Chérie seemed to take him seriously. He was quite sweet and stricken. "Like me when I was young and hopeful," Seth said. "Poor guy. He still feels he had some control over the outcome." They offered Seth a front row seat with all of them if he'd just leave me on my lonesome in a back pew. I regretfully declined for both of us. So Seth and I sat together at some distance from the casket and listened to his children extol Lila's virtues, praise the intensity of her new husband's grief—with no mention at all of Seth's considerable contribution over more than twenty years to their mother's survival.

"We'll never know if she meant to die or not," Tom said at one of the edgy post-mortem dinners at the local Waffle House. "So, if it were me, I'd probably choose the interpretation that gave me the most peace." He held his cup of coffee up for the waitress to refill.

Even then I could tell, by the way he held Chérie's eyes, that theirs was a done deal, just like Seth and me. I'm not a romantic, but one of the mysteries of my middle-age has been discovering that real, instinctual, sustainable love does exist—even for me. But taking in my current good fortune also lets me know how fixed the past is, that its consequences are, in essential ways, irreversible.

On this Thanksgiving, four years later, I could see it in how Solomon cased up Tom, trying to get a handle on his undefended earnestness, so different from Solomon's own guerrilla approach to hope.

"How is Chérie taking to living in Kansas?" I asked.

"It's only another year and a half," Tom said. "Then I think we'll try to move back in this direction." I could feel a fist closing down around my intestines.

"And Rêvé?" I asked Tyler. "Does she like Gainesville?"

"She's used to college towns. She's wanting me to set up practice where she used to live."

"And you, what do you want?" I asked seditiously.

Tyler was a good Southern boy, as adequate in law school as he had been in college, but no more. Rêvé had met him at the local pizza parlor her last year in high school. He'd been a junior in the college where Seth taught. I sometimes wondered if he kept her a little immature, as if her dreams for herself never developed beyond those she shared with him as a teenager in the days just following her parents' divorce.

"What everyone does, I guess. A steady income. A happy family. Close ties." Tyler looked at me reprovingly. "I'm trying to talk her into moving back to Columbia where we have good family support." And his father had a law firm that hired on camaraderie as much as grade point averages.

"What do we have here?" Tom asked. I thought at first he was asking about our dining room, but he was actually greeting Serendipity and Keith, equally tangle-haired and yawning.

It was Tyler, though, who put his arms out for the baby. Tom who shook Serendipity's hand.

"I'm Grace's other," Serendipity said. The look she threw me was amused and, as usual, a little admonishing. I'd never been able to case out her expectations, let alone meet them. Perhaps that is just how it is between mothers and daughters. I know my own mother, who was perhaps even crazier than Lila, felt the same way about me. The difference was my mother blamed me, while I, faced with Serendipity's disappointment, however mild, blamed myself. Don't get me wrong, my daughter loves and respects me as I love and respect her. It's just that some essential kindredness has always been lacking. I've often ascribed it to her lack of imagination, which is what allows the rapid flow of empathy and play between Solomon and me.

As I took Keith from Tyler I felt that powerful and perfectly simple surge of love babies evoke in me. Serendipity, who had put her arms out for the baby, stepped back with a look of relief. I wondered whether Serendipity and I would finally find our ease together through shared love of her son.

"And your husband?" Tyler asked Serendipity. "Is he here?"

Oh, I did want to take a pin and prick his little bubble of convention.

Solomon put his hand protectively around his sister's shoulder. Serendipity lifted her sharp little chin and flashed them her most ravishing smile. Her recently shaved head gleamed like a hedgehog who had shed her spines. "There's no husband, no identified father. I just hope he doesn't develop a Christ complex."

"He could do worse," Tom, bless him, said with a laugh.

"Well, he's certainly the light of my world," I said.

"We come from a distinguished line of matriarchs," Solomon said. "Serendipity is certainly not without models and precedents. I'm not worried about Keith either. Just look at me—right, Mom?" He winked.

"Hors d'oeuvres? Apéritifs?" I asked as I headed off, baby on hip, to the kitchen.

"Orange juice, green tea, Wild Turkey, Budweiser," I crooned to Keith as I prepared the tray.

When I came back in, Tyler was asking Serendipity about labor and delivery. Solomon and Tom were talking about whether tattooing was more influenced by the desire to self-mutilate or to beautify.

"I don't know if there is any kind of self-expression that doesn't come without a certain degree of pain. Maybe they're just acting that out."

"Eighteen hours into it and I was begging for a spinal block—"

"Brie, morbier, chêvre with pepper." Unobserved and unheard, I set the tray on the table.

"Anybody home?" Seth called out, pushing the front door open with a flourish. "We have a hungry horde here."

The family, I thought, a wave of righteous matriarchal rage rising as I turned to greet them. And then it just passed away as I saw them, huddled together, their faces red with the cold or the emotional pathos of their day.

"Welcome," I said. "You're long awaited." I held out my hand, wondering if any of them would take it.

Jason did. "I tried to get them to come back a little earlier, but the twins kept running into friends everywhere we went," he muttered. Our relationship has always been distant but sedulously polite. But this evening his customary poise was frayed. He couldn't stop patting at his windblown hair, although it danced more wildly with every attempt to tamp it down. However much in the past I had found his concentration on conventional appearances a little slick and distancing, I could suddenly see the protection it offered him, like the sea otter's need to constantly groom its fur because of its essential unfittedness for sea life. I wondered when, if ever, he would come out to himself, let alone the world.

"Let me introduce you," I said. "Or reintroduce you, as the case may be." I covered his proffered hand with both of mine.

"I thought you two would be waiting for us at the hotel," Rêvé said, pushing her way in, belly first. She was in her seventh month, Chérie only in her fifth—so for the first time in the sisters' development, Rêvé was the frontrunner. "I was scolding Daddy about coming here first, but he said he wanted to get back and give you a hand." You, I thought. Is that a step forward or back? She wasn't looking at me as she talked.

"How thoughtful," Tom said, coming around to give Chérie a kiss on the cheek and to shake hands with his father-in-law.

Seth and I stared at each other, the distance between us questioning and painful. There was a momentary silence in the room as everyone took in our awkwardness.

"Solomon," my son said, stepping forward to shake Jason's hand, then Chérie and Rêvé's. "My sister Serendipity you may remember, my nephew Keith, you can't."

"Our first born grandson," Seth said, walking over and taking the baby from Tyler and giving him a heartfelt nuzzle.

Rêvé gave Tyler a meaningful look. *Usurped.* I'd never met her mother, perhaps I never needed to, since I imagined her so clearly in her younger daughter's every gesture.

"Ours is going to be the first on my side," Tyler said, putting his arm around his wife and pulling her closer.

"Ours will, I guess, just be part of the throng on both sides," Tom said with a laugh, placing his hand lightly on his wife's small, tight belly.

Chérie smiled comfortably. "There's something to be said for company. With all these cousins, they'll feel in the swim immediately. It will make the next one easier I expect."

"How can you be thinking of another already?" Rêvé said to her sister. "I can't get my mind around this one yet." She looked with a combination of wonder and defeat at her large belly. She was one of those women, like me, who carried everything in front, so at seven months she looked ready to deliver tomorrow. And she was, her puzzled expression clearly indicated, feeling unprepared.

"I don't know if it's worth trying to get your mind around it," Serendipity said. She put her hands on her lower back to balance the unsettling weight of her milk-engorged breasts. "You can't imagine something you haven't experienced yet. The reality is so much simpler—and more complex—than any of the thoughts I had at four in the morning when Keith was battering away inside me like a champion kickboxer."

"We were just talking about her delivery," Tyler said. "Better you than me is all I can say." He took a big swig of his Wild Turkey. "Weaker sex nothing."

"Thank goodness nature kicks in, for men and women," Seth said. "I remember with Jason here what it felt like to take him into my hands in the delivery room. All those months, I felt like Serendipity—and Rêvé. I thought I wasn't ready. But the minute he opened his big mouth and started bawling me out, an amazing confidence filled me. I knew just what to do. Don't know where it came from, but there it was, all this raw affection just when I needed it most." He patted the baby's back comfortably as he talked.

I could see Jason and Rêvé and Chérie visibly relax. Seth has a most seductive voice, but it was more than that. It was as if there was a part of each of them that was as receptive to Seth's every move as was little Keith burping happily away on Seth's shoulder.

When I looked at Solomon and Serendipity, I could see a similar expression, but there was something startled in it as well. Paternal bonding wasn't something either of them were familiar with. They obviously found it attractive and disturbing in equal measure. Since it was where Seth and I met, and separated, I too felt a clash of emotions so powerful I left the room. It wasn't only my children who had never known a father.

In the kitchen, I took stock of what needed to be done to bring the feast to the table. Gravy. Tossing the salad. Whipping the cream for the pecan pies. Through the door, I could see all my vivid stools. I started thinking what a foolish notion it was to have made them. I had an urge to sink down on the floor in the pantry and find some equally dark unpeopled space inside myself where I could hide until this was all over.

When Seth put his hand on my shoulder, I jumped. "Didn't mean to startle you," he said. He leaned down and kissed my cheek. "I can't thank you enough."

"It's not over until it's over," the irrepressible skeptic in me said. "So I want all the strokes I can get for good intentions."

"I've always given you that," he said.

Wasn't that the bitch of it. We both had. And it hadn't prevented us, again and again, from reacting angrily, convinced we were living with a complete stranger: "Why do you have to support them in their callousness?" "Why do you have to put the worst interpretation on everything?" "Why do they never ask me a personal question?" "Why can't they come and stay indefinitely—isn't that what families are for?" "Why do they never talk as if there is more than one family here—another whole, wounded history?" Drowning out the questions we never dared ask aloud: Why, why, why are *we* hurting each other so consistently and so deeply? *Why can't we stop?*

And *they*, this throng of successful, self-sufficient adults easily—or cagily—engaging in conversations in the other room, had no idea, absolutely no idea, of the anguish we had put each other through.

"Gravy?" I asked Seth. "I'm out of practice." I'd been a vegetarian since I had left Solomon and Serendipity's father.

"I used to do this by myself," Seth said. "It's nice having a companion."

That's not, of course, what his children remembered.

"My mother—" I heard Rêvé say.

"My mother," Serendipity responded. There was some weird bonding laughter.

I started up the mixer to drown it out. I sprinkled the powdered sugar on as the cream built itself up into peaks, like a stormy sea.

And then, without warning, the tiger came and set her teeth gently on my neck. *I, Grace, had a mother who wanted to stuff my children's mouths with stones. I, Grace, had a mother who wanted to do even worse to me.* What home had room for that reality? What home would ever be strong enough to wall it out?

"Where do you want me to set up the video?" Solomon asked from the doorway. He held it to his eye, recording the two of us busily whisking and whirring.

I took a deep breath. My voice, when I spoke, was warm and even.

"Behind my chair," I said. "But don't start it up yet."

"Take your places," Seth called out. He switched on the electric carving knife and began slicing the turkey while I carried out the platters of braised anise and onions, nutmeat pâté en croute, sherried sweet potatoes with walnuts, salad, and sourdough bread and set them down the center of the table.

Once everyone had served themselves, Seth raised his wine glass. I held up my hand to stop him.

"Now," I told Solomon, who overturned his stool as he got up to start the video.

"For the record," I said to Seth. We stared at each other, such a vast, peopled distance from one another.

"At long last," Seth said. "We haven't been together like this—"

"Ever," I said.

"It's been my deepest wish that we could get to know each other in this way, make a new unit."

"Daddy," Rêvé said, "can we eat before we get maudlin?"

Seth looked a little put out, but lifted his glass higher.

"To the future," I joined him, feeling unexpectedly, fiercely protective of his good intentions.

"What else is there?" Solomon joined in.

"Well," I asked. "What are people looking forward to most this year?"

"A day job with benefits," Serendipity said. "And reliable day care." She spooned a little pureed spinach into Keith's open mouth. He grimaced, letting it drool off both sides of his tongue.

"Finishing my classes and passing my law boards," Tyler said. Then, squinting with pain, as if someone had pinched him, he added, "And, of course, fatherhood."

"A show," Solomon said, "with a good review in *ArtNew*s and more than my best friends in attendance."

"An easy labor," Chérie said.

"That and starting a graduate program in counseling," Rêvé said.

"Say what?" Tyler said.

"I don't want this baby to hold me back," Rêvé said. "I don't want to lay that on her." She looked at her husband with an expression as indomitable as the stag I had painted on her chair. "It's a terrible thing to lay on someone—to make them feel as if, without you, their world would have been so much better."

"We should never have gone to the grave," I heard Jason mutter.

"It was her idea," Chérie said.

"I wanted to clear the air," Rêvé said.

"Right," Chérie and Jason said in disparaging unison.

"Sometimes the first step in taking hold is letting other things go," I said, surprised at my quick defense of Rêvé. "Making a healthy family, a healthy life is so much about choosing,"

"Like you chose to have us?" Serendipity asked.

"But I did—just the way you chose to have Keith," We shared a steady look, my daughter and I, that brought us both back to the recovery room in the hospital in Seattle where Serendipity held Keith to her breast weeping, "What on earth am I going to do with him, Mom?"

"Let me help you," I had suggested. "Move back closer to me."

"It would be another new world," she'd said, exhaustion blanching her face, making her look a decade older. "I don't have the energy."

"Let yourself love him," I said. "Whatever else you do, let yourself love him. Don't hold back. It can't hurt you. It will be your safe place in all the years to come."

She shook her head helplessly back and forth. "I know I'm years older than you were when you had me, but I don't feel up to it."

"It's not about rising," I said. "It's about sinking in, taking hold."

"What do you—" she started, the rebellious refrain of her adolescence and early adulthood. Then she stopped, for we both knew that I did know. "I'm glad you came."

"I can stay as long as you need me. I can come back again."

"I didn't mean to have it happen this way," she said. And I knew what she meant—because for all my daughter's need to get to the other side of the continent to find herself, for all her wild nights with her band, she had a conventional soul. She wanted a bungalow, just like the one Seth and I were now living in. She wanted someone who could pat her son on the back, bringing those painful bubbles up. She wanted a life she had no reason to expect—one where she was seen, not seen through.

"He's beautiful," I had said, touching my grandson's pulsing, vulnerable skull. "Perfectly beautiful. You've done well by yourself, honey. Time will tell."

And that was when, remembering that day with Serendipity in Seattle, I felt a ghost sit down on the stool behind me—not any of the ones I expected. Not the one I had just felt breathing on my neck in the kitchen. Not poor, furious Lila. Not my ex-husband and lovers en masse, magnificently similar in their indifference. My ghost was me as a young mother, alone in the recovery room after Serendipity's birth. Three in the morning. They had taken her away to check her vital signs, and all I could think about was how detached I had felt when the doctor lifted her up for me to see. Alone in that dark room, I couldn't see, twenty-three years old and on my own with two little ones, how I was ever going to get through this. Coming from where I had come. Being who I was, someone who had as a child, just by breathing, just by being, inspired such pure, murderous animosity in her own mother. And then the nurse came back and put Serendipity in my hands and all this love just washed through me, something larger, safer and surer than I was, something solid that could hold both of us. I think that was my first experience of God—and it made me fierce. "I want you to be alive," I told her. "I want to be your mother."

But what did that ghost of mine have to share with anyone at this table? Who, except me, would know her as my own?

"Yo, Mom, other than making the room feel like a slalom course, what did you have in mind with these stools?" Solomon asked.

"I've been wondering that for the past month," Seth said.

"It was an idea I had whose time may have come and gone."

"Don't be coy, Mom. You're too old for that. We can pan it if we don't like it."

"Maybe that's what I'm afraid of."

"I'd think your skin would be thick enough by now." Solomon said.

"Not on the homefront."

"I'm sure we'll like it, Grace," Chérie said sweetly. "I like our stools. They're kind of folk arty and quaint. I'm sure the art therapists in Tom's clinic will be interested in them if we ever figure out a way to get them there."

"Maybe we can hand deliver them," Seth said. "I was thinking Grace and I might take a road trip this summer and drop in on each of you."

"Maybe by then I might have a love life you could put a crimp in," Jason said.

"If so, you could send them on to me," Solomon said. "I don't even need to set visitation terms, since few people want to stay in my studio for more than a day or two."

"You're welcome to stay with us. But I'd like to get back to this cryptic saying," Tom said. He gave me his best therapeutic smile, made authentic by the farmboy in him. "Ghost gnosis, Grace?"

I was glad the camera could only catch my back. I doubted I would ever hit replay.

"Do you ever feel that you are living out someone else's story?" I asked. "The person looking at you sees someone so completely different from the person you know yourself to be, you begin to feel as if you are living in a world with no gravity, no boundaries? Every word you say gets twisted around to mean something completely different. Every action you take has the consequences you most intended to avoid. It's like, right here in the middle of your own life, you have turned into a ghost—and the real ghosts, the past selves, imagined selves, old relationships, have taken over and are running everything to their own satisfaction."

I ran my knife along the table cloth, making sharp regular creases, like the bars of a cage as I talked. "When that happens, sometimes I just invite the ghosts to come back in and have their say publicly—so I can get my body and my life back."

"I think we call it projection and transference and counter-transference," Tom said. "But I know what you're getting at."

"They know things, those ghosts. If they could speak directly, I think we would all be the wiser for it. But they resist, you know, because to speak out like that, they have to admit that they're dead and we're still living."

"And we do too," Rêvé said. She rubbed her stomach gently. "With this baby coming, my dreams have been really crazy, but the mood carries over into the day. Sometimes I'm not clear whether I'm the real dream. Knowing

I'm going to have a girl, I begin to remember my mother so clearly—not like I wished she could have been, but like she really was."

"Don't start, Rêvé," Jason said sharply.

"Why not?" I asked.

"She's a totalitarian of memory, just like Mommy," Chérie said. "You have to remember it just her way, or she throws a fit." She put her fork and knife down and sat, her hands, fists clenched, on either side of her plate.

"Isn't that what she's getting at?" Solomon asked. "She's beginning to remember it differently."

"Like one of Solomon's shows," Serendipity said. She waved her fork back and forth like a pick-axe. "There you are, a neutral observer, sucked into the heart of some sexy or threatening scenario that Solomon has written and had enacted. There you are, right at the center of it. He slips you in there into the heart of someone else's drama without asking. *Without asking.*" She smiled complicitly at all these strangers, scrupulously excluding her brother.

"Like I did," I said. "All your innocent childhoods. Like I'm doing now. I apologize. Let's drop it."

"No," Seth said. "I'm kind of intrigued. I really don't know who I should invite as my ghost tonight."

"I don't think it is about inviting, Dad," Jason said. "More like possession."

I looked at Seth's son, surprised at his quickness. Jason looked anxious but also exhilarated. He put his hand up toward his dry flyaway hair, then suddenly fanned it out almost brushing Serendipity's cheek. "I know who my ghost is," he said. "It's me, but I'm about eighteen. I'm spending Thanksgiving with my roommate's family. He has one of those picture perfect families—you know, a mother who belongs to the garden club and a Bible study group, a father who is a successful lawyer, an older sister who is in medical school, a younger brother who is a high school football star, and my roommate himself, who made a perfect score on his SAT's and also was class president. Their dog doesn't fart and their cat doesn't scratch the upholstered furniture to tatters or leave half-eaten mice on the doorstep. They have no skeletons in their closets. After we sit down, the mother asks me to say something about my family—and I can't speak. It's not like I'm ashamed, really. I'm filled with this unbelievably fierce protectiveness. I see all our flaws, my mother's craziness and my father's equally crazy loyalty, the way Rêvé is pretending nothing is happening, and Chérie is taking an all-is-flow attitude that is letting all the joy flow right out of her because she refuses to count on anything, and there is me, finally out of it—meaning the chaos of my family—and completely at sea in this big, high-powered university. I look at my roommate's mother and say, 'We aren't picture book quality. We just are.' Everyone thinks I've made a joke and they laugh. When I went to call you all that night, I felt sick with remorse but I couldn't say anything about it. I could just imagine how Mom would take it—or any of the rest of you. I stayed up all night flooded with waves of shame,"

"For what?" Seth asks. "You were right. We were definitely not picture-perfect."

"Did you ever think there might be something wrong with the picture?" Solomon asked, tapping his gold eyebrow ring gently.

"Like what?" Tyler asked belligerently. "What's wrong with a happy family. Mine is."

"Sure," Rêvé said.

"Are you being a smart ass at their expense?" Tyler asked, his chest puffing out his pastel yellow shirt.

"No," she said. "At mine. I think Solomon has a point. But I know what Jason is talking about. I lied you know. After Mommy died, when we went back to college that last summer to make up our exams—"

"We both did," Chérie said quickly.

"You wouldn't if I hadn't made you—"

"I don't know if that's true," Chérie said.

"You didn't lie to me," Tom said. "Or did you?"

"What did you lie about?" Serendipity asked.

"We said she died of cancer, that we'd been expecting it for a long time," Chérie said. "We made up these stories about what she told us on her death bed."

"We got really good at this," Rêvé said. "We never planned it. I don't think we ever did it by ourselves, but if we were together, these things would just start coming out of us. We could get everyone crying within five minutes with how noble and loving she was, how she only wanted the best for us, how we were going to work all our lives to realize the promise she was never able to."

"Oh my darlings," Seth said. Tears were running down his cheeks. "If I had known—"

He reached a hand out to each of them, except their husbands, and the turkey, were in his way, and the sisters had their eyes fixed on each other, their hands folded in exactly the same way high on their bellies.

"You wouldn't have liked it, Daddy," Chérie said without turning her head. "You didn't come out looking too good. We said you left her for Grace, that you'd had this secret affair going for years. She went a little crazy, we admitted, trying to hide the truth from us."

"I kind of like this picture of my mother as a ruthless homewrecker," Solomon said. "I hope you made her tall, svelte and impossibly elegant."

I gestured to him to be quiet. Not now, I thought, completely engrossed by what was emerging.

"But once we knew the truth about Daddy and Grace, we told them," Rêvé continued, "everything made sense. Why she went to Birmingham and found this other man. The drinking. All the wild outbursts. All the crazy spending. Her possessiveness of us."

Chérie took over. "We would have done the same, we told them. It was only natural, we said. All our friends would nod with sympathy."

"We felt so *female*, so united," Rêvé said.

"We couldn't stop ourselves," Chérie added. "We had no idea where this was all coming from, but once we started it all flowed so easily."

"God, it was worse than bulimia," Rêvé said.

"And we couldn't look at each other afterwards, we would be so horrified. But the next opportunity that came up, we'd do it all over again. That was when we knew we had to get away from each other," Chérie said.

"And I always thought you married me for love," Tom looked as spooked as a sturdy farmboy could be.

"Me too," Tyler said. He just looked pissed.

"We did," the young women said.

"We do," Chérie corrected herself.

They turned then and flashed their husbands identically bright and engaging smiles.

"Care to top that?" I asked Solomon.

"I might, but not tonight,"

"You think there'll be another chance?" I goaded him.

"A little more than you bargained for, Grace?" Solomon asked.

"Not on your life," I said. "For the first time, I'm beginning to feel at home," And I was. I could feel a face, both familiar and not, taking place in all these fragments.

"I wonder what stories you are going to make up about me," Serendipity murmured to Keith, who began happily banging on his high chair.

"Scary idea, huh," Solomon gave his sister a light-hearted nudge. "What goes around comes around."

"Kind of freeing too. The one thing you know is they'll be different from anything you ever imagined," I said.

"Which is why we all need to hang around to hear them," Seth said. "Join me?" He held my eyes.

"You're going to listen to our little traitors too, aren't you, Grace?" Rêvé asked, looking at me directly, perhaps for the first time.

"With pleasure," I said without hesitation.

I felt at that moment the same wave that had once washed over me when I first saw Serendipity, except that now there was no fierceness in it, just a startled and bemused awe at what life makes of us, we make of it. Except when I looked at Seth, then all that fierceness flooded in again, and with it the deepest relief because I knew what to do, that it wasn't a question of rising to the occasion but sinking into it, letting it lift us. I knew we would find our safety there, year after year after year.

DUTY BOUND

It's interesting how people are so eager to put words in your mouth. The more ambiguous the situation, the quicker they are. Take lingering death, for example. Or, more exactly, lingering dying.

"After all these months, years really, it must feel anticlimactic," my mother said coming in the front door as the men from the funeral home wheeled Sven out through the garage.

My mother has a taste for highs and lows. I have dedicated my life to everything that lies between these extremes, as close to the median as possible. "A tortoise has more bravura," is the way I heard my mother once describe me.

"My sweet certitude," Sven said last week as he rose to consciousness briefly before slipping back into the morphine haze that would see him through to his next, best, life. He didn't even have to search the room, he knew where I'd be sitting, in my armchair at the foot of the bed, facing him, the morning light from the window gleaming down on my book.

"Now it's *your* time, Laura," my best friend Justine said as she helped me make arrangements for the funeral. "Leif is on his own. You're going to learn to spread your wings."

"So you think champagne is in order?" I asked, looking up from my shopping list. "Or should we stick to coffee and tea? Mulled cider?"

I'd tried to discuss the arrangements with Sven, but he just yawned and said he would leave it up to me.

"Just don't get your hopes up about attendance, Laura," he warned me. "People have written me off for several years now." There was no rancor there. It was just a statement, a fact of life. Sven is—was—an engineer. He took calm satisfaction in facts, emotional as well as physical. We are who we are was Sven's opinion. It doesn't matter why. What matters is functioning, each of us, at our best. A screw can't do what it's suited for if it's being asked to be a nail. He knew us all and never blinked, loved us because of, not in spite of ourselves: my mother, chemically imbalanced in a way lithium couldn't effectively control; our son Leif with his fine mind, good heart, and a stubborn streak that could turn oppositional at the least resistance; and me, above all, me, with the temperament of a work horse, willing to assume any yoke, steady in my incessant round.

"It's time to kick your traces," Justine said as if reading my mind.

"Do you really see me as a beast of burden?" I asked her. "Nothing was imposed on me, you know."

"Don't I though. You're my best friend—who has *chosen* to spend most of her life, scratch that, *all* your life, thinking about others." Justine rearranged her glittering orange and red pashmina shawl, her gold earrings making a cheerful clatter. "But we're going to change all that."

One thing I loved about Sven is that he rarely said we. He usually said, "Laura and I—"

"We're doing fine," I would tell people the first time Sven went through chemo. "Thank you for asking."

"Remember, Laura, *we* are not sick. *We* are not dying," he would say. "There's such a thing as taking togetherness too far."

"Thank you for sticking by me," he said last spring when we learned the metatheses had gone to his brain as well as his spinal column, that this time—our fourth in ten years—there were no more options.

"Don't thank me," I told him. "Anyone would do it." Anyone might have done it, perhaps, but that wasn't why thanks weren't required or appropriate. Thanks imply volition—and it wasn't a choice for me. It was a necessity. A personal necessity. I couldn't fathom my life without him. I still can't.

"Don't sell yourself short, Laura," he said to me. "What you have done is a great kindness. I see it. I appreciate it."

Sven had wanted me to call in hospice months earlier than I did. He didn't want me to take leave from work.

"This has very little to do with you, Sven. It's what *I* signed on for. In sickness and health. I know you would do the same for me.

"Yes," he agreed. He was making his usual breakfast of oatmeal and toast. He was still able to get around on his own at that point. He was wearing his pale blue pajamas and a red silk paisley robe. He was, even in illness, a snappy dresser. "But I wouldn't mind being thanked for it, having it seen."

What *I* wanted as Justine helped me plan the memorial service and reception was that people could see how much Sven had given me *all* his life, even these last few years when, it is true, many of our acquaintances had written him off as dead, worse than dead, really, because of the care still required. Monthly lawn maintenance at the cemetery would have been easier to acknowledge than all those bedpans, stomach tubes, IVs, the sheer time it takes to die, the drudgery of it.

But I'm not like Sven. I don't accept our limits. I want us to improve ourselves, do the work of nails even if we are screws. At that moment, for example, I wanted to be more like him. Instead I was seething at Justine and my mother's tactlessness. I was wondering what was keeping Leif.

We are just having a small memorial service and reception. Sven's parents were older and died before he got ill. The minister at the Unitarian church we have attended sporadically over the years is going to officiate. Several of Sven's colleagues from the state environmental office where he worked for twenty years are going to come and speak, although they seemed a little abashed when I asked them. How many years, they were wondering, had it been since they'd last talked with him. (Sven had taken early retirement, two years ago, after his second recurrence.) My colleagues from the library are coming, and Justine, who is going to sing "Wind Beneath My Wings." Leif is going to say something as well.

"And you, Laura? You knew him most intimately," the Rev. Marilyn Moskowitz said when she came to discuss the service. Justine had just left with the shopping list, kindly taking my mother with her.

"I could never put it into words," I said.

When she looked puzzled, I added, "What it means to me that he's dead. What I wish it meant to others as well. It is the deepest loneliness, knowing that no one except Sven ever knew me that way—the way that can hurt like this—and that no one else ever will."

Reverend Marilyn was thumbing through her book of interfaith funeral readings. "Rumi? Heschel? Buber? Kahlil Gibran? Mary Oliver?" She looked up and smiled sympathetically. "This sounds like Rumi, I think."

"No, it sounds like me, Laura Sorenson, married for two-thirds of my life to a man who, like me, was in no way extraordinary, but who saw me in a way that made me feel that I, my life, *our* life, was extraordinary—a way that, for the life of me, I cannot do alone."

Rev. Marilyn looked at me assessingly. She was sixty-five and happily divorced for many years, the mother of five: two ardently righteous Unitarians, one equally ardent and righteous orthodox Jew, one new age Sufi, and one socially tolerant evangelical. "Sometimes I wonder if I'd found my calling earlier, they would all be happily unchurched and we could eat a holiday meal in peace," she'd once said in a sermon on the challenges of holidays in interfaith families. But at this point, Rev. Marilyn was brushing back her unruly gray hair, straightening her embroidered peasant shirt and trying to decide if I needed a suicide watch.

"We have bereavement groups at the church," she said quietly. "And I know most hospices offer them too."

"Don't worry," I told her. "I may feel bereft, but I know my responsibilities. I have a son I need to set a model for, a mother and father who soon will be needing my active support. Sven's death isn't all about me. You don't need to point that out."

We both took deep breaths, shocked at the real venom in my voice. But venom at whom, at what? How could I *not* be prepared for this moment? *We* had been fighting this cancer in all its cruel and malicious insinuations and onslaughts for a decade. There were living wills, power of attorney, funeral plans, trust funds all in place.

"Can we proceed with the service?" I asked, my voice softer, steadier.

I lifted the teapot and gestured at her cup and Rev. Marilyn nodded, relieved but still wary. She added some sugar, stirred it, looked around our dining room.

"This is a warm and restful space," she said. She looked at the photographs on the walls. They were very large, of spring flowers, flowering meadows.

"Are they paintings?"

"Giclée prints on canvas."

She looked at them and back to me, another expression, different but equally assessing. She had a robustness about her I liked—not just of body but of gesture, voice. It could have been earth motherish except her mind was too analytic. For example, at present she was clearly trying to decide if the work was mine or Sven's or, possibly, our son's, and what each of these possibilities might mean—and what impact it might have if she phrased the question inaccurately.

"I like them," she said. "There's something distinctive, fresh about them—but I can't quite figure out how it gets there. The subjects are conventional, but there's something that makes you look at them more closely—and then more closely at what's around you too."

As she said that, I realized that's what I wanted the memorial service to do as well. I could do that with an image, I had no idea how to do it in life.

"Did Sven have a favorite?" she asked, seeming to read my thoughts.

"Just take them, Laura," Sven would tell me. "I'll curate." And decorate. For two such ordinary people, we had a vivid house and garden. Sven took responsibility for the house, I for the garden. This gender reversal surprised others and suited us both. I began to take the photographs during that sad time in my thirties when we tried so hard to conceive. I would focus my camera on a lily or rose, willing the redness of my menstrual blood to recede from consciousness, willing my eyes, still blurred with tears of fury as much as despair, back into focus. Once we adopted Leif, I stopped photographing with any regularity for a decade. Returned to it as Leif entered adolescence and Sven began his losing contest with his insubordinate cells. Each month I'd bring Sven the images that I'd shot that month, and he'd choose one for us to enlarge, print and frame. Leif would hang them, making wisecracks.

"So, does this mean we're going to reupholster in fuchsia, Dad?"

"Puce," Sven would answer with his rich laugh, so at odds with his thin, worn face.

Leif, always quick on the uptake, would say, "Got to do the rest another day, Dad. I have a hot date with my band."

"There's one in the study he was really fond of," I said, rising. "Let me show you."

I led Rev. Marilyn into the study, which was decorated in straw and blue. The photograph was of a large, still lake we had visited in New Hampshire one summer. The lake reflected the sky, both a clear accepting blue, surrounded by deep green pines, and the three of us standing at the end of a wooden dock, Leif towering between us, his right arm loosely around my shoulders, his left more firmly supporting Sven. He was fifteen and already six-three, ebony black, ravishingly handsome, assured. It was typical of Leif that just by his presence, the energy he exuded, he made Sven and I, both so wan after the winter and that first round of chemo, look radiant as well.

"Smile," he said. "I don't want to run and set that remote again."

But he did, without complaint, twenty more times, until we all agreed we had created an image of us as a family that couldn't be improved. We were all laughing, at ease with one another and with the occasion, *up to it* in some way we hadn't realized until then.

Rev. Marilyn looked at the photo. It took up much of the inner wall, seeming to resonate with the clear sky visible through the sliding glass door behind Sven's desk. Sven titled this one, I told her: *Love Before, Love After*.

"Have Leif bring it over," she said. "We'll put it in front of the pulpit."

After I showed her out, I went back into the study and sat at Sven's desk and stared at the photo again. We were of a height, Sven and I. Equally thin, undistinguished in feature. As was our habit, our windbreakers matched, a bright red that year. Leif's, for once, did too.

The balance in the image was perfect. The three figures, the length of the lake, the reflected mountain encasing us. I wanted with all my soul to turn around and dive into that lake, break its perfect surface, sink like a stone.

I heard the door bang, Leif calling out loudly, "Where you be, Be? I've brought someone I want you to meet."

Everything about Leif is too much for our house, our lives, and once he had come into them, neither Sven nor I would have had it any other way, could imagine it any other way.

"Coming," I said, but Leif met me in the living room, a tall, pretty, very thin young woman with what I thought of as a chemo cut, an elegant one, in tow. She had on skin tight jeans, a waist hugging red leather coat.

Her name was Cocoa, Leif announced. "For obvious reasons," he added with a smile.

Cocoa stepped forward and put out her hand. "Mrs. Sorenson, I hope you don't feel my presence is an intrusion at this time."

"I insisted, Be," Leif said. "This is such an important point in our lives. I wanted Cocoa to be part of it." He put his hand on her shoulder. They both looked, compassionately, down on me.

I looked straight into Leif's chest as I spoke. "I'm sorry you couldn't have come earlier. Leif's father would have liked to have met you, met anyone so important to Leif, before he died."

I didn't really care how they read this since I couldn't decipher my own feelings, they were coming in such a rush. Since *when?* Why now? What do you expect me to do with this?

"Will you be staying with us, Cocoa?" I asked, eyes still fixed on the half-pulled zipper of Leif's black windbreaker, after a long, discomfort inducing pause.

Cocoa glanced hesitantly at Leif.

"The guestroom," I said. "The sheets are fresh. I just changed them this morning."

I had changed them for myself. The guest room was where I'd been sleeping these last six months since we'd moved the hospital bed into our bedroom. Sven had wanted it the other way, but I wanted him to stay there, exactly as he was, where our marriage bed had once been. I'd still not arranged to have his bed removed, or our own bed returned. I didn't think I wanted that. There was no going back now, no use pretending either.

Leif looked as if he was going to say something about sharing a room, but I forestalled him. I wasn't going to do a bed check, of course, but I wanted some indication that the purpose of this visit was Sven's death, not the obliviousness of young love.

"Take your suitcases up, will you, Leif? Then I could use some help down here." I added, "You can take all the time getting settled that you need, Cocoa. I won't put you to work immediately."

I went back into the kitchen, where I was beginning to prepare ginger muffins.

When Leif came in, he enveloped me in a hug and whispered in my ear, "Trust me, Be. I have my reasons. I miss Bop as much as you. If he were still here, I'd have been bringing Cocoa here to see you both."

"What is she to you?"

Leif was always bringing people home with him, had been since he was a boy.

"It's his way," Sven said. "Doesn't mean we have to accept all of them."

Like the Russian, Andrei, smelling of piss and sweat and cheap wine, his hands grimy with oil, who Leif had met waiting for an oil change. He'd just been fired. "Without coss. Without coss," Andrei insisted. Leif wanted Andrei to be his Russian tutor.

"A native speaker," he said excitedly. "Here in Marietta." Leif was sixteen, already chafing at the constraints of our small Ohio town. Andrei, when he left five days later, relieved us of our entire liquor supply, our old TV and a tape player, and we felt we'd gotten off easy.

Undeterred, Leif brought home a college football star, Bummer, who he was teaching to read. "He only tests at fifth grade," he confided to us. "But he knows when people are scamming him, and he can play all the games he's ever been in forward and backward in his mind. In three dimensions. Wild!"

After college, where Leif majored in sociology and minored in psychology, he volunteered for Teach for America. He decided to go back to graduate school in social psychology. He's fascinated by how completely what we feel drives what we think.

"It all happens without ever hitting consciousness," he would tell us. "Whether we decide someone is trustworthy or dangerous."

The way I did with Cocoa. One look at her and I knew. One look at Leif, and I knew that he didn't. Maybe never would. And that it was impossible to bring it up. Ever. Hadn't he already warned me: "It's not about reasoning, don't you see, Be? It's not about talk. It's about intuition, temperament, tuning in, and resonance." Oh, how intensely I had missed Sven as I looked at this lovely woman who, I knew, had my huge, credulous son wrapped around her slender index finger already.

You would think a boy with Leif's history would grow up angry, deeply distrustful. But he didn't. There isn't a person in the world, I've come to believe, that Leif wouldn't give the benefit of the doubt.

At the same time, I've never felt, at least until now, that I had to protect him. In part it is his size. He's gentle but he's also very fit, so at six-foot three there is always this tacit potential for force that creates a protective field around him. In part it is his social acumen. It's not that Leif doesn't see what's going on, it's just that he gives people, and the stories we're always weaving in and between ourselves, the benefit of the doubt. Hope, it seems, is hard-wired in him.

By the time he was three, when he came to us through foster care, Leif had been abandoned five times by his mother. Reunited as well. She was an addict, eighteen when she died, killed not by heroin but by a boyfriend's blow to her head. When a neighbor found them, the door to their apartment wide open, Leif had been sitting beside her lifeless body for six hours.

"She wake up soon we have Fruit Loops. My momma like to take her time," he told the neighbor, Mrs. Coombs. He was stroking his mother's cool cheek. "My momma very pretty. This time round she be good, she be clean, she not leave her Leelown."

When the police asked about the boyfriend, Leif put his hands to his head and rocked back and forth, repeating, "He sorry. He so sorry. So sorry.

So sorry."

We wept when we were told this. But the boy who was brought in to us was as tall and as poised as a five year old. He gave us a radiant smile and climbed right into my arms.

"My name Leelown. I come home with you."

And he did, and he never left. It was our first—and last—foster placement. Given how quickly and passionately both Sven and I attached to him, we wouldn't have been good candidates for foster parents. We didn't have a flow-through mentality, a cosmic trust. This dear boy had had enough trauma, we decided, for an entire lifetime. We were not going to leave him vulnerable to more. There was some objection to a cross-racial adoption from DFACS (not to endless limbo, mind you, just to permanent, cross-racial resolution). But since his mother's immediate and extended family didn't want him and his father was unknown, and he had already developed a close bond with us as the judge observed, DFACS's objections were duly noted and then over-ruled.

Sven and I were delighted, relieved, and we also had no illusions. Leelown would have been just as happy with any other couple who responded to him as warmly as we had.

We watched him so closely those first months, ready to talk to him about the terrible trauma of his mother's death, those six hours he'd spent patiently grooming and mollifying her corpse. We readied ourselves to deal with any behavioral manifestations of distress over all those abandonments. But there were none. There were two constants in Leelown's short life. His mother left erratically and just as erratically returned—and the world, white and black, reliably took him in during the interims.

He came to us in September, and he and I spent those next two months out in the garden. That's how he got his new name. He was in love with the changing leaves of the maples. I'd given him his own garden plot and as I turned beds, planted chrysanthemums, he would race wildly around the lawn chasing the leaves as they fell. He would take them over to his plot and carefully set them down on the turned earth. When he captured another one, he would take it back and revise his pattern on the basis of the size, color, and number of the leaves.

I would come over to watch, fascinated by his concentration.

"Lee me lone," he would say. "Lee me lone." I could hear his mother speaking. It was eerie. Painful. His shoulders would hunch a little in a way

I understood. He wanted to burrow into that pattern. That was the only defensive stance I ever saw him take. When I stepped back a few feet, his shoulders expanded. He could arrange and rearrange his leaves contentedly for hours at a time. I could watch him equally contentedly.

"And what did you do today?" Sven would ask in the evening.

"OCD therapy," I said. "We both feel much better."

But there was this moment first thing in the morning when Leelown went out and saw that his vivid leaves had turned brown overnight when something like despair would cross his trusting face. He would turn around, look up at the trees, and stretch up his arms beseechingly.

"Leelown leafing. Leelown leafing," he would cry.

I would take his hands and swing him around in circles. "Laura turning her new Leaf. Laura turning her new Leaf."

"Flying," he'd yell. "We be flying like the leafs."

And we were. Soaring free. So, when the adoption papers came through, we changed his name. No more Leelown. Leif among the brilliant leavings of the maples. I took a photo of him, on his haunches, arranging his leaves. Another of him emerging from the huge pile of leaves Sven raked and raked again for him on the weekends that fall.

Within the year, it was as if Leif had always been with us. When people would glance at us on the street, these two rather prim white people in their matching jackets and their exuberant black child wearing whatever fed his fancy, it would truly surprise us. It was as if we had collective amnesia. For us, there had been no life before Leif. For Leif, there had been no life before Be Bop, the names Sven had strategically but playfully given us (to avoid any association with mom or dad). Leif had gleefully adopted them.

"Where you be, Bop?" he'd call to Sven.

"Where your bop, Be?" Sven would call to me and I'd start dancing.

We didn't lie to Leif, but we deliberately misled him about the circumstances of his adoption. We told him his mother had been very young when she had him, which was true. We said that she'd been in an accident and had died when he was three, which was true.

"What kind of accident?" he would ask.

"A sad one," we would say. "She loved you very much."

"But she died," Leif would say. "And now you are my family."

"Forever," we would all say.

When Leif was fifteen he was beginning to ask more questions and

Sven and I were trying to decide how to answer him. We were wildly reluctant to give up the story we had made, by omission as much as anything else, of a young, dedicated mother relinquishing her beloved child only through tragic early death. Of course, there were holes in it you could drive a dump truck through. Leif knew that; we did too.

But all that got tabled with Sven's diagnosis and the tough year of treatment that followed. The possibility of losing his father was of far more immediate concern—although Leif, being Leif, refused to let us brood on that possibility.

He went to the library, went on the internet. "You're in charge of the basics," he told me. "Food, water, vomit, clean sheets. Dr. Gramsci is in charge of pharmaceuticals. I'm head coach for holistics."

He bought vitamins for his father, had him out walking or practicing tai chi in the garden just as soon as the nausea eased after treatment sessions. He shaved his head in solidarity when Sven lost his hair and bought them both a range of fedoras, straw hats, and bandannas and had them each pierce an ear. He rented funny movies and had us watch them together every evening. And he became calculatedly needy over his last years in high school. He needed our advice about what AP classes to take. He needed us to read through his research papers. He needed us to go on college visits with him. To read the essays he was writing for his college applications (about how much he was learning from Sven and me and our responses to Sven's illness). He needed Sven to teach him how to tie a bow tie for prom night. He needed to have me help him choose a corsage. He needed both of us to go to his karate demonstrations, his band performances, his graduation. He needed us to welcome his human strays, like Andrei and Bummer and Machiavelli, the schizophrenic grocery clerk at the natural foods store.

Even through college, he spent all his vacations and summers with us. When we suggested he might want to travel, he said, "Look, this is *my* choice and it's a selfish one. I like the amenities of home. I know they have a time limit. I've got to be on my own sometime soon. I'm just staving off the inevitable." He looked around the house, gestured to my latest photograph, to the big black lounger Sven had bought to try to ease his chronic neuropathy, to the flat screen TV. "Hell, I'm greedy. I want everything you're willing to give. Free laundry. Catering. Can you blame me?"

And he meant it. I heard him once with a girlfriend we'd never met. Her name may have been Jasmine. Leif talked about his girlfriends often, drawing us into discussions about the "psychodynamics of juvenile romance," but we rarely met them. His strays were all male. He showed us photos of his girlfriends, though, and talked with them openly on the phone; he just never brought them home or invited them to join us when we made rare trips to Philadelphia to see him at Penn.

"I just don't want anyone to get their hopes up," he said. "I'm not ready to get tied down. I'm loyal, but I'm a free agent. I make that clear."

It was, obviously, not always that clear—and the girlfriends, given Leif's natural warmth, tended to blame us. There were occasional calls late at night where one or the other of them couldn't believe he was out. "Would you just hand that phone over to him, please. I *need* to talk with him," one of them said to us.

The next day, I heard Leif say, "I keep telling you, this is my choice. They're not asking me to be here. They're certainly not coming between us—and I sure as hell don't want *you* coming between me and them. I *want* to be here. They've given me so much, I want to give back what I can. And the time is now. Something happens to my dad, I don't want to look back and say, 'I should have—' I don't want that on *my* conscience. I don't want that unfinished business in *my* bag."

"Sorry about that," he told me thinking I hadn't heard. "She won't be calling back."

At the time I was shocked. Sven was three years into remission at that point. We—or I at least—at the time still naively believed in cure. And Leif had been the one who had been the most adamantly, genuinely upbeat about Sven's chances. Honestly, I felt betrayed, like Leif was leaving some opening, however small, for those malevolent cells to infiltrate our lives again. I had, however unreasonably, expected more of him.

Sometime in August before his senior year in college, something happened between Leif and Sven. It was like they had come to some private agreement that this was to be Leif's last summer with us. Sven had learned that his cancer had returned. A single lesion on his lung they thought they could treat successfully with radiation. No metatheses. But he didn't want his own health to sway Leif's decisions anymore. He talked to Leif about all this before he did to me. It took me a long time to get over that.

From then on, Leif started talking about what he was planning to do after college and his hometown did not factor into it at all. In prospect, the world was his oyster. Teaching English in China. Graduate school in

Amsterdam. A back-packing trip through Turkey and Greece. Human rights observations in Sudan or Sri Lanka.

Sven took up each suggestion with gusto, genuine seriousness. It was when Leif decided on Teach for America and was assigned to an inner city high school in Detroit that the questions about his mother surfaced again.

"I look at these girls in my classes, BeBop," he told us on a conference call. "They're fifteen years old and flaunting bellies big as basketballs. They have no idea what they're in for. No idea what those *babies* are in for. It makes me crazy angry. Sad I could understand. But angry?"

Sven and I looked at each other, trying to decide who should speak.

"It's the situation," Sven said. "You're angry because it is so hard to intervene on something so diffuse, so systemic."

"With such personal consequences," I added.

"We're duty bound to tell him," Sven said. "I'm sure somewhere in him he knows what happened."

"We're duty bound, we always have and always will be, to keep him as safe as we possibly can," I said.

"No," Sven said flatly. "He's a man now. We're not duty bound to do anything, Laura, except tell him the truth—and love him, as we can and as much as we can." He reached over and took my hand. We were sitting at the breakfast table. It was early spring, just a few crocus blooming close to the ground, the daffodil stalks pressing up quickly, so very green. "Leif isn't asking us to protect him from his past. He's wanting to free himself by knowing. Who's to say he doesn't remember? Maybe not in words, or even in images. But somewhere in him he knows abandonment, he knows violence in a way we never can."

I felt such a sense of desolation wash over me that I had to leave the room. Sven found me in Leif's room lying on his bed, staring at the stars we'd glued to his ceiling twenty years earlier.

"When my mother would go into the hospital," I said, "I would lie like this in my own room, in my own bed. There were no stars on the ceiling. There was a crack that had the habit of looking exactly like what it was—a dividing line. It split the room in half. I would run my eyes up and down its ragged length, checking to see if it had widened. But it was always hair thin. It ran from the beginning to the end of my room, dividing everything."

Sven sat down beside me and put his hand on my head as if I were still that little girl. "Like Leif's mother's death divided his life for him. Like my illness divided my life for me."

"For *us*," I wanted to say. "Like it divided our blessed new life *for us*."

Instead, I said, "My dad would let me lie like that for an afternoon, sometimes even into the evening, then he'd come in with a legal pad and say, 'Laura, your mother is going to come home again before you know it. Before that we are duty bound to complete the following—'

"He'd have this long list written down there, half real tasks, half fun or crazy things. Do the laundry, sort nails, eat six ice-cream sandwiches each, get to school and work on time, read eight story books aloud to each other, see five movies, vacuum, defrost the refrigerator, clean the toilets. There was a box to check beside each item. And we did, you know. Each time, we checked them all off—even if it meant eating four ice-cream sandwiches in a row the night before my mother was released again. It became our code. When my mother began to get manic or insensate with depression, I'd just get a legal pad and pen and hand it to him and we'd begin the process again."

Sven smiled at me as he stood up. "So, when we tell Leif the truth and nothing but the truth, what duty bound list do you want to give him? I think life has already given him a pretty long one and he's already busy checking them off, don't you?"

But I had not wanted our love to be an assuagement for Leif, much less a chore. I wanted it to erase everything that had come before. A desire as totally unrealistic as my desire that Sven be cured once and for all. As all-encompassing.

When Leif learned more about his mother, he started a pregnancy prevention class for young men at the school where he was teaching. He also got interested in trauma and early child development, getting involved in early identification and intervention programs.

"I feel duty bound to stand up and say, 'Risk isn't destiny. Just look at me.' These scientists and counselors, they don't know it, but even when they say they're being positive, there's this conviction they have that people are irremediably marked, permanently *damaged*. I just can't accept that," he told us on one of his increasingly infrequent visits.

Just like cancer, I remember thinking. This was during the third of Sven's remissions. I had looked from my vibrant son to my relaxed husband, tanned from our recent trip to the beach, ready to return to work. I was so delighted in both of them. Hope was still instinctual.

"What *is* she to you?" I asked Leif again.

"The one," he said simply. "The only one I've been willing to bring home. That says something, Be. But I'm not rushing things. Although I wish I'd brought her earlier. Bop would have liked her."

But *why* was she the only one he'd brought home? Why did I have such a bad feeling about her? *Was* it a chemo cut she was so stylishly sporting? Was it something else?

When Cocoa joined us in the kitchen, Leif showed her the legal pad. "This is duty's bound. The rest is ad lib, ad hoc."

"I'll help you with the photo," I said.

"Cocoa's taller."

I just nodded, returned to my baking. I scanned my list trying to decide where to focus next. Sugar cookies. Apple Brown Betty. Cranberry scones. Mulled cider.

Sven had died on the anniversary of the day Leif first came to us. I was making all their favorites. I looked out on our back lawn, yellow and red with unraked leaves. It suddenly felt unspeakably important to tend to them. Immediately. I left the creamed sugar and butter in the mixer, the flour in its bag, the baking powder in its tin.

While I was raking, Leif came out to ask me for directions to the church.

"I can do that when I get back, Be."

"It soothes me," I said.

"Cocoa is coming with me," he said. I nodded, my attention already back on the leaves.

When I finished raking, I selected some of the brightest leaves and laid them in an erratic path from the door of Sven's study all the way across the lawn. Before and after. I just couldn't decide which side of the lawn was which.

Why, at this moment, was I responding to Cocoa's presence as if it was more tragic than Sven's death? All it was—was unexpected.

"Laura," my mother called shrilly. "What happened?" She pushed the kitchen door open.

I stepped across the line of leaves. I still didn't know which side was before and which was after, just knew, as usual, that I needed to be on the opposite side from her, so beautiful, so flamboyant, so unpredictable, even at eighty-four.

And alive, unjustly alive while Sven, *my* Sven was dead.

"I took the muffins out. They may be a little too dark, but with that molasses, it's hard to tell. I've never seen you leave your kitchen like that. I couldn't help but fear the worst."

"Which would be what, Mother?" I shook my head before she could answer, went back into the house, surveyed the kitchen, checked the baking list again and set to work.

Justine, who reads behavior fluently, came up and whispered in my ear, "See you tomorrow. Meet you at the church an hour early so we can set up."

"Are you taking her with you?"

"She just wants to help. Have her cut cookies. Your dad will be here in an hour."

But I felt, after almost sixty years, unwilling to be my mother's keeper for another minute. I was quite aware that as soon as Sven's ashes were scattered, all the eulogies said, I was duty bound to turn my attention to my aging parents. But not that day. Just that once, whatever I said to Rev. Marilyn, I wanted it *all* to be about me. I felt as if I was breathing dirt. I didn't know it would hurt this much. I didn't know it would hurt this way, as if I were paralyzed, being buried alive, a shovel at a time. It was the slowness that was getting to me. The end looked like oblivion. Oblivion looked like heaven. But it was a damned long way off.

Before leaving, Justine got my mom busy in the dining room folding napkins, counting plastic spoons, forks, knives. But as soon as her car pulled out, my mother was in the kitchen again, girlishly pulling a chair up to the counter where I was rolling out the cookie dough as if she was ready for a heart to heart. I pushed my hair from my face, the dough catching in my bangs. My mother looked pained.

How my mother's exquisite features led to ones as ordinary as mine was a question she had openly and repeatedly pondered in my presence since I was a child. But today her attention was elsewhere.

"So what do you think of Cocoa?"

"How do you know about Cocoa?"

"We passed Leif on the way back and he pulled over and introduced her. What a lovely girl. You must feel so good about this."

I took a deep breath, brushing my hair back again with my floury hand. I had a cookie cutter in the shape of a little hand that I hadn't used for years, but I dug it out. I kept punching the dough, pulling the extraneous dough away, leaving empty hand after empty hand as my mother chattered on.

"I was never sure, the way he grew up, whether he'd come home with a white girl or a black one. Seems like he came up with the best of both worlds, what do you think? I think she looks a little like that famous model, don't you?" my mother prattled on.

"I think I miss Sven," I said. "I think it would have been better for Leif to wait a week before bringing her here. She doesn't need to attend the funeral of a total stranger."

I'm sure Sven would see just what I do: she's sick.

After dinner, which Leif ordered in from the local Thai restaurant, Cocoa said, "I have to thank you, Mrs. Sorenson, for raising such a wonderful man. He's been a godsend to me this year. A lot of guys would have run when they learned."

"Learned what?" I answered so quickly my heart didn't have time to sink.

"My grade point average," she said and laughed with abandon.

Cocoa was in Leif's program. A year behind, but catching up fast, he joked. She, too, was living proof risk wasn't destiny.

Cocoa was one of eight children her mother had, over the years, surrendered to foster care. She'd never been adopted, just graduated from private homes to group settings, which she claimed to like better. "I was always popular, either setting, but in the group home I had a larger sphere of influence—with both the kids and the caretakers—and I liked that. It was never boring. And it was great preparation for what I do now." Already she was managing one of the intervention projects for foster children.

Cocoa remained at the table with me while Leif went off to prepare his remarks for the service.

"Besides your grade point average, what might Leif have run from?" I asked.

Cocoa looked directly at me. She turned her water glass in her hands.

"I have Crohn's disease. And lupus. The prognosis for each is poor. They are chronic and progressive, but worse than that they are erratic. Some day, some time, I'm going to need help. That's not exactly a turn on."

Except for someone like my son, I thought.

I said goodnight to the two of them early and went upstairs into our bedroom and lay in Sven's hospital bed. I pulled the sides up around me and turned off the lamp. The curtains were open and the window perfectly framed the rising moon, a thin crescent. I lay on my side, framing it yet again between the bars.

I had been prepared, once Sven died, to accept more responsibility for my parents who, well into their eighties, were still living at home. My mother was remarkably healthy given the wide range of medications she had taken all these years to try to control her moods. My father had had both knees and one hip replaced and was considering replacing the other one. I'd been thinking of moving them into our house, perhaps in two years if I took an early retirement. But my father told me as he was leaving that evening that he had arranged for them to move within two months to an assisted living facility with graduated care.

"That way, if something happens to me before your mother, she will have company," he said.

When I started to object, he said, "You did too much of that as a child, Laura. You don't have to do it now." He put his hand on my shoulder, partly for support, partly to reassure me. "There's no question that you would. And I don't want there to be any question that you should. You shouldn't." When he saw me starting to object, he said, "The papers are signed. I've given the deposit. Sven and I talked about this several times. We were of one mind. Neither of us wanted to saddle you with that responsibility."

The thought of the two of them discussing me, my best interest, should have angered me. Who were they to decide? But it didn't.

I pulled my legs up under my skirt, tucked my hands inside my sweater. The days were still warm but the nights chilled quickly. I should make the bed, I thought, but the inertia felt insuperable. I had no idea I was so tired.

I felt Sven leaning over the bed, brushing my hair. I kept my eyes on that sickle moon. I didn't know if it was waxing or waning. I could feel my finger running slowly, dangerously, over that whetted inner curve. I could feel my wrist repeating the same movement, testing the same sharp edge.

I was never so free as when I cared for you.

Sven took a deep breath. "I know, Laura," he said kindly.

But it isn't the freedom I want for my son, I thought. But thinking isn't the right word for this knowing which was faster than thought, searing as a hot brand.

I was fifty when Sven was first diagnosed. I knew my limits. This challenge to help Sven fell squarely inside them. We had already been married thirty years. The same freedom wasn't, couldn't be, available to my son at twenty-five.

Had I, with all my talk of duty, of the inevitability of my own choice, foreclosed Leif's life so dramatically? The idea, just the idea, felt more unbearable than the reality of Sven's death. Indeed it felt like the death of everything Sven and I had fought for. We had never wanted to burden Leif. We had wanted to do the opposite.

I could hear Leif and Cocoa talking downstairs. Leif had put on some Bach cello that Sven had particularly liked. They were laughing about something. Their voices sounded so young, so heart-rendingly young.

I thought of Leif, little Leelown, sitting beside his mother, stroking her cheek, ready to wait an eternity for her to wake. A dark wave rolled over me, icy cold. I didn't want him to sacrifice himself for anyone, ever.

"You must promise me," Sven had said to me toward the end, "That you will express your freedom differently next time—that you will show you can say no as well as yes."

I rolled into a ball and pushed up. Lowered the side of the bed. I went into the guestroom to get my laptop, which I stored in a drawer in the end table beside the bed. Cocoa had arranged her perfume and makeup on top of the bureau, hung her clothes neatly on hangers in the closet, shoulder to shoulder with my own. *Didn't waste a minute did you. Made yourself right at home,* I thought.

She had even set two framed photos beside the bed. One was of an older woman, obviously related, still a beauty in her old age. Mother? Grandmother? I wasn't sure. The other was of a little girl who also bore a marked resemblance to her. I had just gone over to look at them more closely when Cocoa pushed open the door, Leif close behind her. I pulled the laptop close to my chest and turned. My own house, my own bedroom, and I was acting like an intruder.

"Sorry. I needed some things for the night."

"That's more than all right," Cocoa said magnanimously. "Can I help you carry anything?"

"Leif can." I pointed to the two photographs on the wall, the one of Leif with his fall garden and the one of him emerging from the leaf pile. "Would you mind bringing those with you?" I asked him.

"Is that *you*, honey?" Cocoa asked going up and looking at them. "How sweet."

Sweet. I thought of the intensity of Leelown's concentration as he tried to find a place for everything that was sweeping down at him from the sky, rising up from the ground. The implacable patience with which he returned, day after day, to arrange and rearrange until something true and sure could enter him and something else leave and he could finally turn and enter the world again. I thought of me sitting there with my camera for hours studying him with an equally implacable concentration. *I wanted to be ready.*

Leif lifted the photographs from their hooks and followed me. I set the laptop down on the bedside table.

"Just put them up on the bureau," I told him. "Do you have any memory of that day?"

Leif turned to me, smiling. "You know, I actually do, Be. It was the day I decided it might be worthwhile to let you in. The day I decided to live again. Not that at three I put it that way. I just remember something falling into place, and it was like a key turned in me, I felt safe. I think it's the way Bop made you feel up to the very end."

He turned and took my hands. "It's the way I feel with Cocoa, Be. When I understood that what she needs fits so neatly with who I am, something opened up so wide in me. I feel free in a way I can't explain. If I hadn't seen how you and Bop were with each other, especially how you were with him, I don't know that I'd trust it."

"But why *her*, Leif," I blurted. "Why not someone who has only one chronic disease?" I stopped, horrified.

He stared at me, too big for that room, too big for that house, too big for my diminished life, just as he had always been, and started to laugh—and I did too. "You know the answer as well as I do. Because it *feels* right. Because being with her *feels* good. Because it makes me feel like *me*."

There is a moment when you are taking a photo when you know all the elements are in perfect balance, that if you click the shutter the radiance will be sealed in there permanently. It is a perfect stillness and a perfect exhilaration, both. You know it, you experience it, and yet you don't move a finger because this way your continued presence, your continued awareness are necessary for its continued existence. I felt that this was such a moment for Sven, that even now he held us in his attention just so, and I knew Leif felt it too and that to know ourselves as willing parts of that radiance made up for so much.

"There's going to be a day, " Leif said, "years from now, when we'll share what you said with Cocoa and we will all laugh. I *promise* you that, Be."

I blinked my eyes to clear them. Click. I could see the fullness of the moon flowing out, soft, milky, from its brilliant, knife-sharp rim. Click. I could see my son's dark hair haloing wildly as he turned to meet his risk, his destiny as freely as Sven and I ever did. Click. And there would be more, I knew, to follow.

Where's your Be, Bop?
Where's your bop, Be?
Flowing.

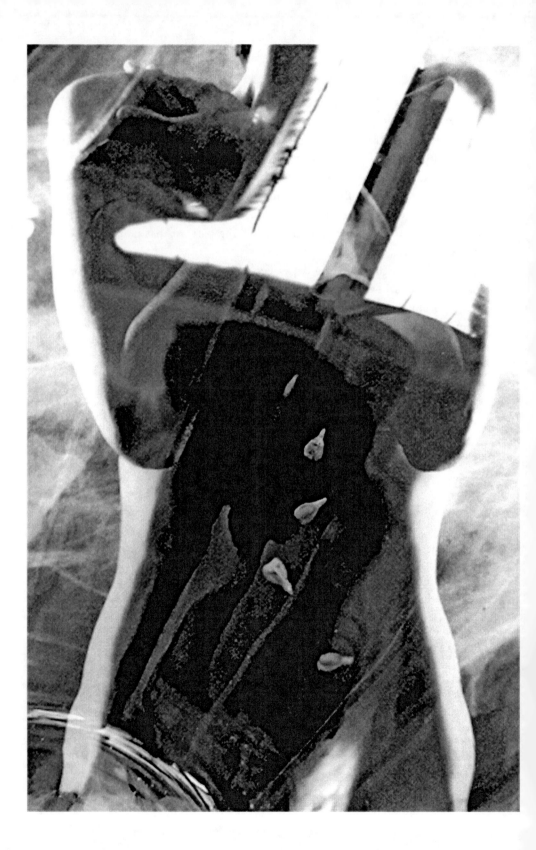

IT WASN'T MEANT TO END THIS WAY

It wasn't meant to end this way. That was all I could think. *It wasn't meant to end this way.* I felt so ashamed.

My friend Donna told me whatever I felt, whatever I wrote to relieve myself, *not* to push send. But I'm a passionate person—all Latinos are. Something touches our heart and it all pours out like a *chorro*—love or rage or despair or joy. Of course, I didn't listen. Of course I pushed that button. I knew it was a mistake, an irreversible one when I did it. But you hope, you know. Even at your wildest, your most childish, you hope.

I had never expected to feel this way again. Sitting there, reading that message over and over on the computer screen, I wished I never had.

For the past year, my son Luis has been making plans to have me move to Orlando where he lives now with his wife Sharon. She is expecting. He wants me to take early retirement to help them with the baby. Sharon is a lawyer and will want to keep on working. I told him, "I'm not retiring without full benefits." My friends think that it is ludicrous that I'm even considering for a minute giving up my job in the clinic to play nanny for my grandchild. I am a family medicine physician and work in a county public health clinic. I don't make a huge salary, but it is nothing to laugh at either. But I can understand Luis's reasoning. It is customary in our country. And my son doesn't think I have that long to live, that my talking about retirement is actually a form of denial. He also does not like the habits I have fallen into in the last ten years, the way I go to bed by six in the evening, seven at the latest, then get up at four to watch the *telenovelas* I have TiVoed before going to the clinic at seven.

"That's despair, Mamí."

"I love my job, my little Cariño who treats me as the center of his little doggy universe," I told him the last time he brought it up. "Believe me, Cariño will let everyone know if something happens to me and interferes with his walk or doggy treats. And you are a wonderful son, Luis. I know you will not forget me either. So I am quite happy the way I am. I am too old to change."

"This is not the woman who raised me," Luis said flatly. "The one who had people over every weekend, who was always out helping someone, the one who accepted help, who knew all her neighbors, who could salsa and mambo until the early morning. The one who read constantly, recited poetry, not the plots of *telenovelas*."

They took her away with my breasts, I thought. They shocked her out of me during the depression that followed.

"This baby of ours *needs* you, Mamí. We need you to need her as well."

I had a beloved aunt, Gabriela, a woman who never married (although I know she had many lovers). She was married to her career as a physician, but didn't mind a little romance on the side, preferably *picante*. She loved me like the child she never had. I have always used her as my model. I wonder if that is the relationship my son is imagining for me now with his child, the one Gabriela might have had with him if she had not chosen to stay behind in Cienfuegos. If history had not divided us, if I had stayed in Cienfuegos or Gabriela had fled with us, she would have stopped her work to help me with my son Luis. I am sure of that. I wouldn't have thought twice about asking her—although perhaps I should have. We are so perfectly egoistical when we are young. It needs to be matched by the egoism of age.

It is surprising to me how one part of me accepted my son's invitation so entirely, imagined myself into their basement apartment, putting on even more weight, always ready to hold the baby, no trouble at all—my whole life organized around them the way little Cariño's is organized around me. And part of me rejected the idea entirely—but for what, this life that from the outside seemed exactly the way Luis described it, the life of a zombie or sleepwalker, but from within was a succession of small, sensual pleasures? *My* sleep, *my* bubble bath, *my* dinner, *my* telenovelas, *my* office beautifully decorated with *my* art collection, *my* plants, *my* lovely public persona, so full of endearments and prescriptions for tired mothers, sniffling children, *my* Cariño, so totally besotted, in his snuffling, shaggy Shih Tzu way, by my every move. Really, what's missing?

Luis is right, of course. My body is very old for sixty-two. Even with all the medicines I am taking daily—three anti-depressants, a sedative, tamoxifen for cancer prevention, Synthroid for thyroid, insulin for Type-II diabetes, an ACE-inhibitor and a beta-blocker for my blood pressure—I often feel as if I have been swimming all the way from Cienfuegos to Miami and am just in sight of land, but know I have no more inner resources and won't make shore. But this knowledge is sweet and quiet, so very sweet, so wonderfully dark, all I want to do is move into it like a lover's embrace.

Or that was how I was feeling before Carlos found me on Facebook three months ago. It has been for me, this surprising reconnection, these emails we've been exchanging, like an amazing rebirth. Facebook is a wonderful invention for those of us who live in caves (however sensuous) and whose lives have crossed countries and continents. It is easy to forget we have lost anything, that we haven't always lived in empty lairs. Carlos's family were friends of my family in Cienfuegos. He was a few years older than my sister and me, and his family left two years before we did. In the States, my family settled in Miami and his in New Jersey, but we both went to medical school in Spain. (We came to the States in our teens, too late to become fully proficient in English in time to study here.) Our paths crossed for a few years in Barcelona. We did not keep in touch. He practiced for many years in Northern California, in Santa Rosa, and then bought a small vineyard in Sonoma—in other words, stayed as far away from his family as he could. He told me he loved them but needed to reinvent himself. Lately, he's been working as a consultant specializing in boutique practices, ones where the doctors stay in close touch with their patients, charge more, but limit the number of patients they see. "See it as an upscale version of Castro's medical system—a doctor in every gated community," he joked with me. In the email, I could not see his wink, but I could feel it. And then he was serious. "Sick is sick, Luz, however much money you have." When not advising others, or keeping up with his own smaller practice (that he was slowly phasing out as his patients died), he was out in his vineyard with his workers (who were all legal, he assured me).

We wrote in English. When we talked on the phone, which was less often, we stuck to English most of the time as well. I am not sure of the significance of this since in Spanish my thoughts are eloquent, in English just serviceable: they have no glamour, no nuance. Even so, a romance bloomed between us. It all felt very real even though we had not yet met in person.

When I went on his Facebook page, I could see Carlos, looking very fit for his sixty-six years, in jeans and a T-shirt working in his fields, or looking very handsome and tailored at a professional meeting in Miami or Indianapolis or San Antonio, as if he could be a Wall Street banker or one of the sexy but impossible *prepotentes* in my *telenovelas*.

But there was nothing *prepotente* about Carlos. From the beginning, he asked me about myself—and he responded to what I said. This is not usual for Latin men, even gay ones. I was more hesitant to ask him about himself—but he told me anyway. Carlos's marriage lasted twenty-five years (my own to Luis's father lasted only a miserable six). Carlos's ended in an amicable divorce ten years ago. He regretted they had no children. Since his divorce, he said, he had enjoyed his own company and an occasional intimate friendship or two. Looking at his photos, I thought he could be tactfully underestimating the number of intimate friendships. And why, I wondered, was this handsome man writing a fat medical school classmate he hadn't seen in thirty-five years?

Family pressure was the answer. It would take a Cuban to understand how powerful that can be. "My mother and sister met up with your sister at a party in Miami last year, and they all decided that we needed to reconnect," he told me when I asked him in my third email. "I am a good son—and they may have a point, you know. Shared history is its own kind of aphrodisiac. When I saw your face on Facebook, so many memories came back to me. I write you and I remember the hopes I had back then—hopes for my country, the world, hopes for myself. I know you had them too."

I did, but I couldn't draw them so easily or painlessly to mind, much less body. They were only hopes. Fidel and Raul dodder impenitently on; no one in my large condo complex speaks Spanish in their sleep; and my patients face social ills more deadly and untreatable than anything I diagnose and medicate them for and I am incapable of changing that. I often feel I am, just as my son Luis fears, only counting off the days to my release from this earth, this life, this body that are all so much less than what I was led to expect.

But when I read those words of Carlos's—here in my beautiful apartment looking out on the lake with its inseparable pair of swans, surrounded by my vivid paintings, my flowering plants, my poetry books in Spanish, my large picture books of Cuba and Spain, my large television screen—for a second, with his words, with what they woke in me, I lived in another world completely. It was as if I had slipped into the closing *capitulos* of my favorite *telenovela* and it was all going to end happily after hours and hours of conniving and unrequited yearning and missed chances and despair. Reading Carlos's words alone in my luminous apartment connected me to the woman I was before I was Luis's mother, and she was beautiful, vivid, and as Carlos was not afraid to remind me, thrumming with hope and a libido that animated everything—politics, personal life, career. They were all a most intimate, irresistible *charge* to me.

Until Carlos, I'd forgotten entirely. But I sat there—it was already eight, so late for me but the summer twilight was such an intense, romantic blue I couldn't leave it—and I thought, ah, this man, whatever his years, whatever his experience, is not afraid to love again. At least I can be his friend. So I wrote him, from that point on, directly from my heart.

I wrote him about my work in the public health clinic, about deciding to take a job in South Carolina to give Luis more room and to create a little more distance between me and my family: my parents, who at eighty and eighty-five, were always fighting, separating, reconciling again and my three sisters and their tumultuous families. I felt my role as the oldest sister, the fixer, was devouring my 'real' life, which I must have imagined as one of peace, quiet, beauty and romance—a *boutique* life. I told him about the silence that nearly devoured me when I finally had what I had dreamed I wanted. About the ineradicable poverty of the children I treated now, poverty that had no hope in it, that was poverty of spirit, of will, far more than money—how it made me realize what a gift leaving Cuba had been for me (although I fought it fiercely at the time). It gave me a sense of possibility. The *world*, not a poor little island, was to be my future.

I wrote about being diagnosed with breast cancer—but not about deciding I wanted a double mastectomy. (How clear I had been about all this. My romantic life was now over. One or two, what was the difference? "Why cling?" I asked the doctor. I refused reconstructive surgery.)

But I told Carlos how, afterwards, the isolation of my situation, the distance from my family, from Luis, living in a strange city that felt more provincial than Cienfuegos, the conflicts at work, and those long months of radiation and chemo all combined—how it was not just breasts I was missing then, it was my soul. I told him about going into the hospital for treatment for depression (but not about the suicide attempt or the electric shock). "It was a very difficult time. Sometimes I feel it is now all in the distant past, but sometimes, my friend, *Tengo un miedo terrible de ser un animal de blanca nieve,*" I wrote him quoting César Vallejo. How long had it been since a line of poetry had come to me?

And Carlos promptly wrote back, "Ah, but we surprise ourselves, don't we, with our resilience? For example, today, this line from Vallejo came to me: *Me viene, hay días, una gana ubérrima, política, de querer, de besar al cariño en sus dos rostros. . .*"

"What are you telling him?" Donna asked when I shared the email with her. (I was so happy I could not keep it to myself.)

"I have a fear of being an animal of white snow."

"And what did he answer?" she asked handing the email back to me.

"It comes to me, for some days now, a desire, exuberant and political, to kiss love on both cheeks," I translated.

"Oh, he works fast," Donna said, blushing a little. "Watch out, Luz, will you? You're more vulnerable than you think."

I could see real concern on her kind, round face. Donna is a physician's assistant and one of the few white women working in the clinic. She is Roman Catholic like me. She's been married since she was twenty and has two girls and two boys. The boys are already off at college; the girls are in their early teens, those worst years when your mother is a constant shame to you. Her husband has a bad back and a weak heart. I think she sees in me a future she fears for herself, so she takes what happens to me very seriously. She had been encouraging me to date again—but clearly she had her doubts about Carlos.

"He never says the wrong thing," she said in explanation when I asked her why she objected.

"Why should he?" I asked. "We have known each other forever."

"I thought you didn't know him so well, that your families were friends and you hung with the same crowd in Barcelona, but weren't personally close."

"There is an intimacy you feel with people who have known you, even at a distance, in important places and at important times in your life."

"Luz, don't let your imagination fill in too much. He's still a guy, you know. And even at sixty—"

"Sixty-six," I corrected her.

"They can just be greedy for attention. Once they get it, they're on the prowl again."

But *I* am the one greedy for attention—and the one who is ruthless when she does not receive it.

"If you don't want to know, don't ask," my mother used to warn me with my husband Raul. "If you know for sure, you're going to have to act. There's no going back."

She was right, of course. That is how Raul became my ex. Yes, there *was* an explanation for his working all those late nights even after the tax season, and her name was Lisa. She was as American as Hostess cupcakes and moon pies. She was a receptionist at his accounting firm. She had a very long nose and narrow eyes and breasts smaller and buttocks bigger than mine. Most insulting of all, she was dull. "Insipid," Luis affirmed loyally. "Completely insipid, Mamí." What more can you expect of an accountant, even a Latino one? They never change their columns, just add a little flesh here, subtract a little flesh there, deduct a substantial quantity of white and gray matter, twelve years, add fat lips and an appeasing manner, and a baby in utero. Sum total: change of household.

But that was almost a quarter of a century ago. I've had relationships since them, none of them live-in, of course. First because of Luis, then because my family was always looking over my shoulder, camping out in my house. I may have had fantasies when I moved away, but for the first two years, work consumed me—and then the cancer, the double mastectomy, the long depression. I wasn't sorry, you know. *Telenovelas* were easier, more fulfilling really.

Or so I felt until I began receiving Carlos's letters. I read them and that space where my breasts once were began to tingle, leak hope.

"There's a difference," I told my mother, dead these last eight years and eternally hovering, eternally scolding, when I heard her say, "Think again, Luz. Do you really want to know—"

There *is* a difference between asking out of fear and asking out of hope.

"We have been writing daily for three months now," I wrote Carlos, "talking weekly for two. Don't you think it is time we meet in the flesh? I have a medical meeting in San Francisco next month. Why don't I come visit you and you can show me your vineyard."

His answer was not what I expected.

"My dear Luz," he wrote me after a day's delay. "I would like nothing more than to see you and spend time with you—but it is not possible at present. As I told you, I have had over the years a few intimate friendships.

Even though we no longer share passion, these women are my dear friends. One of them, Rebecca, has just been diagnosed with metastatic breast cancer, Stage IV. She has never married, has no children, and has turned to me for support and friendship at this very difficult time in her life. I have, of course, promised to be there for her. I think having you visit me at this delicate time, just after surgery and as her chemo begins, would be difficult for her."

"*Cabrón*," I wrote immediately. "*Bruto. Traicionero.* You have led me on infamously. You've written or called every day for three months. I thought you were a man serious, a man honorable, a man *leal.*"

"I am a loyal man, Luz," he wrote back. "And a caring one. Can't you see how difficult this time is for Rebecca? She is not like us. She has no one. We have each other, our families. *We have time.* As a physician, if not as a woman, I would expect you to empathize with Rebecca's situation."

I didn't see why he had to constantly use her name. It wasn't even a pretty one. And what did he mean, as a physician, *if not as a woman.* Why did he think this time in *her* life meant more than this time in mine? My own son could hear my life-clock ticking. Why couldn't he? I'd told him about the cancer. Perhaps I had underplayed it to sound gallant, brave. Attractive. *Double breasted.*

"That must have been hard, Luz," he'd written back quickly. "But ten years remission. That's very good. Looks like a cure." I'd been pleased at the time.

"He said the two of you have time, Luz," Donna said when I showed her his letter. "You haven't written him back yet, have you?"

"Of course I wrote out all my thoughts. My blood was boiling. I had to do something. It is all down there in black and white. I just have to spellcheck. I told him I had had enough of traitor men and I never wanted to see him again. The infidelity, it is in their blood, these Latin men. I've told you that is why I did not want to date them. They are like babies—like my lazy Cariño—you have to cook and clean for them. And then they piss and shit and run around poking their penises in any dark hole they can find."

"Luz," Donna said sharply, pointing to the office door. "Keep it professional. And whatever you do, don't push send."

There was a knock on the door and Qualtee, my nurse, pushed the door open and said, "Mrs. Warren in Room 4. She wants to talk about changing her blood pressure meds."

"That should help bring yours down a little," Donna said, touching me on the shoulder. "And it's a good question he asked you, Luz. Why *can't* you have a little empathy for her? Wouldn't you like him to do the same for you if ever, God forbid, it was necessary again?"

You too, I thought. *Traición.*

But Donna stared straight back at me, unblinking. "When Ken was having such trouble with his back, you were great with him. You hadn't been out of the hospital long, but you were *there* for him. Talking to him on the phone for hours about his options. No question too silly. No hour too late or early. He still talks about how great you were. 'If every doctor could be like that,' he says. Don't you think you could do the same with her? You've *been* there, Luz."

Alone, I thought. I was there *alone.* He has no goddamn fucking right to remind me. I told no one about the cancer, you see, not until it was all over. Not my son, not my sisters, not my parents. I did not want to worry them. Even more, I did not want it to be true.

For three days after I sent my angry email, I fumed, I stewed, I talked to myself as I walked Cariño, as I cooked, even in my sleep. I would wake and hear my own voice echoing.

"I *am* a kind person."

"I *am* an empathetic woman."

Traicionada.

Abandonada.

Sola.

Sola.

SOLA.

I began to feel terribly ashamed of what I had said to Carlos. I had quoted from *La Mariposa*, a tango my aunt had liked: *No es que esté arrepentido de haberte querido tanto; lo que me apena es tu olvido y tu traición . . .*

Alone in my apartment at four in the morning beginning the next installment of *Soy tu dueña,* the next line would rise: *me sume en amargo llanto.*

But was it *his* forgetting, *his* betrayal that threw me into this bitter sorrow? Or was it the truth of my own condition? Truly who *did* I have besides Cariño? Was I punishing Carlos because he was a kind and generous man and I, Luz Montenegro, wanted to be the exclusive recipient of that generosity, which I felt was powerful enough to rewrite my past, transform my present?

I wrote Carlos back on the fourth day to apologize: *It is my Latin blood, my beloved. It is my desire for you, for the love that is possible between us, that drove me to say what I did. I regret it sincerely. My shame at my words is great. I would erase them all if I could. Your friend Rebecca will become our friend. You are right, mi amor, we do have time, time that we can afford to share with the less fortunate.*

I went on Carlos's Facebook page to see if I could find out more about Rebecca, perhaps friend her so Carlos would see how sincere my intentions were. But when I looked, I received a terrible shock.

There was a notice there I could not believe. It had been posted four hours earlier: *Carlos Gutierrez died in a tragic accident at his vineyard this morning. He was found an hour ago. His body has been taken for autopsy. It appears he was the victim of a hit and run. We will post further information here as it becomes available.*

I screamed when I read the words. Cariño barked and came over and circled around my chair. I couldn't take my eyes off the computer screen.

My Carlos. *My* Carlos. How could this have happened?

Cariño kept whining and circling my chair.

"Not now," I told him. "For goodness sake, not now." But he just became more frantic, running to the door and back.

My hands were shaking as I attached his leash. I would not carry him to the elevator as I usually did (he is a fat and lazy dog), I just tugged. In the elevator I kept looking at myself in the mirror. "This was not the way it was meant to end," I said to the woman staring back at me. I said it with the tone of voice I use with one of my patients, the one we all trust, and I could see the woman in the glass begin to respond to it.

I could *hear* Carlos as I walked Cariño around the lake. I heard his voice saying words he had never really spoken aloud to me, "As a physician if not a woman, Luz."

And then I understood. I needed to go to California. I needed to help his family. I needed, as a physician, to understand exactly what had happened to him. I needed to speak, in my professional capacity, to the coroner.

I returned to the apartment full of purpose. I booked a flight to San Francisco for the following morning. "It is a family tragedy," I said in my message to the clinic. "I will be away at least four days."

I called the Canine Comfort Spa where I leave Cariño, telling them I was leaving him that afternoon and reminding them of the special diet he needed for *his* diabetes and high blood pressure.

I went back to Carlos's Facebook page, but there was nothing new there. Only comments.

"Oh Carlos, I can't believe you're gone," wrote Annelise.

"We were going to the theater on Friday," wrote Lauren.

"There must be some mistake, my son talked to me this morning," wrote his mother.

I wrote down the names. I called my sister Alicia to see if she had Carlos's mother's phone number. She did. I called Carlos's mother's house. His niece Lourdes answered.

"*Estoy desolada,*" I told her.

"We all are," she answered. "You wouldn't believe how many calls we've had already."

"We had such a special relationship, your uncle and I," I told her. "I must go there myself to see what can be done. This cannot go unexplained. I will help everyone in every way I can."

"The funeral won't be held until they release the body and everyone gets there," the girl said. She sounded a little bored, but I was sure that was stress. "Tuesday, Wednesday. You don't have to hurry. If you give me your name and phone and email, someone can contact you with the details."

"He would want me there as soon as possible," I said. "He would want me to help with the planning. It is the least I can do. Our relationship was very very special. A once in a lifetime thing."

"Let me get my Mom," she said.

Carlos's sister, also named Lourdes like her mother and daughter, thanked me. She understood why I needed to go immediately, that I would be able, as a physician, to explain to all of them what the coroner was saying. Despite our shared history and natal language, we were all talking in English to lessen the pain. "We're none of us prepared for this. We're all in shock. But I can translate those sad words," I assured her. "I can explain."

To them, I thought. Never to myself.

The rest of the day was a blur of activity. I dropped Cariño off at the spa without a second glance. Back at the apartment I spent several hours choosing the right clothes. Black for the funeral of course, but blue for meeting with the coroner. A dark print for the meeting with the family. A more stylish and vivid one for meeting Rebecca. I tried them all on. Luckily they were all made of forgiving fabrics since I had clearly thickened since last wearing them.

"No sooner did I find him than I lost the love of my life," I said to the mirror, deciding on gold rather than silver jewelry. This love between Carlos and me would never have tarnished. It was the real thing.

I cleaned the refrigerator. Reserved a taxi to get me to the airport three hours early—and was out in front of the building anxiously waiting for it at 3:30. The dark was intense, moonless. I had not slept. I could not imagine sleeping again.

If I didn't sleep, this news could magically rewrite itself, the film reverse. My repentant email would come back to me with Carlos's reply: *"Ah, my hot-tempered beauty, I accept your apology. Love makes us whole—jealous, cruel, generous, humble, unforgiving, glorious. I want it all. With you. 'Debajo tu piel vive la luna,' as Neruda says."*

There would be no Facebook entry. There would not be, as there soon was, the reality of Carlos's body on the sliding tray in the morgue at the Sonoma County Coroner's office.

I did not tell the man who brought me, as Carlos's fiancée, down to the morgue to view the body that this was the first time I had ever touched his face with its trim white beard, its high, unlined forehead.

"*Mi amor*," I said, weeping, pressing my hand to his blue cheek. I went to pull down the sheet.

"I don't think you want to do that," the attendant said. "It's pretty grisly and they haven't even done the autopsy yet."

Then I was all business. I asked when the autopsy was to be conducted and asked to see the report when it was completed. I asked to talk to the coroner so I could let him know how important this was—that someone with knowledge would be watching him to make sure he gave Carlos all the care he deserved.

They called a Deputy Sheriff of Community Oriented Policing and Problem Solving instead. They escorted me up to an interview room. It was a faded beige. All it had on the wall was a framed copy of our Miranda rights. The detective was overweight, late, slow of speech. His name was Roberto Marín. He didn't speak Spanish.

"We're treating this as a suspicious death, Dr. Montenegro. It looks like Dr. Castillo wasn't hit just once, which could have been accidental, but was driven over by the winery's own truck at least twice. We've just matched the treads. That clearly shows intent, malice."

"Who would hurt Carlos?"

"That is the question we're asking everyone. As far as you know, did Dr. Castillo have any enemies?"

Oh, those terrible words in my email flashed before me: *cabrón . . . bruto . . . traicionero*. I knew he could never understand.

"No," I said quietly, professionally. "I would not think so. He is, from my own experience, a very kind and generous man. But our relationship, although intense, has been relatively brief."

"I thought you were his fiancée."

"It has been a whirlwind romance," I acknowledged. "But at our ages, we know what is right. This was right. For both of us."

"Can you tell us about his friends? His colleagues? His family? The workers at his vineyard?" Deputy Sheriff Marín was tapping his pen on his clipboard, ready to take notes.

"Can you tell me what happened to his body?"

"I just told you. He was run over. More than once." Deputy Sheriff Marín looked at me as if there was something wrong with me. I knew this look well. In the United States I have received it frequently. Too often. In Spanish, my intelligence is obvious. In English, my heavy accent makes me seem slow of understanding.

"I am a physician," I said. "I want to know exactly how he died. I *need* to know."

"Why?" the deputy sheriff asked. He had large brown eyes with large bags under them. He may have been my age. He wore no ring on the hand that went to smooth hair that was no longer there.

I couldn't explain, but it made a difference to me if Carlos's death was instantaneous or slow, if what killed him was a sliver of shattered rib that stabbed into his heart or a welling of blood in his brain or a crushed windpipe. Every detail mattered. It was all I had left.

"So I can believe it," I said. "I still can't believe it. I'd like to attend the autopsy."

"We can get you the report. You've already been to the morgue. You've seen him. If we were to do this with everyone—"

"Carlos isn't everyone. Neither am I."

"I don't want to insult you Doctor," he paused to skim his notes,

"Montenegro. I know you're hurting. But as a physician you have to know there isn't a body we have stored here that isn't as precious to someone as his is to you—and, we gather, to many others as well. This death has shocked many. The morgue is not the place to come to terms with it. In addition to yours, we've had ten requests to view the body so far. It has to stop somewhere. We're not a funeral parlor."

The look on his face wasn't unkind. I had my hands in my lap, but my thumbs kept running over the other fingers, baby to index, the way a child churns a blanket. But there was no flannel, no transitional object, always and only skin. My skin touching my skin. I reached down to get my purse and placed it on my lap. I flattened my hands against the smooth leather.

"I need to let you know that two of those requests have come from partners in his practice, eight of those from women friends, two of whom have claimed the same relationship with Dr. Castillo that you have, Dr. Montenegro." His face was red, and he was looking at his hands.

"Amante?"

"Fiancée."

"I am above and beyond your suspicions," I told him coldly. "For thirty-five years, I have not seen Carlos in the flesh. Since that time, I have never seen him alive. Our love has all been through the phone or internet."

"You're not a suspect," he said. "None of you. I just thought you might like to get this straightened out a bit before his family arrives. It's a lot to sort out. We don't want anyone to be embarrassed, do we?"

"I am the one to do that," I said. "His family knows me since the childhood."

"From what I understand, he was their only son. They will want to think well of him."

"We all do," As I stood I pulled down my dress, which was a little tight and a little too short for this purpose. "I will do the best. Can you give me the list of the women who have already visited him. I will be in contact with each of them."

But as I smiled, shook hands, that refrain was starting up again. *No es que esté arrepentido . . . cabrón . . . traicionero . . . bruto.* It wasn't meant to end this way, with all these words that could never be taken back, this view of myself that was even worse.

And it didn't. The funeral was held three days later. The coroner's report, which was issued with compassionate speed given the tragic circumstances, reassured us that Carlos's death was immediate, painless, due more likely to a heart attack after the first blow of the truck to the chest. The crushing of the bones came later.

None of the women, just as Deputy Sheriff Marín indicated, were implicated. He was done in, my kind Carlos, by his own act of charity. He'd taken in a homeless couple, from Fresno, to work on the ranch. I don't know where he ran into them. He offered them work, free housing. But they couldn't stop drinking, snorting meth. Carlos had finally had enough and ordered them out of his truck and off the winery. They'd turned on him instead. He didn't see it coming. Honestly, I doubt if they did either. I went to see them in jail, shabby, frail, their hair straw yellow and brittle, their faces white beneath the freckles, thirty-five but looking older than me. Already haunted.

It felt to me Carlos's fate was kinder than their own. He died instantaneously, with a dramatic flair, handsome, vigorous, beloved, unsuspecting, ripe with life. Several hundred people attended the funeral, which was held at the vineyard. The decision was made to scatter his ashes there so his zest could nourish his new vines.

All the women on the list Roberto (somehow Deputy Sheriff Marín and I had shifted to a first name basis) gave me were there. I'd talked to them all individually. I found them surprisingly compatible. Carlos wasn't secretive about his affections. He updated them all regularly about who he was spending time with, enjoying, worrying about. They all, for example, knew about me. But not, perhaps, how serious our feelings for one another were. How complete.

"Ah, Luz," Rebecca said opening her door and inviting me into her house that, like mine, favored white furniture and thriving plants, had a little Pekinese sniffing around my feet. "I am so pleased to meet you. Carlos knew you'd understand—eventually."

"He had the gift," Annelise said, "of making you feel like the most special person in the world, the most beautiful."

"A gift that kept on giving, thanks to Viagra," his ex-wife Mariposa (the only one not to have visited the coroner's office) said dryly as she watched Carlos's special friends each set a red rose beside the small wine cask that held his ashes as she shared one quality she had loved about Carlos.

Carlos's ex-wife and Carlos's mother regarded each other coolly.

"*Amarga*," Carlos's sister whispered to me, squeezing my hand. "Always *amarga*. From the day she was born. Thank you so much, Luz, for setting a good tone."

Tender. Thoughtful. Funny. Caring. Smart. Adventurous. Sexy (this was Fern). Joyful. *Leal* (this was me). I looked at these women as they went forward bending to touch the seasoned oak, to murmur their word. I liked the company I was keeping. We were all different from each other: tall (Annelise), short (Jinghua), studious (Lauren), funny (Jane), maternal (Georgie), dramatic (Fern), glamorous (Rebecca), quiet (Dawn), colorful (me), ageless (Mariposa). But we were all, it was obvious, worth knowing. Seeing all of us together, I understood something about Carlos I could not understand in any other way. Something good.

If Carlos had been an art collector, I wonder if the artists coming to see their works combined on his walls would look at each other the way we were all looking at each other that hot bright afternoon—with a respect that they grudged and felt relieved by simultaneously. Because deep down we all know, we have to, *it's not all about me*. It is as much about the one who sees, who selects the best in us.

"My god, Luz, you look like you went on vacation," Donna said when I walked into the clinic the following Friday.

My phone book was larger by fifteen numbers, my Facebook page richer by an even greater number of new friends (including Roberto Marín).

"It wasn't supposed to end this way, I know. But now that it has, it feels fated. I can't imagine it going any other way," I said to Donna as I pulled my white coat off the hook on the back of the door.

"Murder? Infidelity?" she asked.

"Don't be so mundane," I said. I smoothed my red dress, then covered it with my white coat. Just enough color flashed through the buttons, extended below the hem, to make life interesting.

"He was not a man destined to grow old, I think. So I'm glad he never held back—that he gave people what they needed out of this big freedom in his own heart."

"I can just hear you at Don Juan's funeral," Donna said. "Bill Clinton's. Dominique Strauss-Kahn's."

"Carlos was not a womanizer. He was a womanist. We all agreed on this (except perhaps his wife). He accepted us, that was his gift. He just accepted the beauty in each of us. He magnified it for our own benefit."

"Are you taking something," Donna asked. "Something new that might be interacting, making you—"

"Poetic?" I smoothed down my coat, where my breasts used to be. They were beautiful, my breasts. They gave me great pleasure. I miss them every day. They can never be replaced. I knew all that before I met Carlos. What he taught me was that my breasts were all that was taken from me. My heart continues to beat, tumultuous, hot, *salvaje*, inside its cage. My spirit still soars.

"When I think of Carlos, the effect he had, his reasons for doing what he did, all I can think of are some lines from Neruda," I told Donna. "He loved Neruda, you know. 'I have a mind to confuse things . . . mix them up, undress them . . . *Hasta que la luz del mundo tenga la unidad del océano . . . .*,'" I murmured.

"Are you sure you're not manic, Luz?"

Qualtee knocked on the door then pushed right in. "DeShawn is in Room 2, Dr. Montenegro. Asthma."

As I followed her out, I called back over my shoulder, "Time will tell."

I am already busy planning. I will start applying for jobs in Orlando. I like the woman in me who prescribes and consoles. I'm certainly not moving into a basement flat to be at Luis and his wife's beck and call. I will move into a retirement complex where everyone knows that it's now or never and whatever we've got left, it's best to flaunt it. Perhaps I will follow Carlos's lead and open a boutique practice there. I will entertain my grandchild, who I will privately call Carlitos or Carlita, on weekends, date on weeknights.

I can already hear Luis complaining, as he did so often as a child, "You are always going, Mamí. You have time for everybody else, but you never have time for me." And we will laugh, the two of us, with relief.

FROM THE OUTSIDE IN

My other children are always asking why I don't use the hearing aid they bought for me. I tell them that it makes it harder to hear because it indiscriminately amplifies everything. It also feels strange in my ear, like I have a bean stuck there. The truth is Addie's voice carries so, I have no need for one since she's come back home. I have no desire to have her voice amplified further. It seems to echo inside my mind just like her father's did. I know she thinks she's doing me a good service by coming back to live here. It's not like she doesn't have choices. She earns a good salary as a dentist and she has another eight years until she retires. Longer if she wants. She's in a group practice in Dahlonega.

The truth is I've been a peaceful woman since Olin died. I've been able, at last, to think my own thoughts to completion. I shouldn't say it, but the luxury of that is better than sex. More expansive. The thought doesn't even have to be complex. Something as simple as thinking, "I'm the center of my own universe," as I blow on the steam rising from my morning coffee sitting out on the back porch watching the sun rise over the fallow fields. "I, Addie Belle, am the center of my own universe." Deep breath. Bees buzzing. Cicadas cresting. A wind sighing in the stand of pines. And me at the center, silent and free.

That was my life at seventy-nine. It feels a century ago, but it's only been two years. After her last divorce, Addie decided it was up to her to save the family farm. She's decided to grow pumpkins, sunflowers, and build a corn maze and a winter wheat labyrinth to take advantage of the fall traffic to the mountains. The labyrinth is for the Episcopal priest, a woman who Addie has also befriended by joining the choir (as I said, she has a carrying voice that can also carry a tune) and becoming a member of the vestry.

But I am the primary focus of Addie's good will. "I know how much the farm meant to you and Daddy," she said when she arrived for what I thought was a weekend visit only to learn that she was planning on moving back in permanently. "I figure if I can bring it back, your grandchildren will be able to keep it running." A generous thought, I grant you. But Addie, as is her way, never bothered to consult, unless she and Olin had a séance on the sly. She didn't ask me or the grands, that's for sure. It wasn't like she didn't care. It just never occurred to her there could be a difference of opinion. She's been that way all her life even though she has two of the most independent-minded siblings imaginable, both of whom, just like her, left the farm as soon as they passed their SATs and earned their scholarships to the University of Georgia and Georgia Tech. Their own children have no desire to go back to what their parents fought so hard to escape.

I was the only one, besides Olin, who ever lived on that farm voluntarily—until Addie took it into her mind to come back. I should have run when I could. But Addie would be hurt and people have always been the pull for me, not dirt.

I was a farmer's wife for fifty-one years. A competent one. More competent, if the truth be told, than Olin was as a farmer. But the lines of authority were clearly drawn. The house was mine to do with as I would. So was the children's schooling. Everything to do with the fields, the barn, the farm equipment, the choice of crops, the sowing and harvesting were Olin's kingdom. And he treated them that way, imperiously. Olin, like his oldest daughter, had a taste for the absolute. When I first met him, I confused it with confidence and knowledge. And, I can see now, with my own daddy's ways as lawyer, judge, and sheriff. I was accustomed to men who felt they *had* to lay down the law. Difference was their systems. My daddy saw himself as a servant of a larger order. Olin, alone in his fields, felt alternately like Job, a hapless punching bag for the Lord, and like a law unto himself.

"Ain't he the be all to end all," I heard my son Junior whisper to his younger sister, Annie Lou, out in the kitchen. Olin was going on about the latest soil analysis, the drought hardiness of soybeans, how to plant to profit most from the current subsidies. And on. And on. I knew then that I had to get Junior away sooner rather than later. He was sixteen. I'd felt the same rebelliousness toward my own father. That's how I ended up marrying Olin after only three months acquaintance. As a twenty-two-year-old college graduate with an honors degree in home economics, to me Olin felt lawless.

His baby sister was my student. I made home visits to see the students' projects, so I came out to their farm. She was raising sheep for their wool.

"In Georgia heat, would you believe it?" Olin had scoffed. He wasn't tall but he was muscled, thin, and he had this smile that lit up something deep in me, something exciting and reckless. My father would not be pleased.

I defended his sister. "There's money to be made," I said. "If she can learn to spin and dye it, there are craft people settling in the mountains now who will buy."

I had his full attention. I liked that. And I could see his sister relax. She wanted something of her own desperately. The family never got around to naming her for anything but her relationship to Olin, *Sister*. That's why I had her name my second girl. When it was time to get Annie Lou away from the farm, I sent her down to Marietta to board with Sister for the summers. Annie Lou went to summer enrichment school down there to help with her advanced placements, although we both told Olin she was helping Sister with her shop. Sister actually had a successful yarn and handicrafts store at that time. Annie Lou, in college, used her aunt as the subject for an oral history project in women's studies. Sister talked about what it felt like, a woman without a proper name, to earn a proper income on her own.

Addie took away from the farm a completely different lesson than the one the farm taught Junior and Annie Lou. It's always an amazement to me how the same event can mean such diametrically different things to people. Annie Lou saw me as her daddy's willing chattel. Addie saw me as the power behind the throne. She'd like me to have the same status now.

"It's *your* farm, Mama," she bellows. "Tell me what you'd like to see growing here."

"Sunflowers," I tell her. "Corn mazes. Winter wheat labyrinths. Pumpkins."

"Butternut squash, winter lettuce and roses," I add, afraid she'll think I'm mocking her. But I don't need to be concerned in that way. Addie just thinks great minds think alike. She has a calculator out before I finish speaking and is working out acreage, costs of seeds and fertilizer, potential yields.

"We'll do organic," she says. "Niche markets are in these days. We'll focus on arugula and radicchio."

I look at her fondly. Addie's face, especially with her short haircut and the menopausal weight gain, is so close to her dad's it's uncanny. Even so, I have this sense of her at twelve, how proud she was when he asked her, a *girl*, to drive the tractor for him. She was as proud when I had her put on a change apron and run the fruit stand during apple season while I made the apple butter and cider. That was what being grown-up meant to Addie. It was *doing* what the grown-ups did. Making money at it.

I still think it's what Addie understands best about the world, a series of physical transactions. It's all rote. X-ray. Drill. Fill. I love my daughter, but it's like she's the shell of a person. There are no sweet murmurings, no second thoughts, no furtive flurries of sexual excitement, no vivid flashes of anger, no tinglings of curiosity, no stings of doubt or regret. *It is what it is.*

I'm not saying Addie doesn't have feelings, isn't even driven by them, but she doesn't recognize them for what they are, can't put them into words, so they come to her as self-evident urges. Like this one to revive our blessedly fallow farm. What she's hungering for, I believe, is the self-importance she felt at twelve when she was able to do what her parents could do—till and make change. She was glowing with pride at those times—like Sister with her wool years before. There was a place for her in the world.

The real reason Addie is living in this big, ramshackle house with me when she can easily afford a glamorous home of her own is that she's hurting in a way she has no name for since her second divorce. This time, there isn't another woman involved. I think that might make it worse. The first time Addie married, she'd just finished college and was starting dental school. She married her high school steady, Gus Crosby, a popular linebacker. She married him because she was twenty-two and that was how old I was when I married. Her marriage ended a year after she finished dental school. She had made it clear she had no intention of having children and insisted Gus come and be her office manager. (He had been coaching high school football even though he had a business degree.) But balancing accounts had less interest for him than physical activities, so it was no surprise that he ended up doing calisthenics in the supply closet with the dental hygienist. The two of them took off—their first baby already incubating—with half of Addie's savings as repayment for the support he'd provided her in dental school. "We wanted different things," is all Addie ever said.

Then Addie and her sister Annie Lou shared an apartment for several years until Annie Lou got a grant to study women's empowerment in India. Then Addie moved in with Dalton, who had been working for her for two years and who she'd been seeing on and off for a year in a romantic way. "It was better for the other staff," she said. She said the same when they married. That's as close to romantic as I think it is in Addie to be. Dalton joked that she gave him a raise as well.

The bottom line, though, is that as independent as she seems, Addie has never lived alone. It comes as a surprise to me, but it shouldn't. What is a woman who only knows herself as the gleam of pride in someone else's eyes going to do surrounded by the indifferent regard of walls? She'll dissolve. Addie has the wit to know that, even if she's at a loss to know how to keep it from happening. If she didn't move in with me, where would those needs and gifts of hers fit best? The military? A women's prison? A mission camp in Uganda? Peru?

She won't mention Dalton, says the decision to divorce was mutual, but I can feel she wakes up some mornings and misses something she can't name, something that after more than a quarter century came to feel like home. Dalton not only ran her office for twenty-eight years, he also ran their life. He was the office manager, bookkeeper, cook, interior decorator, and social secretary. In other words, he was to Addie what I was to Addie's father. Addie doesn't think I know the whole story, but Dalton and I communicate regularly. Always have. We have a fast epistolary friendship—or now an email one—whose secrecy feeds us.

The only one who didn't know Dalton was gay was Addie—and that was because he performed his conjugal obligations at a frequency and level of proficiency that satisfied her. To this day, if anyone said it outright, she'd deny it. Say, at most, that he was occasionally confused in his sexuality. She can't deny it absolutely because he was arrested twice in Dahlonega for public indecency. That's what led to the split. She had a professional reputation to maintain. What amazes me is that they kept it all up as long as they did.

You have no idea how hard I tried, Dalton wrote me when he informed me about the arrests. Dalton was always straight with me, no pun intended. You have to remember that Stonewall happened in New York City, not in rural north Georgia, so even fifteen years later, when they married, Dalton felt he had few choices. Then, with AIDS, even fewer. Not to mention that Addie, along with being his cover, was his quite generous employer. Besides, he had a genuine bond with her.

What Dalton felt for my daughter was respect and sympathy and gratitude. A woman with Addie's disposition has great social vulnerabilities. Dalton could always step in, smooth ruffled feathers, mend fences. After he left, she had such trouble with her private office, she joined a group practice as a contract employee.

"It just wasn't worth the hassle," she told me. "Here they take care of all that. They have a slew of techs, two office managers, a bookkeeper. I just come in, see the patients, do my work, leave. It leaves me plenty of time for the farm, Mama."

How could you have done this to me? I wrote Dalton late at night. Dalton lives now in Atlanta with a lovely man, ten years his junior, named Craig. Craig is a lawyer. Dalton used his half of the proceeds from the sale of the house to buy an office building and create a dental practice. He acts as an equal partner and manager with the dentists, does all the insurance billing and staffing and advertising. *They're happy. I'm happy. Everyone's gay!*, he writes me. He and Craig practice salsa every Wednesday night at a local bar. They're thinking of adopting a child—or fostering.

Dalton didn't create the fix I'm in. I don't begrudge him his current happiness. It couldn't have happened to a better man. I think sometimes of the pressure Dalton must have experienced during those awful years. The ones where his agreement with Addie kept shifting—from never, to only looking on the internet, to only out of town, to not in our bed. Which is what led to the arrests in the local park, exposure in the local newspaper. The awful shame of it all made worse by Addie's naive and ineradicable belief that not acting was the same as not experiencing.

I can't tell you how often I sat at the table with Olin, something in me threatening to rise, so wild an energy it was almost orgasmic. My breasts would tingle and my lips would relax and I just felt something wild as a love cry would come pouring out. Like I was spitting lizards. I'd blink my eyes, yawn. Stand up to clear the table, and Olin would look at me. "Addie Belle have you taken leave of your senses? I'm still talking."

I'd sit down and send the energy down to my toes, just wiggle them. Smile while I did some Kegel exercises. It had nothing to do with sex. It had to do with me. The essence of me. The force it required to suppress it.

I feel so clean, Dalton wrote me after he met Craig. *It's like the inside and the outside can finally match, all that energy has a place to go—and the whole world glows. I am <u>good</u> for something, good for <u>someone</u>—and good for myself.*

I never left Olin, never consciously thought of it, but experienced his final absence as the sweetest release. A truth that still tingles in me the way those images on the internet, men seeking men, must have done for Dalton.

Addie still grieves for Olin. "Wouldn't Daddy be proud of us," she says looking up from her calculator. She has an appointment with the state agricultural agent in an hour. She is truly happy. I am too. For at least two hours I'll be free to return to the novel I'm writing.

It's the last of a trilogy. They're what they call now young adult fiction. They're about what it felt like to live another's dream while suppressing your own. They're about finding the courage to move on and claim your own destiny. The first is about Sister, the second about Annie Lou. By the end of the first, Sister is a successful business woman, and by the end of the second, Annie is a college professor who collects women's stories from all over the world and shares them back with them so they can see their own hard work, and worth, clearly. The third was going to be about me—about the hard work and even harder choices it took to stay on the farm. But now it's turning out to be about something that never happened. I'm taking the truth of Addie and Dalton—and making it Olin's and mine, so Addie's coming back wanting to revive the old ways has a whole different meaning.

What if I'd stayed married so long, stayed so many years with someone so clearly my intellectual inferior not because I first lusted for him and craved the independence from my own family he promised, then out of loyalty toward our children (misguided my daughter Annie Lou will say), and then some genuine fondness that was impossible to separate from pity? And sheer bone weariness.

What if, instead, I'd never lost sight of the bright flame burning in the core of me, just knew it needed to burn in the deepest darkness where it could burn brightest, shed the most light? What if, deep inside me, I had a secret like Dalton's? What if it wasn't Olin I loved, however imperfectly, but Sister? How would that have changed how anyone understood my choices? What would it have meant for my children if, at eighty, it all came out, if, for example, Sister died and asked to be buried next to me with a gravestone saying Beloved Wife of Addie Belle Crowe—or if I did the same? Addie, beloved wife of Sister Parsons. What would the effect be on Addie? Junior? Annie Lou?

These are the kinds of questions that liven my day, bring a smile to my lips as I watch Addie adding in fertilizer costs or subtracting shipping from her sunflower estimates.

Since this book is a little conflagratory, I've taken to putting the chapters in different files on the computer. Addie has, you wouldn't be surprised, taken to using my computer as if it were hers. "To keep the farm and dental practice separate," she says. As if there are no other factors in her equation—like the inner life of her octogenarian mother, or simply private property.

Dalton is the one who is keeping it all in order. I send him each chapter as I finish it. He's my biggest fan, especially of this book. He wants me to title it *What Goes On Under the Scuppernong*, but we don't have grapes here, we're a little too high. I like *Sunflower Song*. I think it would lure in the unsuspecting. *Why Addie Belle, you're cunning*, Dalton writes me back. *I would never have suspected.*

Craig suggested *Living Labyrinths*, but that brought up snakes for Dalton and me rather than the vivid green winter wheat that Addie mows into shape. Right now I'm just using the working title *Mom's Memories*.

What I like about this story is what it does to the two earlier ones I've written. It makes you see Sister's move to the big city differently—and Annie Lou's focus on women's empowerment differently as well. I am, as Addie likes to imagine, the power behind the throne. I am the core. Sister leaves to protect me. We both act to protect Annie Lou's spirit and integrity and her innocence. It empowers her to see me as helpless, as one of the women she has to work to 'save.' But where does this leave brusque, credulous Addie who, just as smart as me, bought her daddy's view of the world so completely?

Last week I decided it's time to begin publishing the books, so I wrote Create Space and Xlibris and i-Universe for quotes. At my age, I have no time for agents or editors.

When I came down for breakfast this morning, I found their responses neatly printed out and set in front of my place mat.

"So, now I have a personal secretary?" I asked Addie. I was beyond ticked. Since when did my personal mail start getting hacked?

"We have to talk," Addie said seriously.

"Not until I've taken my blood pressure medicine and my Metamucil," I said. "Maybe I'll take the time to scrub my dentures too."

"Mama, what's gotten into you?" Addie went from looking stern to looking frightened.

"It's not abrupt onset Alzheimer's," I said. "I feel like someone rummaged in my lingerie drawer. You use *my* computer at *my* convenience, Addie. You don't go prowling around like a cat burglar." That was unfair.

Prowling takes physical grace, some awareness of what's around you, a sense of predatoriness or potential threat.

"I was just trying to be helpful, Mama. I thought we might want to discuss the business implications of these contracts, that we could go over the fine print together. What is it exactly you're thinking of publishing? Recipes? We could sell the book at the stand. I think that's a grand idea. If you want, I could edit."

"That won't be necessary," I told her. I straightened *my* silverware and stood up. I went to *my* refrigerator and pulled out *my* milk and *my* orange juice. I poured myself a small glass of each and carried them back to the table.

Addie watched me carefully, her hands clasped together and resting on the table. Her eyes were sharp. I could tell she was reviewing the signs of stroke. I smiled at her.

"My speech is clear. I'm oriented as to space and time. My smile is bilateral, dear. Mama's all here—and then some."

"But there's this unaccountable mood change, Mama. It's not like you."

Oh Addie, honey, I thought, how can you possibly know what's like me and what's not? I had this sudden image of myself at Addie's age—out with Olin in the back field. It was early spring. We were inspecting the rows of soybean seedlings. It was a clean, clear day, the sky a vivid blue, the clouds like snow-capped mountains towering weightless above us. I said, "I dare you." Just like I had when we were young. And Olin looked at me, a little sweaty and dirty from the planting, and suddenly the young man I'd loved came back, sly as a thief, in broad daylight.

I carried my two small glasses back to the table careful not to spill a drop. I sat down opposite my daughter and clasped my hands together and set them before me just as she had done. I observed her as carefully as she had been observing me.

How was she going to go on without me? Where was she going to find the closeness I had found in my writing? In my epistolary friendship with Dalton? With my grandchildren?

"Addie, dear, I'm happy to sell you the farm," I said without any preliminaries.

"Oh, Mama, you don't need to do that. A family trust so no one can sell it is better, I think." Addie was serious, fair.

"No one *wants* it but you, Addie. Junior and Annie Lou hated living here. Why do you think they keep inviting me to their houses?"

"They're trying to persuade you to give up your independence," Addie said protectively. "I won't let that happen. Not on *my* watch."

"But it's *not* your watch, Addie. It's mine. It's *my* home. *My* farm. I opened them up to you at a difficult time in your life. I held onto them two years longer than I should have, given the economy. For you."

"I want to take you in for an MRI, Mama. This is all so out of character. I'm wondering if you've had a TIA in the frontal lobe. Your judgment is off."

I smiled then, with genuine affection. I could see why Dalton had stayed with her so long. Addie was a deeply decent person. I don't know if dentists swear the Hippocratic Oath, but she could have. She didn't intend harm. She just didn't know how to help.

I'm a mother to the bone. There's something in me that can home in on the deepest fears of my children. Sometimes I can make them safe. Sometimes I can't.

"I can sell you the farm, Addie. I can't give it to you. And I won't share it with you any longer. What do *you* want?"

"But where would you go, Mama? What would you do? The farm keeps you alert, alive. It gives you purpose. You stay with Junior or Annie Lou and soon you'll feel dependent. Suburbs are suffocatingly lonely."

"Speak for yourself, Addie. I'll speak for Addie Belle."

I got up and walked, slowly, over to the coffee maker and poured some coffee in my mug. I leaned against the counter as I spoke.

"The realtor and I set an asking price two years ago. I'll call her and see if she suggests we change it. You can make me your best offer—and then it's going on the market. You're welcome to stay with me until it's sold."

"But where will you go? What will you do?"

"Those are *your* questions, Addie. I'm not part of the answer for you anymore."

"But why *now*, Mama? Why tell me now?"

What was the answer to this?

My own plan had been set for years now. I was going to live in the same home that Sister had chosen in Marietta. It was within easy distance of Athens, where Annie Lou lived, and Dalton and Craig's condo in Atlanta. It had a writer's group and a book group. I had my laptop and my trilogy. But what about Addie? Why *had* I, without inner forewarning, decided today was the day?

It wasn't sharing the fields, or the house that had pushed me to action. It was the laptop. It was Addie's proximity to my stories. It was the need, at my advanced age, to keep them hidden from the one who had the most to learn from them—and couldn't. Just couldn't. Whatever questions I had about publishing my stories, tangling fact inextricably with fiction in a way that would change them both permanently for me and all who knew me or thought they did, any thoughts I'd had about using a pseudonym, they were all gone now. I saw them, these questions, like a flock of large, rapacious crows finally rising from the shorn cornfields and taking on a beautiful symmetry as they reorganized for flight. And I, Addie Belle Crowe, at eighty-two a soon to be published author, watched them rise. Standing securely—and openly—at the center of my own universe, I warmly waved them adieu. Those coarse, glistening, ravenous, magnificently soaring creatures.

"Let's think about you, Addie. Given my plans, what's best for you? If you're running this farm for *you*—not for me, not for your father, not for your nieces and nephews and future generations, what would *you* grow? More importantly, who would you invite in to help you?"

The fear in my daughter's round, middle-aged face was heart-stopping. For a second I was tempted, as I had been again and again with Olin, to wedge my own desires back into some dark cubby hole. It was a mistake then. It was a mistake now.

"It's safe," I told my daughter as the emptiness and grief inside her finally touched the emptiness outside. "There is an answer and it is safe to grow into it. May I suggest two radically different alternatives to help you as you're trying to decide." I opened up the kitchen drawer and pulled out the brochures I'd been putting up like chow chow and apple butter for just such a time. "Take a Mediterranean cruise. Sign up for a dental mission trip to Bolivia or Bhutan. Whatever you do, move on before you move back."

ACKNOWLEDGEMENTS

Existential thanks to William James for *being* William James—and to César Vallejo and Pablo Neruda for the same.

Special thanks to Kerry Langan, Michele Markarian, and Kathleen Housley for their generous, astute, and encouraging readings of this manuscript—and to Charles Brockett who has provided steadfast support every step of the way.

HEATHER TOSTESON, a writer and visual artist, is the author of *The Sanctity of the Moment: Poems from Four Decades, Visible Signs, Hearts as Big as Fists & Other Stories,* and *God Speaks My Language, Can You?* She has received a Nation/Discovery prize for her poetry and fellowships for poetry, fiction, and photography from MacDowell, Yaddo, VCCA and Hambidge. She holds an MFA in Creative Writing (UNC-Greensboro) and PhD in English and Creative Writing (Ohio University). She has co-edited eight Wising Up anthologies, including *Daring to Repair: What Is It, Who Does It & Why?; Complex Allegiances: Constellations of Immigration, Citizenship & Belonging; View from the Bed: View from the Bedside;* and *Families: The Frontline of Pluralism.* She lives in Atlanta with her husband Charles Brockett.